MY TRAVELS IN DING YI

SHI TIESHENG

Translated by
ALEX WOODEND

ACA Publishing Ltd

Paperback published by
ACA Publishing Ltd.

eBook published by
Sinoist Books (an imprint of ACA Publishing Ltd).

University House
11-13 Lower Grosvenor Place
London SW1W 0EX, UK
Tel: +44 (0)20 3289 3885
Fax: +44 (0)20 7973 0076
E-mail: info@alaincharlesasia.com
Web: www.alaincharlesasia.com

Beijing Office
Tel: +86 (0)10 8472 1250
Fax: +86 (0)10 5885 0639

Author: Shi Tiesheng
Translator: Alex Woodend
Translation consultant: Yuan Haiwang
Editor: David Lammie
Cover art: Daniel Li

Published by ACA Publishing Ltd in association with the People's Literature Publishing House

© 2018, by People's Literature Publishing House, Beijing, China

ALL RIGHTS RESERVED. NO PART OF THIS PUBLICATION MAY BE REPRODUCED IN MATERIAL FORM, BY ANY MEANS, WHETHER GRAPHIC, ELECTRONIC, MECHANICAL OR OTHER, INCLUDING PHOTOCOPYING OR INFORMATION STORAGE, IN WHOLE OR IN PART, AND MAY NOT BE USED TO PREPARE OTHER PUBLICATIONS WITHOUT WRITTEN PERMISSION FROM THE PUBLISHER.

The greatest care has been taken to ensure accuracy but the publisher can accept no responsibility for errors or omissions, or for any liability occasioned by relying on its content.

Paperback ISBN: 978-1-910760-39-0
eBook ISBN: 978-1-910760-53-6

A catalogue record for *My Travels in Ding Yi* is available from the National Bibliographic Service of the British Library.

MY TRAVELS IN DING YI

SHI TIESHENG

Translated by
ALEX WOODEND

ACA PUBLISHING LTD

1. Title Explanation

This so-called 'Ding Yi' could, according to custom, be considered one of my names or one of my roots; it could be understood as a particular time in my life, a place I passed through or a burden I bore. Let's put it this way: during my long, perhaps endless travels I arrived upon countless lives, and Ding Yi was one. My travels in Ding Yi were numerous and complicated, clamorous and frightening, and I often found myself at a crossroads, and this is why they left such a deep impression on me. Now in distant Shi Tiesheng, I often dream walk, grasping across the vastness of time and seem to land once again in Ding Yi. So, as I start to write down these impressions, I don't think they'll make for a good novel or even approach literature – if I had to choose a genre, I'd say memoir. So as we have *A's Experiences in Some Life Stage*, *B's Time as Some Occupation* and *C's Travels in Some Place*, this work shall be called *My Travels in Ding Yi*.

But let me be clear: I had no intention of writing up this account at the time, so I have no notes or records. It is inevitable that, as I look back on Ding Yi from the distance of lifetimes, I'll get some things mixed up.

2. Quotation and Recollection

"In the beginning, when God created the heavens and the earth, the earth was a formless void and darkness covered the face of the deep, while a wind from God swept over the face of the waters… then the Lord God formed man from the dust of the ground and breathed into his nostrils the breath of life; and the man became a living being." – **Old Testament, Genesis**

All in all, I come from there. All life comes from then.

"Then the Lord God said: 'It is not good that the man should be alone. I will create a helper to be his partner.' So out of the ground the Lord God formed every animal of the field and every bird of the air, and brought them to the man… but for the man a helper could not be found as his partner. So the Lord God caused a deep sleep to fall upon the man, and he slept. Then he took one of his ribs. And the rib that the Lord God had taken from the man he made into a woman and brought her to the man. Then the man said: "This at last is bone of my bones and flesh of my flesh…" – **Old Testament, Genesis**

Since then, Adam and Eve knew each other and depended on each other.

There, in that garden, the man Adam and the woman Eve were both naked, but they never felt ashamed. But one day at dusk "they heard the sound of the Lord God walking in the garden at the time of the evening breeze, and the man and his wife hid themselves from the presence of the Lord God among the trees of the garden. But the Lord God called to the man and said to him: 'Where are you?' He replied: 'I heard the sound of you in the garden, and I was afraid because I was naked. And I hid myself.' The Lord God said: 'Who told you that you were naked? Have you eaten from the tree of which I commanded you not to eat?' The man said: 'The woman whom you gave to be with me, she gave me fruit from the tree, and I ate.' Then the Lord God said to the woman: 'What is this that you have done?' The woman said: 'The serpent tricked me, and I ate.'… Then the Lord God said: 'See, the man has become like one of us, knowing good and evil. And now he might reach out his hand and take also from the tree of life, and eat, and live forever' – therefore the Lord God sent him forth from the Garden of Eden." – **Old Testament, Genesis**

And thus they left their place of birth.

Thus our Adam and Eve set out separately, like migrating birds promising to return. We promise to look for each other.

Thus they lost their eternal life and through cycles of reincarnation became 'my' heart and soul as it continued on its endless journey.

3. The Spirit Never Dies

As water shouts through the sand, or wind blows through the soul, desire gathers in nothingness – the spirit never dies. I know I'm about to enter another form.

Gently swaying, floating, waving. Gently spreading, escaping… There's a voice saying something, coming in and out in waves, I can't make it out. Or it's just a kind of idea on the edges of yearning and dread… And when I gently start to get close or feel more and more weighed down, the nothingness transforms, the mist suddenly takes shape: a glorious light seems to emanate from some point…

Then the sound of a bell rings forth, followed by the sight of bright-white paper covering window panes divided by dark lines, dots of light and silhouettes of tree branches… From near and far I hear Ding Yi cry, real and fake, I see Mother's silhouette.

4. Ding Yi's Arrival

When I first entered Ding Yi he was still small but not a newborn. I took him from having just the basic survival instincts – crying, eating, sleeping – to being responsive to the outside world.

When I came he'd just opened his eyes. To be more precise, his opened eyes just started to form images. At that time Ding Yi was like an untamed land, wild but harmonious and full of hidden life. Looking back, I realise I broke his serenity. Like moving into a new apartment, I looked around here and there and found all the newness fascinating, so I got carried away and broke out into song. That turned out to be a problem. I wanted to sing, but he cried and cooed with no melody. Then I realised Ding Yi was still shrouded in ignorance, was still a wilderness.

Finally one day he obeyed my wishes and started to call Mother; he did so blindly, but I eagerly awaited Mother's loving gaze and gentle fingers. He couldn't even talk, a stupid mess, while I was restless. I told myself not to be restless. I told myself to wait, wait until this Ding gets his faculties in order in the way a bud becomes a flower – only then could I expect him to accurately carry out my intentions. I knew Mother was waiting too. Mother patiently told him over and over: "Say 'Mama', say it! Ma, ma. Ma!" An attempt to wake up the me in Ding Yi. I really wanted to tell Mother I'd arrived, I'm right here, I really wanted to respond to her call, but no, my response had to go through Ding Yi, and Ding Yi was still confused, unable to understand me. I was so restless I wanted to shout, which made him cry and Mother worry. Hopeless, really hopeless. With great effort I made him smile, made him give Mother a wave with clenched little hands.

The sun, that warm, bright circle, cast a beam on Ding Yi's young pupils. Outside, the silhouettes of trees nearby, mountain ridges far away and the winged dawn beyond the mountain ridges. I kept sending Ding Yi's eyes in that direction, wanting us to gaze together, awaiting the future where we would walk there together.

5. Human Tool

"A worker wanting to be good at his job must first prepare his tools." OK, OK, so Ding Yi, this human tool would do!

The tool wasn't quite ready for me, which made its user lonely, but watching its adult counterpart moving or stopping, thinking or wondering in their glory, I couldn't help but feel pleased. But like a good boat navigates an open river on its own, or one can sleep soundly in a solid desert hut, or the functions of a computer go from storage to associations, communication and playing games... I anticipated my Ding-rich future as the master of Ding Yi.

I see some 'primates' unworthy of the name. How could they possibly be 'prime'? 'Rodere' and 'coelenterata' are aptly named, they chew and crap. It's ridiculous, but on my long journey I've actually mistakenly landed in an ape's body – that useless tool! It led me around all day eating, sleeping, climbing. No passion, no love! Weary ignorance was always tied to me like a rope.

Another time, I was almost pitched into water, panicked and sent my spirit into a fish – oh my, that blockhead sure was a dull tool. Distended from eating their own kind while trapping and slaughtering any other species, a life adrift until dying in unutterable disgrace. How about a dog or a horse? My God, those lost soul distribution centres are no better than fish! Being a fish is like being drugged by jimsonweed or beaten with a big stick. In a dog's body you're much more awake but can only use its four paws for walking and frightened eyes for looking. Even when they wander around and seem to understand something, they end up just lowering their heads and barking a couple times and that's it. The inner turmoil of helplessness.

Now look how great this human tool is! Not only does it have food and shelter, it can laugh and cry; not only can it look near and far, it can prepare for danger in times of peace; not only can it hunt, it can farm. Take this hand, it's exquisitely designed! Its fingertips are so sensitive they can pick up a hair without the aid of sight but are so tough they can withstand intense heat and pluck a chestnut from a fire. And this stomach, it not only absorbs useful nutrients and separates them from waste but automatically vomits out harmful contaminants.

But that's nothing. What do you think the most prominent advantage of the human machine is? It's play! It's recreation! Moreover, it's thought and taste! Poetry and painting, literature and drama, song and dance… there's nothing this tool can't do. Even baseball is amazing, the way the bat strikes the ball so precisely, you can't help but marvel at the Lord's unique creation. Let a computer try it, let a robot try it, let any other tool try it – not even close! So I came to Ding Yi.

So Ding Yi and I started our ten years of inseparability together.

6. Together

Ding Yi and I together – that sounds simple, but it's actually complicated, with many implications. To put it most directly: we breathe the same fate, and share the same pleasures and difficulties. In short, until he was scrapped we were completely dependent on one another, inseparable for even an instant. However, inseparable things are not referred to as being 'together'. This implies another possibility: Ding Yi and I could sometimes go it alone. Take dreaming, for example, that was usually my thing. During that time I'd roam heaven and earth doing whatever I wanted. And Ding Yi? It was plain to see that the beast was sound asleep.

But it would be unfair to say he was uninvolved. For example, if some porno videos made him restless the whole night I'd have trouble dreaming freely. His lust would even make me dream of ripples in the water caused by a spring breeze, dream of dazzling colours. Another example. If he got obsessed with a video game, clicking away all night, how was I supposed to dream? Of course I could ignore it, drift into the void, be nowhere. But as soon as I'd go my own way he'd curse. It was my fault if things got messed up. He'd slap his thighs and forehead, shocking me, ruining my fun, forcing me back to reality. Call it a hardship or a burden, in the end it was a constant lack of freedom from all sides. Like when he met his boss, I couldn't let my mind wander (for fear of being fired). Like when he stands at a podium, I couldn't get restless (for fear of being laid off). And if he walked down the street, I had to maintain his dignity (for fear of others looking down on us). When he went to meet friends, I had to mind his deportment (to keep him from seeming like a crass fool). Especially when he wanted to drive, I had no freedom, unless I should decide to abandon him and run off. But what fun would it be to do that? Moreover, what was the rush? I'd visited many lives. You certainly leave when the time is right, but having just come to Ding Yi, already thinking about leaving – it would be appropriate to cite the ancient maxim: "Might as well."

Since the decision was made to be together it might as well be done with dedication, through thick and thin, no matter how difficult. If not, why bother coming? If not, why would he get grumpy when I'm unhappy? And where would it be any different? Didn't someone say freedom is relative, lack of freedom is constant? Ding Yi wouldn't have understood such a saying when I first arrived, but I had experienced so much of life I couldn't forget it – all the hardship and suffering allowed me to know what freedom was. And how would I have made Ding Yi so frustrated? Like when answering questions at school, later doing maths and writing, staring with a furrowed brow in the light of a desk lamp, brain straining in different directions, what's going on? Simple: I was tired. Sorry if I had to get in a little rest! If not, I'd have just thought of something else – drifted into the void or become restless. I see it this way: when others are around I work tirelessly to maintain your dignity, Ding Yi, and when no one's around you should settle into my mood, make sure my hobbies are accommodated – it can't always be just doing what you want, right? But he tried to keep me awake by soaking me in warm water, then splashing me with cold water. Everything short of stabbing me. But nothing worked. I'm really tired, or I'm just really not interested in that stuff. But if Ding Yi's stubborn, what can you do? Seems twice as much effort gets half the results, like trying to get a dog to jump over a wall that's too high. Like foreign languages: I remember this Ding put in no small effort, memorising words from dawn to dusk, very pleased with his mutterings. And what came of it? He just scraped through. But I'm interested in art. He was naturally good at things I was interested in. I've always liked painting, so it didn't take much for Ding to get praise from the teacher. The art teacher patted his shoulder and cocked his head to get a better look at lines that seemed to be forming with God's help. "Hey, you're all right!" Complimenting him in that vague way, what did he really mean? Why are foreign languages not all right, spending so much effort and still not all right? Why is art good, even just fooling around and the teacher says it's good? I smirked: no need to be vague here, it's me! Got it? But it was no use. The guy wouldn't understand.

7. Fairytale Show

I'll just say here: what Ding Yi was best at, or what Ding Yi and I cooperated best at, was performing, that is to say theatre, singing and dancing.

One year on Children's Day, the children performed *Snow White*. Ding Yi was the prince, and a good-looking girl played the princess. A witch puts the princess to sleep and she can't wake up. The prince hurries over on his horse, bends down and presses his lips to hers, and rescues her. Who knew that, on seeing her closed eyes, pristine body, her soul would depart? Ding actually thought it was real, and before that pair of eyes framed by straight hair, his feet trembled. I hurried to remind him: *It's fake, man! A play, this is a play!*

But this Ding was in such a state with infatuation building up in his heart that he was already head over heels. How could he possibly hear what I was saying? I just saw him storm across the stage like a mad bull, then slump to the ground, crying loudly. The teachers were at a loss. They saw the crowd whispering. The director shouted: "Pull the curtain! Pull the curtain!" But just then an unexpected and heartwarming scene took place on the stage: the princess heard the prince arrive, but why hadn't he bent down and kissed her? Seeing that Ding wailing away in the pitch dark, panicked and afraid, the princess rose like a spirit leaving its body and rushed towards the prince, embracing him and saying: "Hey, hey, I'm not dead! I'm not dead! Look, do I seem dead?" The audience was stunned to silence. On stage, it seemed to be the prince who'd died and come back to life as the two children hugged. The director had an epiphany. "Hurry, hurry! Music, music!" The glorious closing number was played, clearing away the darkness, soaring through the sky, making the traumatised little couple break into tears. Thunderous applause broke out and didn't stop. They shouted: "Bravo, bravo!" Great what they did with the script, and what incredible acting! So much less contrived than that romantic kiss, right? Much more mature and progressive.

8. Spring and Autumn

I've already forgotten that good-looking girl's name, so let's call her Spring, because that Snow White woke up to a world bathed in sunshine and because her sister was named Autumn. Right, Autumn. Autumn was more than ten years older than her sister. But Ding Yi and I never actually saw Autumn, we just heard the sound of her voice, just saw her picture. Spring's family had a room filled with pictures of Autumn dancing.

"Wow, had her picture taken so many times!"

"She dances," Spring said. "And she's attractive."

Autumn's poses really were attractive. Her body was really attractive too. But it was hard to make out her face.

"Is she as pretty as you?"

"Mum says Autumn's a hundred times prettier than me!"

A hundred times? Ding Yi couldn't understand. *What would that look like?* I said: *It's nonsense, that's why you can't figure it out.*

Then the sound of a piano could be heard.

Spring led Ding Yi out. Walked past the quiet hall, walked past the deep courtyard, walked past bees and butterflies dancing in the branches of a Begonia covered in pink and white flowers, to the sound of the piano. Spring said: "Shh. Be quiet." She gripped the door as she peered inside, then called Ding Yi over.

But there was no Autumn. Through the door crack a man could be seen from behind, on his shoulder the fluttering feathers of a large bird.

"Did you see, my sister?"

But there was still no Autumn. Only the sound of her dance steps, only the sound of her breathing, only the sight of the white, wispy feathers, swaying back and forth with the gentle flow of the air…

"Who's the piano player?"

"Big Brother."

Ding Yi straightened up. "Your brother?"

"No, no, it's Big Brother!"

That Ding looked at me. *Big Brother?* I pretended not to understand. *Why are you making such a big fuss?*

But Spring gave a tight smile. After a moment, she spoke into Ding Yi's ear. "That's a secret."

"Secret?"

"Yeah" Spring tilted her head to listen to the piano. "Can't tell you now."

"Why?"

"Because, because, uh… I don't know either." Spring giggled, apparently unaware of the truth but also somehow having a degree of understanding.

I suddenly felt Ding take a long, deep fall, then there was emptiness, like lush grassland suddenly turning into desert.

"Let's go, I'm bored," he said.

Spring, however, seemed to have forgotten the whole thing about the secret. She bounced around, telling Ding Yi: "It's like this every time. Every time Autumn dances, Big Brother comes to do the accompaniment. They close the door and don't let anyone go in. But sometimes they let me go in. Maybe if you weren't here today they would have let me…"

Whatever had gotten into this Ding made him just hurry away, grumbling: "Bullshit, he doesn't even play well…"

Spring stopped short. "Excuse me?"

"I said he doesn't play well at all!" Ding Yi said, still walking.

Spring, offended, followed.

Ding Yi had a point. That piano music didn't fit Autumn's dancing, didn't fit the elegance and turbulence of the white feathers…

9. Hazy Dream

Was it because of Autumn that Ding Yi had this dream? Or did what happened that day touch on some deep past concern of mine? I don't know. I still don't know. Afterwards, that Ding used the 'dreams are your department' defence to dismiss it. What he meant was that dream and him and Autumn and that day were all irrelevant. OK, OK, regardless, it's hard to find evidence. But I remember the dream clearly. It happened on some night of some month of some year that Ding was sleeping well. Suddenly, a nameless woman appeared and danced with me.

All was silent, all was empty, apart from the fluttering white dress.

"Who are you?"

The night was dark, but in the dim light reflected by the white dress I thought she looked familiar.

"Have we met before?"

She just smiled silently, still dancing smoothly and precisely.

I turned and whispered to Ding Yi: *Hey, who is she?*

That young Ding was sound asleep.

I danced and danced with that woman, and music accompanied us. Until the distant dawn light unfurled the nearby fields, villages, the criss-crossing paths. It was a magical dance, and though I was afraid of the woman, my feet couldn't help but move forward and back with hers, uncontrollably. Like that line of poetry I read when I was in Shi Tiesheng: "From wrong to wrong the exasperated spirit / Proceeds, unless restored by that refining fire / Where you must move in measure, like a dancer." – **TS Eliot,** *Four Quartets*

I looked at her intently, saw her smile seemed to hold sorrow or hide regret. For a long, long time she said nothing, just danced like that from start to finish, as light as the wind, like the peace of night. But with the expansion of dawn her elegant face began to blur, her slim figure seemed to melt, and her white dress and the daylight melded together...

"Hey, what's wrong? What the heck is wrong!"

I screamed, wanting to grab her, be near to her, hold her tight, but my hands were empty, the woman already gone.

I looked all around, near and far, on the streets, in the city, in the countless buildings: "Hey, hey! Where are you? Where are you?"

Ding Yi started awake and sat there, confused.

Hey, you know that woman?

Young Ding Yi seemed to think blankly about it.

That woman, you've seen her?

Ding Yi gave a drowsy 'Yeah' but then shook his head.

Why did she seem so familiar to me? I thought to myself.

When I thought to myself, that Ding was already heeding his mother's call to dress, excrete, wash and eat.

This was one of the first dreams after I came to Ding Yi. In the end, it didn't matter if this dream had anything to do with Autumn. From then on, that unknown woman came frequently in dreams, harassing Ding Yi.

10. Innate Affection

When it comes down to it, of all the human forms I've taken, one thing that stood out about Ding Yi was that he was innately affectionate.

Ding Yi's affection was already evident in the *Snow White* performance and has now been reconfirmed by the hazy dream. But why, you may ask, must we choose an affectionate residence? I'll tell you. This place has an old saying: "True genius comes from good cheer." For some reason, the affectionate cannot be fools. But why is that? Aren't fools even more happy? Alas, once bitten by a snake, twice shy of rope. The fool couldn't help but make me think about the times I strayed into the bodies of primates and fish or transported my soul in a horse or dog. Such senseless lives were just wanderings, blind and hopeless like endlessly weaving a headless, tailless, colourless rope. Ding Yi's rope also had to be woven, but it didn't include a different kind of body, it was a compatible machine. For example, beasts such as primates, fish and canines spend half their lives nodding their heads at themselves, walking back and forth, and sooner or later end up in a trap. The human path isn't like that. The human path is full of change and colour, with infinite possibilities giving way to infinite hope, and though the pain is greater than that of beasts, there is surprise, honour, appreciation and feeling as the rewards. So I say it's worth it. So I settled on Ding Yi, admired his affection. Why is the human path full of colour and possibility? I say it comes down to feeling.

Another point: I like this Ding's honesty. Fools don't tend to be cunning. I think this Ding is reckless, silly and maybe even a bit stupid. This kind of person is usually honest. Honesty does not mean no privacy, no tricks, everything being out in the open – not at all, just that Ding Yi and I didn't deceive each other.

Really, man? Of course, of course. I think you're not only genuine but clear-minded. You think fools are all honest? Yeah, yeah, the more of a fool one is, the more clever one must pretend to be. Fools are foolish because they always deceive themselves.

11. Metabolism

The words 'Ding Yi and I together' would suggest that difference or conflict would be inevitable. Are we able to reach mutual compromise? Of course. Sometimes. Sometimes compromise is necessary, but there are also major problems. Why? Because being an immortal spirit, I always find inspiration in hope, but the human-born Ding Yi is blazing desire.

Like smoking. I've always been against it, but he wouldn't listen, smoking a cigarette and humming a little tune, absolutely pleased with himself! I mean, think of your lungs, buddy! The lungs are yours, the heart is yours too, from head to toe it's all yours, just think it over. You know what he said? He said what the fuck's it got to do with you? I thought, fine, fine, fine. OK, Ding Yi, go ahead and smoke. What do I care if you smoke yourself to death. It's like the local song about her love dying in the morning and her following him to the afterlife in the afternoon. But really if you die, Ding Yi, I'm still me, I have places to go. An immortal spirit has little to learn from your short life. So I'd say the smoking wasn't my responsibility. Why did he never smoke in dreams? Dreams are my jurisdiction, I don't smoke. He can smoke a dick! When he gets up and doesn't listen to my advice once more, there's nothing else I can do.

Then there's gluttony. When walking down the street, if he saw something tasty he'd freeze, regardless of whether the thing was clean or not, his eyes would suddenly light up, saliva running over his lips, stomach grumbling fiercely. I mean take it easy, buddy, that's dirty. I mean look at these flies, more numerous than your teeth, that just came from the toilet! But by then he was already sitting down, all my advice just hot air, as the food hit the nose, mouth and then stomach. Did it matter what the result would be as it continued on further? Alas, good advice is hard to take!

When it comes to compromise, sometimes it's necessary. You have to. Take food, food is necessary, when in Rome, right? That I understand. Without provisions, the body breaks. First a little gossip: this place has a story that says there was a well-known philosopher who one day hosted a banquet for all his friends, but when they arrived they saw a bag of food blasphemously worshipped in the main hall. They were all stunned, because this went against the scholar's reputation. The scholar asked: "What's this called?" The guests were displeased, thinking he was teasing them. But then they saw the scholar remove his hat and kneel, bowing to that thing and saying: "Without it, there is no elegance!"

But while eating for me is a last resort, the people of Ding Yi's realm turn it into a performance, or even a badge of honour. To say "Have you eaten?" is considered a compliment, or a good wish, but if spoken reluctantly it can also be sarcastic.

Honestly, the act of eating is really absurd. From spring to winter, from birth to death, a good smell here, a bad smell there. Some organic matter visits the body like a tourist destination, turning the stomach into a runway. How did Ding Yi's people acquire this custom? They say it's life, that it's one of life's necessities. But in my many travels, would you believe I've been to a place with no need for such base concerns? What? You don't think that could be called life? OK, OK, let me ask: why live? How did life happen? I understand you can't answer. I'll tell you: in general, if ceaseless reproduction and regeneration isn't life, what is it? Everything is metabolism, rolling and flowing, endlessly. Everything is eternally spread, everything is a slice of eternal spreading, a point, a ring, a ray, a simple desire for stillness!

Borges said this could all just be an image or side of something infinite. The problem is the image or side are unknown to one another. Like the bookcase filled with millions of books, millions of stories, each with the same origin, but each independent of the other. The metabolistic way is simply multi-faceted. When used to seeing a three-dimensional body, others can't recognise you. When you hear about another way of life, you don't believe it, you don't understand it. You can't imagine it even if I explain it to you. You see the world from the perspective of your own cosmic dimension, like looking at the stars from the bottom of a well, see it self-righteously. You experiment, make guesses, speculate, but you'll never know how other dimensions exist, how they spread. In modern physics there is the anthropic principle, which basically means: isn't it amazing the world is like this (conducive to human existence) and not otherwise (unconducive to human existence)? The answer is: because the world is the way it is, humans are the way they are, and humans can make such observations and ask questions about the world, or such questions and observations about the world make it that way. For example, another metabolism wouldn't necessary feature the verbosity, shabbiness or dangerousness of Ding Yi's realm.

12. Spirit and Tool

Telling you all this has made me realise something: the reason why apes, fish, dogs and horses have more difficulty evolving could be because those apparatuses spend too much time eating. They run wild, digging, peeling, biting, searching and seeking – all of that and more in the name of finding sustenance! Eating all day, chewing all night, where's the time to do anything else? So the mind can't develop, thinking has no way to develop, feelings cannot emerge, and thus, even with a spirit inhabiting it, the material has difficulty acting. Eat, then sleep, eat, then sleep, then defecate. Even mating time is squeezed in between other activities and done in a panicked, perfunctory way. If it weren't crucial for the survival of the species, they probably wouldn't do that thing either. How did people develop? How did people become people? One view is that is has to do with labour. Jeez, the ignorance. I see it as ignorance. What are you working for? Isn't food and drink enough – look at apes, fish, dogs and horses, what's the point of making yourself busy all the time, plotting and scheming? If feeling isn't part of the driver, heroes and cowards would take the same kinds of wives – who doesn't know 'no pain, no gain'? Another view holds that it's because of language, which is obviously much deeper. But why do you want to speak? Who do you most want to speak your heart to? If it weren't for the lure of feeling, would this mouth be busy enough just eating? A whole life of silently shaking your head and tail like a fish? Of course it's because of feeling! And then because of love! Because of loneliness you long for others, because of fear you seek companionship with them. "Knowing one other in life is enough", so you want to see if those bodies like yours have the same yearning you do. That's why language was created. That's why work came to exist. That's how people stopped being satisfied with eating, drinking and multiplying, and separated themselves from beasts.

In fact, bodies are all beasts. Qin Han (I'll talk about him later) said: "The difference between people is larger than that between people and pigs." This irritates some people who think it's insulting to humans. Actually, there's no malice in that remark. It points out a fact: no matter how a body is constructed, what organs it's equipped with, its physiological features, there isn't much difference between humans and other animals. It's said that the genes of mice are very similar to those of people, while those of chimpanzees are just a tiny bit different. The true difference, or the most important difference, is mood, is longing, is thought and feeling. And in those aspects, who could be more different than one man from another? Another piece of evidence: people are sometimes more aggressive than beasts, more heartless; an example everyone knows is Hitler, isn't he more like a beast than a human? Alternatively: doesn't the human body necessarily contain a soul?

Yes, yes, not every human body contains a soul. How can we check? Actually, it's easy. Just see whether or not the body can fall madly in love, whether or not it's full of love. Regardless of a human form, even a beautiful one, if like a beast it blindly easts, sleeps and multiplies, follows the law of the jungle, it can be shown not to contain a soul. Another example is the insatiably greedy, who adhere to the idea that the ends justify the means, those flatterers, bandwagoners, people who wouldn't give a hair on their head for the good of the world. What should you call people who gorge themselves into oblivion all day? The walking dead! That's right, can't get more accurate than that! That's the definition of a human body devoid of a soul. Their thoughts and feelings are like a fallow field, their love and desire rotted away, without even the smallest dreams. No, no, I'm not referring to the haughty self-righteous, fully independent train of thought; that is like walking down a dead end or the esoteric theory even someone like me doesn't dare involve himself with. But, in my opinion, those people who say they want to cut off desire are mostly unable to bear the intensity of human life and so take to the wild and run off. There's also a type of person who hears love and speaks exhaustion. You say love, they shout exhaustion: "Man are you done yet?" "Man are you stupid!"— Heh, when you've seen enough you'll understand it's not just the result of getting one's hopes up and having them dashed. Truly soulless bodies fail to understand such words, including all that about being tired or having enough, it's all lost on them. You discuss feelings and love with them? OK, listen to me, talking back and forth they'll still see that is a kind of special food (such as a 'film feast', 'cultural feast', 'arts feast' and other common phrases you find on the screen or in newspapers). Now that is a soulless body, a godforsaken place where, though life was breathed into them, the soul never illuminated. It's like a computer filled with features but without software. No one ever came to operate it, so they never had any desire to run it. Your solemness won't allow you to say it's not a computer, but it's total rubbish.

That's right, bodies are all beasts, they function in largely similar ways, with minor differences – the big similarities are eat, drink, excrete, mate, sleep; the only small differences are a strong or weak memory, the speed or slowness of the power of understanding, and the flourishing or waning of the power to procreate. Though the human body has relative advantages in these aspects, the key to making humans human lies elsewhere. A computer's memories are clearly greater than a human's, but they're still not better than beasts. The crucial thing that makes humans human is the power of imagination! The power of imagination's abundance is still depressed, its flow is still stagnant, its vastness is still constrained. Yet this power of imagination was born in all its glory from nothing, or to be more precise was driven out of feeling. So no kind of robot whatsoever can match it.

Ding Yi was a bit confused: *What do we do about this?*
Do about what?
Soulless bodies. If we encounter them, what do we do?
No need to worry. My man Ding is actually unlikely to encounter them.
Why?
Think about a computer. You turn it on, but nothing appears on the screen no matter what commands you enter. Would you consider that an encounter? Think of a human form. You discuss feelings and love with them, and they just shout about food and drink. Have you encountered them?

13. Shi Tiesheng Interjects

At this point, Shi Tiesheng had some serious veiled criticism: "Why just feeling?"

Maybe later I'll write *My Travels in Shi Tiesheng*, but now isn't the time. Wherever this Shi's travels finally led, however he had been reduced by them, the final nail still wasn't in the coffin, like the officials in this Shi's realm would famously say: first, "Can't say"; second, "Hard to say"; third, "Still can't say".

"Hey, I'm asking you!" That Shi looked stern.

"What?" I said. "You tell me."

"Like 'spirit' isn't as important as your 'feeling'?"

Heh, I felt annoyed: this Shi seemed like a great one.

"Oh, Old Shi," I said. "Don't bring up the boundary in your parts, OK? You're always crying about your empty 'spirit'! But there's always either nothing or everything in there. You guys get yourselves all mixed up by relying on that word too much. How can spirit be more important than feeling, more splendorous than love, broader than thought? But let me ask: without emotion, love and thought, what could 'spirit' actually be?"

That Shi was briefly at a loss for words. "Of course there's a... whole lot, like strength."

"Strength, what for?"

"You know. Strength, first of all, is a virtue."

"So that Hitler wasn't strong?"

"But strength is definite... definitely better than weakness, you must agree with that, right?"

"Not necessarily. Ding Yi is weaker than that artist Z in *Notes On the Obscure*, but I'd rather have Ding."

"That's just you! I think Z is more ambitious..."

"Come on, ambitious! Is hatred also ambition? No wonder your realm is such a mess! No wonder your realm is out of great people! Spirit conquers spirit, bullets shoot bullets..."

"Then I'll also ask: thought and love, are they not spirit?"

"That's why I can't speak as inanely as you."

"So let me ask again: the 'thought' you're talking about isn't inane? Z doesn't have thought? And Hitler didn't have thought? You reckoned hatred wasn't thought?"

"Hatred is an instinct. Don't get it wrong, Old Shi. Hatred is a psychological reaction, much like a wolf showing its teeth, much like a dog tucking its tail, it's actually fear, it's wariness or a way of taking the offensive. Of course it's necessary sometimes, but it's definitely not thought, how could fear and wariness be considered thought? But when hate turns to love, and follows it, thought is born. Love, in that case, isn't an instinct, it's wisdom."

"Now you're talking about feeling again, come on!"

"I don't think you can have love without feeling."

"Don't you think you're overemphasising feeling now?"

"I'm just saying, spirit without feeling can be anything but love. Spirit without love can be anything but thought."

"So what's to be done?"

"Don't people in your realm usually start by raising a spirit flag?"

14. Challenge Yourself

But there's a problem: Ding Yi and I are not one, so who does the brain actually belong to? That's a really good question, something a discerning person would ask. But this question can't be answered in a succinct and satisfying manner.

Put it this way: you sit in front of a computer, wanting to write an article and also wanting to play a game, what's the result? The result is you either write an article or play a game. No, I'm really not joking, it's the truth. The truth is, my conflicts with Ding Yi often started from here: both contending for use of the same brain.

Everyone wants their wishes to be its commands or make it run in accord with their own life. In truth, the difficulties of travelling in Ding Yi often stemmed from here. Why did I sometimes hit his head? Why did he often drive my exploits to confusion? Again, it's like the most popular catchphrase in Ding Yi's realm – 'challenge yourself'. But few people have thought about who the challenger is and who the challenger is challenging. Really, it's simple. If I say I challenge Ding Yi or Ding Yi challenged me. One time competing in the high jump, the pole went up to 1.45 metres, and that Ding said: No way, no way! I said: No way? Come on. You're all right! Then he jumped right over, nice and easy. The pole was raised again, to 1.55 metres, and he said: No way, no way again. This time for sure. I said: Don't be so sure. Listen to me, my man, jump! So he jumped over it again. Then it was 1.65, 1.75. Every time he said no way. Probably not gonna make it. I said: Why are you worrying about that? It doesn't matter, we're going to try anyway! So he kept jumping, up to 1.77 metres! That's what 'challenging yourself' means. That was me challenging Ding Yi.

Did Ding Yi challenge me? For example, I sometimes resented his stupidity, complained about his incompetence: why can you never get more than an eighty in foreign language and always barely pass chemistry? Why can't you be like Chen Jingrun in maths, like Carl Lewis in the hundred metres, be as tall as Yao Ming, or look anything like Alain Delon? At those times – you could say he was quite reasonable or you could think that Ding was brimming with many virtues – he tilted his neck to one side and said: I'm Ding Yi and just Ding Yi. That's the way Ding Yi is, take it or leave it, man! I couldn't disagree. I chose Ding Yi, yet I complained about Ding Yi. What was the point? Like if we played cards, but I dealt them all to you, would that be fun? The issue is, if you get a bad hand don't you still play? If there's no way to avoid losing, brothers, let's make a show of it! That's how he challenged me, that is the effect Ding Yi's challenge had on me.

But since I've long stopped inhabiting Ding Yi, and he's long since become a point in my past to examine, that brain should be his. Recently

I've been in Shi Tiesheng, so Ding Yi's brain has gone off with Ding Yi, and Shi Tiesheng and I now share one. Just like being in Ding Yi, this Shi and I are often at odds with each other. For example, now I'm writing *My Travels in Ding Yi*, and that Shi is really against it. He's always being a cynic: "Did you include this?", "Did you include that?" "Oh, hey, why are you always emphasising the good parts?" "Why didn't you talk about certain things? You forget, or are you too afraid?" But there are some things I wanted to say yet he wouldn't let me. He worried other people would think they're things he did, which would implicate him, cause him to be ridiculed. I just said: "Hey, if it's not about you, stay out of it. It was between me and Ding Yi when he was alive, and now that he's dead it's all my responsibility."

"But some things about me," that Shi muttered, "you seem to have written in too."

Apologies, apologies, I really apologise. But I have a response ready: looking back at Ding Yi, who lived his life and left this earth, inevitably causes instances of mistaken identity.

Literature is like that. Literature isn't news, it isn't reporting, it isn't a factual recording of a life or an experience. People often talk about 'imaginative powers'. What makes one possess imaginative powers?

Then there's 'fiction'. Where does fiction come from? Simply put, literature doesn't come from the human body. It comes from the common experiences of the eternal soul's endless journey, its imaginings, thoughts, difficulties, hopes and desires. Literature exists in me, or you could say I exist because of literature. Don't you have to answer to the words you put down? Remember: this literature thing, fundamentally speaking, is unlike the responsibility, the form that Ding, that Shi, and those like them, take. That Ding is already gone, already scattered by the wind. This Shi will sooner or later become nothing, off in a puff of smoke, so I'm the only one who is able to speak to these things.

15. Danger and Cover

Let's get back to Ding Yi. This Ding Yi's realm was full of hazards. The metabolic danger was nothing, nothing more than the danger of eating unclean food, nothing more than the five elements being out of balance. The real danger was even more frightening. The real danger was revealed the first time Ding Yi and I left the house, the moment we walked into the outside world.

"I hobbled out of the house, walked into the yard. The smell of the sun-scorched flowers, the smell of the sun-scorched masonry. As the wind blew the sunlight danced, flowed. Two intersecting grey brick paths joined the four houses around the yard and cut it into four equal pieces of land. Two of the pieces each had a jujube tree, while the other two were planted with blue passion flowers. The large, lonely petals of the blue passion flowers bloomed. Surrounded by layers of petals, bees drilled into the middle, buzzing as they mined. The butterflies flew here and there leisurely and elegantly, silent as a phantom. The wavering shadow of the jujube trees was covered in bits of its flowers. The greenish-yellow jujube flowers were like a layer of powder covering the moss on the ground... I crossed the high threshold, struggling to walk out of the courtyard entranceway. Before my eyes was a small, peaceful road – slim, tidy. The outlines of two or three unknown people walked past, towards the rising sun in the east, towards the sunset in the west..." **Shi Tiesheng's *Gently Leaving and Gently Coming***

This is me in Shi Tiesheng encountering the atmosphere of the outside world. But all the same this could be me availing myself of Ding Yi's help, or Ding Yi heeding me and stepping into that seductive world atmosphere that we gazed at together in swaddling clothes.

Distant mountains are still unreachable, the flowing glow behind distant mountains are no nearer. We still gazed. With Ding Yi's innate desire and my constant praying, speculating about everything in front of and behind that mountain, imagining the area behind the back of the flowing glow. And the key encounter, or the real danger, was arriving at that moment.

Then, strange eyes suddenly flashed within the silhouettes of the nearby trees. Their gaze was quite unusual, unlike the softness of Mother's and the frankness of Father's, and even more unlike the kindness and affection of Grandmother's. The eyes gradually increased in number and surrounded us, watching us intently. Some came right up to us, pointing, sniggering and whispering. Whenever it was, young Ding Yi was standing outside the door of his house, the two of us observing the strange, hidden mysteries of the world, hidden mysteries that seemed to hold a clue to...

A voice said: "Look at him, standing in the street with his bum exposed!"

Though the voice was soft, its eyes were like a sword and caused a shiver to run down the naked boy's body. What? What's wrong with the bum, I thought. It can't be exposed?

"Ha, not bad little guy, you just let it stick out for everyone to see?"

They giggled then hushed before shamelessly fiddling with the little sprout below the boy's belly. Is that weird? He was born with it, is it really that funny? I noticed Ding Yi was at a loss too, but that little sprout was sticking straight up, and a wave of inexplicable pleasure washed along its land. That pleasure was like a cut, and like danger. I looked at that boy again and saw he was lost in a daze. I also got confused, momentarily unsure of the cause, forgot it. Young Ding Yi was naturally more shrouded in ignorance, only feeling the daze grow step by step, helplessly moving towards terror but also heeding an irrefutable call. Could the little sprout really be that sensitive and alert? It was shocking. Young Ding Yi couldn't imagine its future, magical use. Look at it, like going forth into the wind and rain, like the thoughtful indicator of an immediate want, all of heaven and earth are outlined in its shape which holds the bounds of time. Suddenly I saw that boy look ashamed and use both hands to quietly cover that sprout – Ah, then I got it: Adam! Adam and Eve! Naked Adam and naked Eve and those two fig leaves that floated out of nothingness...

Oh, yes, yes, that was the beginning of my travels! Then I had been in Adam. I had set out from Adam. Right, it was because of a snake, a vitriolic snake that spread temptation. The cause was a tree and the fruit on the tree. Because the fruit was stolen and eaten, I left home, left Eden and set out from Adam, then happened to unexpectedly land one day in Ding Yi. Ah, it's been so long, that beautiful garden! A paradise built without shelter that fostered virtue without honour and disgrace; all the flowers in the garden, the trees, all the hearts and bodies, spirits and tools, were without exception naked, content, happy and awash in the peaceful elements. It was the snake's word that forced Adam and Eve from their home, made us permanent drifters, travellers.

We broke up outside the entrance to that garden and left behind the names Adam and Eve. To put it another way, we made the break-up of Adam and Eve into the start of the journey. This point is very important. From then on the seamless dream world was split in two, from then on Adam and Eve were notably different, from then on we were scattered to the four corners of the earth and searching for each other became the committed purpose of our setting out. That's why, when Ding Yi quietly covered that marker passed down to him from Adam's genes, I suddenly remembered our departing ceremony: two fig leaves floated down and covered two different flowers...

But if Adam and Eve's different markers were obvious, why cover them?

Oh, right, right – while being punished, they were also gently urged by God: your built-in dissimilarities make you different; cover them so you can call each other on your search; taboos represent openings. This way you may be able to walk the path of stirring your effervescent souls to life.

Maybe I had worked out why the ceremony must be taken seriously: the snake's secret could not be taken back, but this severe punishment and gentle urging could remedy the world's pride and carry forth the profound meaning of life. But, to be exact, what is that profound meaning? Can we actually ask what this endless journey is exactly? I don't know. I don't know. Starting when Adam and Eve separated and travelled long and far and endured the hardships of climbing mountains and crossing rivers, I was making guesses.

Right, cover! I could only say to that boy Ding Yi: *This is the ceremony that was necessary before setting out.*

But that Ding was still dazed, standing alone in the vastness of time like Adam covering his flower back then with a shameful and horrified look. I'm not blaming him. I have to make guesses about that opaque deep meaning, so of course I can't blame him. And not to mention that, while I was guessing, I frequently came to the human world and entered lives by many names, right? Again and again setting out, again and again praying, again and again feeling apprehensive.

16. Natural Lust

Before this I only valued love's genius and overlooked love's natural lust. I simply believed that love couldn't possibly be foolish, while forgetting that lust's adherents are behind the times, unreasonable and that some foolishness is inevitable.

What is lust? Attraction to something's shape or appearance. But those who are truly addicted to beauty are greedy. Ding Yi wasn't greedy. His lust was only for elegant, beautiful women, the beauty of the opposite sex. How would I know? How wouldn't I know! I'm a clear-eyed bystander with regard to Ding Yi and an old pro when it comes to being a bystander.

As the seasons passed and Ding Yi grew, his vision solidified, and I noticed he wasn't at all hesitant to hone in on women – little eyes suddenly gleaming as they groped the opposite sex in exploration; searching; gazing at this one, staring at that one, like he was carrying out a plan.

"Come here, come here, come here and kiss me!"

Grown-up women teased him, played with him, liked him. This actually posed a problem – is kissing that easy? Putting men aside, are women incomparable? If a woman ignores a man, does she become irresistible? Women were constantly expressing their feelings to him, and him? He either cried to scare them off, acting like he didn't enjoy it, or pretended to be indifferent about whether or not a pretty woman held him. But if the human form is eager and a beautiful woman appears in a flash before them? Ah-hah, so you take a look, this little guy's gaze is suddenly full of affection, and he is ready to spread his wings and fly to the promised land. I silently said to him: *Hey brother, don't be so blunt!* And he naturally didn't understand, nor did he understand the opposite of bluntness, just snuggled in that wonderful embrace, singing his babbling love song or grasping a button on a blouse, like he was playing or studying – who knew the creature could undo it.

When he got a little older, this Ding's natural lust astonished me. For example, when his mother was giving him a bath he cried every time and made a fuss like the world was ending. But some days there was the rare opportunity for a girl to come over and play. It was hot as hell, and Ding Yi's mother told him he had to wash. As soon as Ding Yi heard, sadness brewed deep in his heart. But to his surprise his mother said: "This little miss is going too, OK?" What, really? Ding Yi was elated, the sadness disappeared, and he voluntarily undressed, then happily took the girl's hand and jumped into the tub. The girl sheepishly sat in the corner. That Ding cheerfully splashed around like a fish. His mother learned quickly and often invited the girl to go with him to bathe. But one day the girl's family went on a long trip and didn't come back, so Ding Yi's mother had to get a boy to lure him into the bath. This boy was always a bit thick. As soon as he was standing naked next to the water, he had no idea how he was supposed to act and was eager to go home. That time Ding jumped out in his birthday suit as soon as he saw the boy next to the water, and he wailed, shouted, scaring his bath mate so he cried too. After the boy left, Ding Yi's mother cleverly urged him not to waste a good bath full of water, and he had no choice but to obey. He hurried to finish washing but didn't smile again for the rest of the afternoon – like he was thinking gloomily, hoping futilely, dumbly wishing to wash his past cleverness away. The scene made one inevitably think of that legendary (fake) gem in *Dream of the Red Chamber* – meant as an engagement gift for Lam Mui Mui but behind the red curtain was a Jiao Da. Alas, Ding Yi's mother and I realised the guy didn't want someone to accompany him to the bath, he clearly just wanted girls – a little girl who would wear no clothes and not hide!

This Ding's yearning for the opposite sex often embarrassed me.

When his mother got pregnant again people would ask him: "Do you want a little brother or a little sister?"

"Older sister," he'd say firmly.

"Oh, that's impossible! It can only be a little brother or a little sister."

"Little sister," he'd answer, undeterred.

"Why?"

"Little sisters are girls," the gentleman would say.

"Wow, this kid! Grown up..."

The neighbourhood had groups of both boys and girls, but Ding Yi was determined to join the girls. He never tried to take advantage, it was just running after girls, trying to be their servant. The girls sang and danced, had their well-ordered fun as this Ding followed blindly, sweating, carefree.

Furthermore, I think this Ding Yi was born with this naked desire (incompatible with the departure ceremony). There were signs from when he was very little. A prominent example is the winter before he started primary school, new year's day. His mother wanted to replace all the clothes he had on with new ones.

"Why change into all-new clothes?"

"It's new year."

"So what if it's new year?"

"Everyone gets new clothes after the new year."

His mother had barely explained, but her loving demeanour stuck with me, was buried deep in my memory, became a symbol of coming festivities. His mother's joyous nature also infected Ding Yi. He'd never been so agreeable: he kissed his mother's head as he let her take off his clothes one item at a time. But at that point, between when the old clothes were removed and the new ones put on, the only sound was a screech as he cast his mother aside and burst out the door, naked as the wind. Outside, snow was swirling, and this Ding cut through it, waving his arms and galloping, jumping with both feet in the snow as he shouted and laughed, now insane, mad, ecstatic and delighted. Then – without altering his path – he rushed headlong into a well-dressed group of the opposite sex. The girls were wearing new clothes, kindly touching each other to inspect them. Seeing this Ding jump out in his birthday suit, they all stood and watched, laughed at him, thinking the flowerbud below his belly was really wonderful. Either that or funny. His mother chased after him and, with no small effort, got him back in the house. These events caused me deep anxiety: did this Ding Yi realm contain hidden dangers, sleeping ghosts? I arrived so carelessly, did I make a rash error? Is it safe to stay here long term? I had a lurking feeling that the coming problems would not be few.

17. Scary Title

As a result I was always on guard with him, and always admonishing. Some bad behaviour, some unbecoming desires, I always tried to keep them hidden from others – this Ding was young, after all, one couldn't neglect to safeguard his future.

Or this forgiveness was already mixed with connivance, which was a hidden encouragement to his bad habits. On some day of some month of some year, Ding Yi saw a beautiful woman on his way home from school. The narrow road was long. The woman was walking ahead in fine clothing, with a graceful gait. Suddenly this guy felt a dizzy longing for her. Since I had no control over him, the kid chased after the woman like he was possessed. If the woman walked quickly, he walked quickly; if she walked slowly, he walked slowly. Not seeming to have control of himself, he walked wherever that woman went.

I said: *Hey, hey, what are we doing?* He ignored me. I said: *Wait, wait, what are you trying to do?* He still ignored me. I got worried, shouted: *Rascal! Why don't you go on home?* But he didn't seem to hear anything, he just kept staring blankly, silently focusing on that woman's back. The woman finally reached a gate. She unlocked it, pushed it open, turned sideways, and only then did she realise there was an impetuous child on her tail.

"Who are you looking for?"

Ding Yi shook his head.

"Do you know me?"

Ding Yi shook his head again.

"Where do you live?"

Ding Yi withdrew timidly.

The woman smiled, closed the door and disappeared from sight.

After standing there looking at the mysterious, secluded yard a little longer, the guy looked around and finally felt some confusion: *Damn, where is this?* I said: *Who the hell knows, let's just figure out how to get home.* We could only go off our impressions to fumble our way towards home. On the way I said: *What's been going through your head all day?* He didn't reply, like he was ashamed and also like he was excited. I said: *How old are you now? It'll be shocking if these dirty thoughts of yours don't get us into some real trouble in future.* He didn't reply, like he was sorry and also like he was satisfied. We got tired of walking and sat down to rest at an intersection. That Ding was still dazed out of his mind. *Hey, hey, what are you thinking about? Do you think this woman used to be Autumn? Did you know her before? Or that future Autumn would look like that?* This guy certainly didn't lack imagination.

Another time, flipping through a magazine in someone's house, there was a colour photo insert: on the shore next to clear blue water a graceful, strong woman in a swimsuit. Alas, as soon as this guy saw it he was shocked, thinking how could such a splendid woman exist? So he turned the image this way and that, looking, falling short only of letting his eyeballs drop out onto it. Then, having asked the owner where the magazine came from, he turned and left and walked down the street and bought a copy. So far, so normal. I didn't say anything to him. But the true perversity is still to come. After he bought that magazine, turned to that page, looked at it over and over for the whole afternoon, can you guess? Admiring the spectacle wasn't enough: just like the most precious stone cannot be perfect, the woman's face didn't look beautiful enough. He thought and thought until he came up with a plan and rushed to find another picture, cut out the film star's face and made a collage. Did that make him satisfied? Yet, however, but, did the swimsuit still cover too much? So he went to get paints and a brush, stroke by stroke made that swimsuit shrink, shrink... Ahem, might as well just paint the whole thing in flesh tones. Then he straightened up, contentedly squinted his eyes, took a few steps back to get a better look... I had a realisation: *Ding Yi, what are you doing?* That guy snapped out of it, finally felt ashamed and hurried to close the magazine. *You close it and all's well? Then what? Why not burn it!*

So things like that, those kinds of thoughts or activities happened a lot, and I helped him hide them, prevent others from finding out. And privately I often advised him: these kinds of wants are never enough, but you have to understand you're still too young, it still isn't time. How can love be so simple? We've long since left Eden, it's already been a long time since we left. Do you still remember, when leaving, why the fig leaf ceremony was necessary? Right, you still don't quite understand, but you can picture it clearly, so you have to be patient, be cautious. The kind of trouble you could stir up if you act rashly is beyond your comprehension at this age...

Education and persuasion were necessary, of course, as was enlightening, as was warning and even strictness – he couldn't be pampered. But with progress comes greater challenges. Instincts, instincts are always undervalued. Sure enough, this Ding Yi didn't let my worry go to waste! One spring day after I entered him, this guy finally caused a scene so big that all the neighbours found out – an uproar so large that even I couldn't help him hide it if he tried. What happened? That will have to be said later, and there's plenty to say. In short, that year, as the eastern wind suddenly gathered the first burst of spring light, this Ding did a very imprudent thing, which earned us a terrible title: 'hooligan' or 'rotten scoundrel'.

18. Cruel Spring

Because of this title, Ding Yi's spring became cruel. Happiness was suddenly filled with frustration. Just as the world was brightening and the flowers flourished, this Ding Yi's sky was lowered and filled with clouds as a fierce wind picked up – mocking words like a sandstorm gathered in our head and swirled around us. Wherever we went we were met with the faint sound of the title, buzzing like mosquitos or flies. In every crowd, cold faces rose to the surface, contempt flashed in eyes and familiar figures turned away. The spring wind was cruel, bracingly cold. "Warmth that suddenly turns cold is the hardest to recover."

In that period Ding Yi tucked his head in his collar, walked by himself in a lonely, sad panic, thinking maybe if he walked and walked and walked he could walk out of this society, walk out of this world! As for me, I thought about it too, why not get out of this troublesome place right away?

It's all your fault, I said to him.

Ding Yi was gloomy but said to me in private: *But you said... ugh, I didn't mean any harm.*

Then you just can't control yourself?
I only wanted... wanted to get a bit closer... closer to them.
Well said!
I just wanted to look and see if they were all... real or not.
Look and see? Is this where looking and seeing gets us?
But if you can't... touch, then how do you know they're really all there?
What's it got to do with you if they're there or not?

Ding Yi was speechless. Ding Yi walked gloomily in the spring wind, forlorn in the buzz of the title.

I understood what he meant, really I didn't blame him that much.

In my opinion, even though he was reckless, is recklessness such a big mistake? I even secretly applauded him. Why? Because of his sensitivity? Because of his frankness? Because of his bravery? None of that. So why then? Oh, oh, I just realised, as I think back on that Ding's 'scandal', I feel more longing than regret, more gladness than panic, vaguely feel there is incomparable happiness and hope there.

They're so beautiful! Don't you think so?

Hey, enough man! You haven't made a big enough mess yet?

Ding Yi looked around confused. It was really a case of the young blindly ascending without knowing suffering, then being unable to express it when they really felt it. But I still knew the things he didn't express. Of course I knew. I'm an immortal spirit on an endless journey. I've been through as many springs as I have lives! What that Ding wanted to say is: They were so wonderful, so moving. But could their wonderful selves be a mirage? Is it possible to get close to such wonder? Are such wonders authentic, lasting, or do they drift off with the wind as soon as one stops paying attention? But he couldn't say it clearly, and innocently speaking unclearly and not being understood, he was coldly exiled from society.

I could only comfort him: *It's nothing, it's nothing, brother, we've still got a whole future ahead of us.* Inside I was thinking: This itty bitty interlude counts for nothing in such a long journey. *Listen to me, brother, the future is bright, a boundless landscape, our best days are ahead.*

But that Ding still looked dejected, it was really like a local folk song says: 'Wait a thousand years for one time.' A thousand years, one time, but Ding Yi was afraid his time was a disaster.

Ahem, don't fret, don't fret. I told him not to think like that.

Don't bother me. Don't fucking bother me, OK? And to himself he cried: Maybe I should just fucking die.

19. Suicide

In Ding Yi's realm, or not limited to Ding Yi's realm, this society, from ancient times to today (including Shi Tiesheng's), is the only one I've seen that tends to commit suicide. One can't just generalise about the cause, the same result is achieved by different methods. Cause of death is the body's ageing or injury, which keeps it from living. Suicide, on the other hand, is the result of the soul's hopeless desperation; or the soul cannot bear the bounds of the human tool, its isolation, closeness, or it can't bear the suspicion of its peers, their slander, hostility or even violence, so it leaves even though the tool is still intact. You can imagine that prior to this the soul must struggle, face deep sorrow, until finally it's unbearable and has to find another way. For example this time when I was in Ding Yi, in this dark and cloudy early spring, under this 'hooligan' pressure, on this forlorn path, there were sudden thoughts of suicide – bid farewell to Ding Yi and search for a better form?

However what is death? What other paths are there? Ding Yi didn't know, I couldn't grasp it either. Based on my past experience, another path could be a little better than travels in Ding Yi, or quite good, but maybe not as good, or even more terrible. Anything was possible. The problem was you couldn't grasp it. Isn't it true that I would have had no way of imagining when I came excitedly to Ding Yi that we'd end up in this situation? To die, or not to die. Leave, or stay? The question was old enough to lose teeth. Some years ago when Shakespeare's soul passed through Hamlet's body, I thought about it day and night.

So, Ding Yi, my experience leads to one conclusion: in the end whether to live or die is up to us!

The situation is a bit like one I repeatedly faced in Shi Tiesheng. That Shi was always getting sick, always had to go to the doctor. His friends introduced him to a lot of doctors, and the doctors recommended other doctors, but which one was the best? Which one can really cure your illness? In the end we had to choose ourselves, the sick man had to choose. Someone who knew nothing about medicine would have the final say.

This was really absurd.

But everything is always this absurd, to be certain is the true absurdity.

So it is with everything. So I said to Ding Yi: *Everything must be decided for oneself in the end.*

Decide! Decide! But what should we rely on to make our decision?
Generally speaking, you rely on me. Of course, sometimes I rely on you.
And now?
Now, there's only prayer.
Prayer?
That's right, man, pray, then make a decision.
Very easy for you to say. What decision should I make?
Any decision is OK.
OK, any decision is OK. Why ask you?
Asking me or not is all the same. Because not deciding is also deciding.
What are you saying?
Truth. Anyway, there's always a path to walk. And there can only be one path to walk.

20. Value and Vanity

Why does suicide only happen in human society? Wrist cutting, jumping, lying on tracks, poisoning, hanging, drowning... why don't livestock do those things to themselves? Why have apes, fish, dogs, horses and so on never done them? People, why? Live but want to die, for what reason?

There are all kinds of direct causes. The most basic reason – in truth, I have to warn you about another more hidden, bigger danger in Ding Yi's realm, and why it exists.

In my opinion it's because of ability, relative ability. In other words value, value's assets and liabilities, the threat that arises from the comparison of value's assets and liabilities. For example, if a store has a lot of stereos on display – with one speaker, with eight speakers, mono, surround sound. From their value and price, the disparity between high and low, the cheap positioned in an inconspicuous place, the expensive in a prominent one – eye-catching, magnificent, makes people gasp and admire. This is the common practice in Ding Yi's realm. But are those that function poorly doomed to be overlooked? But can't those that function poorly be eye-catching? Are the less valuable ones always cheaper? Not necessarily. Depends on what people do. There's a workaround called publicity or hype. That is, upend the previous order – if what's valuable isn't eye-catching, the eye-catching is made valuable. Ding Yi's realm's unspoken rules.

Therefore, vanity is a trend, and this trend is pervasive to the point that it became custom. Someone as stupid as Ding Yi is unlikely to avoid being infected by such a trend. But to be honest, it's hard to absolve myself from the charge of vanity too – you can't flock together for long without becoming a bird of a feather. The reason is roughly this: I say I'm me, and Ding Yi is Ding Yi, but other people don't necessarily see it that way; other people see us as one unit, right? As a result, that Ding's actions were thought of as carrying out my wishes, and that Ding's foolish spectacle seemed to result from my instigation. If this can be tolerated, what can't be? So I say Ding Yi's vanity was really hard for me to avoid. I couldn't remain impassive, and I couldn't avoid suffering for his faults. Just as Ding Yi secretly said to me: *You still don't want to clear your name?* That's right. Once vanity became the norm, everyone became the same. Not to mention he took the blame for some things that really were not my wishes. I helped him cover it up, make things seem less ugly or more magnificent – what seemed like mutual benefit was actually mutual encouragement to do wrong.

Do people have anything private? There are those who give up their gains for honour, but none can give up their honour to give others gains. If your good deeds are done under another's name you can be accomplished and stay silent. But what if another puts their ugly deeds on your head? Even comrade Lei Feng would have to worry. A good name naturally comes from real achievement, is certainly cause for celebration, but fascination with glory makes vanity quietly grow.

As for Ding Yi's vanity, I could go on forever. Let's start with just one: for a time this Ding was keen on meeting celebrities. Put it this way: as soon as he saw a celebrity – didn't matter whether in business or government, a writer or soldier, whether on the left or right, Asian or Western – he was certain to smile and act modest. Calling it fawning might be going a little far, but I could tell his attitude was completely different than when he met normal people. That's not to say it was endless compliments, but it was at least nodding along whether he understood or not. And regardless of who he was talking with, he always tried to bring up some famous people, mention a personal anecdote about some famous person you'd never heard of, implying Ding Yi and them were close, tight, equals, mutual admirers. This made me unhappy, distressed, uncomfortable.

During and after I privately urged him: *Forget it man, is it really interesting?* Even late at night I gave up my dream freedom to make fun of him: *Would you say this is your calling?* His face would get hot, heart pumping, but he'd quickly reject it and show great inertia by remaining unchanged in the morning and going back to his old ways again.

What could I do? As a somewhat better person, you tell me what I could do. I had to help him lie, had to make them believe this guy was by no means sick, not making an empty show of strength. As for us mixing with celebrities every day, our brothers and sisters didn't distinguish between you and me: together making big plans, recording great events, making special friends, commenting on the times, challenging the leading men. As a result we were no ordinary bunch, born in a shabby room, but our character makes it glorious!

Or what? Or Ding Yi gave me trouble, said: *How can you not understand hardships?* That was one. Another: there was a long period of time when Ding kept his origin a secret. I knew – how couldn't I know? I'm not just a clear-headed bystander, not just one who has understood by personal experience, I also have intuition, I also have subconscious knowledge. The subconscious is omniscient. What made that Ding most ashamed was not that his ancestors were landlords and therefore from one of the 'Five Black' groups labelled enemies of the revolution by Mao. It was the fact that his nearer relations were workers: a glorified class with a humble position.

But we're getting ahead of ourselves. Let's first talk about our name. 'Ding Yi' (丁一 or Ding One). It was actually an unauthorised change that came after that Ding began his youth and became familiar with the ways of the world. Our original name was Ding Er (丁二 or Ding Two). One character different, or rather one stroke fewer, reflecting the elegance of vulgarity. Let me explain: This Yi (一 one) character with its concision, its sparse plainness, its unadornedness, already shows its aloofness, elegance. When put with this 'Ding' (丁) character, the name with the fewest pen strokes in the world's specialness is revealed! Sayings with 'one' ('man being one with nature', 'one thousand and one ways', 'one leader', 'one rising above the rest') are all positive. While those with 'two' ('you cannot serve two masters', 'don't walk two paths', 'two-timer', 'second-hand') are all negative. But the truth is, because of Ding Er's parents' education this was, and could not be, considered. Ding Er was therefore entered into the household registry, because Ding had an older brother named Ding Da (da means 'big'). Since they were born they called them 'Ding the Da' and 'Ding Er' so when their father was at the registry, looking at the old man in charge and holding the pen for a long time as he thought about it, the solution came to him: Ding Er!

After a number of years we happily used this convenient name. But one year, during the first windy days of spring, Ding Er fell into a mood that was withdrawn and resentful, and he began comparing himself with others. This Ding was suddenly dissatisfied, then depressed. The tackiness of that name annoyed him no end. In his words: Other people shouldn't hear our name then look at our clothes and think we don't know anything about culture. Then this guy started a series of strategies and plans, rushing to carry out operations.

I urged him to drop it: *Father and Mother gave it to you, and you can't change it, do you think you can change fate? If you change the monk, can you change the temple? Once you change it, and people see you change it, well, something to hide!*

He didn't believe me. He curled his lip, stared and whined: *You're you, I'm me. From now on stay out of my business!*

In one sense he was right. I think names are bullshit. If you want to change your name, just change it. Call me whatever you want. Whatever you're called, you're still part of my road. When it gets rough, who knows if there's a mire or a trap? The road's endless, my history, experiences, hardships or burdens are vast, without end in sight. No matter what people call me, I'm still me, no matter what my name is, it's temporary.

21. Lingling

Ding Er's impulse to change his name, thinking back on it now, was probably because of a woman called Lingling.

Lingling lived on our street, was much older than Ding Er. This woman never caught Ding Er's eye before. But during summer holiday one year Ding Er woke up early, which felt fun, so he went with his brother to deliver milk. Ding Da wasn't as full of evil thoughts as Ding Er. Ding Da was kind, not only good academically but he also learned early to show concern for his parents. That day the big brother pedalled the bike while the Little Brother ran back and forth, delivering a couple of bottles here, a few bottles there through the breeze and sun, the glowing mist.

Ding Er said: "So fun!" Ding Da said: "If it's so fun, you can do it all by yourself tomorrow." Ding Er didn't respond. He felt there was a decent chance something good would happen to him that day. The deliveries eventually took him to Lingling's house. Ding Da stuck his heel on a sticky bottle to force it into the case, while Ding Er sang a tune as he gazed over the horizon. At that point Lingling came out. When Lingling saw Ding

Er's bright, bald head she was truly puzzled and stopped to laugh. She couldn't help but go up and rub his bald pate.

"What's your name?" she said. Ding Er was still naive then, so he said frankly: "Ding Er."

To his surprise, Lingling staggered and convulsed with laughter. At first Ding Er foolishly laughed along, until he slowly got an idea and asked back: "So what's your name?" Thinking: Lingling, right? What's so special about that? But Lingling didn't answer. She pulled his hand and wrote two amazing characters on his palm.

"What, what?" Ding Er said, cocking his bald head and looking at her. "Your name is Lengleng?"

"No, Ling, Ling!" Lingling corrected him, then smugly walked away. Ding Yi watched that gradually fading silhouette as a gust of spring wind blew in his face. As I recall, this Ding Er didn't just begin to have eyes for Lingling, especially for her suddenly enchanting figure, gait and voice, but he also gained a muddled understanding of the elegance and coarseness of names.

22. Name Test

The name of this realm is very particular. From a name you can frequently tell someone's age and background. You can also determine their parents' hopes or their own interests, and sometimes see the imprint of a time period, changing trends.

If you hear the regal names Shouren or Shoulian, you can assume the person is around sixty years old. Their father or grandfather was probably a traditional man who liked to read. That or a traditional man who didn't read but always advocated reading. Or take names such as Jiye and Shengzu. There's a very good chance their family is rich, most likely aristocrats, officials or merchants afraid their offspring will be unscrupulous, become corrupt or squander the family resources. What about Yaozu? By altering just one character, the meaning changes completely. Their family probably always had its dreams frustrated and felt unlucky, so they tried to give twice as much of the family luck onto the next generation. Of course, everyone who has a name like that is no longer young. People around fifty have more varied names; they were born during a good dynastic change and therefore are often called Jianguo, Aihua or Jianjun. But some people are still lingering amid the old naming conventions, which leads to Tiesheng, Zhiqiang, Shuying and so forth. People a little younger often have one-character names: Hui, Li, Wei. The revolutionary mood had arrived and you had to be concise, strong and show movement away from the older generation's inertia and lethargy, the two's irreconcilability. As for people with stacked character names, such as Lili, Maomao, Pingping, one suspects they come from the nouveau riche. Families like that often have servants. Servants gain their masters' favour with such sweet nicknames. The master is then trapped, and these names that cannot grow up stay with their people as they do. Then there's names like Kangmei, Chaoying. Of course such people were born during the Korean War and Great Leap Forward periods. Later still this generation caused an unprecedented revolution. If you couldn't keep up with the situation, accept your name or shame yourself, you changed it! That's how we got a generation of people with names like Jihong, Lixin, Weige and Xuejun.

After that revolution, naming trends largely went in two directions. One sought to show cultured taste: you might find a spirited little fellow with the name Moseng, or a naive little girl named Muchan. Another sought to transcend Asia: Dawei, Zhenni, Dinuo and so on. Of course, some people are quite rash about choosing names, who think as long as you can put some characters on an identification card it's OK – Xiaogang, Xiaoming and Daping, for example… There are some people with the surname Wang who name their child Guo; with the surname Yang who name their child Wei; with the surname Jia who name their child Weimin. One can tell how careless parents can be when naming their kids with homonyms. Then there's the opposite. Some names are truly deep and mysterious. People with these kinds of names are usually artists or writers, or the children of artists or writers. For example how do you pronounce two呆's side by side? Or three又's lined up next to each other, how do you say that? Go look in the dictionary, many of them won't be found. But there are other names that are both ambitious and plain. For example, the writers Guang Weiran, Chen Huangmei and Yan Wenjing. That kind of name is no longer fashionable among writers. They simply don't like that elegant, heroic kind. They want something arbitrary, like Pipi, like Xiaozha – when you hear of a writer with a name like that, you can bet they're a generation younger. Young writers' children then have simplified names that are more rustic than elegant. Names like Chou Niu or Wei Yang. There's no deep meaning, they were just born in the years of the *niu* (bull) and *yang* (ram). Four-character names (not counting compound surnames) usually indicate someone was born in the nineties or later.

As the population increased, so did the number of people with the same names. As the length of phone numbers increased, names added characters. Some even sound like a sentence or nonsense. But the greater number of characters, like whatever-whatever Siji, Sitan, whatever-whatever Fu, Wa, Zi, Lang… There isn't enough space here, and I haven't even covered the uncivilised parts of the country.

They say that a long time ago, just by looking at someone's surname, you could tell their class background. But after I arrived in Ding Yi this norm was already fading away. Only countries such as India and Germany retain it. It's become quite difficult to distinguish between higher and lower surnames. When discussing the high and low of this realm's names, it's important to remember they aren't just a marker of one's house, they show someone's character, tastes, aims, culturedness… In sum, they emphasise the differences between mortals, the differences between values pursued or even different market pricing; and not just names, there are others things, maybe everything.

23. Packaging

As a result, the word packaging is increasingly prominent.

Naming is really packaging. Origins, professions, titles and so on are all packaging, but they're slightly more primitive, slightly rougher, simpler, sillier, more perverse. Until history moves forward into a franker time, all implication, metaphor and shame should be considered excessive, while image, identity and status should be called what they truly are: packaging. How direct and honest, doing away with all the costly, painstaking hiding and covering up! But how did we get to this point? It has to do with commerce finally taking over.

Packaging is totally justifiable and done openly, so counterfeit brands spread like wildfire. Short people can get thicker soles for their shoes; people with small eyes can cut their lids; those with small breasts can get implants; fat bellies can be sucked out; dark skin can be made lighter; people can dye their hair blonde to look like Westerners… The methods of packaging are too long to list, but the idea is nothing new. The ancients had it. For example, there's the cruel history of the Manchu queue order. There's feet binding, which we now think of as horrible but which used to be essential for a woman to be considered beautiful. More recently, around the time I first arrived in Ding Yi, some people sewed two patches on new clothing to support the revolution. Once in an abandoned, ancient park I saw a young violinist with sheet music spread on the bushes, clothing was so patched I couldn't tell what the original colour was – at that time you wouldn't suspect he was a street artist or a starving artist; you wouldn't sprinkle some coins at his feet, or praise his diehard dedication. After taking some time to calm down, it became clear it was also packaging. It's all packaging. Only the specifications, the styles, change with time. Once again, take this guy Ding Yi for example. I remember during one surging year of the revolution, with three swings of a hammer he smashed all the ornamentation off the family's old furniture and won himself some revolutionary pride. But this was also packaging. Nothing new.

Packaging is the second most important thing after survival for this place. This custom can be traced back to when Adam and Eve were exiled from Eden – the fig leaves they used for cover. Well, it will probably go on forever.

How is it nowadays? Worse than ever. If you travel to Ding Yi's realm, mind you this area has long had industry, business, technology and media leading in all aspects of life, not only clothing, hairstyles, decor and furnishings, but also gestures and smiles – all packaging. (That's also how words like 'operation', 'hype' and 'scale' became popular.) Anyway, what's inside no longer counts, what counts is packaging. Food and clothing (for the time being) are rarely a concern, modern people are concerned with packaging. Near and far people bustle about, clamorous – if an emperor went out in disguise and asked what was going on, an obedient staffer would answer: "Must be packaging!"

Culture is the same. For example, your house can't not have bookshelves. You have to act literate, even if you're not. You can not know what the books say, but you can't not know something about the fashionable ideas or famous people they contain. Otherwise at a party or salon, when fancy people mention Heidegger or Foucault, discourse, hegemony or political correctness, my man you will be disoriented, embarrassed and awkward. I'll teach you a trick: suppose someone's telling you some unlikely story, but you're not getting it – don't worry, don't be afraid. All you have to do is have a vague grasp of some trendy idea such as multiculturalism, spiritual pursuits or whatever-ism, and lead the topic in that direction. That's how to play to your strengths and avoid your weaknesses. The trick is to pick out the details that others aren't really thinking about and bring them up. Then ask properly: "Really?" If yes: "Nobody knows." If unsure: "What?" Things get a bit easier to handle. Will these fancy people know that you've successfully executed (or carried out the operation of) exquisite packaging? How would I know? Nonsense! One more time: I'm not just an eternal spirit, or just a consciousness, I'm Ding Yi's secret!

But, in all seriousness, when it comes to that point I lose heart. As soon as I lose heart that Ding starts sweating, his whole body gets covered in cold sweat. Right, right, I'm responsible for that. I taught him how to play to strengths and avoid weaknesses. But with shameful eyes upon him I can't but give him some guidance, right? Afterwards I regret it, feel filthy and say to him: *Come on man, you're not stupid, what are we actually doing?* He'll be stunned awhile, lost in the clouds again. I say: *Whatever we are, we are, what's the point of getting to this mess, saying it isn't what it is?* I say: *If there's an ugly scene some day, you better not throw me under the bus!* That Ding listened, overcome by shame.

At times like that he often got drowsy, yawned incessantly, then dazed into sleep. That's one way of doing it. Don't speak, sleep, forget, just act like nothing happened, which is a common strategy for saving yourself from the dangers of packaging. Another benefit was that it meant I was going to get some alone time. Dreams, how fascinating! Travelling in Ding Yi and Ding Yi's realm, one needs such a stronghold in which to regroup and recuperate. Like the people who left society to avoid war in the first dynasty and didn't know when the next one started. It's also better than an extremely vulgar saying from around here: If you pretend to be asleep while being raped, are you playing dumb or just dumb?

But I never expected dream time was also when one was most vulnerable to attack. That Ding Yi guy actually used this free time to argue back: Is this just my fault? Why haven't you exposed me in public? I earned all my dignity. You just mooch it. Even before people have said anything, you're there accusing me! What'd you say, one day I'll throw you under a bus? So you're afraid of being embarrassed too? Wouldn't you call that vanity? Man, take a look at yourself first! Of course, of course, having my words thrown back in my face left me speechless.

We both sat in stunned silence.

The moon rose.

Then stars began to shine.

Finally I said: *Sleep, sleep, you poor man.*

I couldn't wait for complete silence. I couldn't wait for the peace of dreams. Dream, or a return to the origins of life.

24. Dreamless Night

Unfortunately there were no dreams that night.

That night I slept fitfully, chaotically. I was aware of the wind picking up the first half of the night, and I remember the rain of the second half. The young couple next door argued all night. I understood every word. I just couldn't figure out why – why fight? Why marry? And why not divorce already?

As the sun was about to come up a mediator arrived, an old woman. As soon as the old woman came in she shouted: "What the hell are you doing? What do you think you're going to accomplish? All this about love and feelings! Your uncle and I never even said those three words [I love you], but I still give him three sons and two daughters, didn't I? Get through the days together, OK. What's the point of fighting?"

The old woman's words were hypnotising like music, and afterwards I slept soundly. And no dreams came to me from the darkness.

25. One Truth of the World

After he got rid of the Er and took on Yi, Ding Yi felt calmer, feeling he'd rid himself of crassness and had become refined. Especially since on any list of names or registry, with that name he was always the first – even though there were few strokes in the surname, it was clear and eye-catching, and satisfied this Ding. But this pleasant, cosy feeling didn't last long. Soon he discovered what a name cannot hide. It was hard for people to forget his humble origins, and his sadness slowly returned.

Remembering it now, there were a few things in particular that bothered him. One happened at the beginning of the Cultural Revolution. I remember a slogan suddenly flying out of the air and sunlight: 'Heroic fathers have good kids, reactionary fathers' kids are bastards!' It would be reasonable to say that this slogan posed a threat to Ding Yi, or something that could help him. Though the Ding family ancestors were landlords, as times changed the family declined and found itself short of food and clothing. Father Ding knew Confucius's lesson that those who study often find their strength fails them when they return to work the land, so he took a crash course in cooking. In an example of a misfortune turning out to be a blessing in disguise, cooks are considered workers! As a result, that Ding had a resounding advantage in his ability to carry out core revolutionary work. So one day, when one of the most arrogant revolutionary organisations was founded, he hurried confidently to join. But reality is always more complicated.

When Ding Yi arrived, all he saw was an enthusiastic crowd outside a classroom door. Some natural leaders sat in the centre of the classroom, reviewing the candidates' qualifications one by one:

"Zhang San?""Present." "Origin?" "Revolutionary!" "Approved, Approved, Approved, Approved... Armband granted!"

"Li Si?" "Present." "Origin?" "Revolutionary soldier!""Approved, Approved, Approved, Approved... Armband granted!"

And so on.

A beautiful girl stood to the side of some of the natural leaders. All she did was issue armbands. They were stacked in bright red piles according to texture and width. Ding Yi's eyes widened again. Of course he wasn't looking at the armbands. He was looking at the girl behind them.

Her name was Qin, Qin E. Ding Yi whispered to me: *She just changed the E from the character with the woman radical to the one with the mountain.*

All right, I said. *Got your mind turning again?*

Do you think the mountain or the woman one is better?

Of course the woman one!

Yeah, yeah. I think so too.

This kid was really sincere, didn't ever hear the wild jeers.

Hey, look! How come some of those armbands are silk, while others are satin and regular cloth? And why aren't the widths the same?

How could that guy be paying attention to these questions when his gaze was still fixed on Qin E?

"Wang Wu?" "Present!" "Origin?" "Senior cadre!" "Approved, Approved, Approved, Approved... Armband granted!"

"Sun Liu?" "Present!" "Origin?" "Martyr!" "Approved, Approved, Approved, Approved... Armband granted!"

"Zhou Qi?" " Present!" " Origin?" "Revolutionary soldier!" "Approved, Approved, Approved, Approved... Armband granted!"

"Zhao Er?" "Present?" "Origin?" "Revolutionary!" "Approved, Approved, Approved, Approved... Armband granted!"
And so forth.
"Ding Yi? Ding Yi!"
"Oh yeah, present!"
"Origin?"
"What? What origin?"
"Blah, I'm asking you!"
"Oh, oh, work... worker!"
"Approved, Approved, Approved, Approved... Armband granted!"
That Ding's heart galloped like a horse. He'd long lost track of where he was as he took a few panicked steps forward and received an armband from Qin E's hands. As soon as he touched her hand that guy's body shook as a warm current surged through him.

Qin E was wearing a washed-out military uniform with a tight waist and big chest. Her short hair cut to the ears revealed extraordinary beauty.

That first contact ended so quickly. Ding Yi ran out of the crowd. He had gone quite a distance before he realised: Hey, what happened, why is this armband narrower than the others? Other people's are five, six, seven inches wide. Why is mine only four? Other people got satin, silk, why was Ding Yi's made of regular red cloth? Ding Yi wanted to go back and ask Qin E, but he didn't dare. As he hesitated he heard a disagreement in the crowd: the armband's width and texture varied with one's parents' status!

Ding Yi was momentarily stunned. His thoughts jumped to the end of *Journey to the West*: Master, my brothers have all attained enlightenment, but this old pig is only an arhat? Facing Buddha's majesty you can only dedicate yourself to the precepts. Ah, the Buddhist community was also ranked like this, Ding Yi thought. All you can do is act right, hide that shameful four-inch wide plain red cloth in your arms.

26. A Second Truth of the World

The good thing was that, though Ding Yi felt jealous about the red silk and red satin, he wasn't a big fan of those who wore the red silk and red satin – except Qin E, his feelings were calm.

Those who Ding Yi was on good terms with were friends about his age from his neighbourhood. These friends' origins were neither red nor very black. If they weren't one of the 'smelly nine', they were 'reactionary academic authorities' and couldn't even have a four-inch-wide armband. Though they tried to keep their indignity quiet, they showed deep resentment for the group with the red silk and red satin bands.

The first reason for their contempt: what did that group have?
The second reason for their contempt: that group, what did they really have?

The third reason for their contempt: that group, really, what did they really have?

At first Ding Yi listened to this happily, vented and joined in, but he never understood what that 'what' was really referring to. Some of his good friends were very sarcastic about 'that group', ridiculed and derided them, which allowed them to bond with each other. From then on they were hooked, and wherever they went they expressed contempt for the red silks and red satins. Ding Yi would make some defence of Qin E: "Hey, I'm telling you, Qin E really isn't like them," or "Hey, did you guys notice Qin E really isn't like the rest of the group?" or "Really, I'm serious, Qin E isn't anything like the rest of that group." His friends objected at first, then sniggered, then finally agreed, having taken into account that they should back up their friends who backed them up… "OK, OK, Qin E isn't," or, "Right, right, she isn't like that group," or "True, true, Qin E really has nothing in common with that group, OK?" Then that Ding would feel relieved as he bit his ice lolly in the July sun and strolled with his good friends, and kept belittling the red silks and red satins that weren't Qin E, continuously laughed at how 'that group' were petty social climbers, crooks, bottom feeders.

"If you don't believe me, go to their house and look. There's not a single book!" "Who says? There might be some literacy textbooks, right?"… Gradually, Ding Yi felt a bit off. Why did it seem that a wisp of dark clouds was hiding in the bright, clear sky? The wisp gathered and scattered again – what was really going on? Finally, Ding Yi heard something burdened with hidden meaning. Some of the good friends were making clear implications. Knowledgeable families like ours aren't the norm; scholarly families like ours are the noble ones. Only noble families have stability and longevity. Professors, professionals, students, celebrities… in the way an eagle sometimes flies lower than the chicken, but the chicken can never fly as high as the eagle! When it comes to learning, knowledge, achievements, cultural accomplishments – "Really, that group! What do they have?" This feeling, that refrain, though not suitable to say publicly at that time, wasn't hidden between those good friends. Ding Yi's heart thumped a moment as he suddenly felt uncomfortable. He thought further and felt what they said didn't seem wrong. But as he listened further he still felt uncomfortable and walked sheepishly, eating his ice lolly, and didn't chime in any more.

Ding Yi's silence was suddenly as bleak as the autumn wind, the empty landscape. His body and heart turned cold in waves. He touched the armband and suddenly realised that, whether red or black or some other colour, Ding Yi's was destined to be four inches wide.

The good friends noticed Ding Yi's low spirits. They quickly read his mind and comforted him one after another. "Hey, you're not like that group…" "Workers, workers are so great, you workers are really good…"

"Workers? You guys are the best by far..." Ah, you guys! Us! Them! Ding Yi's brain boomed with the realisation that 'we' are not 'them'; 'they' are also not 'you'; 'you' certainly can't be 'us'... Ding Yi listened and wanted to cry, wanted to run away. But he still stood, still sat or squatted, still smiled. The dim sunlight made the sky seem white. The high wind was unscrupulous. The good friends' words and smiles, though still clear, seemed to slowly flatten, slowly drift off, drift further and further away.

27. A Third Truth of the World

Something else happened not long after this. That day, another slogan suddenly flew through the air and sunlight: 'Who are our enemies? Who are our friends? This is the revolution's first question!' And on that very day the line between good friends and arseholes was blurred. Some old 'heroes' and some old 'reactionaries' all stood on the stage. Ding Yi and those good friends' parents, along with some parents of the red silks and red satins, stood in a queue for denunciation. High cadres, revolutionary soldiers, professors, professionals, celebrities... all lowered their heads together as our 'enemies'.

"What's this? What happened?"

Ding Yi asked his good friend. The friend didn't respond.

Ding Yi looked at those red silks and red satins. Why were even they biting their tongues?

Red flags waved all around, song and revolutionary slogans filled the sky. Then I saw Ding Yi's father appear at the edge of the crowd – in a grease-stained white apron, pushing a cart with lunch for the rally.

Bickering people suddenly surrounded him, handed over meal vouchers, handed over all kinds of lunch boxes. No matter what side they came from they didn't ask his position, didn't ask which faction, didn't bother to think about this middle-aged man's revolutionary status as they rushed him to take care of everyone's grumbling stomachs. And Ding Yi's father? He just had a tranquil expression, looked well-mannered, as if he didn't know there was a rally or didn't know what it was for, just believed the hungry deserve to eat and gave everyone a helping of food, a helping of soup, a helping of rice. He seemed like a wisp of colour in the rolling red waves, a little haven amid the clamour and confusion. Unlike those children who had tumultuous relationships with their parents, I thought Ding Yi, you must be worried about your progenitor now, right?

Isn't that strange? I asked. *What's your problem this time?*

That Ding wanted to cry but he also felt funny, wanted to shout but knew it was irrational, wanted to run away but feared it would be awkward.

What's wrong with you brother, why am I not understanding?

Ding Yi didn't reply. He just smiled, grimaced.

Speak, come on speak. What's too big to talk with me about?
Ding Yi didn't reply, just grimaced harder.
So it seems to me, honour isn't for us, right?
Who would have guessed that Ding would blurt out: *Right, right, 'we'! No, no, it's 'you'!*
Huh? We? You? Who are you talking about?
I mean, why doesn't he stand on the stage?
Him? Who? I mean, you tell me who's better to stand on stage?
Tears flickered in Ding Yi's eyes.
What? Now I started to understand and shouted at him: *Do you know what that's called?*
Ding Yi turned his back.
Ah, so that's how it is! Really he wished his father was on stage, he wished his father was on stage with his head hanging, being denounced, and couldn't stand that he was busy off stage serving food! Poor Ding Yi. Turns out he still envied those good friends, envied those red silks and red satins, envied their origins, their family status. Poor Ding Yi thought he finally understood something: it was more honourable to be a disgraced celebrity than a cook! Denounced senior cadres were more noble than workers! Suddenly he felt he'd uncovered a truth: some lowliness was never-ending, some scorn was deeply-rooted, some guilt was inborn.
Why? Why do you think that?
Because everyone thinks that way, they just don't say it.
He ignored me for a long time, stood there doing nothing, the red waves rolling in his dull eyes, or that four-inch-wide thing was still buzzing in his mind.
Hey, move, you're gonna scare people.
That got him to finally take a few steps, walk out of the crowd.
You're right. In their eyes we'll always be outcasts.
Why?
You're still asking why? Because of mediocrity, lowliness! He squinted up at me: *Are you talking about a little haven amid the clamour?*
He stood down, didn't move, looked at the wind in the trees, looked at the shadows in the water, looked at the ever deeper, ever redder sunset.
You tell me, he said. *A mediocre person, someone thought of as mediocre, also has peace?*
You tell me, he said. *A forgotten person, an overlooked person – what peace do they have?*
You say it, he shouted. *Someone who's never been discovered is definitely more peaceful than a denounced senior cadre or a disgraced celebrity?*
I saw the confusion mounting in his gaze. I saw the resentment sinking into his distorted face. The faraway sunset gradually dimmed. I urged him: *Let's go, brother. Let's go home.* I worried that, if this feeling persisted, he'd end up like the painter Z. He'd always be talking about his resentments

like Z, desiring conquest, desiring anything, a force that could drive him to do anything, without regret.

The sun went down. Everywhere, a light blue haze floated.

All right, all right, looks all right – Ding Yi sighed to himself. Everywhere he looked he saw those good friends, saw those pretty girls, and he didn't grit his teeth and press on like Z.

28. Imaginative Power

This reminded me of a thought I had when I was in Shi Tiesheng. It was during one of his 'writing nights' when he was paradoxically travelling with the painter Z and experiencing his mood.

The painter Z had a lot in common with Ding Yi's situation then, but he did become resentful and desire to conquer others. Why is that? Why did the painter Z's heart fill with resentment? Why did he choose conquest? Because he was more arrogant or meaner? Because his imaginative powers were cruder or richer? In fact not one of Z's friends didn't think he was strong, but the truth is, from my clear, dual perspective as a witness, at that time Z was already completely controlled by humiliating historical acts. That caused a kind of 'spirit' to overwhelm his emotional intelligence, which destroyed his capacity for a richer, vaster imagination.

Ding Yi and Z were very different.

The difference between the travels of Ding Yi and Z quite possibly had to do with the difference in their moods when they decided to leave the crowd: Ding Yi seemed to look back with each step at those friends, gazing at those beautiful girls. So Ding Yi was Ding Yi. So Ding Yi was romantic. Ding Yi couldn't stand for his feelings of camaraderie to disappear, or turn his back on his deeply held dreams and run. Not so with Z. Z never again wanted to see those people who ignored and despised him. Unless he could trade places with them one day and condescendingly accept their praise. So Z was Z. So Z was strong. Z's imaginative powers only went that far.

Looking at it that way, Ding Yi was a lot like that poet L from writing nights. "If on that winter afternoon, on that cold afternoon when the snow began to melt, the nine-year-old Z was in that surprising building, in that nine-year-old girl's room, and carelessly said to that girl: 'Why'd you bring him in, huh? Who asked you to bring him in?' If Z didn't feel the beauty and coldness of that voice but put all his attention on the girl's body, then it's quite possible he wasn't the nine-year-old Z but the ten-year-old L." – **Shi Tiesheng's *Notes on the Obscure*.**

Ding Yi's imaginative powers always used 'feeling' as guidance, to choose, to decide. Like the legendary 'precious jade', the belief that girls had muscles of ice and bones of jade, all born clean and untarnished. Or like the poet L, thinking truth was all in women's hands. So in that moment when Ding Yi was in a very similar situation to Z, Ding Yi was only pining for those girls, still it was those girls. Which girl? No, no, it wasn't one, it was all of them, all those hazy yet alluring ones. Which had yet to be decided. Who it was finally was still unclear. But what is certain is that she was already there. Since Eve and I broke up in Eden, she must have already come into the human world. Maybe she was among those good friends, or it could be that she was even among the red silks and red satins. Of course it was more likely she was somewhere else, in a faraway place, on some path for some reason, walking towards us now. Thus romantics and the strong are different. When Z couldn't help but take the path of resentment, Ding Yi left the gathering, walked home, walked into the dark night and shared something that had been troubling him for some time with me alone: everyone used to be so good, why do they have to be like that?

Right, I remember when Z left the crowd the first thing that came to his mind was his mother, his mother being bullied her whole life – could it be that that didn't come from 'feeling'?

"Don't give in so easily, don't give in so easily!" That Shi's scoffing had turned into gloating. "So 'feeling' can just be anything, account for everything?"

Right, right. If 'feeling' can't move towards love, then it's still an instinct. However, Old Shi, did you notice Ding Yi's pupils gazed even more broadly, more vastly, more obsessively or more deeply? Maybe it was because he had never focused in on any one and was just longing for all the women. He wasn't attached to what he had (such as his mother or maternal love) but was drawn towards others, so he could ask a question like that. So when he asked me that with his teenage craziness, to me it sounded like Ding Yi was overcome with feeling, which at that moment, or in the near future, would become love.

But I didn't congratulate him. I didn't want to disturb Ding Yi. Of course I wasn't without concern. He still knew nothing, but I knew: whether in the past or future, and whether it was a Ding or a Shi, life's travels could/would all confirm the near prophetic verse: "Who then devised the torment? Love." – **TS Eliot's Four Quartets.**

29. Dream

A dream finally came. But it was a strange dream.

It was still dancing.

It was still dark all around.

And it was still that dancing partner – the woman in the white dress, indistinct yet familiar.

"Hey, who are you really?"

"Huh, you don't recognise me?"

"Recognise? From when?"
"A long time ago."
"A long time ago?"
"Yeah, a long time ago."
"Where?"
She sighed. "You really forgot… You're in Ding Yi now, right?"
"Right. And you?"
I tried hard to think back, tried hard to make out her face.

But then the number of dancers increased. They formed pairs, their steps gentle and elegant. From the distance lit by early dawn, from behind the dark, towering buildings, from all directions they swam, drifted, even fluttered as they gathered together. Dresses of every colour blew in the breeze.

Then I suddenly thought I figured out who she was. "Are you that theatre actress girl from years ago? That Snow White?"

Dawn expanded, the sound of the strings and woodwinds gradually subsided. The brass and percussion were immediately deafening, making everyone's steps more agitated, jubilated, wild. The dress flowed in waves, a series of swirling surges.

"Are you Spring?"

The woman in the white dress just looked down and smiled.

"You've been here all this time?"

The woman in the white dress just gave me an affectionate look.

"Hey, who are you really? Can you tell me your name, where you live?"

But the wildly dancing crowd suddenly surged, forcing, pushing and squeezing me to the point of suffocation… Maybe feeling afraid of being separated again, I saw that Ding suddenly take her – take that woman, Spring or Snow White. Take that once childish, innocent, tiny figure and pull her towards him, pull her towards him hard… Inside I thought, No, but without warning this rash Ding Yi was already leaning in for a kiss…

Then everything stopped.

No song, no dancing, no dawn, no people.

The lonely darkness stretched indefinitely. The only sound was a growing hiss. Finally the end of the terrible song was sung: "Wandering, wandering, la la la, wandering, silly wandering…" It was actually sung leisurely, happily, endlessly.

30. Sick

This dream seemed like a sign. Not long after that, this dream and the hooligan song joined forces to bring about more terrible events in Ding Yi's life.

First the scary phrase 'hooligan', the cruel title, had raged like a dust storm since Ding Yi's childhood and hadn't subsided with the passing of years. Then there was the continued harassment from the woman in the white dress or Ding Yi's dreams of her harassment. Either way, the accumulation of sadness and torment of lust finally caused Ding Yi to fall ill.

This is relevant to metabolism again. Ding Yi's illness had to do with an imbalance between generation and decline. They say if some part of an organism goes out of control for an unknown reason, multiplies rapidly, expands at breakneck speed and somehow generates energy, generates, generates... It seizes all the nutrition, resistance from adjacent organs is harmful, blind retreat, blind decline, decline, decline... In a sense, generation is worse than decline, generation takes over decline. This Ding had no appetite for food, he slept fitfully. While part of him flourished, the rest deteriorated... Amid all this I had trouble feeling comfortable too. Resting and this and that wasn't supporting you. Using this and that wasn't respecting you – it was like a car whose gears wouldn't stick, whose oil was too low, whose brakes were unresponsive, wobbling and wobbling. I always seemed to want to fling myself out of Ding Yi – suddenly walk away leisurely or humbly float off.

How could this be good? Gazing at the distant mountains, gazing at the soaring dawn, I walked full of interest and feeling, full of suspense mixed with triumph – how could Ding Yi suddenly want to give up?

He leaned over on the side of the road, panting: *It's over, it's over, man, I don't think I can go on.*

I said: *How about we rest a bit then walk some more?*

He said: *I don't think it's that's simple.*

What do you think is wrong?

He touched his stomach: *Inside, probably around here... something went wrong.*

I helped him up, pushed him on. Have you seen a driver break down in the middle of a road? It was like that. I whacked him, kicked him, begged him, tried to threaten or cajole him however I could. But none of it worked. Somehow none of it worked. Finally he just lay down and sobbed and sighed: *Brother, I think you'll have to go on without me.*

That made no sense! It was infuriating. Wasn't this joke crossing the line a little bit?

I said: *My bro, we already discussed not giving up, why you getting cold on me halfway?* I went on: *What if you were flying home but the plane wanted to drop you off halfway, do you think that'd be OK?*

He didn't respond, just panted, didn't eat or drink for a few days, gave me confused nightmares at night. I'd wake up in the morning and see him still inert, his face ever gloomier.

I shouted at him: *I'm telling you, if we're gonna come apart let's really come apart! What's all this humming and hawing?*

To myself I thought: I took a liking to you because you can run and jump, can think and reflect, can speak and laugh, but if you can't even do this little thing, in heaven's name, how can I rely on you for protection?

He cried in protest: *What are you shouting about? If you want to go, then go!*

Taking a closer look at his mad state, alas, it may be better to just march off. Taking a closer look at Ding Yi's reflection, it was clear he had wasted away to skin and bones, was pale to the point of being transparent. My heart sank, and I thought darkly: This is really a big mess. I suspected he was as stupid as a van, but now the van wouldn't even drive.

I went with him to the hospital.

I went with him to see a doctor.

It's like I said: Among countless doctors, which is good? They all say they're good, they all say they their opinions are sound, but who do you listen to? In the end, it's the sick person with no medical experience who has to decide!

I went with him to be examined – X-rays, sonograms, CT scans, NMRs... such smart people have come up with the silliest things!

The film showed a cluster of flower buds, pale, ugly, but opening.

Our efforts were not in vain for we got word of cancer.

Outside of the sick room spring sun shone boundlessly. Inside the sick room was dim as a rat's nest. Every day we ran around the crisscrossing paths of that maze crying out for help. Each baffling room shone with lights like secrets and hunger. In the dark parts some huge machines ran slowly. The doctors' faces were like smooth sheets of paper. There was always some ticking breaking the silence. In the pale white light silent shadows swam. One of them – like Gargamel in the fairy tale – stirred a cup full of liquid with a glass rod that made a clanging sound: yellow, a stir and a clang; red, a stir and a clang; black... asked Ding Yi to drink it down. Before us was the golden snake dance, flashing red stars, bitter cold and rain, but Ding Yi's face was slowly getting bluer.

"What medicine?"

The doctor didn't pay him any attention. The doctor wanted Ding Yi to go with him.

This made me think of a human trafficker – the child drugged with jimsonweed followed willingly.

Ding Yi stayed close behind the flowing white fabric, ignoring everyone else.

After passing through countless tunnels, countless caves, countless doors and windows and the shrieks that came from them, countless clamorous or delirious crowds of people... Ding Yi found himself in a relatively quiet place and was ordered to strip.

Ding Yi was naked while the person fiddled around. I discovered that his little flower bud, now mature, was still sensitive, now shyly hanging down, now being touched and getting restless – I thought: could this mean he has a chance?

The doctor pretended not to notice. The doctor shone some invisible light on Ding Yi's abdomen, where there were some bright areas already circled in red pen.

"Is this OK?"

The doctor ignored him, and a smile formed on his blank paper face that reminded one of that crafty sphinx.

Oh, Ding Yi, you broken-down vehicle! I complained to myself, regretting choosing this place. The engine was, in fact, rumbling along, and those outside saw a complete human form, but could I stand it? Especially when that Ding cried out in sadness, felt fury in his heart, tumbled this way and that, he still had a young man's hot-blooded temper. But I could tell he was afraid things were headed for the worse. What is cancer? That thing isn't as good as 'hooligan', that thing hadn't left any external signs but internally it was already making trouble – lower blood pressure, increased heart rate and body temperature so erratic that when he was hot it was like he was in a sauna and when he was cold it was like he was in a freezer. I thought, rather than get so mixed up with him, it would be best to end things and look for other prospects, so I went straight to the point and told him: *Brother, I'll just let you go, would be better for everyone in the end.* I just wanted to scrap the broken-down car, break it down, recycle it, suffer in the short term rather than long term. There would be other cars. As there are other proverbial fish in the sea, the world is full of Ding Yi's.

31. Death

I thought hard about Ding Yi and all this.

I thought: just leave like this? Not give it another shot? You'll leave sooner or later, do you have to rush? When it comes to life, there's nothing more certain than death and for me wasn't the way to leave just to leave? Moreover, suppose you bypass that hard road, is it still travelling, are you still an eternal spirit?

Ding Yi really had the fearlessness of the ignorant. This time he was quicker than me, an angry tool preparing to die. First he found a rope, but after thinking about how frightening hanging bodies look, he decided against it. Next he thought of jumping, but the messy scene of blood and guts would be disgusting, so he discarded that idea. What about sleeping pills? Peacefully lie down, feel your eyelids get heavy, be overcome with drowsiness and fall asleep, anticipate some dreams that don't come, and afterwards people come to pack you up and dispose of you, gone in a wisp of smoke before anyone could come and laugh at us... Yeah, good idea. But the pills? The pills were hard to find and, if you didn't get enough, wouldn't they only half kill you and make you a laughing stock? Electric shock! Right, right, right, that's a good one. Bring two poles together, add a timer, drink a bellyful of wine to get sleepy and let the current take over till everything's fine. All right, that then!

But when everything was ready, that Ding's thoughts coincided with mine: what's the rush? Really, he contemplated those tools of death he'd spent all day planning to use without thinking what the rush was. Then he smoked another cigarette, and his resignation became lack of fear to keep living. At least with only that one thing left, everything else seemed more appealing. The wisps of smoke gently danced away, his mood relaxed, and this Ding had some unusual thoughts, especially regarding something he'd never considered: death, what is it?

He asked me: *Death, what's it like?*

I said: *After death, we're free of the suffering of sin.*

Who? Speak clearly, don't be vague, who's free?

You, and I.

But I'm already dead, already gone, right?

Listen to me carefully...

Don't beat around the bush! he said. *Really you're free, but I'm gone.*

No, no, no, it's not that...

If not that, then what?

You've done enough damage!

But... But before you were gone too, right?

Before? When?

Before you were born?

Ding Yi was at a loss for words and stayed that way a long time before he suddenly sniggered.

What are you laughing at? Is there something funny?

He looked at me and smiled more viciously: *But if I die, won't you be gone too?*

Not necessarily. I tried to speak vaguely, didn't want to disturb him too much.

He smiled again: *After death, everything is gone isn't it?*

Of course not.

What's left?

I'm left.

You're saying I'm gone, but you still exist?

No. If he was going to be like this, I'd just tell him directly. *You're gone. I still exist.*

Ha, how funny! So where are you?

In another place. I was in other places before.

Other places? What other places?

I really hated the way he was smiling. It was as if, when he died, the world would stop spinning. If I'm gone, you're gone, he's gone, the endless flow of information just stops.

I said: *Really think about it, Ding Yi, how long have you existed? Have you thought about where I was before you were here?*

Wherever you were you can say whatever you want, but who can prove where you were?

And if it could be proven? If it could be proven that after you're gone I'll still exist, wouldn't it also prove that I existed before you?

Go on. But I can't just take your word for it, who else can provide evidence?

Anyone.

Anyone? I'm not in the mood for jokes.

Listen, listen to me! Whether before you existed or after you stop existing, how does any person address themself? How are they aware of themself? Or you could say, how do they allege themself? That is, from what perspective do they view this world? Forget it, don't speculate, I'm telling you: I! No person can escape this perspective: I!

But that's a different I!

But which one, can't be a different one?

I'm saying that already isn't Ding Yi!

Right, right, this time you're right – Ding Yi is gone, but I still exist.

Ding Yi was a little anxious, he anxiously scratched his head. Like when he couldn't figure out a maths problem he pinched his thigh, tapped his forehead.

I pushed him: *Take Ding Yi for example, who is Ding Yi?*

I.

Good, easy enough. If you ask the next Ding, and the next and the next, all the way to one hundred, they would answer the same way: I.

So... so what?

I, is enough.

Bull! You're enough, but I'll be gone.

One more time: I cannot be gone, I can never be gone, what will be gone is Ding Yi.

This time he was a bit dazed, dumb, confused.

I pushed him again: *Think about music. Music is also never-ending, but each individual note passes. So the note of Ding Yi will naturally pass. Each note passes, so music cannot stop. Each note can pass, but music cannot stop, which means what? It means there can be countless notes – the next Ding and the next Ding all the way to a hundred – in an endless line! That is to say, with Ding Yi gone there will still be countless I's in an endless line!*

What you're saying is, you're music?

I'm an eternal spirit, like never-ending music.

And I'm just a note?

You, Ding Yi, are a note. I've already used countless notes to become eternal compositional movements, in the way my eternal journeys have led me to pass through Ding Yi.

In that case, coming and going, coming and going, notes are just a crowd of insignificant morons?

Notes that cannot become compositions are all noise, believe it or not, they will all be forgotten and buried forevermore. It's because music gives notes meaning, gives them direction. Like that day when I came, you finally opened your eyes, you opened your eyes and were finally able to form images. Like that day when we went out together, walked along the street, felt the world's danger and mystery, the images in your eyes finally requested or displayed – meaning. And just because of this, you noticed yourself, you considered yourself an 'I', you knew life, spoke of death...

But without each note, your music is nothing!

Wow, just like without travels in Ding Yi, how could I be an eternal spirit? The same, without the journey before and after now, how can there be an eternal spirit, and how can I exist?

Ding Yi thought blankly.

I saw a flicker in his dim eyes. Even before he said anything I knew the problem, I already knew what he was going to say.

If that's the case, why are you in a rush to leave me? To use your terms, why would never-ending music want to abandon Ding Yi, this insignificant note?

Well! I had no choice but to secretly applaud this Ding – I never thought he'd set such a trap, cut off my escape.

32. A Suicide Says

But death still had some allure to me. Especially those days living in the hospital, death often showed me its charm. In fact, death is just a fear of the living. To an eternal spirit, it's just a migration to fulfil a promise to return, or a reunion to bid farewell. Of course, of course, Ding Yi couldn't comprehend these things. But there was an inmate who had attempted suicide that actually deepened Ding Yi's understanding of life and death.

That person had been rescued and shared a room with Ding Yi. The hospital director asked everyone not to speak with him. I thought it was outrageous! And right when Ding was very interested in the effects of suicide, it was just him and that man in the room. This guy leaned over, first asked how he was doing, then made small talk, slowly got to know the terrain before cutting to the chase.

"What it's like, man, what feeling?"

"What feeling?"

Ding Yi wrote furiously with a finger on the man's wrist: "Scared?"

"Scared you don't do it. Doing it means not doing it is more scary."

"Why, you?"

The man's response was surprising: "No reason, just wanted to change places and stay somewhere else."

"Change to the hospital?"

The man smiled. "Yeah, sure."

"So where do you want to change to now?"

The man patted Ding Yi's shoulder: "What's up little bro, you want to change too?"

"I uh, yeah…" Ding Yi mumbled. "Tell me, where do you want to change to?"

The man looked Ding Yi over, sizing him up. "I'd say you shouldn't change. I think your place isn't bad."

"So why do you want to change?"

"Ah, my place couldn't be worse."

"What's your place?"

"In for life. And I wasn't falsely convicted."

Ding Yi was shocked.

"To him I wasn't falsely convicted." He pointed at his head. "But I think I was!" He pointed at his heart.

"You're strange."

"I dunno, I never thought of doing that! But later, you do what you never wanted to…"

"What really happened?"

"Little brother, listen to me. Live well. Just be careful when you run into problems."

Ding Yi was confused. "So you really want, want to move. Where?"

"For example, move to your place and live?"

"My house?"

"No, here." He patted Ding Yi's shoulder, then patted his chest. "What's your name?"

"Ding Yi."

"K, I'd be content to move to Ding Yi and live."

Ding Yi still didn't understand, but I understood: this was a wandering spirit who'd strayed into the abyss! I whispered to Ding Yi: *Don't ask him any more, OK. He's either a secret agent or a spy or corrupt.*

The man closed his eyes and seemed to sleep a moment, maybe feeling Ding Yi was endearingly innocent and couldn't bear to see him dumbfounded. He asked Ding Yi: "Tell me, what's the worst punishment?"

"What?"

"I can tell you it's not the death penalty, it's life."

"What did you actually do?"

"Little brother, it's best if you don't know. That kind of thing wouldn't tempt you" – he pointed at Ding Yi's heart – "but it could easily tempt him" – he pointed at Ding Yi's head.

Ding Yi was more puzzled.

"But I'll tell you an approach." The man suddenly seemed relaxed, maybe even a little happy. "Other things you don't need to know, but if you wind up with my luck, just remember this solution."

"Change the place I live?"

"OK, you're not stupid. If you really can't stand the few square metres of that little black room, I'm saying you have a key that can open all doors."

"What key?"

The man wrote furiously on his wrist.

"This, how can this move you to another place?"

"Because you can only change to one place at a time."

"Man, you're strange."

Ding Yi thought he was avoiding the question, but I could appreciate his kindness or cunning – he knew why, if he said "changing places", Ding Yi still didn't understand, but "you can only change to one place at a time" would ring true.

"Not strange at all," the man said, "but remember one thing, wherever you change to will be the same. In the end there are no satisfying boundaries of the heart."

"So you, do you want to change again or not?" Ding Yi drew on his wrist again.

"Depends, it's pretty easy anyway."

"You think it's easy?"

"Yeah, easy. But I have to tell you, little brother – changing is easy, but living is not easy. So don't change unless as a last resort. Because, you know, because you might not be satisfied no matter where you are."

33. Ding Yi Persuades Me to Stay

Maybe because what that man said had an effect, or maybe because the spirit of youth instinctively finds reasons to live, just as I was hesitating about whether or not to leave, that Ding suddenly changed his mind. He solemnly quoted the *Book of Songs* passage about not having to be buried with your ancestors and added that there was only one Ding Yi in the world. Then he quoted my own words: "Every musical note is important." So I think this original movement should be played all the way through. If not, he said, Ding Yi wouldn't be like a man, and I couldn't brag about being an eternal spirit. We'd both suffer, and for what? Finally, he somehow pulled out some epic maxim. The gist was: people only get one life, the only way to turn such a limited thing into a contribution to the limitless, something, something, so that Ding Yi could do this and that – I don't remember all of it, and I'm not too interested in that kind of rhetoric. I simply saw this Ding's age was just right, had a bright future, and he couldn't bear to give up so quickly. Maybe give it another try? See if that colourful medicine and invisible light might work. So I found an appropriate comedic aphorism: you're queueing up to buy tofu, but you're stuffed; and so with death, why try to jump the queue? When Ding Yi thought with such foresight it really surprised me; the words must have come from some other wandering spirit who'd come by.

I have to admit, Ding Yi really persuaded me that time.

When that Ding was sadder, he used his tenacious resistance to convince me to stay, he used his youthful strength to imply a powerful spring, used his stubbornness, or better, his arrogance to convince me, convince me to give him some more time. I agreed. I said then I'll stay a while, and I even promised! I even secretly thanked him, true, true, at that point his desire saved my hope.

34. When in Job

Ding Yi's determination was moving. But that cancer was no game, that thing was like an old whore sucking Ding Yi day and night, exploiting his youthful energy to grow larger, not just to flourish, but to bloom and bear fruit, as if it wouldn't give up until its evil had spread throughout Ding Yi. Fortunately he had colourful pills and colourless light to slow its advance. But the pills and light ravaged Ding Yi, depleted his strength, destroyed his will and confidence. For a period Ding Yi was depressed and discouraged, spending all day demoralised, complaining. It was as if the spring light went out, surging waves suddenly subsided. His arrogant flair diminished, base desires were especially absent, so I feared he couldn't rely solely on his own vitality.

Helpless Ding Yi turned his eyes towards the sky.

Flowers bloom in midsummer, so you can't just look at the sky in autumn when the wind blows incessantly and all is sparse as leaves rustle and think you know the vast boundlessness of this life.

How's it going, little brother Ding Yi?

I'm not gloating but at this time he may have been able to regard me seriously.

He asked me: *Big brother, say, have we tricked or offended anyone?*

No. We haven't tricked or offended anyone, that's why it's called fate.

Then he shouted: *So why is all this happening? Why? Tell me, God!*

Because you're mortal, because you, being mortal, cannot bargain with God.

As soon as I said that, I thought of Job, thought of my experience in Job.

That Ding fought back with the fire of injustice in his belly and forced himself to stay calm: *Brother, this could be it, I don't see any need to keep dragging you along. If you want to go, you should go.*

Don't take it to heart, brother, I said. *We should stay true to our word. We can't give up halfway, right?*

He shouted again: *Great, it's that easy! I should suffer punishment for a crime I didn't commit for no reason?*

Yes, Job! My memory became clearer, I remember a long time ago, before I was in Ding Yi, something God said to Job: "Before I created the world, where were you?"

This voice came from the heavens.

This voice came from far away, farther than anything, to the point of being abstract.

Distant but durable, this voice had passed through who knows how many lives before reaching Ding Yi.

Right, Ding Yi, so you can't complain about God or his creation. That dignified yet tender voice said: God's work is a journey, it's bumpy, and you are just a part of it, an insignificant bump. Or God said: Wherever he goes the road is infinite, a musical composition without beginning or end, and you, Ding Yi? You're just a short stop on an endless road, a small segment, a note in an endless movement. So listen: if the bump complains about the journey or the note complains about the movement, it's not reasonable. For example, if you complain about your father and mother giving birth to you it's unreasonable – if they hadn't given birth to you, would you be able to complain about it? Besides, who can they complain to? So, Ding Yi, you must understand: before God created you, you had no way to complain; after being created, anyone complaining about another is a fool. Ding Yi, this is something it took me weeks in Job to understand.

Right, when I was in Job, when I passed through Job. That time was much more difficult than this one. Job's path was rough and rugged, full of danger. We lost all of our property, then our family left us one after another. Lonely Job had nothing and became severely ill, others gossiped that he must have offended God, committed a grave sin, and gotten what he deserved. Job, he felt wronged, Job, he was lonely and helpless. At that time I was as stricken as Ding Yi, felt indignant for Job, I not only knew Job was innocent, I had no idea why I, being good, had been trapped in this corner with Job. But just at that time, I seemed to hear that dignified yet tender voice: When I created the world, you [little man] were where? Right, God couldn't change his movement for the sake of a note. God isn't your servant, you're God's servant. What God wants you to experience, you must experience. What you don't have to experience is also not what God has to make you experience. The way God leads us is not a way without wind and rain, it's not smooth sailing, but God's way cannot be blocked.

That Ding seemed puzzled. Only later did he ask: *What happened to Job? How was Job in the end?*

I asked back: *You tell me, if God's way cannot be blocked?*

35. Bison

Laying in the sick bed, we watched a show: through endless mountains and vast wilderness a herd of bison trekked thousands of miles, chasing the sun, in search of pasture and water. Hungry wolves hounded them, following behind like a shadow. There was an old bison, still fit, but thin, walking at a slower pace. He tried hard stay with the group and once again survive the snow-covered winter, once again ford the turbulent glacial rivers, once again escape the attacks of hyenas and leopards, survive the dry and arid spring... But when the rain came and lush summer arrived, the bison was old and too tired to eat. It stood silently, staring with both eyes, seeing his fellows drink eagerly, slowly sensing the wolf pack surrounding it. What was it thinking? It knew it had to stay still, couldn't fall over; if it fell over, the wolves would rush. Wolves patiently surrounded it, they were as patient as they were relentless.

I'm the same, that Ding said. *Surrounded.*
By who?
By those wolf-like plants.
Don't kid around, I said. *We're probably not at that point yet.*
Does it matter when?

I didn't answer. The old bison struggled to escape the danger, but as it tried to move, its body wouldn't stop shaking. This gave the wolves the signal to attack. Several strong wolves leapt, dug at its crotch, bit its face, jumped on its body and chewed its meat. That giant body didn't resist. The proud wolves swarmed, the old bison fell with a thump, and in an instant was in pieces, a blur of flesh and blood...

It's all for this?
What do you mean?
All the hard treks, all the patience and resistance, all the running and hoping, all to give the wolves a meal of old bison meat?
But look, right where that old bison died, a calf was born...
What's that got to do with me?
But that old bison stayed standing till the end, brother!
So what?
But this is a crucial note...

That Ding put his hands together in prayer and looked at the sky.
The sky seemed to have a calling, or that sky was calling.

36. Desire

It could also be said that that call came from the sky, came from infinity, but in springlike Ding Yi it was still just desire. Spring wasn't like that, just relied on its natural talent to listen to that old call. But what's wrong with that? No, we should all have a certain level of respect for desire, like no matter how we travel – by horse, by boat or by car – we should be grateful for the capability. Put it this way: life is desire. And desire invariably makes the sky joyous, invariably moves towards infinity, just like a song from this area goes: "I bet my youth on tomorrow." Otherwise, "how can hair on smooth skin attach?" God's drama will also come to nothing. Without desire, why hope and pray? Even life would have no way to continue. The way the spring breeze moves towards life with no thought of death is truly walking with a purpose, heartily, wonderfully, quickly and widely. And life's limits are only noticed when autumn comes; after autumn, or when Ding Yi and I break up, he may finally sense his limits and start to understand my endless journey.

When the forever travelling spirit leaves Ding Yi, continues its long journey, life will fork into two paths, one dissolving into ashes and one the same as mine. Why the same as mine? A tentative life, only when polished into a string of beautiful information, can become an eternal movement, just like noise is wiped out and only beautiful stories are passed on. Or put it this way: that spirited desire, only if converted to love, can become an eternal way. Why? Because only love can guide the eternal search (and relentlessness is just sealed-off information) and thus join hand in hand with the inextinguishable soul.

As for Ding Yi, it was too early to know what path his assertiveness would put him on. Of course I already noticed his abundance of desire, his stubborn temperament. So I knew youthful Ding Yi wouldn't give up, his arrogance and stubbornness, though already showing the brilliance of love, were inherent dictates of desire like relics of prehistory.

37. Unpredictable Future

Floods, for example, are both destructive and nourishing. A tree that dies prematurely in spring, for example, would have continued growing if it hadn't died. Young Ding Yi was like a wildfire, blown back by an unexpected storm but still burning and getting stronger (I'm not sure how big a role Job's warning played). Ding Yi spoke of optimism, strength. I approved of him for the time being, but studying the particulars, he wasn't without a bit of sensationalism and self-congratulation. The future path was still far off, imitating passion, could by no means be sustained. So I said: *Take it easy, brother.* So that Ding wiped his tears away, touched the scar in that strange light and smugly said to me: *Relax, brother, we won't lie down.* Then he spoke grandly (or foolishly) again: *We will succeed, we will absolutely succeed!*

Succeed at what?

He just sniggered.

Wildfire, brother, where are you burning to?

His face was full of determination, like he had it all planned.

Let's say you make a name for yourself, what next? Or in the end? Have you thought of that?

That Ding dismissively clung to his optimism and strength, his eyes staring straight ahead with single-minded focus. I knew my questions went too far, went to infinity, the sky, information too distant for this spring to grasp.

Spring is mostly full of desire.

Spring relies solely on this desire to believe in love.

So when that Ding vowed to turn his gaze upward, I knew what this feeling's expectation was. When I was in Shi Tiesheng, he looked up during one of his writing nights: "Heaven, in the clouds, or the infinite sky, a large, white bird flies, leisurely, strongly, with rhythm." At this time Ding Yi was also looking up at it, looking up at it flying, towards its pride and grace. "The large bird's shadow is cast on the earth, cast on the mountains and river," cast on Ding Yi's face. "Then rain came, from south to north, then wind came, from east to west, the large bird broke through the clouds and fog, white like a lightning bolt." And beneath it, a slice of green in the wilderness, lush, flowers dense like stars, once withered now regrown, once in peril now budding again. Like Ding Yi, whole body filled with strength.

"Hey, at that time, what were you thinking?" I asked that Shi, the master of writing nights.

"What are you referring to?"

"When you looked up at the big white bird?"

"Love."

"Really?"

Spring thought it was love; in fact, it might still just be desire.

In spring, the body rules the soul and often thinks desire is love.

Especially this young Ding Yi, especially this feeling, I know, that call can't yet be love.

But it could be an early sign of love.

Regardless, when that spring's large bird spread its wings and flew, everything was in suspense. Put it this way: can authentic desire in the end become love? Or become what in the end? Because of the so-called clouds and fog, it's not yet known. It's more than unknown, it's an eternal mystery. Amid this mystery Ding Yi and I evened up. Ding Yi's future, or our journey, could be summed up in the phrase: unpredictable future.

38. Great Mystery

What is the great mystery? Looking at it from the end, each person has one path, but looking from the start there are countless possibilities.

What is the great mystery? There's an old saying: the slightest mistake can have big consequences. Then there's the butterfly effect, the sensitive dependence on initial conditions – for example the flap of butterfly wings in New York could initiate a heavy rainstorm in Beijing.

What is the great mystery? The starting point is hidden, the end point is open. But the end point opens what? Sorry: another (^{n}) starting point, that's all.

This made me remember that garden again as if in a dream: a tree, and the fruit in the tree; a snake, and the snake's vile words… And later a road called love. That road seems difficult to walk, with hidden wonders and ever-present danger. But Ding Yi in spring had bright blue skies, wild wind and drunken rain, how could he undertake quiet contemplation? Nights were short and days were long, where could he find a moment of solitude? Ever since I tried to sail ahead, the wind sent me astray, distant memories were obscured by pride. Better wait for autumn, only in the autumn breeze does one see the dangers that surrounded them while under desire's command. Dangers, like desires, hide well, they emerge in the spring breeze, waiting for their chance.

39. Struggling

Carrying those temporarily converging plants, or seeds waiting for their chance to attack, Ding Yi started to apply himself. Based on my repeated life experience, a sick person, disabled person, their depression isn't all because of the ailment, mostly it's from their loss of value. Alas, this human tool is quite troublesome.

Yesterday you were sound from head to toe, beautiful, attracting glances, God knows how a mistake can cause deformity that makes you damaged goods, surplus goods, low-quality goods, everyone's attention comes with good intentions but is no more than pity. That kind of sentiment makes people feel sorry for themselves. That kind of sentiment encourages people to rise up, wake early and prepare for combat. And what's the first thing people determined to rise think of? Writing. Take a line from a TV series: I can't take it any more, I'm going to go be a writer! Writers are rich and famous, an especially admired line of work in this generation. It's used to compensate for some deficiency, increase one's value, and most of all an investment with a quick return. As a result, Ding Yi had a not-so-long-lived literary career.

First he wrote two novels, sealed them up and sent them out. No response. Then he wrote a series of poems, made copies, gave them to people. No reaction.

Cancer in his body and poetry in his heart, Ding Yi observed himself in the mirror, and even I was moved. I poked fun at him: Chinese medicine says this cancer's growing because your heart's damp, which rhymes with 'poetry' in Chinese. I meant well, didn't think it was really a bad sign, who knew he'd get upset: you're fucking damp! Then he threw the pen and stormed outside. I followed him, stayed with him, pleaded with him: *OK, OK, I was talking nonsense, let's just go back and write some poetry.*

Next he wrote a little drama. He wrote about himself. He made himself seem a bit like Job. He wrote Job as an optimist, strong. His hero constantly remembered: we must succeed, we can certainly succeed!

Was Job like that?

Then I won't bother.

God made a promise to Job: "Are you really able to succeed?"

As he wishes.
Moreover, what does it mean to succeed? What is success?
For him to succeed at anything, you have to succeed first.
And then?
Come on, you're so fucking exhausting!

But not long afterwards, this Ding really had some success: an old director read his script and quite liked it, praised it even. "Hero! Model! Really a model of staying strong in the face of adversity." Soon a small troupe said: "If we can get a sponsor, we'd like to bring the play to the stage." In the end they found a sponsor: "Right, right, we have no reason not to support his spirit, we have no reason not to praise the strength of this era!"

Ding Yi was so pleased.

Ding Yi was dizzy with happiness.

After this first victory, Ding had trouble sleeping for days. The first thing he thought of was that chorus singing the hooligan song, how he ought to send them all a letter: What now, everyone? Is that all I am? He also thought about the expressions of those red silks, red satins, others he knew: one by one they all turned and froze, eyes wide with shock... Ah, there really is no better feeling than this!

Really, not even in his dreams, days before we were running scared in the dark maze, subject to the colourful light, drinking colourful liquids, changing between different coloured faces... Now we were on the colourful rehearsal stage: colourful lights, colourful props, colourful scenery and countless colourful beauties! With so many people busying themselves with his script, pleasantly moving according to his words, even I couldn't help but admire this Ding.

What's up, brother, am I talking nonsense? he asked, looking at me triumphantly in the mirror.

There was no way I could fail to acknowledge this Ding's talent for theatre, but the scene before me made me think of another play: Goethe's *Faust*.

Faust, you still remember that, Brother Ding?
Of course, why?
Was that wager ultimately won by Faust or Mephistopheles?
His face filled with disdain: *What's it matter!*

OK, OK, don't worry about it. But I quickly realised that Ding Yi's interest was not in the play; wherever he looked, his gaze fell on the actresses. Alas, I was also confused: here were natural feelings, there were beautiful girls, what was the point of my insight?

I figured I should keep to one side. Who could bury the gift of this natural feeling? Who could repress the youth of this youthful life? Who could block the mightiness of this mighty spring wind? All right, I told myself to observe, a good play really would be performed!

40. The Mighty Spring Wind

What is illness? The spring wind cannot be blocked!

Further, what is optimism, what is strength? (And what is desire, what is feeling, what is recklessness and foolishness?) Also, where do optimism and strength come from? I'll tell you: the mighty spring wind.

The mighty spring wind is like a hormone-made mission. In the sparse, frozen season, that Ding was like a child playing on his grandmother's knee, asking this and that, obsequious, or now and then looking at Eve like me, thinking of Eden, respectfully hearing an old legend. But when the spring wind first blew, suddenly things changed: the sky became bright and sunny, the wilderness vast, the green grass lush, the flowers like constellations... It was as if this Ding had become beastly overnight, full of crude thoughts, dragging lewd desires, what was left for me? The little sprout also grew day and night, or had long quietly opened in loneliness. Ready to make trouble, often high-spirited. And there were so many pretty girls, so many pretty girls! When seductive titbits overwhelmed him, this Ding dreamed of it at night, thought of it during the day. These thoughts and dreams filled me with fear and expectation, kept me up at night. But they made Ding Yi excited and happy, unable to stop.

That old bison seemed to be on its feet again!

Restrain yourself, I told him. *Your illness, your illness!*

Illness? That Ding smiled. *Can the illness be restrained? Is the illness restrained? Moreover...*

Moreover what?

He didn't say. He didn't say, but I still knew: moreover, good times were coming, beauty was coming. It was this beauty that really made Ding Yi feel sadness and regret. He said to me: *I just got here, brother, how can I leave?* He said to me: *I've been hoping for so long, brother, you oughta know!* He said to me: *Is it fair for me to just die like this? I still haven't really experienced spring! I still didn't know where the women are, I still didn't know if they're really there. If I just die like this, I'll never know if they're real or not, I'll always think they're ghosts, brother!*

Alas, poor Ding Yi. Alas, this feeling of yours. This Ding Yi's wilderness, this wilderness' spring sky, this spring sky's wind! I understand you, brother!

But still I urged him: *Restrain yourself, man, some things you have to wait for.*

Wait, wait and wait for what?

Did you forget that grand time?

What grand time?

Eve, before Eve came...

That Ding was discontented. That Ding was depressed. That Ding knew it was inconvenient to argue with me, but his eager eyes overflowed with spring light as he looked forward to the day he would conquer beauty and enchantment. (Tell you a secret: in all of virgin Ding Yi's dreams there was never a concrete woman – especially in that most seductive place, it was always shrouded in fog, mystery.)

There's a folk song here: White clouds lie on the large blue stone, the hardest thing in life is missing another.

Maybe I should just let him go? Maybe I should go with him.

In that case, no matter when I leave, I'll have done right by him.

41. Other People

But Eve, where was Eve?

I was still longing for Eve. What route had Eve taken since I had arrived in Ding Yi?

Eve didn't have an address. Not having an address, the only information I had was that Eve was harboured in another person.

Deep among the masses of people. The bustling streets or silent rooms. All possible roads. In valleys, wilderness, wind and rain, hot sun. In a jostling train or on a ship sailing at night. Some place of emptiness, some kind of emotion – where the history of emptiness and emotion meet, or at a point the history creates, at some moment the emptiness and emotion link together... Eve must be there.

Because of my longing, Eve must be there.

Because of my searching, Eve must be there.

Because of the countless other people, Eve must be there.

Ever since we separated at Eden, ever since that fig leaf floated down, hid our keepsakes, or especially hid lovers' unique language... We became other people.

We all became other people, so we spent life after life searching for each other. But our search was again cut off by countless other people, their hiding, their opposition. Other people? Once, for example, Ding Yi and I saw one pair of strange eyes after another, those pointing fingers, those whispers and sniggers. But not only that. Other people: there's no place they aren't. Both sides of the wall. In other parts of the heart. In the exterior of clothing or manner. In the depth difficult to notice in a smile, or ulterior motives in words. In dreams, even hidden in the dark corners of dreams...

For example near dusk one summer evening, below a large tree, as a child Ding Yi once played happily with a girl, played till his head dripped with sweat, till his whole body was covered in dirt, till heaven and earth filled with innocent, childhood laughter. But the sunset slowly faded, and the stars alighted. The adults said: "No more playing, time to go home." The well-behaved girl went into an adult's arms. But Ding Yi hadn't had enough, Ding Yi jumped and shouted: "No, no! I want to play a little more."

The adults smiled and said: "Tomorrow, is tomorrow OK? Now it's time to go home and sleep." Sleep, is that a real reason? Ding Yi kept shouting: "No! Right now, I don't want to sleep today." Could there be something more important than that girl? But the girl had already taken an adult's hand and headed off, then she turned and smiled at him. Helpless and anxious, the boy grasped his only hope: "Tomorrow then, we'll play again tomorrow, OK little miss? I'll be here waiting for you!" The girl looked at the expression on the adult's face. The adult answered for her: "OK, tomorrow." The next day, Ding Yi went under the big tree very early and waited for the sun to rise, waited for the sunlight to fade, kept waiting until starlight filled the sky. Where was the little girl? There was only long, empty loneliness. So Ding Yi and I noticed other people. Other people didn't take tomorrow to heart. Other people were in a different mood.

Another example is a peaceful afternoon on the small street in front of our house when young Ding Yi was playing marbles by himself. The small, colourful glass balls were crystal clear. His grandmother had just bought them for him. He wasn't that good with them. Before, he'd just watch others play, wishing he could too. Now he played happily alone, knocking one into another, not daring to use too much force, afraid one would roll away. Then a big kid came along. The big kid was surprised Ding Yi had so many new, beautiful marbles and asked to play with him. "Nice shot!" the big kid said. "No, no... you broke the rules." Ding Yi didn't have confidence in himself. The big kid said: "What the heck? I found a moron!" Ding Yi hugged the bag tight, hesitating. I've said this Ding was timid by nature, but he also wanted respect. "What the hell are you thinking about, are we playing or not?" "Well OK..." What happened next is very simple: while the peaceful afternoon was still peaceful, Ding Yi lost all his 'property'. In the emptiness of the street, its narrowness, the big kid went home happy, while young Ding Yi stood serenely, then did what he thought was a matter of course, but was actually absurd: asked his grandmother to find that big kid and get his 'property' back. His grandmother said she wouldn't do that. She said: "I'll buy you more, OK?" "No, I want those, I don't want other ones." Ding Yi stomped and shouted, in his heart were those distinct, pleasing marbles, each like his own flesh and blood. His grandmother had no choice but to go, and she actually got all the marbles back. But surprisingly this led to endless shame: "Look, that's him, Ding Yi!" "It's him, losing things fair and square and having his family get them back!" "Yup, that's him." "Yo! Yo! Give him a good one..." This ridicule and contempt for young Ding Yi was like thunder, shock, defamation, invasion, and it left a deep mark on the rest of our history in the shape of 'other people'.

What else? Also, during one of Shi Tiesheng's writing nights, when an apparently fictional boy and I walked together, we felt like the words that had been carved into Ding Yi's heart had been carved into ours too: other people.

That was the season of melting snow, sunny winter mornings, that boy held the first painting he had ever made, risking the cold but enthusiastically walking towards an incredibly beautiful house, going to look for the girl he'd long held in his heart, wanting to give his first proud painting to her... "Hey, what are you doing here?" the girl said. "Where were you trying to go?" The girl's meaning was: Did you really come just to see me? "Of course!" Was there any doubt in the boy's heart? But the decorations in the house amazed him, and he actually forgot the painting he was holding, forgot the purpose of this journey. The girl happily pulled him into the maze-like house, through the palatial hallways. Passing row after row of solemn bookshelves, passing pot after pot of soothing flowers, opening door after door, opening the doors in the rooms past the doors, passing soft carpets, passing windows made brilliant by ice, passing daylight etched on the floor, and the faint sound of music... On that winter morning, I, or that boy in the book, walked into a house we couldn't have dreamed of. But somehow it was as if we'd also entered some kind of fictitious, bizarre, horror: beautiful yet chilly, elegant yet oppressive, expansive yet seemingly congested... Or it's because, from deep in that beautiful open house came a sound – the sound of other people, or the insistence of differentiating the voice of another: "Hey, why'd you bring him in? Who asked you to bring him in? OK, OK, don't bring him in again..." So on that sunny morning, or rather the thousand-year-long night, a naive heart was doomed to come upon other people, doomed to have an innocent dream and be startled awake by other people. So when I or that boy in the book was on the way home, he still clutched that childish painting – maybe he forgot, forgot what he was supposed to do, but maybe we didn't forget, just suddenly felt that painting was too mediocre and would have no place in someone else's heart...

But what made us feel the richness and mystery of 'other people' the most was something I still haven't figured out: why Ding Yi bothered with an old man he called 'Uncle'.

42. Uncle

Ever since I landed in Ding Yi, we decided to call this old man 'Uncle', despite him being no different from any of the others.

So we called him Uncle.

Uncle really wasn't that old at that time. He lived alone, across from Ding Yi's house, on the other side of that little road where Ding Yi and I first encountered the world. So Uncle made us feel the richness and mystery of 'other people'. First of all because Mother was never keen on Ding Yi going to his house: "Look for yourself, do other people go?" Second of all, when guests did occasionally visit Uncle, neighbours asked one another full of suspicion: "Who came? What person?" Uncle overheard and was vague: "Ah, all to do a favour for someone else." Another reason: Uncle's house always contained a picture of a strange woman. Once Ding Yi asked: "Who's this woman?" I thought Uncle would be short again and say it was someone else, but he didn't. Uncle pondered awhile, solemnly brushed off the photo, held it up and said: "It's a martyr."

Martyr! Ding Yi went home and told this news to his parents, they listened with surprise.

Father asked Mother: "Martyr? Doesn't that mean they're a traitor?"

Mother said: "Men are traitors, so women can't be martyrs?"

"Who?" Ding Yi asked. "Who's a traitor?"

"Don't ask, little boy," his parents both whispered to Ding Yi.

So that episode came to an end. Young Ding Yi didn't think carefully, he just felt Uncle had something to do with a play or a film. But afterwards he still frequented Uncle's house behind his parents' backs – that old man could tell stories.

Uncle's house was the only one in his little yard, or you could say Uncle lived there alone. The yard had a lot of trees, pomegranates, wintersweets, cloves. In the house's three rooms were many pots, large and small, where flowers and plants grew. Among the plants were just three items of furniture: a bed, a table, a stool. I remember a sago palm, which was outside in summer and came in during the winter. Uncle said: "This thing hasn't bloomed in many years. I didn't take care of it well, so it's going to spite me for the rest of its life." There was another plant called a climbing cactus, Uncle said each plant had its own essential temperament, this flower bloomed but only for an hour each time. If it blooms in the middle of the night you have to stare at it, waiting, and if you accidentally doze off, then it's closed up again by the time you wake up. When Ding Yi and Uncle were waiting for the climbing cactus to blossom, he told us many stories. You could even say that, during Ding Yi's childhood, half of all the stories he heard were from Uncle.

43. Magic

Of all the many stories Uncle told, the one about magic has been the hardest to forget.

That day Ding Yi and Uncle sat in the yard. That day there were no special flowers about to bloom. Uncle was unpreoccupied and said: "I'll tell you a story, OK?"

"But," Uncle went on, "this isn't a made-up story, it's a true one."

Uncle said it's totally fine not to believe it, "but I really saw it with my own eyes".

When Uncle was young, he studied in E. The city of E was surrounded by mountains and water, beautiful scenery. One day Uncle went for a stroll and found himself in front of a theatre, heard someone shouting: "Hurry, come look, come see!" A Chinese-American or Chinese-European magician (so-and-so-stan or so-and-so-sky, Uncle couldn't remember) had come back to pay respects to his ancestors and wanted to give a fantastic performance in this theatre. "One show only! Don't miss it, it won't happen again!" Uncle looked up and saw, written like lightning on the poster, the words: 'Incredible, awe-inspiring mystery'. Uncle asked that guy: "What happens?" The guy shook his head. "Don't know." Uncle said: "But you still shout about it?" Then he bought two tickets.

The performance started at seven. Uncle and his classmate friend X got there a few minutes early. It wasn't a large theatre, and half the seats were empty.

Uncle said that, in that chaotic year, it was actually a pretty good crowd.

At seven there was still no movement on stage. After waiting a little longer, the curtain remained closed tight, and there was chatter offstage. Uncle looked at his watch: ten past seven. Someone in the audience asked: "Where is this magician really from?" Someone answered: "I heard he's Chinese." Someone shook their head: "A Chinese person wouldn't have such a strange name!" Someone said: "Foreign-born then." Someone else said: "When in Rome." Another person said: "When in Rome? What about honouring your ancestors!"

At twenty past seven some people got unruly, threw fruit peel onstage.

A little while later the theatre boss walked onstage and apologised to the audience, saying this so-and-so-stan or so-and-so-sky had lived abroad a long time, this was his first time to E city, and he had probably been so charmed by the scenery that he lost track of time and was currently hurrying there from the beach. Someone offstage shouted: "Could he be a crook?" Another said ironically: "A bumpkin trying to give himself a fancy name?" The boss was at a loss, he bowed repeatedly: "No, no, I promise you brothers, definitely not." Laughter rippled over the audience. Someone said to the boss: "What about you? Who can promise you're not a crook?" The boss wiped away sweat, bowed, smiled and spoke politely: "Brothers, this theatre has been around for some years, many of you sitting here are acquaintances, friends. You have my personal guarantee. It is said... It is said this magic is truly extraordinary, you may wish to wait a minute, it is, after all, a rare opportunity..." Before the boss could finish, people were already calling for refunds. "It is said! It is said! You want us all to be awed by hearsay!"

Uncle's classmate X was losing patience, said he wanted to go out and get some air, it was suffocating inside. Uncle said: "Why don't I go with you?" X said there was no need, said he'd be back in a minute.

But as soon as X had one foot out the door, news came: that so-and-so-stan or so-and-so-sky had arrived.

Uncle went out to look but didn't see any trace of X. The curtain opened, and Uncle hurried back to his seat.

The magician took to the stage. Sure enough he had yellow skin, black eyes and black hair. He straightened out his dinner suit and bowed deeply to the audience. "I'm sorry, I'm very sorry, I'm half an hour late." He raised his wristwatch. "No more, no less, exactly half an hour."

Uncle looked at his watch: half past seven.

The magician paced onstage, introduced himself, said he was not only Chinese, but his family also came from E city. Being born and raised abroad, he'd come back now to visit the land of his ancestors. He said that, starting with his grandfather and going back he didn't know how many generations, his family had lived there and worked as fishermen. "It's really a case of seeing is believing," the magician said. "I've travelled all over the world and have seldom seen a beach as lovely as the one in E city. Lingering there is what made me half an hour late." Then the magician stood still a moment as if stunned.

Uncle said that, at that point, he noticed that the lights on stage seemed to flicker before dimming somewhat.

The magician bowed with his hands folded and spoke: "But I suddenly remembered that tonight I would perform for my fellow residents of E city. How could I forget that? So I jumped up and hurried here." He raised his wristwatch again. "Not bad, not bad, didn't delay things for even a minute. Everyone please look, it's seven o'clock sharp."

People looked at their watches and were shocked.

Uncle said he looked at his watch too. "It was really seven o'clock sharp again! Could my own eyes be mistaken?"

The sounds of surprise faded, the magician continued to hold forth, saying that E's scenery was truly enchanting, green mountains and blue water, sea and sky, the beach so clean, so soft, the sun so bright and gentle... The magician closed his eyes and slowly paced onstage, his voice clear and round: "Lie down, lie down, stretch out your limbs, face the blue sky, let the sea breeze and sunlight envelop your body like when you were a child and slept in your mother's arms... Ah, no one else around, just me, the earth and sky, the sound of the waves, the wind flying like magic, the seawater salty and refreshing, the white clouds taking shape as if blown by an ancient wind..." Then the magician opened his eyes slightly. "I suddenly felt dizzy, for a moment I felt lost like I myself was those clouds, those waves, that wind, everything as far as the eye could see..."

Uncle said: "There's no way I'm remembering this wrong." The stage lights flickered again and were as bright as before.

The magician paced to centre stage then sat down on the floor, spoke to himself, the sound suddenly seemed hazy, as if out of reach. "Like this, I'll lie on the beach, by the waves, in the wind, under the clouds, lying between heaven and earth, lying in a corner of the universe. Like this I'll forget everything, even forget this evening, so, so..."

With the audience half asleep, muddled like fog around a cloud, suddenly the stage lights became really bright.

The magician smiled slightly and stood. "So I'm very sorry, I still came late. Everyone please look at your watches. Half past seven. It's really half past seven, I was late exactly half an hour."

The whole audience was stunned and sat silent for about thirty seconds.

Then there was thunderous applause.

During the applause, Uncle's classmate came back, shocked. "Huh, it's over?"

Uncle said: "You left for a few minutes and missed the whole thing!"

X was surprised. "What are you talking about, a few minutes?"

Uncle showed him his watch.

"Impossible!" X stared in surprise. "This is impossible!"

But no one was paying attention to Uncle and X. The magician took his final bow as the cheers continued.

Uncle said it was the most bizarre magic he'd ever seen.

Uncle said that, compared with that magic, everything else was child's play.

"Really," Uncle said, "if I hadn't seen it with my own eyes I wouldn't believe it no matter who told me."

Uncle stopped speaking and leaned over to smell the scent of the night-blooming flowers, then sat back and gazed up without saying anything. A bright moon was reflected in his pupils, then that photo in the moonlight and the woman in that photo. To this day I can still remember Uncle's expression: humble, awed and very calm.

44. Searching for Eve and Three Warnings

This magic is just a short interlude. Other people are my concern, my confusion, my suffering. And not to mention Ding Yi, who has been among those beautiful actresses like a fish in water, forgetting himself.

I reminded him: Eve! Eve, still remember her?

I reminded him: Eve didn't leave an address, Eve is hiding in another person.

But I also had to comfort him: Don't panic, don't fear, since I arrived in you, since we joined forces, Ding Yi, we've walked in to ever-present other people.

I comforted him: But that's exactly our path, Ding Yi! Since we left Eden we must walk this path, must walk this path in search of Eve.

But who would come to comfort the writing nights boy? Who would comfort the old man we called Uncle? I also couldn't sufficiently comfort Ding Yi. And Eve, who would comfort her? Since leaving Eden, where has she gone?

Well, these other people as vast as the mountains and oceans, these other people as distant as heaven and earth, these other people marching endlessly like time are proof of Adam and Eve's lost paradise! As a result I had to tell Ding Yi: *This time, and all times, is the time to look for Eve. Other places and other places' other places are all our route to Eve.*

But there are three warnings, Ding Yi, that you must remember.

First you must remember, always, the difficulties involved in this search: only when you look for Eve will you recognise she is not another person, and before that she and others will seem alike. Second, you can't use the keepsake God gave you to go notice her, can't abuse that unique language to tempt her – for example, people cannot tempt God! Ding Yi, I'm warning you, this is important. If not, you'll be battered among other people spread like mountains and vast as water (he doesn't seem to mind). Third, listen, Ding Yi: in the end we must rely on this token, rely on this unique language to recognise Eden's allies!

So I gave Ding Yi the above advice for two main reasons. First, Ding Yi's feeling. I recognised early on his primary motivation for life – did you think it was optimism and strength? No, fundamentally it's still desire, the solemn promises basically all stem from feeling! And whether this feeling can tend towards love or not remains to be seen.

Second, a soul has no gender. That is to say a soul is not one gender or another, it is an other. This endless journey is rooted in loneliness, this lonely soul seeks only to reunite with others. It's only that a soul needs an agent, a body, and those have genders. Gender has always been a body's symbol, its attraction, a way to make it stand out and call for reunion, a gift from God. The different concave and convex flowers are tokens, codes. And the problem starts from there: a body's manifestation is often hidden in the soul, the body's temptation can be even stronger than the call of the soul! Gender's attraction often turns things upside down, a flower hyperactive with desire can actually ignore the soul, content itself, have its way and bring about disorder in the soul – the body and soul torturing each other!

This kind of story is common in Ding Yi's realm, I've long been aware. No matter what the result, no matter whether this Ding ends up losing himself or falling deep in sorrow, I can never let him interrupt this journey of mine, can't miss the chance to reunite with Eve.

45. Body-Soul Conflict

What is body-soul conflict? For example, I fall in love with A, but Ding Yi only has eyes for B. For example, say I finally find Eve, but Ding Yi doesn't like her current body. Or again, for example, Ding Yi takes a liking to a gorgeous body, but I find out it's not really Eve inside.

Also, around here you often hear about resentful men and women crying: "I know he/she doesn't love me, but I can't let go of him/her!" Huh? Why can't you let go? Or: "He/she is a total jerk, a devil, I know, I know, I know I should leave him/her, but I can't!" Who knows? Who knows whether they should leave and who can't do it? And why can't they do it? Maybe all such incidents are a result of body-soul conflict, thus the heart tortures the body, the body hurts the heart. When a dream is wasted or one gives up halfway on one's endless journey to find their path, this could be the cause of death.

46. Loneliness

The problem is that other people are not the only cause of your terror. Terror is because of yearning, otherwise there wouldn't be terror, otherwise other people wouldn't matter, otherwise no one would pay them any attention. Yearning causes terror. And one of this yearning's primary causes is that Eve is hidden in another person.

Early in Ding Yi's life I was already using his bleary eyes to look for Eve's location – look for other people, look for any girl, so from a young age Ding Yi had feelings or lust (and later that cruel nickname). I also acted this way in Shi Tiesheng. For example during his writing nights I once saw Eve travelling in a beautiful but anxious girl, saw her feeling the loneliness and confusion I felt in Ding Yi. At that time Eve was walking hand-in-hand into the sunset with that girl. They squatted in the grass, at a loss like Ding Yi and me – presumably with the same mood we felt when looking at other people. Who was she? Tentatively 'O'. She stopped by that Shi's writing night, and I don't know where she went after.

I borrowed Ding Yi to look at other people.

I borrowed Ding Yi's looking at other people and looked for Eve's location.

I was lonely, it was innate loneliness.

I would guess everyone else is like that too. Because: "Then the Lord God said: 'It is not good for the man to be alone. I will make him a helper as his partner..." **– Old Testament, Genesis**

For example, when one day you have to leave your mother, you search for the partner God promised you.

At that time loneliness is proven.

At that time finite vision looks to infinite elsewhere, intuits Eve's voice.

I remember a bright spring day when Mother promised to take us to play. Ding Yi and I waited patiently, dreaming of a faraway place amid Mother's hectic footsteps, believing that, when Mother finished every household chore, she'd take us. To where? Either behind that mysterious mountain or in the flowing glow? Bleary-eyed Ding Yi looked at the sun, watched it from morning to noon, go from hot to setting, thinking that his hope would inevitably become reality at some point. But Mother forgot her promise. She kept washing clothes, washing and washing, washing and washing, until the light converged with the top of the mountain and weakened, until I suddenly awoke within that bleary-eyed yet happy Ding Yi – no different from when I was first in Shi Tiesheng: "The surrounding light gradually dimmed, gradually cooled and became gloomy, gradually farther, gradually mistier, I said nothing and suddenly understood a little. I can still feel that slow yet rapid shift, lonely, melancholy dusk had arrived, and I heard the swoosh of Mother scrubbing clothes, that sound's constancy like the passing of time. That Sunday. That very day. Mother found her boy hiding there, still, found him crying, tears falling silently. I sensed Mother shake the water off her hands in a panic and pick me up and hold me in her arms. I heard her say, kissing me and saying: 'Oh sorry, oh, sorry...' The boy squatted next to the big heavy tub, nestled in Mother's arms, closed his eyes and didn't see the sun again, the light was gone irrevocably, desolate." – **Shi Tiesheng's *Notes on Principles.*** That day, on that day, just when Ding Yi was snuggling in his mother's bosom, I discovered I was detaching from her. At that moment, while Ding Yi was still ignorant and half asleep, I was looking into the distance, looking for Eve, missing her in the dream Adam perpetuated, wondering about her, searching for her...

Those were all consequences of saying goodbye to Eden, so this boy named Ding Yi couldn't avoid getting wrapped up in this long-standing torture. Who came up with this torture? Love. For a long time the distant mountains and sunset seemed lonely. So Ding Yi and I (and any boy) sincerely believed that solitude is the natural state in life.

When Ding Yi was crying and burying his head in his mother's arms, I floated off, eager to seek high and low, eager to search heaven and earth. And I believed that, if Eve once passed through O, then regardless of the time or place this would be O's mood too. If Eve's journey had already moved on from O, travelled elsewhere, extended to any girl, then it didn't matter who, she would still be looking like me, for our original separation and pact, always searching, for all of life.

47. Sex

Distance, or difference, is a fundamental aspect of God's creation – only this way could a path be made. Separation followed by searching is the primary intention of God's creation – the only way this path could be maintained. Made various, made enchanting, made captivating, longed for... only then could this path transmit the signal of love. Just like a wise father who sees his daughter pampered all day at home with nothing to do, fears wasted years and wants them to go out and travel in search of treasure. Where's the treasure? The treasure is not other, it is the way of hunting.

For the sake of difference, God separated day and night, separated heaven and earth, separated land and sea, separated the sun, moon and stars, separated plants and animals, separated animals and people.

For the sake of difference, God used the names Adam and Eve to separate men and women.

In order for them to search for each other, God endowed them with different symbols – convex and concave tokens or languages. Because of the wonderful way concave and convex fit, God hoped it would be the way their souls enacted their covenant, the moment when heaven and earth reunited.

"Upon meeting in golden wind and jade dew, they surpassed countless others." Go look in the fields, go look in nature, go look at the edges of the earth, the deserts and rivers, all of life has a similar symbol, all of life comes from the same 'first movement' – desire! Male, female, convex and concave flowers grow together day and night, miss each other, seek life! It's the torment of emotion, it's all love's exhortation, it's all the anxiety of searching and waiting. Waiting until a year or a life's most solemn time, then gently slipping into dreams, with no hesitation to exhaust life's essence, shout in the wind, sing in the rain… Then wilt, shrivel, leave the DNA record's last wish, life after life, life after life spreading, in limitless sunlight, continuing that endless journey in pursuit of love, the path towards love.

But, but, just having two different symbols isn't enough, those two symbols have to be made to long for each other, those mutual longings must never be exhausted, they must never tire, otherwise how can they construct a never-ending future? Look at the livestock in the mountain grass, recklessly bumping together, abusing this unique language, failing to express the gift of their keepsake, abandoning the covenant, celebrating vulgarity, their expression of interest and passionate journey suddenly turning into aimless wandering, the spread of love's message becomes more difficult, all that's left is propagation, propagation, propagation and propagation this oppressive labour. Because of this, two leaves floated down outside the gates of Eden to cover the two different flowers. This hiding or taboo is necessary, God designed it so searching souls attract, so the wonderful longing is protected. "Upon meeting in golden wind and jade dew" I'm afraid is accidental, upon meeting in golden wind and jade dew – then it's good, then it's good, then there can be joy all around, endless charm, the lonely universe filled with happiness.

Amid this listening and comprehension, Ding Yi and I grew up together. Ding Yi and I could no longer, or didn't dare, go naked in the street, and let that bud stand in vain. We understood, or went along with those watchful eyes, those pointing fingers and sniggering voices. We put on clothes. We grew into adults. We even understood dressing up, oh right – packaging!

48. Clothes and Walls

As a result, this world has a big clothing industry; cold or not cold, people always want to wrap their bodies in clothes. Similarly, wall-construction is highly developed; whether wind or rain, people want to build walls for shelter, build houses and hide. Over time this became a custom, or convention, rule – you must dress neatly in broad daylight but however you want within your four walls. Take having sex, for example: it requires removing clothes so it must take place behind walls – Ding Yi's realm calls it 'room business', 'room movement', 'sharing a room', or even 'room skills', that is to say, these activities cannot be done without a room.

The reason it can't be done without a room is not that it can't be done in bad weather and is easy to do in good weather, it has nothing to do with the intrusion of nature and everything to do with resisting the eyes and ears of others. Therefore, when no one is around you can enjoy sex in 'public' or get it on outdoors. So it seems walls and rooms are not needed, what is needed is just the act of hiding – to keep out others' eyes and ears, to ward off their hearts and minds. Or you could look at it this way: no one being around is like clothes, and being alone is like walls. From my experience of being in Ding Yi's realm for ten years, clothes and walls come in many forms, fibres and fabrics make one kind of clothes, stacking bricks and tiles is a preliminary step in making a wall. And the expression, certainly not hidden? How about a smile, is it certainly not concealed? And applause, how perfunctory. Discourse especially has trouble avoiding underground roads. It's all clothes and walls, all hiding, escape, isolation, prevention. Like Ding Yi changing his name, isn't that clothing? Or the half-truths I told to simplify things for him, do they not form an invisible wall?

The philosopher Roland Barthes observed that nudity can be a kind of clothing. For example nude dancing: a nude dancer is stark naked but in fact she wears 'naked clothing'. What's this clothing called? It's called dance or called art. Dance or art can also be clothes or walls and thereby hide her nudity. With her unique attitude as a dancer, with the special feeling of conducting art, she is refined, extraordinary and not just naked. Because of the unique form of the theatre, because there is a stage, lights, sets, rules emphasised by props, the audience is lost in the extraordinary, enters the aesthetic, and naturally cannot but recognise her identity as a dancer, recognise her 'nude clothing'. If anyone still sees her as naked, with her bottom out, then, ladies and gentlemen: you have violated the rules, shown contempt for conventions, and this idea makes you contemptuous, though you have not hindered others. This behaviour also reveals your own wicked thoughts, and thereby makes you – but not others – naked without clothing.

What a bizarre business this is. First, why is nudity shameful? Why does having one's bottom out incite ridicule? Bottoms and those wonderful buried slots are proper body parts, right, organs that human beings need, why discriminate against them, or (actually) emphasise them? Lips can smile, teeth can show, why does the bum need to be carefully hidden? Next, to say that 'naked clothing' hides her nudity begs the question: if she's already nude, what can 'naked clothing' hide? Finally, what can make nudity into clothing and also – wait for it – make clothing nudity?

As Ding Yi grew up I started to understand: it's rules, it's conventions, it's people's consensus or acceptance. If you don't believe me, go to a nudist beach, there you can be naked and open and relaxed, cheerful and calm, but if you point out someone's naked, people won't think you're an honest kid and will instead be surprised you're such an emperor with no clothes. But on the streets, in public places, in any so-called respectable establishment, don't even think about being naked, even if you're wearing just a sliver of clothing (like a bikini), people will stare at you like you're crazy, a moron, or – like Ding Yi – a hooligan! What's the deal? Rules and conventions must be obeyed. To travellers in Ding Yi's realm I would remind you to do as the Romans do, accept them, obey them, lay your thoughts bare when you get back to your room. You must understand one important thing: the issue isn't whether you dress or not, but whether you dress like others, whether you follow rules, comply with conventions, can follow the crowd and hide in other people.

Right, hiding in other people provides safety. So Eve hid in other people, right? So young Ding Yi distressed his father like a dash of colour in a sea of red, right? So there's a phrase around here: black sheep – unlike your predecessors and therefore a bad child! So 'heresy' is 'evil'. So you can't rely on dressing nicely to hide in other people, you have to rely on thinking nicely to hide in other people! Dressing nicely won't always allow you to hide in others, dressing nicely is a way of flaunting, thinking nicely. Whether your bum is out or not isn't crucial; what is crucial is whether or not your thinking can be hidden. So you can dress nicely and hide in nicely dressed masses, and can nakedly hide in a group's nakedness but not the other way around. If you walk naked into a nicely dressed group your nakedness is naturally shameful but not the other way around – if you walked nicely dressed into a naked group? Sorry, you'll still be as ashamed as if you were naked! What happened? What are you exposing? Bottom, aren't your bottom and its counterparts hidden away? However, you've exposed your breaking of the rules, exposed your contempt for convention, exposed the heresy and evil of refusing to give in! So, in fact, clothing can do without clothing, walls can do without walls, as long as there is hiding. Also, the most important thing to hide is not flesh, it's your desire, your deepest wishes, your freest yearnings.

Eve, oh, Eve, this is so hard, this is making it so hard to find you – especially with those three warnings.

Why have walls? Why make clothes? Oh, Eve, how did we fall on this lot? How could we fear nakedness, hide from each other? Before, how did we wait without hiding, meet with such frankness! Eve, you must still remember, in Eden, we were so free, had no sense of shame, our desire, our dreams, bloomed like gorgeous flowers, floated calm as clouds, drifted like rain, were all around like light and air, was there any of today's caution, alertness? This hiding, this fear!

49. How the Snake Lured People

She took of its fruit and ate; and she gave some to her husband, who was with her, and he ate. Then the eyes of both were opened, and they knew that they were naked; and they sewed fig leaves together and made loincloths for themselves. – **Old Testament, Genesis**

In reality, the actual separation from Eve started then.

Because searching started with hiding.

Because it started with Adam and Eve, eternal spirits didn't just pass through a certain Ding or a certain Shi, it was all in order to find freedom again, find the soul's completeness again.

But that separation was all because of the snake's trick. The snake said: "God doesn't want you to eat the fruit from the tree because God knows that when you eat it your eyes will be opened, and you will be like God, knowing good and evil." – **Old Testament, Genesis**

But why is this a trick? Ding Yi asked me. *Should people not know good from evil?*

I thought hard, thought: *Maybe the problem is that people don't have that kind of ability!*

Why not? That Ding shook his head. *No, no, you haven't convinced me.*

During my time in Ding Yi and many other lives, I still haven't resolved this problem.

Only when I now look back on Ding Yi, look back on that realm's vanity, especially after when I was in Shi Tiesheng and saw a scary child, I started to realise the snake's words weren't just a trick, they were two tricks in one! First, the snake knew that even if people ate the fruit on that tree they still wouldn't really know good from evil, like God. At that time the snake also knew that, once people saw themselves as gods, it would be hard to avoid using people's wisdom as evidence to divide them into a hierarchy, or use their own likes and dislikes to differentiate value, and use this as an alternative to divine good and evil. But people, the snake especially knew that people – because of their innate vanity and lust for power, their great ambition – would listen to its vile speech. And what would be the result? The result is that the voice of God gradually shrunk and people used their own notions of high and low to struggle, strive, resist, fight...

The result is that good and evil are harder to tell apart.

The result is that resentment spread, discrimination became pervasive.

The result is that souls became like planets in an expanding universe, farther and farther away from each other, farther and farther yet still not letting down their guard.

So Eve hid in another person.

So Eve, she – they say somewhere in this world, we really don't know!

50. Tree of Knowledge

That tree, some call it the tree of wisdom, some call it the tree of knowledge. I tend towards the latter. One, because wisdom is hard to obtain, while knowledge increases day by day. Two, because wisdom always sees people's regrets, people's sins, while knowledgeable people (intellectuals) are always pretentious.

In fact, the snake's trick not only succeeded, it has advanced over time. Once upon a time, 'intellectual' implied a common standpoint, and this standpoint, without any evidence, was representative of being correct and honourable. It implied bravery or the need for bravery. An example? OK: let's say you're literate, let's say you've passed the civil service exam and had an achievement or two, but you're still not courageous (please remember this place's ancient saying still in use today: warriors die in battle, ministers die speaking truth), you still retain the weakness of human nature, or the hard-to-avoid faults of those with knowledge, so some could sternly say of you: this intellectual's shame!

This can't help but make me admire the snake's knowledge of people's hearts and spirits, admire its thorough, accurate understanding of people.

I would dare say that Ding Yi is this kind of shameful intellectual. And I've only ever known him to be brutal, honest, but I don't know if this guy can not only be ashamed but also reject shame.

You've never been proud of this, have you, Brother Ding?

Of course not. I just think if you're courageous you should go be courageous, if you're devoted, go be devoted. That's why I respect you, but this respect is not because you're some kind of intellectual.

Shh, quiet down, this kind of talk isn't without 'hooligan' risk.

That guy lowered his voice and asked me: *What do you think?*

Forget it, forget it, you want to make more trouble for me?

Like dedication, what do you think? That guy persisted, wanted to get me to say it. *Dedication should be limited to a private virtue. Calling on others to be devoted doesn't sit well with me. What's he relying on, being an intellectual? Furthermore, if someone more courageous than you comes along, you just turn into an ordinary person?*

Shh, you have more than a little guts.

But I believe that tree must be called the tree of knowledge.

51. In Shi Tiesheng I Met a Scary Child

"That short, thin child, why did he make people afraid? He had a sort of cunning talent – so long as the kids around him were ranked, out of nowhere he had power. 'I like you, I like you... and so on' and 'I don't like you,' then the delighted followed him delightedly, the depressed, still depressed, also followed him. I remember it was a longstanding source of fear in my childhood... Life's fear or difficulties, previously seen cleanly from afar, suddenly demanded a strategy from me; I remember my first strategy, it was flattery. But the fear didn't dissipate as a result. The difficulties, as a result, became more difficult. I still remember, I was hugging a broken football that I had wanted to give as a gift, hugging my broken strategy, the sun setting and breeze blowing on my way home." – **Shi Tiesheng's *Longing for the Temple of Earth***

That scary child confirmed God's concern.

That scary child, he took a power approach and my peaceful strategy's flattery, it's the template for original sin. This template is very important for my journey – whether passing through this Ding or stopping by that Shi, you could say they all had decisive significance.

Adhering to the butterfly effect, that scary child had already become all-powerful, already worn everything down, so that all of human discrimination, resentment, guardedness and fighting can see his shadow. As a result, the quotation above not only describes my experience in Shi Tiesheng but also many encounters in Ding Yi.

Where there are crowds there will be struggle, a strong man from this area once said. It should be added that, where there are crowds this kind of strong man will exist. It should be added that, where there are struggles this kind of strong man will be produced. But do these kind of struggles need these kinds of strong men, or do these kinds of strong men need these kinds of struggles? So can you also say that, where there are these strong men there will be flattery, there will be strategies?

What else could there be?

There could be cowards. There could be traitors. Of course there is feeling.

I once heard a strong man say: "Love? That's a toy for the weak." Those words are not without basis, but it could also be that his self-judgment was rushed – based on my endless yet complicated journey I'd say he is not necessarily weak.

52. Shi Tiesheng Interjects

That Shi: Moreover, those strong men or those scary guys invariably use sex to attack you and threaten you in order to manipulate you. Sex is their favourite weapon.

I: Because that is your biggest secret, your biggest weakness.

That Shi: Why?

I: Because sex is bound to involve other people. Or love is what helps most during lonely times. Love cannot but yearn for others. So that is also your biggest fear.

That Shi: Fear?

I: Because you don't know other people will have what kind of attitude.

That Shi nodded slightly. I'd rarely seen him so modest.

Even if you don't have that issue, that Shi said, back to his old arrogance, they make up something like that to attack you.

I smiled and thought to myself: you might not have that issue, but you cannot but have that kind of longing. No one cannot but have that kind of longing.

That Shi looked at me alertly: What are you smiling at?

I put my smile away: No, nothing. Tell me, what you just said, who, for example?

That Shi: For example that scary kid, he seemed to be born with the knowledge that sex is people's weakest point, their biggest fear. So he always created some opinion or spread some rumours, saying you definitely like some girl, definitely are this or that way with whoever, and provide some trumped-up 'evidence', and as long as you blushed...

I guessed correctly again: Why blush? If you never had that issue, what are you blushing for?

That Shi continued: As long as you blush, you lose. Doesn't matter if it's shyness, if it's anger, you lose either way.

Right, I said, and no matter how you fight back, you're on your heels.

Ha, you know!

You couldn't defend yourself against a trumped-up charge, then you were afraid of him, didn't dare to offend him, went along with him on everything, obeyed him, even supported him, right? Of course I know.

That Shi was momentarily stunned, shook his head like he was unconvinced. Not necessarily, you don't necessarily know everything.

I looked at him in the mirror: So tell me, what else don't I know?

Once some other kids and I banded together and set him straight.

Who?

That scary kid, that thin, short kid who always ranked everyone. One time we really set him straight, we also ranked him. We said: 'Everyone, all of us! We are all the best, all better than you!' Then he was really a fool.

Ha, how did you do it?

We conspired for a long time, a bit like the revolutionary generals Zhang Xueliang and Yang Hucheng. First we felt each other out, then... well, what's it matter. You guess what happened next.

What happened next?

He not only surrendered, he did it in a sexual way. He suddenly pointed to a poster of a pretty woman and said to the best fighter among us: I'll always listen to you. No, do you want to make me kiss this woman on the lips? Gosh, do you realise? No, no, I'm not saying kissing that woman, I'm saying he was already counterattacking, ranking us again! Everyone was stunned, but before anyone could think of anything, that guy already had his face against the poster! Then he turned an eye to look at everyone, looked at that good fighter again, said to him: If I don't listen to you, then tell other people about this. Do you realise? You can't realise, he easily defeated us again...

53. Ancient Suspicion

Right, there's always a problem: why is sex, this natural flower, this talented attractor and aphrodisiac, something shameful for humans? But in other species it's always been proper, not shameful at all?

In fact, since Ding Yi was careless and became a 'hooligan', this question started to perplex me.

There's a lot of evidence. Pussy, dick, slut, whore, arsehole, bitch... people use all kinds of sexual insults. And for those who are too casual in their sexual relations or who live eccentric sexual lives, what do people say? They simply say they're not people, they're animals!

The underlying meaning is that animals can have sex however they want. But animals tend not to disappoint, from generation to generation they pass down the practice of mating. All for one purpose: multiplication.

And people, how should people be? People have always secretively concealed their sexual practices? No way, during my endless journey I remember it used to not only be proper but honourable! Intercourse like thunder and lightning, pouring out like a rainstorm, that was strength, was vigour, was dignity and beauty! Since when did it stop being like that? When and why did people lose this freedom? When and why did people give up this openness?

Oh, Eden! Or that snake, that tree, that tree's fruit! Just because Adam and Eve ate the fruit of that tree, people learned shame! Right, right, right from then, because of that, one had to hide, had to be wary, and the paradise without division ceased to exist. From that time and because of that you saw me, I discovered you, and everyone became aware of mutual differences. And from that time and because of that, you hid your wishes, while I concealed my secrets. Because of this we wore clothing, because of this we built walls, used clothes and walls to proclaim our dignity, used clothes and walls to shield the gaze of others, to remind each other to be respectful and vigilant... So being naked became shameful, so people became unpredictable – bodies close, hearts distant.

Right, proclamation! This is all proclamation, it's implication, it's expression, it's discourse!

So separation and shame are the foundation of discourse.

So wariness and inquiry are the continuation of discourse.

(No wonder *Absolute Privacy* could become a bestseller from its title alone.)

So in front of others you have to dress neatly, behave decently; among familiar faces you can unbutton your coat and kick off your shoes, laugh casually; with your family you can even go shirtless, can cry; only with your husband or wife can you express your wishes, bare your heart.

So, openness is discourse's direction.

As a result, Eros is discourse's extreme.

To put it more directly: that smallest, thinnest piece of underwear is the final barrier, or even talisman, it's responsible for the most crucial hiding. People, you have to be careful: this world's most beautiful and ugliest discourse is all hidden in there! (Still remember that cruel game? Behind a closed door could be a beautiful animal or a wild beast!) So from this thinnest, smallest piece of clothing love can be liberated and have no choice but to reveal its plot...

Ah-ha! Shortly after I arrived in this Ding Yi, I already saw the sphinx play this little trick: sex, to people, is the language of life and death. While for beasts it has no meaning without mating and breeding, so they are worry-free and can save their energy to bother with other things. But one who dreams lightly and cannot guess the sphinx's riddle will inevitably end up like Ding Yi, longing for the beasts' openness and freedom, and even going so far as to practise it.

But now the urgent question is, with all kinds of freedom, why can't people be as open as animals? Right, right, no one said they can't. Of course they can. Anything that has happened can be done. It's just that I haven't been in Ding Yi for long, after all, and can't help but worry: in that case you have to give up your dreams and thereby give up language. Moreover, is giving it up enough? It doesn't seem like enough. It seems like you have to completely root them out. Remember when I stayed in an ape and fish, you can't say I was completely without thoughts and dreams, no words day and night; I did have them, they were just sporadic inklings about eating, drinking, defecating, peeing and screwing.

Dreams, those things, do not occur because you want them, or don't occur because you don't want them.

Love is that way too. Are you asking whether one has love or not? Sorry, it comes once it's asked.

Discourse is that way.

Go ask apes, fish, dogs and horses. Whatever you ask them you'll understand what it means to be without it.

Based on the experience of all my lives, in society, the world, that's basically been the case, there hasn't been much change.

But we must get one thing clear: about being an 'animal', there's no malice. First, it's a legitimate name for any non-human species. Second, everything with a spirit – flesh, body, physical being – are in fact, no more than animals. Of course 'animal' can be an insult, but that's a condemnation that comes from a person's regret or reminder: you are someone with a soul, how can you lose control of your animal and let it take over? Like a hardworking wife denouncing her husband's alcoholism: "Why can't you control your mouth!" Or someone in a field of crops shouting: "Hey! Whose donkey is this eating our unit's sorghum?"

54. Peeping

In view of the danger of taking on animals' shamelessness, I suddenly understood something again: people's weakness, giving up, fear, wariness, etc., are fundamentally caused by our attraction to love. Otherwise, who cares. Otherwise you wouldn't have any feeling at all, you'd just be meat – livestock. Of course, you also couldn't have dreams. I'll just mention something: joy and happiness are two different things. Joy is just a physiological response, apes, fish, dogs and horses have it too, but happiness is all in the soul's heartstrings.

So I searched long and far for Eve: whether in Ding Yi or in Shi Tiesheng or when I first set out in Adam – all the same.

But now I was confined in Ding Yi. Eve was hidden in another person. Everyone in Ding Yi's realm was in clothes, everyone behind walls, eyes avoiding eyes, hearts wary of hearts, what can be done?

"Hey, tell me, who are you really?" Ooh, a nutcase, a proper nutcase!

"Hey, tell me, who among you holds Eve?" Huh, moron, ignore him!

"Hey, do you still remember me? I was in Eden? (or *Last Year at Marienbad*, written by the French author Alain Robbe-Grillet, in which the main character was far less lucky than me in Ding Yi. He used dreamy nonsense to bring that woman from reality to the dream world, made her wake up from the reality of death to live in the virtual)."

Ha, this douchebag! Or: Wow, freaking hooligan...

Must be like this. It would be like this.

As a result Ding Yi and I had an intolerable desire – transcend all clothes and walls, see who really lived there. Do they have the same desire as us, the same tendency and the same wish to stop hiding our hearts? Or who is just like us, alone and searching?

So Ding Yi and I kept looking towards the sea of strangers, towards what was behind the walls, towards any hidden place. To the point that we even called out in the dream world, prayed with our imaginations during the day (daydreams), Ding Yi and I searched and searched some more... Imagination, that true life behind lonely walls, imagination, that vigorous body in rigid clothes, imagination, that vigorous soul in a cautious body... Imagining Eve's journey, imagining Eve's arrival, imagining Eve's body...

Imagining that body's moving wonder, and beating inside that wonderful body is Eve's very soul... Imagining her tranquillity and warmth, imagining her usual alertness and calmness when alone, imagining that with our same gaze she eagerly longed for the far side of the mountain... Imagining the precious token she kept from Eden until today, or the promise she guarded for so many years to meet again, imagining her with the old covenant in mind, preparing for the great occasion!

However, however. If this looking was improper, if I was wrong about Ding Yi, unexpectedly fanning the flames of his rising lust, my dream world became an accessory, awakening his long-dormant desire to peep.

First on the streets, public places, wherever people were, I noticed this Ding often stared, and in his line of sight would be an elegant lady or a sexy girl. And then at the beach, the colourful swimsuits on the sand and the glistening bodies in the water dazed Mr Ding all the more, raising his adrenalin to boiling point. Then home again, sitting alone at the desk, sitting alone with the fire of summer or winter, Ding Yi was often stunned into silence, unable to think, then suddenly grabbed a pen and sketched a wild smear – it was really embarrassing – the elegant bodies, everything exposed.

I laughed at him: *Hey, hey, when porn magazines and tapes are so easy to come by, why take the trouble to paint?*

That Ding disagreed: *Don't you see, they are all dead in those media? The bodies in the magazines all resemble corpses, while those in the videos look like ghosts.*

These words actually left me silent, quietly proud, or in agreement.

But who could have guessed that once, or even more than once, I caught that guy suddenly peeping on the opposite sex in the shower? Too far! I shouted at him: *Hey, hey, what are you doing!* He didn't pay me any attention, just waved: *Shh –don't yell...* He was surprisingly focused. I shouted at him again: *Hey, hey, hey.* He didn't listen, was too enthralled. I said: *Enough, man, don't you remember the scandal you caused that year?* That finally made him look. I said I never thought you'd actually do this kind of thing! He didn't pay attention and turned back to the sight, still unable to pull himself away. I said again: *You really are a hooligan!* His feet seemed to stumble, his fantasy fading away, and he looked at me.

What, hooligan? Why don't you tell us, what's a hooligan?

The way you're looking at other people, that's a hooligan!

Why? You're saying you never looked this way?

No!

I'm saying on the street, in public, a sideways glance, an angle people don't notice.

Hey, I said, right, this monster casting blame first: *Come on, man! Why are you implicating me?*

OK, then in your heart, dreams, in your imagination, what's Eve look like?

This question left me somewhat befuddled.

An old woman? Or a pretty little package?

But I didn't peep!

But you mentally peeped. Tell me, in your thoughts, dreams, imagination, what did you see?

Ahem, look at this kid questioning me!

I'll say it for you, that Ding said, *an enchantingly beautiful woman. But an enchantingly beautiful woman certainly wouldn't just dress cute, isn't that right?*

Ha, Ding Yi! So you're here to educate me? I had to strike back: *You might as well do your usual peeping at magazines and videos and leering at the beach.*

That's not the same! Ding Yi shouted, suddenly inspired. *Is anyone really naked on the beach? They're all like you said, covered in naked clothing! When far away they seem proud as wax figures, if you want to get closer to get a clear look, they jump up and call me an idiot like you, hooligan, psycho...*

You don't think you are?

Fine, let's not bicker. To be honest I really wasn't interested in them at first – those beachside stunts, those swaggering yet empty models, attractive yet dead so-called physical beauties, those beautiful ghosts! What do you think pure nudity is, brother? The area of covered skin is limited, cannot be reduced in the slightest, no fluttering or shaking allowed, so apart from nudity there is nothing to see, apart from seeming naked they don't seem like women!

This little guy really shocked me: Ding Yi might have some serious talent.

But have you ever seen a solitary woman? he asked. *A woman showering, for instance, that's quite different! She's so free, outstretched, relaxed, both weak and powerful, both graceful and solid. So weak you want to get close to her, so powerful you feel you can depend on her, so beautiful and true you want to join her... And they're so unguarded, no one else around, holding an incredible warmth in the incredible quiet, warm but private, as old as time, heavy, sad... Time is so heavy and sad, wouldn't you say? But they make it flourish, clever, bring it into their endless comfort and leisure. Their gaze, expression, every part of them and all their movements are all saying one thing... all saying...*

What?

That Ding looked down and thought a long time.

Let me say it for you, there's no one else here, there are no clothes or walls here.

Ding Yi practically jumped up. *Right, right, right, what you said! Wow, all right, brother!*

Come on! Who am I? An eternal spirit! Remember: I'm a journey, rocky, subconscious, all your secrets... Oh, forget it, no need for that. But you're still a hooligan!

What now?

Illegal. Illegal, you know what I mean?

Well, that Ding chuckled, *let's not talk about that.*

55. Not a Miracle

Let's revisit Ding Yi's illness. He was incredible! That optimistic and strong Ding Yi, that young playwright Ding Yi, and that Ding Yi followed by the media and flirting with beautiful actresses like a fish in water, he was really something else: he had recovered from his illness, suddenly fully recovered! Right, right, he was healed and all right. Those ugly symptoms and malicious diseases suddenly disappeared. Everything was fine! It was truly incredible.

Of course he went through a series of tests: X-ray, ultrasound, CT, NMR, blood, urine, lymph, saliva... Hey, why isn't that thing there? So they did it again: X-ray, ultrasound, CT, NMR, blood, urine, lymph, saliva... Gone, still gone. Strange. Frowning and grimacing, the doctors looked as pale as white paper.

One said: "What was the prior situation? It was certainly there!" A second said: "As sure as you're standing before me." A third said: "Then how is it gone? And if it is gone, it couldn't have gone so cleanly." A fourth said: "It can't be gone. Can't-be-gone!" A fifth said: "You're saying it can't be gone now or it couldn't have been gone before?" A sixth said: "Can't be gone now or before." A seventh said: "So we're all douchebags?"

Ding Yi interjected: "There's another possibility."

"What?" The frowning pale faces turned to him.

"It was there before, and now it's gone."

The doctors shook their heads, sighed doubtfully and stared at those bizarre pictures and screens.

Breaking the silence, one of the doctors thumped the table and laughed: "It makes no sense!"

That annoyed Ding Yi a little. "So are you saying you'd all feel better if I died?"

"Oh, no, no, no, it's not that. How can I put it? How about this: I, me personally, must acknowledge, medicine, to this point, is still a douchebag. And you, Ding Yi, are a miracle!"

"It sounds like you're still saying it'd be more normal for me to die."

"Yes, based on our grasp of the situation, that's correct."

"So that means all the lights and medicine everyone was fooling around with all day are to trick people?"

"You could also say comfort, the comfort cure. Making every possible effort."

"Basically, from the start, you knew that stuff would have no use?"

"Comfort is a use."

"Could it be that I basically didn't have that sickness?"

"According to our grasp of the situation, it couldn't have been anything else."

"So, according to our grasp of the situation, where should I be now?"

"This, uh... is hard to say. Can't say."
"Then do say it! Really I shouldn't be here, right?"
"You're a miracle."
"So are you!"

56. Miracle

Outside the entrance to the hospital Ding Yi bought four fried dough sticks, three biscuits, two bowls of soy milk, and bolting them down, thought: Miracle, what's a miracle? If I live it's a miracle, so can I still be a miracle? According to them the normal thing would for me to be dead now, to know nothing, to know nothing is normal, my arse!

He thought and thought then smiled. *Hey, brother, there's a bet you're guaranteed to win.*

What?

Go bet someone that they can't die, bet anything, you'll definitely win – he lives, you of course win; he dies, he's gone and can't collect.

OK, brother! I said. Ding Yi, you're almost a pro.

But he ate and ate and nearly choked, then thought of another question: *If there was no miracle, things were normal, then now I'd be gone. Now everything would be gone. Now each and every thing would be gone. But what is it like for everything to be gone?*

Good, good question! I encouraged him. Think about it, what would it be like? Do you remember what it was like when there was nothing? Do you remember there ever being nothing?

He didn't answer.

I helped him: *So what do you remember?*

I remember... a little bit. Everything was there. First the sound of clock chimes resonating. Then bright white window blinds, the dark lines of window lattices, the swimming spots made by the shadow of trees... Then four walls, a roof, a chandelier and that old clock... then near and far, as if stepping out from a dream, I saw Mother's silhouette...

Great! Ding Yi, now you must understand what it means for there to be nothing? No life, no death, no normal, no miracle. That's truly nothing! And there can also be no nothing, that's true nothingness!

But what's that like?

It has no likeness, it's nothing! How could nothing be like anything?

Then... then... Ding Yi said, *then before I was born?*

Before you were born? OK, I'll tell you. If there was nothing before you were born, then there couldn't have been 'before you were born' either! If there was a before you were born then before you were born could not be nothing, so it cannot be or be not. Do you still remember? Like water screaming over sand, wind blowing from the soul, between dream and reality, desire accumulates, the mind doesn't die... gently drifting, floating, wavering, gently spreading or fantasising...

Then nothingness changes dramatically, the mist becomes tangible, light gathers into an abstract point and suddenly elaborates... Then I came to you, and together we walked to this point...

Ding Yi wiped his mouth, took a breath and shook his head. *But this is all conjecture, legend, rumour, history or other people's memories, myths, jokes. It's all vague chatter.*

But! I'd like to ask you how much of yourself you think you have. How many opportunities have you had to be independent? Apart from your body hardware, what you know, how much of it came from legends, rumours? What you believe is real. How much is based on history or other's memories? Your future, how much is based on hope and conjecture? Ding Yi, you are basically the inheritor of a note in a movement, a paragraph, how could you forget?

That Ding ate and drank his fill, then happily went to relieve himself. It seems the sickness really was cured. His whole body felt fluid and relaxed... But his heart was still puzzled.

What are we really doing talking this much?

Listen, I said to him solemnly, *searching for Eve!*

57. That Phrase

Searching for Eve?

That Ding laughed for some reason, looked indifferent.

That glimpse of disdain, frivolity, made it impossible to regret indulging him; and I couldn't help but think of one of this place's most popular aphorisms: are you done yet, man? The subtext: can there be love on this earth? The second subtext: how do some people die? From being an idiot! The third subtext: whatever you want to do, man, do it, all this this and that – 'eat, drink, and be merry' – it's not worth wasting time over trivial things, idling the years away.

This made me suddenly alert, remember one of my long journey's precepts: the beginning of the debasement of human language.

Language? What kind of language? What language can debase the human world?

Really it's not 'Are you done yet, man', that kind of language. But it points to that language! You remember 'that word' – the obscure names for that concave/convex miracle in Ding Yi's realm's ancient novel: that bud, that flower? More than just vague, in my opinion they're so wise! And I also believe some of my pioneers must have come early to invent such an appropriate title and spread this profound language. 'That word' is a convenient way to tease? Of course not. Think about it: if it was just referring to an organ, a capability, a necessary means of reproducing, why not say 'that thing' instead of 'that word'? What does it say? Pioneers deliberately chose 'word' to describe it, to express it, to name it? So it once said something, and will say something, and what will it say in the end? Why would pioneers choose 'word' to convey high expectations for speech?

Ah, it's been such a long time, the journey so far, I don't remember clearly. But it goes without saying that it's beyond an organ, it's a kind of language! Those different flowers, those convex/concave gifts, be a statement, must contain some kind of unique expression, so not this word, not our common language, textual communication, but that word, that word beyond speech and writing, a possibility besides communication and exchange, words generally have trouble conveying what we intend. That's why at the start of the Daodejing 'the name that can be named' has its 'not the eternal name', 'the road that can be spoken' has its unspoken road. But, alas, since those pioneers, thousands of years of wise naming have been distorted, the profanity of people who claim to be smart but don't understand it (intellectuals?)! That unnameable name has shrunk, become indecent, obscene, molested, beyond recognition...

And that's the beginning of humanity's corruption, you understand, Ding Yi?

But that Ding had already looked away, had stopped listening patiently.

So he was still talking about Eve, like he'd never forgotten, but in fact the core of the covenant had already weakened. His so-called obsession was just for being surrounded by pretty girls and for Eve's potential body – elegant shape, bright white teeth, tender eyes... the wonderful, moving charm. This Ding was in his prime, his body fit and strong, how to prohibit that kind of temptation?

The spring breeze grew stronger. The force could not be resisted, constrained, even neglected. I still kept the covenant, praying secretly that Eve would come soon, and it would indulge without restraint, expand throughout the frozen land, open up strange territory. That wishful thinking Ding Yi, those gusts of life, would blow to every corner of the wilderness, wake up every life or form, dance wildly, toast and thus neglect the long-held wish, bury the unfallen, not strong soul.

Ever since spring grew strong, this feeling pressed on.

Ever since the romantic scene was set, this barbarian repeatedly attacked.

Ever since the day, this Ding's desire became reality: in a noisy corner of the world, in a moment of loneliness, the word 'remove', after thousands of revolutions, finally visited my travels in Ding Yi. Remove sounded like Ding Yi was about to unlock women's secrets. And the movement of removal is to take the blurry millennia and guess how the phantom would be cast into reality on the final day!

I was at a loss. I pulled on that Ding's sleeve. *Hey, brother, our words betray our heart?*

He pretended to be calm. *Hey, this... what's this?*

You still remember Eden's covenant?

He whispered: *Of, of course...*
You still remember the three warnings?
He became evasive: *But, but...*
Then I'll ask: *Are those women Eve? Where is Eve now?*
I felt that Ding's heart gallop.
It seemed he was burning up.
I saw there was fire in his eyes and knew there was something he was having trouble saying.
He looked at me sorrowfully.
I watched him intently.
To my surprise that Ding blurted out something clever. He suddenly found a defensive and aggressive excuse: *Then... then tell me. If not, how will we know who... who Eve is?*

Ah, I had long suspected this manoeuvre! But this really is an old quandary: those in hiding are afraid of meeting without knowing it. Without limits it's possible for many to pass with no sign of one another. It's not the other way around, but who can know which is the way home? If it's such a long journey, again and again, without limits, again and again, removing again, removing, removing... then is the unique language not abused? Abuse leads to mediocrity, mediocrity leads to failure, and fear of the long-awaited reunion is inevitably reduced to planning and strategising, or just an intoxicating configuration, an elegant assignment.

That Ding saw me struggling and turned to discuss: *Brother, maybe there's no harm in giving it a try?*

That Ding saw me vacillate and turned to encourage me: *Brother, this is life, this is life!*

That Ding saw me frustrated and turned to mock me: *Why not, why not, why not? If we die talking nonsense, does that make us martyrs?*

58. Remove

So remove came, gently, with a tremble, like this world finally would reveal its truth, an ancient secret brought to light... So remove came, without sound but ringing, heart beating like a drum, hopeful and fearful... So remove came, as if peacefully breaking out, silently crying, gently compelling, rudely complying and thereby dizzying, with the sound of screams through brains, with a soaring tide flooding the wilderness... As if drifting through the empty sky, like an imaginary illusion, like a waking dream, to the point that you don't even know if you're real or fake... Ever since that Ding's stupid question: *Really? All this, that concealment can be laid bare? That inconceivability can actually become reality...*

Ah, right, right – clothing falls away like water, soft and heavy, as the solid yet virtual humanoid falls away, as the bright and clean or snow white falls away, falls away, falls down and away... In the dim radiance of twilight the spirit hatches and I see: naked Ding Yi and a naked girl, together within four walls...

Nakedly facing, suddenly overwhelmed.

As if forgetting why.

Why then?

Just to be like this?

Is everything too simple?

Could it be that there is, that something... something went wrong?

Well, maybe everything was too fast, too hasty, not as grand as was expected?

I originally thought this period of openness should be long. I originally thought remove should be wavering, complicated, should be hesitant, as fearful as that fig leaf floating down, as hesitant, delayed, slow... That's the right way. That way I could hear if Eve was inside.

But Ding Yi's flower was already in high spirits, and forced me to look at that girl – see her wonderful rise and fall, see that smooth body, rolling skin, the contrast between the white and tan from her clothes blocking the sun... Slender and plump, flat to the point of being curved, the hidden places in the curves like dark, lonely valleys, spellbinding... Silent toes and hair tips, silent fold around the belly button, silence around that mature section, that cry and burial, and that fleece flourishing on that forbidden turf... I felt wonderful, I felt pleased, yet suddenly I heard a storm starting from nothing, like a huge wave sweeping the wilderness, roaring, banging and was caught off guard – ha, I haven't misspoken, that human form was actually a wild beast! That Ding suddenly pretended I wasn't there, just leaned towards the forbidden sign... It was as if as a matter of course he couldn't resist, as if it had been unavoidable for a long time – right, I haven't misspoken, that wild beast was young after all, not only revived, not only healthy, but unstoppable! Suddenly I felt the rudeness and outrageousness of life, felt the sharpness and sensitivity of Ding Yi's flower, thrilling, horrifying... I could only listen to him, accompany him. Though I still remembered distant Eve, but as you have to let your own cattle graze and be satisfied, honestly I liked it too... Just felt space had been condensed into one point, time compressed to nothing, wind rising and waves surging... But after some smooth talking I suddenly couldn't help flying out of Ding Yi. That Ding shrunk like an empty shell as I scattered away, scattered away freely, scattered away deep and far yet seemingly empty, scattered away ecstatic but also panicked, flew. Flew, flew, boundlessly to I didn't know where... When I looked back I just saw that Ding looking terrified, drowsy; turning my ear to the side he seemed to shout something breathlessly. It echoed and rang all around... Oh, was he calling me back? Yes, yes, he seemed to be calling me back. Just as I hesitated slightly, was stunned slightly, the boundless emptiness took an edge, took on a shape, took on the world's atmosphere... It seemed rain and clouds converged as I slowly landed. It seemed the wind subsided and the trees were still as I returned to Ding Yi.

The furious beast was already limp.

Dead silence all around, two pale bodies on the settee.

What else? The wind, as always, slanted the noise of the bustle. The sun, still functioning, separated day from night. Time, tick-tocking, tick-tocking, never stopped. What else? What else exactly? It seems there should still be something else! But what?

Could it be that only farewell remained?

To say goodbye?

Then hide in another? Dressed to the nines, exchange a smile when meeting, repay the debt?

I quietly asked him: *Now, Brother Ding, what are you thinking?*

That Ding was silent, like he was still caught up in emotions.

I quietly asked him: *How's the naked clothing? And Eve, where is she?*

That Ding didn't respond, still basking in memory.

Hey, I shouted, *I'm asking you!*

That Ding started awake. *Oh, oh, what are you saying?*

Eve! Is that woman Eve?

As high as the sky reaches, the Han river is far away.

That Ding sat up and looked at the woman next to him as if thousands of miles away.

OK, OK, he said drowsily. *I love, I just love her.*

Hey, that's not just for you to decide, I screamed at him. *I'm here too, and I'm telling you, I don't love her!*

That Ding sat still, eyes swimming, a puff of loss on his face.

I tossed and turned that night, disturbing Ding Yi. I kept making noises in his ear. *What about me? Me...* I kept grumbling inside him. *I don't love her, don't, don't, love her.*

59. Remove and Nude

I might be a bit like Tomáš from *The Unbearable Lightness of Being* by the Czech writer Milan Kundera. That guy has a soft spot for 'remove', has the dearest love for the word and its sound. The motion of removing, the attitude, its meaning and atmosphere. Tomáš's passion for it never abates, it never fails to move him. I'm a bit like him, or in this regard I'm like Milan Kundera. No one understands that Tomáš more than me.

Remove isn't simply nude – Tomáš and I agree on this.

What is nude? I think all of nude's charm is in remove, otherwise it would be easily confused with anatomy or physical examination – and these aspects have already been calmly and carefully investigated in medicine and education.

Calm.

Right, calm! Why do education and medicine require calm? Because they are only concerned with the human form, just the body, not the soul. Calm gets to the point. Because nothing of the soul has been removed, the soul is still wrapped and hidden in naked clothing (but this time it's not called dance or art, it's called education, called medicine). And a purely naked body does not convey one's spirit, so in order to avoid misunderstanding the soul, calm is used to resist its swell. Teachers or doctors must maintain calm, must not disturb the soul, otherwise it's hard to avoid committing a crime – you can imagine, if you have a desire to teach something, you don't want to cross the line into fetishism or desecration. Like with nude dancing, if you say they're stark naked you're not showing adequate calm, maybe even to the point of being inappropriate.

So what about during sex? During sex it's just the opposite. What's required is passion, heat, indulgence. Calm is powerless.

During sex one soul – via the flesh, or even transcending the flesh – meets another soul. So simple nudity or calm nudity are unrelated to love. So in medicine, education or in preparation for intercourse, multiplication and reproduction are primary. With 'room business', 'room movement', 'room sharing' and 'room skills', calm stifles the call of the soul – maintaining standards requires a method, just like preparation in a pharmacy or laboratory, or workmanship in a carpenter's repair shop, really quite calm.

By the way, I've always wondered how some people just see ED, the English abbreviation for 'erectile dysfunction'. Is it impotence? My conclusion after long, extensive travels is that sex comes in a variety of forms, but those that revere intercourse are not open-minded. But in people, described as convoluted mountains traversed by winding rivers, shadowed willows revealing brightened flowers, has sex long been a strange kind of casual language? But its strange casualness, wonder, is what makes it creative and romantic, like joining hands in a barren land and climbing the summit of a snowy plateau. That way, and only in that way, can the soul have that homecoming surprise. Only sex? Ahem, what's that called?

We said before: that's an animal! Of course things that multiply revere sexual intercourse, of course focusing on sex is a way of mastering stupidity, and if confused people cling to this mastery they will truly be impotent.

We're a bit off topic now, let's get back to remove and nude. So can there be pure nudity? Can there be nudity without removal? And there is removal solely for the sake of nudity – whether to teach, practise medicine, share a room, all convenient. But there is also nudity fundamentally for removal – this is not for convenience. On the contrary, this aims for complexity, don't be so simple, so quick. For example when I first felt joyful in Ding Yi, I always believed removal should be long, complicated, hesitant. It should be as horrible as the two fig leaves floating down, delayed, sluggish. But what is that for?

Yes, to tell!

To deeply question and to answer.

To recall or confirm.

For a distant inner path, for the reunion of old souls, for the foundation of a past or future glance.

So remove can be a kind of expression, nude is usually a convenient tool.

So remove is a lasting development, is the soul's unceasing memory. Nude, on the other hand, is memory's interruption, end, or complete lack – after convenient use, walls are walls, nudity is clothing.

So relaxed nudity is the most popular, complicated, hesitating, remove is hard, tiring – more often suffering or lonely.

Especially around the twentieth year of my time in Ding Yi, as spring was turning to summer, nudity was suddenly in full swing. Intentional nudity, unintentional nudity, intentional unintentional nudity, baring it, selling it, list price, bargain price... Or with much fanfare, the word spread, posted about or bundled into boxes, wholesale, mail order, sold on a faint, dark alley. So very quickly, nudity takes the shape of meaning, but in the glossy print or beautiful skin's swagger, struggle, exhausted charm, lack of luck, what can open the soul? What can fulfil the wish of Tomáš and myself?

Open? Open what? Simply nonsense – it's packaging, it's planning, it's operating, it's humanity's liberation, it's the spirit of the age! What opening – where are you actually from, an isolated village or another planet?

Right, Ding Yi, did you forget? Pure nudity we already said: a small piece of the skin's packaging unable to be expanded at all... Does it make sense now? Heavy nude clothing buried the heart. Opening already covered by dazzling nude devices, its suspension even destroyed.

Luckily, remove is still around (Ding Yi has apparently forgotten).

Luckily, remove and nude have always had different interests.

So remove still has glamour. Remove, if not stopped prior to nudity, what is removed is not simply clothing or walls, but endless hiding, countless people's obstruction, the isolation beyond Eden, the centre of this world and the heart's defences.

As a result love can sprout eternally.

As a result remove spreads, lovers are moved.

As a result remove, this trembling sound, this sincere action, this endless hoping and seeking, makes the hearts of me and that Tomáš tend towards the holy.

That lover's secret language and mottos, it's the soul's expectation to return to the path, the happy call to gather and reunite!

60. Dazzling Spring Light

But don't expect miracles. Ding Yi was normal, never miraculous. I said it a long time ago: the human tool is often more attractive than that covenant, flowers in full bloom can make one disregard the soul. Dazzling spring light, the power of its rushing waves is like a prophet once said: Unless Vulcan saves you, like a dancer, you will jump there with the beat. Nothing was what I expected. That Ding Yi taught himself amid flowers and under dresses, all that bedroom stuff was instinctive. Moreover, his severe illness had passed, the spring light was just right, that irresistible natural beauty. What did he need me for, what did he need Eve for, what did he care about Eden's covenant? So there was a time when this Ding Yi was an unstoppable force, frequently astonishing.

Lucky in love, it seemed this guy's time had come.

Except I'd always wondered why this Ding was attractive. Why, whether innocent, forward, polite or irritable, would there always be cute girls who like him? Just because he was fond of them since birth?

But this place has an ancient saying – results don't lie – and that Ding sure had talent. Early when the spring wind first began to blow he secretly looked at porn, and as the wind grew, after he saw a video, he often complained to me in private: Man, these directors, what's so great about them? Their imagination is like a cube, no matter how you turn it, it's the same height... And dirty, so dirty and unoriginal from beginning to end! And this sexual knowledge, gosh, can that be taught? The scariest is 'room skills', controlling orgasm. Beasts just go with the seasons, how can these people delay it, do it on a tight schedule?

So tell me, how should it be?

Come on, man, art! What are you talking about? Pranksters are better than them.

Pranksters? Tell me, what kind of pranks?

Pranks? That Ding laughed. *Think for yourself!*

Can't.

Shit, I don't believe you can't. If you can't think of something, you're really thick.

Then I laughed.

Then he laughed.

And I knew what he was thinking, and he knew what I was thinking. But we didn't say anything. Because as soon as we did, it would be 'that word' and 'that word' was not appropriate to say openly.

Good news raises the spirits. Ding Yi was now like shining sun and bright moon, pouring rain and gusting wind. His boundless spring flew to every corner, his every second filled with sexual messages. But the two of us didn't speak of it, walking among people calm as usual, trying to look innocent and ignorant. Only when no one else was around, whether sitting in the woods or walking through wild fields, the two of us were relieved, could freely follow the inclinations of our childhood to watch the distant mountain and winged dawn. The difference was the blinding spring light. From whatever angle you looked, I noticed, our private thoughts were always farther than that distant mountain, more gorgeous than that winged dawn. As a sage said: "Infinite and unmeasurable things move and distract us."

We often fell into that kind of imagining, hot blood pumping, trembling with fascination, but we didn't speak. We spent a long time enjoying that imagining, soul floating, dreams flying, but knew it could not be spoken. We kept imagining into the night, developed it into dreams. A branch of red apricots extended out over the wall of a spring garden that could not be closed. But we were silent after we woke up. Lessons from the past were too deep, experience from the past warned us: other people, other people, other people and other people! Ah, inscrutable other people, you still haven't had enough? We feared they could again join in unison to sing that long, scary hooligan song.

But in early summer, the advent of the season, that Ding's desire galloped, talent unresistable. Next, inevitably, I followed him to a beautifully colourful experience. Though I don't dare call it supreme happiness, it was at least lucky in love.

I was guilty of being timid, still fearing – would this triumphant advance take us further from Eden's covenant? So I drew on my extensive memories and experiences to remind Ding Yi: remove and nude are not the same, but remove and remove are also different. Remove, this word, this sound, this action that sex cannot do without, actually has many meanings. Many meanings, Ding Yi: could be admiration and could be humiliation. Could be holy and noble and could be wretched and obscene. Could be love's comfort, and could be evil's execution. Maybe it's free will, and maybe it's power and possession. Maybe it's adventure, intent, involvement, and maybe it's reward, pleasantness, but after momentary joy... In sum, this remove word could meet nude sincerely, and could be nude clothing. Why are you so confident, unalert?

But that Ding was hard-headed, sceptical and suspicious of me: *What? What is all this you're saying? In my opinion, it's just seeking truth, can't be as complicated as you think!*

Truth? But? Just?

What? I'm saying they are no longer phantoms, no longer horrifying, can't kill you with one touch then float off with a screech...

They don't call you a hooligan any more, right?

Right, why?

Nothing, I'm saying this probably feels great, but...

But what? They don't run or hide, you don't think this is amazing? Look at them, they have texture, weight, temperature, they have light yet firm breath, they have real fragrance or musk... Just like those erratic dreams suddenly gathered, real and tangible, right next you...

Real?

Real!

Tangible?

No doubt!

Right, right, the grace of Lin Lang's beautiful shape, its plumpness, its vibrancy. Needless to say that Ding was moved, and even I trembled with agitation, lost myself, had trouble resisting... So with sincerity, I acquiesced to Ding Yi's excuses, Eve's possible host!

61. Shi Tiesheng Interjects

This is that feeling you guys care so much about? That Shi, on the sidelines, finally caught up.

Then what, I asked him, do you care a lot about?

Well spirit, for one, is much more noble than your feeling, and much greater too!

Tell me, what does spirit signify? And where does it originate from? And where does it end up?

No response.

While feeling, in my view, is man's most beautiful starting point. Can you think of a better starting point?

But look what following feeling has done for your Ding Yi now!

What he's gotten into that has you this worked up?

He fundamentally doesn't understand love.

I hope you mean he doesn't understand love yet. It's quite possible he is closer to love than that spirit of yours is.

Sheesh. Anyway I've met people like Ding Yi, they're destined to stay hooked on lust, and fail to aim higher.

No interest, no value, people look down on them, and finally they're abandoned by their generation, eliminated from society, that good enough?

Anyway this Ding Yi of yours disappoints me. I thought that your so-called beautiful starting point would lead to a beautiful result!

This actually made my heart thump a moment. Careful, careful, now I didn't even know where this Ding would finally end up. Based on my countless life experiences I'd say love really is a difficult road. I could only secretly pray for Ding Yi.

62. Confusion

Ah, that Shi really loves thought and contemplation, but unfortunately he's wrong. Let's get back to Ding Yi.

But what about him? His countless encounters, frequent adventures? His invincibility, triumph? However... but... actually... how can it be said? The frequent adventures ended where they began, the frequent encounters were quite routine, not much to talk about. Maybe some 'raw footage' will say it all.

Now distant from Ding Yi, looking back on those frequent encounters, I'm already confused, already all muddled. It's like days, one follows another and another. If there's no sign of wind, frost, rain or snow, no reminder of birth, ageing, illness or death, a thousand years later would you know how much time had passed? Remove is like this, skin comes into contact again and again, shoulders rub again and again, bottom-up excitement and top-down exhaustion... If there are no unusual feelings, no enchanting sensations, remove can also lose its charm or transform into nude. A thousand people in the same style, casually encountered like on an assembly line, remove has actually stopped already, is already gone – with the exact same naked clothing, how is it possible to remember who is who?

Not to mention this young Ding Yi still wasn't thinking deeply. Just as spring slowly turns to summer when the flower leaves are thin, green and weak, his imaginative powers were still budding. When it came to sex that Ding was self-taught. Once saw him thinking up strategies. He was not nearly as clever as those directors he scoffed. He managed to make those film clichés slightly three-dimensional, but they were still only space wrapped in skin that could not be expanded. First, relying on his style with no substance, he had some courage, but his heart slowly tired, his fierceness dwindled and his energy was gradually spent.

Damn, what happened?
Bull, do you always have to do things this way?
How?
There's a mirror there, see for yourself!

In the mirror there were two naked human figures entangled, limp, somehow a little strange and funny. It was like push-ups or sit-ups and even brought to mind an acrobatic rehearsal...

At some point this feeling came quietly to Ding Yi, then lingered.

I didn't want to pay him any attention. Especially considering I didn't know where Eve was, I really didn't want to deal with him.

But I still advised him.

Hey hey, I once heard someone say the unfamiliar is sexy. Don't see any of that here, mechanical like a hole puncher, is that all you do? That word! That word, do you remember?

Shit, you instigator.

Fine, fine, you go ahead. Hole puncher, I mean, is this your job?

That Ding refused to be cowed. But again and again, during the running in of the concave and convex, only Ding Yi's flower was high-spirited and the howl of a herd of wild beasts was heard, with no longing for news of that special day.

By midsummer Ding was growing fatigued, inspiration already dried up.

I glared at him as if to say: What next?

He looked at me, short of breath: Yeah, what next?

I rolled my eyes then looked around, as if to say: What else is there?

He looked suspicious, glanced left and right: Yeah, what else is there?

But there was nothing around except the ticking of the old clock; on the settee, two pale human figures silent as could be.

Actually naked clothing was confirmed once again, that flesh is a boundary and our confinement was confirmed.

Actually I was again told: any kind of extreme discourse, once abused, is confused with gossip.

Actually I again realised: Ding Yi and I have different interests! He's obsessed with beautiful vessels, I long to encounter Eve's soul.

My weariness, even disgust, made that Ding more lonely and helpless. That guy running this way and that on his last legs, searching helplessly, gradually lost the tremble he felt with remove, lost the surprise, the sensitivity. Remove, done without hesitation, logically – the world just so, today like yesterday, forbidden to walk the familiar path – how could that call even seem more and more like drums deep in the night, or just an opening bell? Remove, once the operation is perfect, straight to the point – kisses are like pretences, like a warm-up or an appetiser before the main course – how can you reach the summit with only a partial struggle? Remove, remove, remove... everywhere with Ding Yi, it seems to have nothing to do with me. I was just bored in a corner of him, going along with the ups and downs, like listening to rain on a window, or watching fire on a distant shore. When the turbulence got bad I would recall the time my soul flew off, longing for that interesting trip... However, however, that bird had already grown tired from flying, grown dull, was flying mechanically, numbly... That empty vastness, ethereal and turbulent – I longed for it more, come quick, but the clouds converged, silence reigned...

Ding Yi still thought this was an occasional thing, temporary, maybe even my fault.

You were always there talking and talking, saying what?

All right, all right, I won't talk. Go ahead.

Go ahead my arse! That Ding angrily sat up and hit me with irony. The general idea was: You think you're a fucking saint? You fucking know love? Eve, Eve, always Eve! Go talk pretty with someone else, you think I don't know you? When the bitch wants to put up a statue, I'm telling you, I'm not that big of a hypocrite. All this you and me, spirit and flesh, I'm done with it. This fake Daoism is past being old, if it even made sense back in the day! I'm tired of this hypocrisy, I want reality, reality, reality,

reality! What? I'm a little fucking tired now, look how pleased you are...

Fine, fine, fine, you go ahead. To myself I said: You go ahead and see what tricks your little girl's going to play!

63. Other Places

After all, that Ding was young, could take a breath and look to other places.

The unfamiliar is sexy, is something he actually strongly agreed with. So, I kept on travelling with that Ding Yi into oases... You wouldn't call it playing the field, but there were many nights he didn't sleep in his own bed; not always with the most amazing women but certainly new ones.

But what else – other places, other places and other places' other places? His hard work was like a tireless survey team. His futility a bit like a certain Apollo mission – how was the moon's surface? But does it count as another place's other place's other place? But when you fly and see it, all round, is still boundless! Ah, another place but this area of another place, this area but another place's other place. Though there were often new partners, it was still the same traditional or skilled movements. "OK, remove." Or: "All right, come." And: "Hey, hey, good?" Even: "Faster, faster! Cut the crap?"... Mandarin, you understand I understand pretty quickly. Happy awhile, then think, naked, it was still like push-ups.

That Ding wasn't convinced, was bitter towards me: *Leave it, that's just your opinion, your feeling!*

OK, OK, it's still that phrase: You go ahead!

Maybe it's like the last light of sunset making the sky look brighter, that Ding going all out, that Ding motivating himself, like a labour of love, seeming to enjoy it, continuing to indulge in his beautiful vessels, indulging in heavenly flowers, indulging in the joy of the concave/convex union... Now I think, if not for my hesitation, who knows how much thirsty earth Ding Yi's flower would have sown (or desiccated).

Right, right, tiredness is certainly my mood. For example, dreams are my domain. During Ding Yi's abnormally exuberant days, I dreamed of Eve. While Ding Yi wandered through all deserted or fertile land, I was always thinking of Eve, imagining her journey, her anticipation, her anxiety, her arriving... In short, since separating from her at Eden, I never stopped thinking of Eve, thinking of the still wandering dream of her.

Surprisingly, this thinking almost ruined Ding Yi.

I've already said Ding Yi's lust would interfere with my dreams. So naturally my dreams could also influence his emotions. When? A sunny day, water wide and long, that Ding suddenly felt unhappy...

I remember that pleasant summer weather, and nothing unhappy happened, but on that very day, Ding Yi was moseying along as usual, his spirits high as ever, when suddenly, a question rose from his depths:

Who is she? This Ding immediately slowed down, then felt defeated, his gaze spread over that beautiful human form in front of or under him, like research, like inquiry, like deep in a maze... and that beautiful human form turned cold, dazzling white and empty.

From the emptiness a response reverberated – that girl asked in horror: "What's wrong?"

This is one I can remember out of thousands, or one of the fruits that survived the storm.

Because of my dreams, my interference?

But maybe the cause is much more profound.

In sum, that time, Ding Yi suddenly felt removed. Like he and I floated into the void, suspended above the two entangled figures, watching with me.

Then he couldn't help but ask: "Hey, who are you?"

Couldn't help but ask: "I, where am I?"

Couldn't help but think: All this, for what reason?

Then that woman livened up and suddenly smiled. "Who am I, is it important?"

She slowly dressed. "I'm just one of them."

"Them?"

"Yeah? Do you want to ask all of them who they are?"

Why did "they" seem to sound so loud to Ding Yi?

"So don't ask me," the woman said. "It's not important to you."

They, we and you, Brother Ding Yi, this is what your friends said!

"So I won't ask you either," that woman continued. "Neither of us will ask the other, OK?"

"But we're friends," Ding Yi said.

"Friends?"

Shh – don't be an idiot, Brother Ding. She's saying that you're not important to her either.

That woman glanced at me and smirked like she'd read my mind.

I thought OK, OK, OK, then why not just make things clear or this travel in Ding Yi will end here!

But unexpectedly – at first I thought this kind of 'progressive' woman would long have her unrestraint – who would have guessed that, after her smirk, she would turn and start to cry.

"What's wrong?" Ding Yi asked.

"Ha, friend!"

"Can't we be?"

"Right. But it's like 'people', when you can be everything, when you can be nothing."

"What are you trying to say?"

"For example, friends can't be sold, right? But when they have to be sold, you just say they're not enough of a friend and it's fine."

That Ding was shocked, broke out into a cold sweat – I knew what he was thinking.

"The real is only now!" that woman said.

"Don't ask about the past, and don't ask about the future," she added.

"Really, there is no past or future, only now," she said.

Ding Yi then sat, seeming not to hear, to be ignoring her.

I wished I could rush out of Ding Yi and speak directly with this woman.

But her face was already covered in tears.

She was speaking as she dressed. "I'm just your present joy."

She combed her hair. "We are just the other's momentary condition of joy."

She wiped away her tears, smearing her beautiful face. "Remember, we have no shared history."

She slowly got dressed. "Don't be like that, OK? Don't ask. Don't be one of those who talk to me about love."

She looked at herself in the mirror from different angles. "No, I'm here. When I'm not here this woman will be gone."

She looked at Ding Yi in the mirror. "A famous person said there are two kinds of lives. One is tragic, the other is very tragic."

She turned around and smiled slightly. "A woman has made part of your life happy. Or because of a man, part of my life isn't 'very tragic'. That's it."

But she suddenly broke into tears. In that crying I heard a hidden, frightful history.

A moment of great peace. The wind, as before, set the busy marketplace in motion. The sun continued its eternal journey, dividing day and night. Time ticked on incessantly.

Then she furiously turned and left.

The door opened, a blinding light broke the gloom.

She walked into the crowd of people – dressed to the nines, hidden in others.

Ding Yi! Hurry, catch her! Might she be Eve?

That Ding didn't move. He looked blankly at me.

At least, at least she... she might know where Eve is!

Why?

Didn't you hear her? 'Don't be one of those who talk to me about love!'

So what?

I thought: I've already been in Ding Yi more than twenty years. Is Eve getting worried waiting for me? I thought: Because I have been misbehaving like this in Ding Yi, Eve has already been heartbroken, hasn't she? I thought if one day Eve came, what would she say? Would it be: Don't talk about love with me again!

64. Where Am I?

Then, you, Shi Tiesheng interjected again, where in the world are you?

You want to ask where the soul is, right?

For example, what part of Ding Yi were you actually in? The brain? You said no, you said you and Ding Yi often struggled over the same brain. In *Notes on Principles* Doctor F did countless autopsies, puzzled by this very question.

Oh, I'll have to think about that, uh... how to put it?

Some people say the soul weighs twenty-one grams. People have done tests showing that the body weighs twenty-one grams less as soon as the soul leaves.

You might want to think about it this way: when I'm recalling something in the past, where am I? When I describe some kind of future, where am I? When I speculate about other people, understand other people, even can't help but imitate other people, where am I? When I imagine another possible life and my emotions surge, where am I? When I believe a delusion and confusion fill my gaze, where am I? Or put it this way: when I'm missing Eve, where am I? When I'm missing Eve but don't know where she is, where am I? When I'm searching for Eve and go astray, and ask another, and forget all I was interested in, where am I then? If I go see Eve, walk through mountains and rivers, walk down road after road, but I have no idea where I've walked, then where am I really? If I see a beautiful place in my dreams but it simply doesn't exist in reality, where am I then? If the reality before my eyes is woven from and constructed of countless secrets, then where am I? If some kind of real action started from a dream, then again where am I?

I'm just asking what part of Ding Yi you're in!

Or to put it simply: What part of Ding Yi am I? Which tissue, which organ, which function of that organ or tissue, right?

You could put it that way.

Listen, the news on the radio – have you heard it? There was a coup somewhere.

Don't get all mysterious with me.

This news is in what part of the radio?

I get it, I get it, you're saying all components, what all components are made of is what finally receives, what finally transmits this news.

No, not just all components, but all of history, all of the present, all of reality, all dreams and all secrets... Now tell me, where is the news?

Then how do you explain weighing twenty-one grams less after death?

Maybe it's because of implication.

What implication?

Like tides. Like dreams.

65. Title Interpretation

So 'My Travels in Ding Yi' could also be understood to be one of my implications, a kind of dream. Or put it this way: a dream I entered via Shi Tiesheng is tentatively called 'Ding Yi' or 'My Travels in Ding Yi'.

So taking this a step further, is 'Shi Tiesheng' another dream?

The problem is, who dreamed of whom? Did I see that Ding in this Shi or the other way around?

Neither. Really I dreamed of this Shi and dreamed of that Ding. To be more exact: these two dream worlds (and there may be more) intersect along a horizontal and vertical axis. Their intricate weaving made me – made the immortal soul.

So that Shi and this Ding don't necessarily have a successive relationship, rather it's more likely that my dreams colluded, immersed, overlapped.

Dreams are unrelated to time, everyone knows that. Dreams transcend time, which is why this endless journey provides infinite possibilities.

If time is the fourth dimension, could we suppose that dreams are the fifth dimension?

66. Border

In the following days Ding Yi was always tired and listless, or walking alone in the wilderness or sitting in the wind or simply inside. It made me a little nervous too: had that vicious flower not been eradicated, so that its scattered seeds germinated again? We hurried to the hospital to get checked once more. No, definitely not. Clean and clear. Then what had happened?

Oh, had this Ding seen the emptiness in everything and his radical thinking made him avoid the hustle and bustle? Extremes lead to their opposites – this kind of thing happens. But speaking honestly, if that was the case, I still had reservations.

Brother, what's this about?

Ding Yi shook his head helplessly.

Were you really moved by that [woman]?

Ding Yi shook his head again.

Then what else could it be?

Ding Yi hesitated.

Someone offended you, yeah?

Ding Yi said he was a mess and asked me not to bother him.

So I sat with him in the sunset, in the weeds, the mountains and trees reminiscent of childhood.

But it was not childhood. The old days were long gone. Ding Yi's mood now, or in the future – for example in the thoughts of the one who signed things 'Shi Tiesheng', you can see clues of this.

"The body is without restrictions. But the forbidden fruit is gone.
If the forbidden fruit is lost because of freedom – 'What can I offer you, my lover?'
The spring wind is strong, the spring wind is omnipresent, but flesh is a boundary!
You and I are two cages.
If the forbidden fruit was released by the flesh – 'What can I offer you, my lover?'"

– Shi Tiesheng, *Rock and Writing For Example*

Or, this was just the Ding Yi I understood in the one called Shi Tiesheng's dream.

In that helpless summer, Ding Yi went several days without a word, occasionally eating a meal like he was chewing wax.

He wandered madly, I just followed.

At any moment he would sit down, and I could only go along.

I urged him to take care of his body and especially be careful with that once rampant flower.

But he didn't respond, simply nodded to show he understood my reminder.

I had no alternative but to repeat his own words to inspire him – 'optimism' and 'strength' and 'we must succeed, we definitely will succeed', etc., etc.

Abruptly, he said: *The unfamiliar is sexy. What son of a bitch said that?*

Is there a problem?

Bullshit! I'm telling you, this is bullshit!

Bullshit is bullshit, I thought to myself; as long as he finally starts talking.

The unfamiliar is sexy, the sexy is unfamiliar, is there any end to it?

You're asking me if there's any end to it?

You mean if the end is still unfamiliar, what are we planning?

Right, right, right, what are you planning?

That's why I told you it's bullshit!

OK, OK, that's fine... but, but why?

Ding Yi was anxious as he tried to find an answer.

I feel like I talked about this with you a long time ago, you weren't paying attention: the soul doesn't have sex, the soul is only other, so how could the reunion of the heart and soul merely rely on sexiness? Furthermore, what people call the unfamiliar – does it merely refer to flesh? You yourself are fooling around while you say they're bullshitting. But... But... Man, it's a good omen! Thinking and thinking I suddenly felt a flash of insight: is this prodigal Ding Yi looking back and seeking refuge in the soul?

But Ding Yi was confused and could only find doubt.
Tell me, what can be more real than the sense of touch?
Than the sense of touch? More real?
I'm saying, is there still a way to have firmer proof of reality than the sense of touch? Something closer than closeness, more entered than entering – is there? To put it directly: is there a way to make that feeling of entering last longer than an instant?

Ah, Ding Yi once again made me see him anew. He was talking about that unique language! He was saying: Flowers fly and flowers fall, what is that language for? OK, OK, sure enough, this Ding had great talent, I wasn't wrong about him. He's saying: What's that language for? How does that language wither? How does that language endanger? That language, what was it once for? Today, in the future, in the end, what is it all for?

I was secretly pleased.

But that Ding was still sad: *One-size-fits-all, one-size-fits-all, tell me brother, is there anything fresh left? Remove, remove, remove! This, that, that, this, who hasn't yet? Other places are just other places' this place, this place is just another place's other place, I have to hand it to you, brother! You start somewhere, and you end up there too, but where are we really trying to go?*

"Flesh is a boundary, you and I are two cages.
Enraptured again and again, helpless again and again.
Again and again, that boundary is more obvious.
...
All vocabulary has gone pale. All movement has withered.
All entry has entered the absurd."

- **Shi Tiesheng, *Rock and Writing For Example***

The wild wind grew elusive again, unlike before, better than before.

Ding Yi's thoughts went back to the beginning: Dead, it's all dead, can't you tell? It's all remains, all phantoms... The space covered by skin cannot expand at all, can't flutter, waver...

I myself thought of Eve again: if that repeated opening is just naked clothing, how can I identify Eve? If that unique language is repeatedly confused with games and jokes, confused with drums to mark the beginning of night or bells the morning, what else can prove Eden's covenant? Or when that grand season comes, can I still say to her: This unique language waits for you after a thousand years?

67. Quotes and Guesses

"Why have sex? The answer seems simple – it's the best way to pass genes on to the next generation while maintaining its diversity. But this explanation has a fatal flaw: sexual reproduction is a short-term waste... Some generations later, cloned offspring will outnumber their sexually reproduced counterparts and eventually make them extinct. In the short-term battle for survival, sex represents a defeat. Of course in the long term that is not the case. Without two sexes coming together to mate and shuffle genes, a species accumulates harmful mutations and soon dies off... But this is not a satisfactory explanation for nearly ubiquitous sexuality. Natural selection doesn't care about what happens several generations later. Some biologists think the pattern of cell division that forms sperm and eggs evolved very early in the history of life and only later became the means of reproduction. This is a promising but incomplete answer. From a certain perspective this explanation only shifts the mystery to another issue: how did gender first evolve? This question will keep us guessing for at least another hundred years." – **Reference News, 22 December 2004, 'Ten Unsolved Mysteries of Life'**

Ha, Ding Yi! My eyes flashed. *Did you know the cell division pattern that forms sperm and eggs evolved early in the history of life and only later became the means of reproduction?*

That Ding looked at me in horror, still not understanding the news' great implications.

In other words, sex doesn't exist for the purpose of reproduction!

Then, then what's it for?

Why, you say why? Are you stupid? To search, to search for Eve!

"Then the Lord God said: 'It is not good that the man should be alone. I will create a helper to be his partner.' So out of the ground the Lord God formed every animal of the field and every bird of the air, and brought them to the man... but for the man there was not found a helper as his partner. So the Lord God caused a deep sleep to fall upon the man, and he slept. Then he took one of his ribs... And the rib that the Lord God had taken from the man he made into a woman and brought her to the man. Then the man said: 'This at last is bone of my bones and flesh of my flesh.'" – **Old Testament, Genesis**

God thought this was good, gave them a language, an expression, or a ritual – sex, the reason for the concave and convex flowers!

68. Nurturing Spring Rain

But language started when man began. That language's confusion, making expression petty, making the ceremony popular. Instruments limited to instruments, even the gift of language loses its charm. Bored, tired, people follow others or don't understand, making the once imminent flower weak.

Ding Yi's flower was so sensitive, strong, tireless! Now it seems exhausted and hangs pitifully.

I just waited quietly for it, watched it, looked forward to it.

All human tools, in my opinion, most want to submit to this flower's uncanny craftsmanship, carefully carved! It makes people confused, makes people excited, makes people perplexed. Comparing Ding Yi to a cage, I think this flower is the weak point; if Ding Yi were a tomb, I think this flower is where the ghosts would come and go; if Ding Yi were a purgatory, a danger zone, an island, then I think it would be the only place you could call for help from passing boats. Oh, maybe there's a narrow gate to heaven here? If not, then why is it so attractive? So powerful, so secret? So foggy, so dreamy?

How's that ancient song go? "The carriage came from heaven and took me to my hometown... The carriage came from heaven and took me to my hometown."

Sex or sexiness are just expressions of the human tool, are God's inspirations for souls to seek one another, but there's a problem – for example if you get caught up and lose yourself, they're Mephisto's traps.

Look at that flying, uncontainable soul, look at the helpless beauty of the tool – anxiously entangled, colliding, oblivious to the rules of the day, rolling and howling, ignoring life and death... All for what? Just for sexiness? Just for having sex and breeding? It can't be – God's inspiration and the devil's traps aren't so simple. If it were just 'sexual attraction' and 'self-replication' then why go through so much trouble, such heartache? Then, really, why is it? I think it must contain extraordinary creativity, God must have had high expectations of these concave and convex flowers!

But what were those high expectations exactly?

What discourse is that word?

Has that discourse already been forgotten? Already trapped in the tool, making the heart and soul inaccessible, resulting in the loss of God's equipment, devastated and dying?

In dreams or in the past, I became aware that, regarding the endlessly wandering soul, the difficulty lies not in the declared desire for returning home but in the darkness overcasting the road to home. Looking in the distance at dusk, where is my home? the pioneer sighs.

So Ding Yi and I looked again, looked around the sea of people, wistfully – looked through the thick walls, looked through the many clothes and the boundaries of flesh... looked through other people, looked for traces of Eve hiding in others, looked for the souls hiding in others!

But if you expect another soul, if it's expressed in clothes and flesh is a wall, this looking is just a peep.

But this time the peeping being undisciplined, Ding Yi's gaze focused on one.

But this time the peeping being refuge, Ding Yi joined me in Eden.

He seemed to see that solitary woman, same as always: she's that free, lithe, weak yet strong... Weak enough to make you want to approach, strong enough to feel reliable. She was unguarded, alone, with unimaginable warmth buried in the incomparable silence... The warmth was not public but long-held, as heavy as time, even sad... But that sadness was channelled in her vigour, liveliness, in her endless ease... Her eyes, her expression, every part of her and all her actions were all saying one thing –

There's no one else here?
Right, no one else.
There are no clothes or walls here?
Right, no clothes or walls.
The whole past can be told to her?
Sure, can tell it all to her.
Can you look at the vast future with her?
Of course, of course, we'll look together.
If flesh is not a boundary either, then the two of us aren't cages any more?
Ah, that's so great!
I told Ding Yi: *Who's that? That's Eve!*
Ding Yi looked around, teary-eyed: *Then she, where is she really?*

This really made me overjoyed! With this sincere question Ding Yi became enlightened; with this sincere question the covenant became apparent, the eternal soul expected to return...

69. Dream: Night Without Walls

Rain drifts into dream, arouses a dense, boundless cry: where is she? Where is she? Where? Where...

The rainy, misty city recklessly unfolds towards the mysterious day. The dense windows are like dust, flying in the air before being knocked down by rainwater, row by row, string by string, pile by pile, opening empty eyes. Empty and mysterious.

I walk the streets alone – or the rain just wanders in the wind, the wind just wanders in the rain. The only sound is a call from nearby, though it always seems to be elsewhere.

No one is on the streets.

No people, no cars, not even a single sign.

Where is this?

Even I seem not to exist – the rain becomes footsteps, the wind becomes soulsteps, only that call proves I'm here.

Or could there be Bergman's blank clock? Or Dali's deformed clock? Bergman, the famous Swedish director, in the film *Wild Strawberries* shows a clock on the street with no hands or numbers. Dali, the famous Spanish artist, paints distorted clocks in *The Persistence of Memory*. Also without. Just walls. Continuous walls. Continuous walls become streets, become alleys, become vast cities, become the inescapable cry outside the walls – perhaps time consists of this call?

Freedom is a maze; wilderness is also a prison; people are destined to become the dead – a wise man named Borges once said.

Walls, real and strong. Made of granite, marble, iron or concrete, they make a sound when struck. But there are no people. I hit the wall hard – or just the wind and rain hit, but no one responds. There is still that lingering cry, brushing the wall, brushing the eaves, brushing the path stones and steps, sometimes hissing, sometimes screaming.

I sit back against a wall – or is it just the wind stopping, the rain stopping? The rainwater accumulates in front of the building, spreads like a mirror, which is constantly smashed by rain, rippled, then suddenly flat as ever. It goes back and forth like this. In between the back and forth are light and shadow – ah, the moon!

The moon has come out.

The moon breaks through the clouds and fog, sometimes bright, sometimes faded.

In the air, the pure light floats. On the ground, the shadows of the leaves blur.

When the call in the distance goes quiet, noises rise up nearby. Behind this is emptiness. I almost fall back – what happened? The wall, what happened to the wall?

When I turn to look, I can't see any wall, just a group of unsupported human figures hanging and floating!

And the wall? Gone without a trace or never was?

But those people are not alarmed, living up and down, left and right, each doing as they please, all turning a blind eye as if the wall was still standing... The empty wall was traversed like a three-dimensional stage...

Some washed dishes.

Some drank tea.

Some read the newspaper.

Two played chess against each other.

A group of four sat around a table, maybe playing cards.

An old person sat alone in the gloom, a flickering screen occasionally lighting up his stiff face. But is he watching TV, or watching the girl behind the TV? Behind the TV the light cuts through the gloom...

In the light the girl is busy in front of the computer, sometimes contemplating, sometimes smiling, click-clacking on the keyboard. Above her, a teenager steps onto a stool to change a light bulb. Lacking care, the bulb slips from his hand and is about to hit the girl's head when it shatters in mid-air. The teenager looks on helplessly... In the direction of his gaze, a young couple are playing darts with their child, laughing and cheering. The dartboard is really too small, and the darts seem to be flying towards the man in front. In front, that is, behind the dartboard, the light suddenly goes dim again –

In the dim light, the man sits on a toilet, leisurely tapping his foot to a beat, presumably humming some song. Darts fall vertically by his feet, some steadily suspend in front of him... And a bright light shines on him from below –

When the light went bright, the wine vessels clinked, a group of young people shouted in some kind of celebration, or memorial... And behind them, a sliver of light –

In the candlelight a portrait covered in black lace could be seen, next to it sat an old lady, like a statue; as if there were no hustle and bustle nearby, or it simply couldn't disturb her recollections... Farther on, there were two dark, empty rooms, or a waiting bridal bed.

The moonlight showed big red 'double happiness' characters on the door, and faint strings of beads and balloons... And below the empty room was another string of fluttering balloons –

The fluttering balloons surround a sleeping baby. Is this child dreaming of rain, or where is the shallow sound of water coming from? Oh, it's underneath, a little farther, there –

There, water splashes in swirls, water mists spray. In a soft, green light a woman is bathing, carefree... (How can that elegant silhouette seem so familiar?) I looked at her obsessively, like Ding Yi did. Looked at the black hair sticking to her white shoulders, looked at the curtains of water spread over her towering chest. Looked at the bubbles gathering in the place where they fell, gathering, and finally moving along the bend as the stream washed them away... A thin stream dripped on her hindquarters, flowed over her legs, over her toes, spread out flat, cradling her turbulent body... Just as Ding Yi said: "She's that free, lengthy, vigorous..." Then the sound of the water stopped. She slowly rubbed her wet hair, rubbed all over, arms, the curve of her lower back, knees, gently jumping... (Why did it feel like I'd seen this jumping gesture before?) She walked naked out of the bathroom, walked through the hallway, walked through the sleeping flowers, walked through vigilant time, footsteps gentle, all her skin flowing like waves... Just as Ding Yi had hoped she had "that vulnerability, no one else around", all her movements were that calm, scarily sincere... She walked into the bedroom, walked up to the bed, sat peacefully alone, absentmindedly picked up a fan to drive away the hot summer night... But she suddenly jumped in front of the mirror, no, not to primp, to look at herself. (Why did she seem a bit like... like who?) She gently turned around, looked at herself... Just as Ding Yi expected, "incomparable calm was buried in that unbearable warmth..." She stretched her arms, stood on tiptoe, admired herself, admired Eve's host body. Ah! Is it her? Eve? Could she be Eve? Could it be that Eve was already stationed in her? But just at that moment, someone rang the doorbell –

In the dark corridor was a postman, shouting: "Telegram! Telegram!"

"Hey, coming!" Eve vanished from the mirror... "OK, got it!" Naked Eve reached left and right. Though she looked kind of ridiculous, she didn't try to hide it... "Sorry, please wait a second, wait a second, OK?" Embarrassed, Eve dressed in a panic, put clothes on haphazardly, fastened them... That scene was truly frustrating, sad – at that moment she became something other than Eve...

The postman leisurely hummed a song.

The doorbell rang again. The door opened with glaring white light.

But when that woman came out, Eve was already hiding in another person – dressed to the nines, smiling properly, solemnly cautious...

I jumped up and threw myself towards her – perhaps in an effort to stop time, delay time, bring this woman back to freedom, back to before, back to Eve. However, the open wall suddenly closed like a stage curtain...

Closed into a wall.

Outside the real, sturdy wall, only I remained.

Clouds flowed, suddenly surged.

The moon like a boat disappeared instantly.

The rainy, misty city remained, with its rainy, misty streets. Remaining also is the wind that carries the flying soul, and the rain that carries the walking me. Piercing cries roamed along the wall: *Where are you? Where are you? Where? Where?*

There! Ding Yi woke from his dream, sat up and shouted: *She, she's there!*

Where? I followed his gaze. *Who?*

Ding Yi looked blankly at the sky as if still in a dream.

Who? Ding Yi, who did you really see?

The... the woman in plain... plain white.

Oh, well, you know her well! I asked him again: *Where? Tell me where she is.*

The play... in the play!

Play?

Yes, the... play! She's there. That Ding stared straight at me as if to say: You should understand.

Are you talking about Snow White?

No, I'm saying the... play!

What play?

That Ding yawned and seemed to fall back asleep as if in a trance.

I quickly shook him, tried to support his heavy body: *Hurry, say it! Which play?*

Might not be... which, it's a... a play...

I zoned out a bit, and that Ding was snoring again. It seemed his dream was erotic, didn't want to let him go.

Alas, I was momentarily confused. It took me a while to realise this was good news, it really was good news! Dreams were originally my domain, it seemed this Ding really was a prodigal son who wanted to return to my command. OK, wow, then let him enjoy himself in his sleep and dreams.

Night's eyes see more vividly, night's ears hear more profoundly.

Only 'play' came oddly – nonsense? Or prophecy? Ah, don't worry, that will have to wait for later – later Ding Yi and I were destined to enter the play, comprehend its mystery, or hear the meaning of life from it.

70. The Continuation of Truth

However, Ding Yi's low spirits really did have a deeper meaning, since 'sell out' came suddenly and in a situation similar to the one that year! "Friends can't be sold out, but when they must be sold out, you'll just say they weren't enough of a friend." That woman's casual sentence touched Ding Yi's secret, poked his old wound.

Now we can discuss Ding Yi's 'scandal' from that year – that is to say, the thing that brought dark clouds to early spring that he has always kept secret and hasn't even dared to think much about. Everyone knows he later earned the name of hooligan but don't know about another hidden layer. Now that things have changed and Ding Yi has boasted repeated successes in the realm of love, recalling the old case will not cause much harm.

The sound of slogans filled the air following the meeting. I can't remember the exact time. In any case, it was after the winter when Ding Yi thought he'd seen through to the heart of the human world. Do you still remember, at that big gathering, quiet Ding Yi suddenly erupted, angrily saying to me: *It'd be better if he were on stage?* He was talking about his father. He would prefer his father being denounced on stage than standing offstage quietly selling food. Of course I know his preferred situation would be for his father not to be offstage selling food or onstage being denounced. Thinking that his father was even too humble to qualify to be onstage with a bucket on his head made Ding Yi incredibly sorrowful. A worthless cook who no one knows. Apart from seeing you when they go eat, who finds you any other time, who would have any other expectations of you? So, they won't have any accusations or demands of you either and won't expect you to have any views or opinions. Thinking that far, the incredible sorrow had become a serious wound. I know he was still jealous of those friends with professional, authoritative or famous parents, and was jealous of those 'red silks' and 'red satins'. He was jealous from the start and still jealous now. Why? Because now they still had reason to be prouder than a cook's son, that is to say – if I don't say it will still be thought or judged in this manner – "You workers, you workers are really pretty good..." Ahh, "They", "we", "you"! Ding Yi knew hostility, knew scorn and disregard, knew deep-rooted, knew sticking to his guns.

The thing happened not long afterwards, a winter Sunday.

It snowed hard all night and cleared up at dawn. At sunrise that Sunday I went out with Ding Yi, walked aimlessly on the clean snow.

The weather was great, the blue sky stretched far, open, so blue it almost seemed fake. The snow sparkled in the sun's glare, creaked underfoot. One's mood was also penetrated, made as clean as the air after the snow, and stimulation made it feel like there was something to look forward to. The wind was still chilly, but it was undeniably spring as pigeons circled leisurely, sprinkling the whole sky with clear, bright whistles. Ding Yi didn't stop, and I continued to walk farther with him.

Without realising it, we already reached the outskirts. When walking past the city wall, I remember seeing some people flying a kite; it trembled, lonely and aloft. Approaching the moat, I saw some people skating. My eyes were drawn to the flashes of the girls' flowery headscarves. We walked down the bridge, up to the river bank, in open fields and saw a group of children playing in the snow. Their laughter, spread by the wind, was crisp and sweet. An overgrown, winding path led Ding Yi to a deserted park.

The park was full of ancient, frosty trees; abandoned halls, carvings like ice sculptures. There was no one around, and that Ding shouted. The sound echoed... There was no one else, and we seemed to have dream-walked into another world. But what about long-awaited Eden? Or a new paradise? But I was definitely still in Ding Yi. I was in Ding Yi, there was no doubt about that – the sun cast a human shadow on the snow, it rocked up and down with us, reminding us not to get carried away. But it was definitely a good place, a wall of pines, a winding path. I walked slowly with Ding Yi, sometimes sang low-pitched, leaned against a wall, against a railing... Throughout the morning we enjoyed our freedom apart from others.

Ding Yi even said to me: *We could even get naked here, you think?*

I said to myself: This kid seems to be a real exhibitionist.

Forget it, you! I pointed at a faraway window and said: *Do you know who's looking right at us?*

Let them look, Ding Yi said. *Either way we won't recognise each other.*

Do you dare?

Do you?

If you do, I do. Psh, I'm not afraid!

That Ding looked around like a rat. *You're saying there are definitely people in those windows?*

If you dare then there aren't, if you don't dare then there are.

Then we both laughed, neither of us dared. Maybe it was fated, maybe it was a curious coincidence that, right when Ding Yi got tired and hungry and we thought about going home, that Ding found a set of footprints in the flat snow. The footprints seemed hesitant and aimless, winding, advancing and retreating before finally disappearing into a dense forest. The trouble started there. The trouble started with this Ding's feelings. He said that the footprints looked familiar.

You recognise them?
Yeah, I've definitely seen them.
Whose? I laughed sarcastically. *Tell me, whose?*

That Ding stooped over and said something surprising: *Girl, guarantee they belong to a girl.*

Ahh, that brave feeling, you can't blame this guy for bordering insanity. I had to follow him and those footsteps into the woods.

This is called fate, this is called a curious coincidence. Right there, that day, deep in that forest a red headscarf suddenly turned towards us.

"Hey, what are you doing here?"

"Ha, I knew it was you."

I already said, on the day of that gathering, when the truth of human affairs was revealed, when the painter Z felt the surging sensation of future conquest, Ding Yi was only dejected, or aggrieved. As a result he looked at those girls more anxiously. The feeling he had at that point, looking around, I understood: why, why is it like this? Could it be that we cannot be as intimate as before? I'd long had a presentiment: the identity of the girl inspiring Ding Yi was not clear, but she already existed, perhaps among his few good childhood friends.

Sure enough, when the red headscarf turned towards us, the person I saw was one of them: Yi. He Yi.

"What are you doing here?" Yi asked.

"I came to look for you."

"No way, no one knows I'm here."

Ding Yi just smiled. Ding Yi was overjoyed.

"How did you find this place?"

"I recognised your footprints."

"Really?" She looked at him with surprise.

"Why did you run off to this place alone?"

"See for yourself!"

To a drawing board was clipped a canvas, on which there was a hazy sketch of an old cypress tree.

"A tree?"

"I like trees."

"Why not draw people?"

"I don't like people."

"Don't like people?"

"You do?"

"What's wrong with people?"

"You're asking what's wrong with people?"

"OK, then you draw."

"Where are you going?"

"Nowhere. I'll watch you draw."

"I mean you should go."

"Go where?"

"Do I care? Go wherever you want."

"Can't I just stay and watch? I promise I'll be quiet."

"Don't make a sound."

"I promise."

"And what if you do?"

"If I do, you don't have to say anything, I'll scram."

Yi giggled.

Through the sky the pigeons passed, their whistles passed, the clouds passed. The faint shadow of clouds crossed the woods, crossed the drawing paper, crossed the old cypress tree on the drawing paper. Ding Yi would remember the peacefulness of that moment for the rest of his life, remember the tranquillity of the shifting light, remember the shifting light's hidden fragrance. I sensed Ding Yi's feelings, smelled the warm fragrance floating through the woods, coiling, and soon found her source...

"If you drew people, you would definitely be good at them too."

"I won't!"

"Our art teacher said people are the most beautiful and best at representing a particular time..."

"Hell with that, people are hypocritical."

The day of the assembly suddenly flashed in Ding Yi's mind, the truth of humanity.

Noticing he had stopped speaking, she stopped drawing, looked at him.

"People say one thing and think something else, don't you agree?" Yi asked.

Ding Yi nodded mechanically, still quiet.

Yi said: "Today, my dad's students or disciples, they cluster around 'Mistering' you all the time, but once you're in trouble, they denounce you more fiercely than anyone else in order to distance themselves."

Do they stand offstage selling food?

Shh, Ding Yi! Yi doesn't mean any harm.

"That's human nature!" Yi said.

"I don't see anything good about people," Yi said.

"Tell me, what's good about people?" Yi asked.

"But look at these trees," Yi said. "So real, so magnanimous. They tell you all their difficulties, memories and desires directly, don't hide behind empty words."

"My dad said this is true language," Yi said.

"Drawing it is listening to it speak." Yi looked at Ding Yi again.

"Can you hear what they're saying?" Yi asked.

"They're having a discussion. In their dreams they pray for peace. In their winter dreams they silently pray for spring, mulling over the green of mountains and plains... Hey, what's wrong?"

Ding Yi bent forward, hands on knees, eyes fixed on the drawing, and noise filled his ears – maybe the sound of pigeons whistling in the sky was too loud?

"Hey, you goof."

The old cypress in the drawing grew blurry.

"Hey, did you hear me?"

Ding Yi didn't move, his eyes were still, he was afraid that, if he moved, tears would pour down.

Yi put down her pencil, pushed him: "What's wrong with you, are you OK?"

Ding Yi finally snapped out of it, forced a smile, but he couldn't shake off his mood.

"What are you thinking?"

"Nothing? Nothing."

"Bull, liar."

"Didn't you say people all say one thing and think another, so why ask?"

"I wasn't talking about you."

"You weren't talking about me, I'm talking about me."

Yi tilted her head, looked at him.

"I didn't qualify and say other people."

Yi turned and faced him.

"You're right, trees are better than people. Trees are just trees, only people differentiate between rich and poor."

"What are you trying to say?"

"What can I say?"

"Why are you thinking something and not saying it?"

"People say everything they think?"

Yi put the pencil in her box without taking her eyes from her friend.

Ding Yi walked around an old cypress, looked at the sky, looked in the distance, glanced occasionally at Yi.

Yi looked at him the whole time, waiting for him to speak.

"Does the peace you pray for include us?" Ding Yi finally uttered this sentence, and as soon as it was out, even he was terrified.

"We?" Yi asked him. "Who's 'we'?"

"Do you think that people who are humble or average also deserve a prayer for peace?"

"'You'? I don't know what you mean."

"You don't know what 'average' means or you don't know what it feels like to be looked down on?"

"What are you talking about?"

"Then I'll tell you. Average means receiving compassion, comfort, consolation, praise, before being discovered."

It looked like Yi understood. The proof of her understanding was the sudden change in her face, but she just bowed her head, didn't argue. I think she thought of what happened (on that sunburnt July), or she never forgot what happened that day (arms around each other's shoulders and eating ice lollies on the street, and Ding Yi suddenly going silent). Though it wasn't intense, it often came up in her mind ('you', 'we', 'they'). Seeing how Yi looked, I felt a little sorry.

Hey, Ding Yi, stop it!

But that Ding suddenly got ruthless: "Do you know what it's like to be ignored? You thought being deeply average, humble, always being looked down on, was better than being denounced onstage? You say you pray for peace, but I dare say no one can pray for... for us average people – despised, forgotten and then... comforted!"

Wow! Since when did this guy have such clear ideas, such a sharp tongue? Even I was shocked.

"I didn't think that, really, Ding Yi. None of us thought that..."

"But you said it! You said: 'You workers...'"

It looked like Yi had long been expecting this sentence. Her face turned pale. I would guess that Yi thought of that sentence more than once after that day, trying to figure out what it meant. It certainly had more than one meaning, but what were they? She couldn't figure it out, maybe she didn't dare. But now she asked Ding Yi to explain it.

"Really, I'm truly sorry, but I'm just not like that." Yi's pale face suddenly blushed.

Ah, so that's how pretty she is!

What, you just realised that?

"I don't really understand how, but I know we hurt you... but don't take it seriously, OK? Really, I'm really sorry..."

Ding Yi was dazed. Ding Yi had thought it was over; when a discussion reached this stage, the friendship was broken. If Yi hadn't said that, his next move would certainly have been to escape, escape on instinct, but at that moment his instincts deserted him. Ding Yi stood staring stupidly, his mind blank...

But that emptiness was like the forest snowscape, spread flat, spread clean, peaceful, some of the strong noon light shining through, and there was even sound, was it a pigeon? The sound seemed to come from far away, to evoke distant memories – distant where? And who? Eden? Or Eve?

The distress that followed made it impossible for me to remember what happened next. Suffice to say, when Ding Yi and the girl He Yi reconciled, when that "we", "you", and "they" were made right, at the edge of the woods, the hooligan song sounded. Or when Ding Yi finally found the source of that warm fragrance and sank into it, someone else entered the woods! I remember when Ding Yi finally looked up after his heart-thumping first kiss, he discovered space-time had played a tremendous joke on him: not only had the strong sun turned to sunset, the woods and snow had disappeared, the setting had changed to the dark cabin of a 'revolutionary committee'. There Ding Yi was – not on the surface but in the heart – labelled a 'sellout'.

71. Sellout

'Sellout' is a far worse label than 'hooligan', so for a long time Ding Yi was willing to accept the latter, while keeping the former secret and even trying to erase it from his own memory.

But it was no use. It turned out to be impossible.

As for Ding Yi's selling out, others can say what they think. Some said it was caused by violence, law-breaking, the times. Some said, under the same circumstances, there are traitors and heroes, so each must know their responsibilities. Some said the pursuit of survival and peace is human nature, so Ding Yi's weakness was understandable and forgivable. But regardless, this sellout behaviour could not be erased from Ding Yi's history. The fundamental reason it could not be erased was Ding Yi and I could never remember...

When the light in the dark cabin went on, several people filed in.

"Ha, quite young to pull a stunt like this!" Several strangers sat down one after another and began to mock Ding Yi before their bums hit the chairs. (Right, they definitely started from this perspective – a sexual perspective! That Shi was right: that scary child had already grown up and spread everywhere.)

Ding Yi was so ashamed he didn't dare to look up. I remembered our first encounter with the world. Then the shame was because child Ding Yi was naked. But why now? Because young Ding Yi's first kiss exposed our wishes.

"Talk, what else?" those people said, looking serious.

"Nothing, sir, really nothing."

A string of sniggers.

"Women, you know what they're like?"

Ding Yi looked at them, confused, even reflected innocently: what are women like?

"That reactionary professor's daughter didn't talk about anything else with you, did she?"

A long time later Ding Yi was able to understand that the 'revolutionary committee' members targeted Yi, targeted Yi's father.

"No? We're just saying... about her drawing."

"What did she say?"

"She said she likes trees, she likes to draw trees."

"And?"

"Nothing."

"No? You guys were in the little forest all day and that's all you said?"

"Really, sir, if you don't believe me, ask Yi."

"Of course we'll ask her. But now I'm asking you, to see if you're honest or not."

Ding Yi's awareness was beyond my comprehension. I urged him to be honest, but he refused: *No, no, saying some things could cause trouble.*

"There's really nothing else, we just talked about her drawing."

"Looks like you want to do it the hard way, huh?"

Ding Yi looked down, silent.

"Don't think your worker status will protect you. You don't think we know your father's status?"

At that point I felt Ding Yi's heart rate start to speed up.

"Strictly speaking, status lasts for generations. But not many, no more than a couple. What are you?"

At that point I felt Ding Yi trembling, shaking uncontrollably from the inside out.

"You're considered workers, this could very well be a mistake, we could certainly correct this mistake. Maybe your father is an alien class element who infiltrated our workers!"

It was 'you' and 'us' again. And Yi? Naturally 'they'.

"This has nothing to do with my dad, really, sir, it's not my dad's business!"

"What business? Talk! What's not your dad's business?"

Ding Yi was at a loss for words. At that point our brain started to get more confused.

"It seems like we'll have to call your dad in, right?"

"No, sir, don't! Let me think about it, let me think about it, OK?"

But that brain seemed to disobey any commands from me or Ding Yi. Such things have happened during my long journey: somehow you can't help yourself, become mindless, the brain neither obeys the heart nor listens to the soul, but magically takes orders from someone else. When lured, for example, when terrified, for example, when caught up in the crowd, all using one mind... Then the brain seems to be at a loss, like a dead leaf on water, flowing at the mercy of the waves.

"For example, Yi's father said something to her, right?"

It was a sophisticated group of interrogators, they got to the point. While our brain was a like a dead leaf, they were waiting.

"Her dad said... said trees don't say empty words, but people..."

"People what?"

"People all... say one thing, while... while thinking another."

"The mouth does one thing and the heart another?"

"She said her dad's students were all over him yesterday, but then her dad got... got into trouble, and she said they cursed him fiercer than anyone else."

"And?"

"Nothing."

"Do you know what this is? Not being content with circumstances!"
Surprisingly honest Ding Yi nodded.
"What else has your dad said?"
"Not my dad, her dad..."
"What else did her dad say?"
"He said, he said something about hell with... hell with the times."
...
Is this selling out?
Of course it's selling out!
Because of this, the interrogators increased the charges against Yi's father. Not long after, all of Yi's family was exiled. And because of the sellout, Ding Yi was exiled farther – this kind of exile was not limited to space or time but permanent in the soul; guilt, fear, confusion were parts of his life from then on.

During the 'revolutionary committee' days and nights, we were deeply disappointed in Ding Yi, this friend of Yi, deeply embarrassed by the word 'friend', had deep doubts about trusting people. But it may have been lucky in the end – simply because this disappointment, embarrassment and doubt was not due to others but due to our self, was not pointed at others but at Ding Yi. As a result there was not resentment like with Painter Z. If one day you discovered you were another person, you couldn't be trusted, you're inevitably a sellout, a traitor, what would you do? Doom and gloom, only doom and gloom. Pure despair, pure hopeless despair. Awake and asleep, Ding Yi and I were always asking each other: What's the point of living like this? How long can this go on? In that dark hut we cast ourselves aside and sincerely prayed for peace for Yi. Sentimental Ding Yi, on the brink of tears, thought of one thing – if I could still go out I'd hurry and find Yi and tell her: It can't be, it really can't be, Yi, please believe, this world cannot be without reliable friendships because of this...

But during spring of that year, when we came out of the 'revolutionary committee's' dark room, Yi was gone. Yi had already moved away from this city. Other people had moved into the Yi family home. We heard Yi and her parents had been exiled to the border. But where was the border? Or which border was it? There was no way to ask. Poor Ding Yi had been grounded by his father and was constantly lectured: "Don't interact with other people any more, be a good boy at home."

So for a long time we could only look out the window: trees near, mountains far, the winged dawn... and the border underneath the winged dawn, and Yi and Eve at the frontier...

72. Traitor

'Traitor' is the world's scariest label, scarier than 'hooligan' and even a thousand times scarier than the ugly, poisonous flowers that came later.

Cancer is still a natural disaster, while being a traitor is an unbearable, self-inflicted wound. Hooligan, meanwhile, just requires putting up with others' scorn, you don't have to hate yourself too; like if you're really a hooligan you can go back to being a prodigal son, but a traitor is exiled forever, with no shore to return to.

Where is the shore? Of course it can't be where the enemy is, of course it should be where your people are. But, but! Where do you have your people? The reason traitors are traitors is because they betrayed their own people; their own people have long seen them as enemies, and enemies cannot be your people. For this reason a traitor's exile is not a distance in space, is not a length of time, but being outside of people. Once someone becomes a traitor it's as if God had created a new species – they are not like people but some other type of animal that walks upright. Based on my observations Ding Yi's realm has three kinds of animals that walk upright: people, penguins and traitors. (Dogs and bears don't count: bears occasionally stand when angry, and dogs do it to tease.) There are indications that traitors are not human – though they have the body and soul of a human, they are not considered human. Though they eat human food, live in human dwellings, they are not some kind of pet. To put it simply, they are garbage! Hooligans and beggars form their own groups – has anyone heard of a traitor's association? Some people are concerned about chimps, giant pandas, Tibetan antelopes, Siberian tigers – has anyone asked how the traitors are doing?

Ever since Ding Yi sold out, I often felt afraid that my endless journey had entered a kind of purgatory. Inadvertently becoming a traitor is definitely worse than falling into a fish or a dog. How can we move forward? Where is the soul of a traitor, where did it defect to? Can a traitor still go see their Eve?

One afternoon shortly after that incident Ding Yi was bored, and we went to watch a film together in which a 'comrade' somehow gradually became a traitor. This 'comrade' had been through thick and thin, trials and tribulations with his comrades for many years, but a moment of neglect ruined his good name. That second this 'comrade' suddenly became emotional (damn, emotion!). God knows how he made that big, careless decision: go see his sweetheart, go see his Eve, go visit his fiancée once again. After he was assigned a dangerous mission, while walking home, walking towards that second – he suddenly felt that everything around looked so familiar. Did the air even carry an intimate feeling? He sniffed hard like a dog... ah, I got it: he was close to his fiancée's little place. The subconscious was bringing her before him! Only then, after receiving his orders, did he realise that he couldn't get her off his mind, which was a problem: would he ever see her again in this life? So this 'comrade' sat down on the side of the road, lit a cigarette, hesitating and hovering before that second. He pondered for a long time. Finally the word 'emotion' filled the wind and gently blew him to that cruel second: the moon was dim, stars thin, the night like a black curtain, silence all around. He thinks it won't be a problem, right? And this way could be goodbye forever... He walked towards his sweetheart's little place. As that song goes: "A young girl sent a soldier to fight, / they said goodbye in the dark night / but just before that step... through the faint mist / the youth saw in the girl's light / the light still shining..." Right, right, outside that kind of window this comrade's enemies were waiting.

What happened next, alas! I really felt this 'comrade' greatly lacked imagination – if you've been prepared to give your life thousands of times, how have you not prepared to withstand torture thousands of times? Leather whips, soldering irons, bamboo skewers, tiger benches... Who did you think you were? When you were alert, you preferred to die rather than give in. After not being allowed to sleep for eight days, do you know which way is up? You despise the enemy's torture, do you despise your loved ones' torture too? You have the right to choose to die, do you also have the right to choose for your loved ones?

When we left the cinema I realised Ding Yi's face had turned white as a ghost, his eyes had dimmed, and he wore a dazed expression – the cinema was dark, hot and stuffy, and overrun by the smell of sweat mixed with farts. We struggled to make our way to an ice cream parlour. After eating seven ice lollies, this Ding was panting: *God dammit!*

OK? I asked him. *What if it was you?*

That Ding was stunned. After a while he said humbly: *Shit, don't fucking turn on me!*

I mean, what if I did?

Ding Yi looked up and down and thought a little longer, then said honestly: *Probably under duress.*

Are you that weak?
The whip might work.
What about bamboo skewers and the soldering iron?
Enough.
Not being allowed to sleep for eight days?
Eight days? After three days I'd forget my own name.
What then?
Die! OK? Just let me die.
You're easy! That guy was probably just anxious to die!
Shit...
Or what if they tortured your family in front of you? For example...
Stop it with the 'for examples'! I'd crack regardless, OK?
OK? If it's OK, then why avoid being a traitor?
I know, I know. Shit, just stop talking, OK?

OK, then I'll stop talking. Better I won't think. Think nothing, just look at the people passing on the road. Look at their leisurely or hurried steps, the variety of trousers and shoes, the scraps of paper on the ground, the cigarette butts, the phlegm and dust, listen to the hawkers and singers shouting over each other: "The moon leaves / Oh, I'll leave / Oh, I'll see my big brother off / Oh... this way the mountains are high, the road is long / This way I won't be back for eighty years..." But this way will Big Brother let your enemies catch you, turn you into a traitor? For example, that brother from a minute ago. Though he's a traitor he could certainly be a girl's big brother... I said I wouldn't think, but really I still thought, and thinking, became depressed, then looked at the sky. Looked at the pigeons in the sky and cats on the roofs, listened to the plaintive pigeon song, looked at the listless flag beside the cats... As the evening breeze slowly passed, there was only one thing to be thankful for: thank God we were not that traitor.

Also we aren't thought to have done something, right? that Ding said. *Otherwise, someone would have caught us.*

But you were already caught, man! And you already sold out your friend.

Ugh – that Ding sat down again.

Despair. The dark evening breeze was full of despair.

Tell me, how can we make sure we don't sink that low?

Unless...

Unless what?

Unless you don't have any enemies at all.

I never thought I had enemies?

Or if you never have any... any of your... your people.

That night we went to see Uncle. It had been a long time since we'd listen to him tell stories. Meanwhile we wanted to see the woman in that picture – who was she really?

73. Fu's Story

"Now, apart from me and Old Liu," Uncle sighed, "no one knows who she really is."

"Now, apart from Old Liu," Uncle said again, "no one can prove who she is."

"She isn't a martyr?" Ding Yi asked.

"Only I think so," Uncle said. "Only I think she should be a martyr."

"How did she die?"

"But my opinion doesn't matter. How can you prove a traitor is a martyr?"

"What about Old Liu, where's Old Liu?"

Uncle put on a tea kettle and asked Ding Yi to sit down.

Uncle said a cactus was going to bloom soon, if not tonight, then early in the morning.

Uncle said Ding Yi guessed right, the woman in the photo was his lover. But Uncle immediately corrected himself, saying, no, he should say he was the lover of the woman in the photo.

"What's the actual difference?" Uncle asked Ding Yi. "I'm hers or she's mine?"

"Mutual. Lovers are always mutual."

"Ah." Uncle took another long sigh and smiled bitterly. "If you love this girl, but she dies never knowing, tell me, what's that considered?"

The woman was called Fu, Uncle's high school classmate. It could really be called a case of love at first sight. Uncle fell for her as soon as he saw her and it stayed like that to that day. But Fu didn't know. Uncle never told her. At that time Fu had short hair, wore a plain white dress, sang and laughed – pure as an angel. Uncle said: "Letting your eye linger on her felt profane, how could you talk to her?" One day Uncle finally decided that he would talk to her no matter what. He gathered his courage and approached her.

After exchanging greetings, the words were about to come out when someone else came along... Uncle said it was fate, pure fate! He missed his chance to speak this time and would never get another one again. After that, Fu suddenly disappeared.

"Disappeared?"

"Disappeared."

Fu seemed to be gone three or four years, maybe longer. Not to be found anywhere. Uncle asked around everywhere, asked everyone, but it was no use. No one knew where she went, had no information about her. It was really as if this person had evaporated into thin air.

"And Old Liu? He would know, right?"

"Man!" Uncle didn't consider Ding Yi a boy, they were speaking man-to-man. "Man, if you don't believe me, listen close as I talk it through."

I could sense the bitterness in Uncle's speech. He was saying: Even if I finish and it comes to nothing, let me enjoy the telling.

One day, Uncle said, Old Liu asked him if he thought maybe Fu had died. Uncle said it was impossible. You can't die without anyone knowing! Still later, Old Liu said: Even if she's alive you might as well consider such a heartless person dead, don't you think? Uncle still wouldn't accept it. Uncle didn't believe Fu was that kind of person. Uncle couldn't imagine where she'd gone. What was hardest for him to figure out was, regardless of where she went, she wouldn't have been able to leave without a word.

"Then where did she really go?"

"Many years later I found out she went to a senior official's mansion."

"Senior official? Did she marry the guy?"

"Patience, man. Hear me out."

Oh, I understand! I nudged Ding Yi as he said to Uncle: "She must have been sent behind enemy lines, undercover, as a secretary or something."

"How'd you know?" Uncle's face took on the expression of a surprised child, as if, had he figured it out earlier, that his life would have been different, but unfortunately he did not have Ding Yi's agile mind.

"Otherwise," I said, "how would she become a martyr?" I poked Ding Yi: *Did you forget, the movie is like that, right?*

But Uncle's smile slowly faded, and he took on a look of deep regret: "Ah, I'm so stupid. How did I not think of that at the time? Afterwards, I thought, Old Liu was trying to give me hints, but it couldn't get through my thick skull."

I also thought this old guy was pretty stupid. I had started with the answer and figured out the riddle, while you didn't even know where she ended up.

Yes, undercover agents, also known as underground workers, penetrated the enemy. But Uncle said Fu wasn't a secretary but a babysitter.

"How could she be a babysitter?"

"To put it more nicely, she was a private tutor, but in reality she was a babysitter. To put it less nicely, she was a maid. Taking care of three children, two young ladies and a young gentlemen who didn't understand anything."

Uncle really couldn't understand. Uncle wondered what had gone wrong with Fu. Don't you usually think clearly, Fu? It's a waste of talent at the very least, don't you understand? Fu was smart, beautiful and capable, with ambition and ideas. Uncle thought she was a princess, a queen, for real! In school she was top of the class. Uncle secretly struggled to keep up with her. Why would you become a private tutor? Why would you become a maid? So Uncle couldn't stop looking for Fu in the hope of urging her to leave. Can't you go anywhere? Can't you do anything? Do you understand what I'm saying, Fu? But Fu always talked around the issue and evaded him. Her expression was harder to read or perhaps more vigilant, not bright like before. She seemed to be a completely different person.

Uncle said: "I was really so stupid."

Uncle found her on the corner of a little street. It was completely by chance, like finding a needle in a haystack. To put it crudely, all thanks to having to go for a crap. That day Uncle went to some book stalls and was wandering around when he felt an urge to go, no option but to find a place to relieve himself. Uncle went into a small alley, passed through one after another. Thank God there was a public toilet. Happily finished, Uncle slowly walked through the alley. It was a clear, bright day. The trees shone in all their colours. The quiet alley burst with children's singing... the picture of peace. Uncle was full of emotion, knowing that fate wanted him to walk to that place. Fu! Standing in front of a large house, singing songs with two innocent children.

"The flower shakes, oh,
The first of the month,
The old lady wants to see the lotus glow...

The flower shakes, oh,
It's May the fifth,
The old lady wants to eat roasted sweet potato."

Uncle said he'd never forget that sound as long as he lived, never forget Fu's shocked expression when she looked back. Beneath the clear, bright sky among the colourful trees Fu froze, her white dress flowing in the breeze... the scene still often came to Uncle in his dreams.

The two of them looked at each other a long time. Before Uncle could speak, Fu took the children into the big house behind her. The children were excited, though. "Miss Wu, Miss Wu," they kept shouting. "Miss Wu, let's play some more."

Ha, Miss Wu! Uncle nearly fainted.

From that point forward, Uncle often went to that corner to wait for her. Uncle asked Fu if she was going to be a maid like this for the rest of her life. Uncle told Fu that she used to be so idealistic, so ambitious. Are you short of money? This still isn't worth doing! Uncle said you should go to college and keep learning. If you're short of money, I'll talk to my dad. Uncle's dad ran a family business, but behind closed doors Uncle would tell you he was his dad's boss. But Fu refused and didn't say why. Fu said: "You go your way and I'll go mine. I only ask one thing – don't come looking for me again. I'm not who you think I am. I'm just a regular person who wants a quiet life." But Uncle kept visiting her. Fu didn't come out. He just waited on the corner. Fu didn't come out for a whole day. Uncle waited a whole day. But Uncle never went into the big house for fear of making trouble for Fu.

It was like this until, one day, Old Liu came to talk to Uncle and told him not to visit Fu again. Uncle asked why, what's it have to do with you? Old Liu said it didn't, but the organisation asked him to say it. Uncle asked if the organisation had to tell him what woman to like. Old Liu said he didn't know, he just knew the organisation wanted him to break off his relationship with that woman and he could go ask himself if he didn't believe it. Uncle shouted at Old Liu: "Who can I ask? You're my only higher-up!" Old Liu looked at him sternly: "Good you know it, I also only have one higher-up, and I tell you what he tells me."

"Tell me how stupid I am," Uncle said. "I mean, I never thought Fu was behind enemy lines."

"No one's stupider than me," Uncle said. "I mean, I never realised Fu has long been my comrade."

"It seems I suspected it for a time," Uncle said, "but I couldn't believe that innocent Fu would hide the fact that she knew Old Liu and me."

"I must be brain-dead," Uncle said. "From then on I tried to force myself not to think of her, to never think of her again, to consider that vulgar woman, that fallen woman, that maid behind enemy lines, dead!"

Of course, Uncle could never forget her.

When victory was near Old Liu gave Uncle an address, asked Uncle to dress up as a knife sharpener and go to a certain house on a certain street and meet with someone named Miss Wu. Uncle asked why. Old Liu said no reason, just go to the meeting first. Uncle asked one more thing: Did you say Miss Wu? Old Liu said yes, that's Miss Wu's house.

"It must have been God's will, it had to be God's will," Uncle said, slapping his forehead. "I never thought who this Miss Wu might be."

Uncle found the street, went to the right alley, found the house number. When Uncle shouted "Knife sharpener, knife sharpener!" at the entrance to the mansion, he thought, huh? Where am I? Quiet alley, colourful trees, Miss Wu? Who's Miss Wu? If it wasn't the woman singing about flowers with the kids, who else could it be? Uncle slumped down on the steps and sat stunned for half an hour.

Uncle said: "If I'm not mistaken, can you believe it, man? Seven years! It'd already been seven years since I called on her."

"Then you never married?" Ding Yi asked.

Ahem, way to make it harder for him, Ding Yi!

"If I never married, would you call me Uncle?" To Uncle's slack face was added a touch of sorrow.

"So, Uncle, was it Fu?" Ding Yi pressed on.

"But Fu had already died."

"When?"

Uncle looked at the entrance to the mansion and forced himself to calm down. Uncle urged himself not to show emotion or the slightest unusual expression. It would bring danger to Fu. Uncle also told himself that Fu was now Miss Wu. I am just a knife sharpener. Uncle took some deep breaths and felt better, then began shouting again.

But the person who emerged from the mansion was not Fu but a man, who gave two kitchen knives to Uncle. Uncle bent down and began to sharpen one of the knives and quietly asked the man: So, Miss Wu's busy? The man asked back: You know Miss Wu? Uncle said they were from the same hometown: Miss Wu took care of me, always gave me knife-sharpening jobs. The man looked at Uncle: But you still don't know? Uncle said: Know what? The man said: Miss Wu has passed. What?! Miss Wu passed. The knife in Uncle's hand almost fell on his foot. Last month, the man said. It happened last month.

"How?" Ding Yi asked.

At the time Uncle felt dizzy and let his tongue slip: Fu... Fu... Fu died? Luckily the man misunderstood Uncle's words, because 'fu' can also mean rich in Chinese. Do people die rich these days? It would be more accurate to say she died poor. The man told Uncle: Miss Wu had been sick for many years. She had a constant dry cough and later coughed blood. Miss Wu spent all the money she earned on doctors, but couldn't be cured.

The family was afraid her illness would spread and wanted her to resign, so Miss Wu asked others to buy her medicine and stood firm, said she couldn't possibly lose this job.

"You must know why!" Uncle said plaintively with a bitter smile as he looked at Ding Yi.

"This was her mission," Uncle said. "What had she been doing all those years? Apart from taking care of the young miss and young master and straightening up the rooms, she didn't do anything else – why? To act like an illiterate person, who understood nothing, asked nothing, cared about nothing. Only then would the enemy let down its guard."

"But then what use would she be?" Ding Yi said.

"At the very end, at the crucial moment, the organisation would give her a directive. At that point, for example, she might gain access to some sensitive materials... and no one would suspect a simple maid."

"But she never expected to get sick," Uncle said. "People always get sick. Underground workers are people too, and they can also die of illness. But Fu also knew she couldn't ask the organisation for money for treatment. If a maid spent a lot of money on treatment, wouldn't the enemy get suspicious?"

"What illness was it?"

"It isn't important. It's no longer important."

"Then what happened next?"

Uncle took a few sips of his drink, squinted, apparently looking at a flower in front of him.

His expression became harder and harder to read – it seemed helpless, self-mocking, falling into deep absurdity...

"Fu left a note, four words: Who am I really?"

"What's it mean?"

"You're smart, Ding Yi. Do you need me to explain it?"

Uncle said that, one day, Fu felt she was not OK, couldn't go on for more than a few more days. If she didn't die she wouldn't be able to do any work, but the organisation still hadn't sent anyone – still no news from the sharpener. Maybe deep in the night with no one around Fu turned the matter over in her mind and wrote these words, hid the note in a knife handle. Uncle said he guessed she must have been thinking: if the knife sharpener really comes, if he's smart, he might find this note.

"But what do the words mean?"

If someone else happened upon the note, they wouldn't be able to understand it either. If the organisation found it, it would mean: I've been waiting and waiting for a directive and cannot die in peace! And if no one found the note? "It would be spoken only to herself," Uncle said.

"Spoken to herself?"

"Or a question for heaven."

"Uncle, I still don't understand."

Hey, hey, Ding Yi, are you really stupider than this old man?

Uncle was silent a moment, then asked Ding Yi: "Tell me, man, who was Fu?"

"Wasn't she a martyr?"

"That's what I said. But she wasn't killed by the enemy, right?"

"Then she was a... a regular underground worker?"

"But she didn't provide any intelligence at all."

"Then, then she was just Fu, just herself, OK?"

"Right, she went to school for twelve years and did all her work well, but for the next seven years, until she left this world, she only wrote those four words."

"At least she was your lover."

"But I never even told her."

"But you always remembered her, even loved her, right?"

Uncle, Ding Yi and I all looked at the picture on the wall, looked up at Fu, that young, innocent but awkward and sorrowful face. Was she a real person or just a picture? Was she a myth or someone who had a soul? When she had this picture taken, where was I? At what point in history was this? This beautiful human form had already disappeared, but had that authentic, sincere, firm, persistent and anxious soul already disappeared? I saw that Ding Yi was caught up in these endless questions or trekking along the endless road of history.

All right, Ding Yi, I secretly said to him. *This way you can understand who I am.*

What's this got to do with you?

Well, if you live a year and get a year older I experience something, hear some information and expand my existence... What, you don't believe me?

Ding Yi hesitated, seemed unsure.

OK, you will believe it. One day you will believe it.

Really, when?

Then Uncle suddenly slapped his thigh. "Wow, my flower!"

At some point a cactus had bloomed and already withered.

74. Newer Needs

Really there was no need to wait for that day. As soon as Ding Yi and I heard the above story our lives had already matured, our moods had changed, our way of looking at the world was unlike before. Thus the soul expands its journey, continues its progression, enriches its existence.

The soul like that endless news is like a river, constantly born, constantly converging, improvising to expand and spread, weaving an unpredictable net... And at one of its knots I long for Ding Yi. For example, if Ding Yi is a knot, I am somehow inextricably linked. If Ding Yi is part of the net, I am laced in this net's hologram.

Sometimes people feel they've suddenly grown up. How's that happen? The flesh can't grow that quickly, but the soul can. Once the soul integrates with the age-old news, one feels they've suddenly grown up – especially when you hear some of the news come from the chaos or when something eternal comes from noisy history.

Later, Ding Yi asked Uncle: "So Old Liu, could he certify Fu's loyalty?"

Uncle had already closed his eyes as if he were still regretting missing the blooming of that flower.

"If Fu died without doing anything," Uncle said, "what would Old Liu certify?"

"Fu was waiting. Does Old Liu know this?"

"Anyone could certify she was waiting, but who can prove what she was waiting for? Just the opposite – if someone wants to use Miss Wu's business to certify that Old Liu recruits traitors, wouldn't that be more logical?"

"That'd require seeking truth from facts, right? Old Liu couldn't be that selfish!"

"But he suddenly fell ill."

"Can't sick people still talk?"

"Stroke. Mute from a stroke, got it? Old Liu is practically a vegetable."

"Then... then... then his superiors?"

"Right, I started to look for his superiors, and spent no little effort trying to find them. But when I finally did, man, guess what?"

"What?"

"You have to believe in fate. You have to believe there's something in this world that no one can resist."

"He died?"

"You should add a sentence – he'll always live on in our hearts." Uncle smiled bitterly.

The sun was already coming up. Uncle cleared the drinks and snacks – put the leftover liquor back in the bottles, poured the leftover food in a pot. He carried his burden so well, it was as if the past didn't exist.

I whispered to Ding Yi: *Did you see? The soul dies out like this in some places.*

What do you mean?

Some knots, like withered roots, no longer spread the news.

But Ding Yi's thoughts were still on the tales.

"And you?" he said, summoning his courage to ask Uncle.

"What about me?" Uncle didn't stop his chores.

"Are you really a traitor?"

"Really," he said as if he were talking about something insignificant.

"How?"

"Afraid of dying." He spoke so easily it didn't seem he could be talking about himself.

Uncle started watering the flowers, patiently, pot by pot.

The first light came into the room, shining initially on the wall, later on the flowers closer to the ceiling, still later hitting Uncle's white hair.

Then I heard words tremble in the sun: "But I don't know if I'm afraid of dying or if this man you call Uncle is afraid of dying."

These words moved me deeply. I knew the soul still lingered inside Uncle like withered roots that still hold a long history of news. Furthermore, this news was bound to make the sellout Ding Yi more exiled.

For example, if Ding Yi realised he and Uncle suffered from the same ailment.

For example, if Ding Yi believed he was just luckier than Uncle.

For example if he also thought: Yi, how is she now? Yi, how will she be later? One day Yi could become a picture, and who would know the beautiful image once had a soul?

And that the beautiful soul was betrayed by a friend?

That Ding was quiet, just ashamed, just looking sad.

I began to really love Ding Yi. He didn't blame others, not even me. What about me? Alas, I was really worthy of vigilance: a long-wandering soul can also be carved into cunning, maybe it's not as good as fresh life, which is so pure and frank! I came to understand the need to update: the reason God renewed life over and over was out of fear that this long journey or rich experience would turn purity and frankness, surprise and absurdity, into treachery and calculation. That way, whatever you see seems normal, like the TV show title: *Move But Don't Be Moved*.

Tell me, Ding Yi asked me quietly, *where could Yi be?*

Don't know.

Tell me, can we still find Yi?

Yeah, I don't know.

75. False Truth

How could you tell the sellout Ding Yi had been exiled even further?

You'd have to wait till later when he overcomes those bad directors and actors, and his fresh experience with sex makes his imagination overflow with colourful fantasies to notice the clues, see it clearly. And now, in the refreshing spring air, that Ding is just tired of romantic affairs, is just questioning the truth, irreverent towards the strange dreams of youth: is this truth? Could so-called truth be this way? Is the so-called truth you seek just a physical boundary? If the soul and history's abundance are covered by these boundary lines, what's true about it?

Good sign! I thought this was an excellent sign. But hopefully this Ding would not stop at this superficial questioning. Usually this is the first step of life becoming soul. Of course taking one step doesn't guarantee there will be a second or, 'Warmth that suddenly turns cold is hardest to recover'. This second step could certainly be some distance away.

For example, to this doubt, this guy added a hobby: alcohol.

But this didn't mean anything definitive. Alcohol can make people lethargic, make people forget themselves, even become perverted, but alcohol can also help one escape reality and discover realms outside of truth. Put it this way: the real must be recognised, but is what lies outside recognition all false? For example, dreams are unreal but not fake. Alcohol has a false reality to it. Who decided the true was always real? Why must the true always be limited to the real? And not the virtual? For example, the sky – vast and empty – isn't true? The real is constrained; the virtual is wide open. As the so-called quiet life was a kind of drunken daze, and midsummer approached, alcohol helped Ding Yi make a comeback.

This guy was excited, not picky about the type of alcohol. As soon as he started sipping he began to feel loose, mysterious, and become more and more powerful. His face looked better, and his mood was gentler. Alcohol is best enjoyed with lots of food, but by the time the dishes were ready this Ding had already given up on them or was in a bar walking and drinking, muttering – this was when he still hadn't drunk much. When he had drunk a lot he walked incessantly, talked for ages, crisscrossed the streets and alleys, his clothing and gait unkempt – making him look like a piece of rubbish blowing in the wind. Occasionally he even sang.

This time he sang lyrics from an exotic ballad. All that could be made out was: "I always lie to myself, but you've already left me..." I don't know what they're from.

I said: *Hey, I haven't left. I'm here!*

He raised the bottle and spat: *I wasn't talking about you, bastard!*

Son of a bitch! I didn't know whether to laugh or cry.

He wasn't upset and went back to the song: "I've always lied to myself..."

The streets on that sultry summer night were flowing with people. This Ding sat down in the busiest area and took one sip after another while far away, rich dishes were being removed one by one. This guy was drinking no small quantity of alcohol, so passersby looked at him, thinking he was just thirsty.

The train station bell reported another day's arrival.

As the people dispersed, the day gradually cooled down.

I said: *What's up, staying out?*

He said: *Damn, arsehole!*

OK, OK, OK, then just sit, don't fall over.

Under the shining street lights I recall a few strange women were swinging around, making me dizzy.

Ding Yi rubbed his eyes to get a better look and make sure he wasn't dreaming: *Motherfucker, 'chicks'!*

I said: *Right, chicks! Nothing to do with Mother.*

The guy laughed, laughed rudely. But unexpectedly his laughter made me feel relaxed like I was floating, already among the treetops in fact.

Hey, what's going on? Hey, what's going on?

I was horrified, but that guy didn't move. He just laughed and made eyes at those bad women.

Hey, brother, why don't you help me!

That Ding just shifted on his bum, didn't even lift his head.

Ding Yi! Are you fucking deaf or stupid?

He did not get upset, was completely indifferent.

Ah, now I understood. I suddenly figured out what happened. I could leave him for a while, I could be free awhile! Good news, good news, so good I could cry. I could make him suffer some days. Since everything lost its charm, Ding Yi's town was no exception. Just sitting alone I was so bored I almost went into a fish or a dog again. OK, OK, that's leaving the real for the virtual, at least you can take a nice breath.

Instantly I felt free and rejuvenated, finding myself sauntering in the sky. I flew up and down, to and fro, stars rushing by and wind brushing my sides. I could reach anywhere any moment: roofs, treetops, spires... The unknown, fields, villages... The surface of water, mountaintops, desert wilderness... As classic sayings go, I could "hold the world in a glance", "see as far as the end of the earth", "daring not to speak aloud" and "reach the heavenly bodies with my hands"... Did you think the night was endless darkness? You thought the night was lifeless? No, no, in the dead of night dreams come alive and we ride the wind... The countless restrictions on the souls are released and we go free into the night.

Many souls wander like hope and expectations, acting like flashing stars.

Many cherished longings that come and go in fits and starts have become wind to mingle with the clouds.

Many unfillable wishes that sound like crying and singing are turned into the sound of heaven.

Ah, this is night's drama, night's promise, night's lamentations and confessions.

Night's drama calls the shots. Night's drama plays it loose. But this night's drama cannot be watched idly.

Otherwise you'll avert your eyes and hear nothing.

Give up the rules of the day, give up modesty. Even give up respect. The night wants you in your real role.

Otherwise it will not be believable.

Because, look, even the homesick, nervous apparatus that always snores under the guard of night, earnestly, has abandoned the vigilance and discernment of day. Because, look, everything is tangible and infinite in the night, without shelter, without beginning or end, with all of day's names removed.

Of course, soon they'll wake up. When night ends, the soul will be

trapped in the human form and can't help but go where it's taken.
So, don't let go of such a good time.
How's the song go? "Hurry on my boat before day breaks..."
Night has always been the time when souls unite.

76. Soul Searching for Long Night

"Ah, the night is like water and dreams are like boats. Drunkenly paddling, heart flowing long...
Look at the moon wandering, clouds flying, all but amorous rendezvous.
Look at the stars and shadows shifting, all the song and dance of the heart and soul.
Listen to the stranger's words from the heart, listen and you'll weep with joy.
Listen to that distant dream encounter, crying through the long night.

Ah, the night is like water and dreams are like boats. Drunkenly paddling, heart flowing long...
I see souls riding a flying leaf, hovering under the moon, expecting to meet a good companion.
I see souls catching a light wind, gently blowing the curtains, sneaking into the woman's boudoir.
I see souls become the sounds of nature, tapping the window, fleetingly peering.
I see a lonely soul with a candle, lingering with tears by the beauty.

Ah, the night is like water and dreams are like boats. Drunkenly paddling, heart flowing long...
I see souls transcend the walls, hesitating, not sure where they're going.
I see souls break through the walls, searching, not sure what for.
I see souls go in dreams, sailing towards distant shadows, the ends of the earth.
I see souls retreat in moonlight, sighing against the wind for the desolate countryside.

Ah, the night is like water and dreams are like boats. Drunkenly shaking, heart flowing long...
I see souls leaving the comfort of their homes, transferring their love to others.
I see souls unable to sleep alone, dreaming erotically.
I see souls emotional as teenagers, making solemn pledges of love.

I see souls old but strong, searching for girls near and far.

Ah, the night is like water and dreams are like boats. Drunkenly paddling, heart flowing long...
I hear souls of love suddenly reunited despite the barriers of mountains and rivers.
I hear souls destined as lovers instantly fall for each other despite the wind and rain.
I hear birds sing day and night among the flowers and trees.
I hear the chirps and roars of mating creatures in the vast wilderness under the sun.

Ah, the night is like water and dreams are like boats.
I must be the moon and stars, right? I'm spreading light for miles and miles at night.
I am this eternal, infatuated soul! Forever and always, hoping and dreaming.
Ah, drunkenly paddling, heart flowing long...
But I don't see the path back to Eden.
But I don't see any sign of Eve's spirit."

77. Abandoned Land of Delusion and Absurdity

I was wandering as I sighed and pondered when there suddenly came a burst of sound – drum music?

I listened closer. It seemed that someone was sad and was repeatedly sighing.

When I walked closer to look, it turned out to be an abandoned land of delusion and absurdity, populated by desolate lost souls. How do I know? Listen, those sad sighs were almost heartless. Look, the singing and dancing were insincere.

I wanted to talk with them. Before I could ask, the song and dance laughed at me. "Where'd this drunk come from? Talking about love! What, have you seen that thing?" Before I could respond, a sad sigh urged me: "Love, love, do you have a low IQ, brother? Talking about that, and even taking it goddam seriously!"

For a moment I felt as dumb as a piece of wood. What else could I say? In the past, all who knew me said I was passionate, while those who didn't know me called me a hooligan. Now it's better, whether someone knows you or not, as soon as you talk about love they call you a drunkard, an imbecile. Ah I'm just afraid that over time the night will no longer be night, the soul no longer the soul. But think about it, I might leave as well. The stubbornness – I quote a sage as one who can understand me the best.

Who could expect that my initial thought would invite much

sniggering? It seemed the disgraced person was me. I had no choice but to ask them courageously. I asked the song and dance why they were song and dance.

Somehow this caused the song and dance to stop. For a time the joyful spirits were still – some were speechless, some were tumultuous, some felt lost, some were stunned and some angry... After a lengthy silence, I heard words come sonorously: Be optimistic, brother! You know what optimism is? Another witty tongue argued helplessly: Hey, laughing is better than crying! Right? Can you tell me what's wrong with that, brother? Another loud, lofty voice said: Freedom, freedom! I can do whatever I want, all right? A group echoed: Yeah, yeah, well said. Then the playful singing and drumming came back.

I dully thought to myself, was it jealousy or abandonment? Thickheaded, I asked those sad sighs why they were sad and sighing.

I didn't think this question would be more troublesome. For a time the wind begrudged and tragedy lamented – there were those who sobbed, those who wailed, those who looked away with suspicion and those who covered their faces in embarrassment... After crying, a feeble voice asked: Why are we women always the ones who get hurt? Why, why, why? Then a shrewish voice spat: Heck! Where can we find a decent man? None is faithful! Or another voice objected: Women? Women are all as darn vicious as vipers! Still another voice sighed in cadence and made me cynical: Come! Forget your emotions, be at ease. Don't you see that women come in different forms, but no matter how good they look, they all eventually die. As the years pass by in thousands, isn't all that's left are desolate graves and ugly bones? Well, this question didn't seem without foresight. I thought about it, yet another painful shout sounded familiar: I know he doesn't love me, I know he's lying to me. But I can't leave him, can't leave him...

Who was that? I wanted to look, to see if their situation was consistent with my previous speculation.

Then through the walls, looking for the sound among the many – sure enough, sure enough it was a pair of conflicted haunts! Maybe their hearts were in sync, or just looked similar but were very different. Looking closer it seemed to be the latter: though they slept in the same brocade bed, there had long been a feeling of separation, their dreams diverged! While the physical forms are entangled with each other, their souls have long been wandering apart. One seeking love from another place with his soul, while the other facing the walls of solitude with her sorrowful heart.

"People long for the shapes when they part from each other, hate their actions when they come together, you know?"

"They pine for each other when separated and are tired of each other when reconciled. No need to elaborate. I understand."

What to do then?

As soon as I wanted to say 'then leave', I remembered one of the place's old adages and retreated. What's the old adage say? Something like: "One would rather destroy a temple than separate a couple."

The stars were sparse, the moon forlorn, dawn breeze spread sleepiness, I thought it might be best to go back to Ding Yi and sleep awhile.

When I was close to home, I saw that Ding still hadn't come back. (I'll add here: the soul departing is seen by Ding Yi as a passive thing, but to me it's active – when the soul departs, it goes in search of new vessels.) As for Ding Yi he'd probably just fallen asleep somewhere, still not over jetlag from coming from the western to the eastern hemisphere. I wasn't sure if I should wait for him to come back or go look for him. Then from the peaceful night I heard a loud shout like a warning: "Just a couple passing the days together, what is there to fight about?!"

Where? Who? Who was making such a racket?

Ah, next door! It seemed that old woman had come to mediate again.

The other couple seemed to be engaged in a cold war while this one was in close combat – mutual vitriol and groaning with scratches and bites. The other couple appeared united but was separated at heart, and what was happening to this one? Listen closely. If I tell you I'm afraid, you won't believe it. Here were three human tools with no soul! Let me explain: the so-called human tool doesn't mean the spirit travels while the tool waits (as dreaming and drunk) and doesn't mean the spirit stays a long time and suddenly leaves (as in death and return), but these three human tools were soulless! It's no wonder such situations exist: the spirit never enters for some reason or somehow takes a detour, and so is left wandering, alone. It's also like a computer (as I've said). The hardware's ready, colourful, even beautiful, but the program has never been loaded, only tested a few times during production. So the old woman's exhortation was nothing new: "What's wrong, you're not satisfied with a full belly? Love or not, how the hell have I never heard that word before? Don't just listen to people blather and take everything seriously. Be happy you have food and drink. Live in peace for me. What's better than having children? Turn out the lights and go to sleep."

Then everything seemed still.

Then the moon fell and the stars faded.

Now and then a baby cried or a dog barked.

Hopefully the crying baby was visited by a faraway soul – as when I first entered Ding Yi, and the soul wanted to sing while that Ding cried. But the barking worried me. Could a wronged soul have wandered in, with no way out, and yelped?

And I couldn't help but think: was the dog tool filled with the soul's bitterness, or the empty human form sad? But there's another: a human form with a canine soul – that's an even greater disaster! This reflects that the small-minded often live in shame and sorrow. Also the dog barking situation, virtual sound situation, inflammatory potential could all be signs of a dog soul in a human form. Such a spiritual configuration tends to go with the flow, is the most unthinking, always gobbling up whatever they can get, and as a result their core characteristic is being afraid to look inwards. Right, once the animal soul is clear, what can be done? It's better not to drift off, go soul-searching. Focus on reality.

So I'd better go look for Ding Yi, I guess. How late can this guy stay out? I hope that, in my absence, he didn't make a fool of himself.

78. Night Encounter of Returning Souls

The sky slowly lightened in the east. After a night of unrestrained freedom, at this time, a wandering soul can often enjoy returning. I met them, asking from time to time if anyone had seen Ding Yi.

One spirit laughed at me: "You're talking about the drunk guy?"

One spirit pitied me: "Hurry, don't let that thing drink any more!"

Another spirit felt bad for me: "Huh, you're in Ding Yi? Heh, why'd you go there?"

I couldn't simply explain, so out of politeness I asked back: "Everyone, where are you going?"

They said Zhang San, Li Si as well as Liu Wu, Wang Liu, Chen Qi, Shi Ba...

So, you've been OK?

A spirit said: "Ah, my human form doesn't misbehave. He's just lazy, eating, crapping, screwing and watching TV. I'm so bored I can't wait for him to sleep so I can go."

A second spirit said: "That's nothing, you're lucky. My place is really something. Every few days something goes wrong. Once the rubbish chute got blocked (obstructed intestine), and then the sewer got blocked (uremia). I nearly suffocated."

Another spirit said: "There's nothing wrong with my place other than being stupid! He can't get out a whole sentence (lexicon incomplete) or already forgot the words he learned yesterday (can't save or retrieve)."

Another spirit said: "Your places are all better than mine. Mine, ah..."

"What about your place?"

"Forget it, he and his mistresses fight all day. He's comfortable, but I don't like being scolded and bullied."

Everyone rested a moment now, expressed understanding and reassurance, and really didn't want to disperse.

Our gathering attracted more returning souls to join in.

One said: "Don't complain, haven't you heard the saying that every family is a hard nut to crack?"

"What's your place?"

"Carl Lewis, a famous track athlete, winner of nine gold medals."

"Ah, you have nothing to complain about! Everyone was jealous: healthy and chic, accomplished, how many better places can there be?"

"You think it's an ideal place?"

"OK, forget about me. Leslie Cheung, the deceased movie star. Everyone knows him, right?"

"Of course, why?"

"How's that place?"

"Isn't it obvious? Cheerful, talented, blessed, blessed!"

"But what happened in the end? Jumped off a building!"

Everyone sighed.

Then another spirit asked: "I really don't understand, what was he thinking?"

A spirit said: "Remember what every famous person has said: 'I do it so people respect me.'"

"What do you mean?"

"They're still afraid of evaluation? Value comparison."

Another spirit corrected them: "More like price!"

Everyone was silent a moment, all feeling the same.

"Not necessarily. I think it's insatiable greed."

"But what could a place like that be dissatisfied with?"

"This human animal! They want what they don't have, and if they have everything they think it's meaningless."

"True. Whatever we seek, is it not because we lack it? If in the end we lacked nothing, hey, what do you think we'd do?"

This startled everyone.

"No, impossible. How can you lack nothing? No way!"

This made everyone relieved.

"But if it's impossible, why are we still seeking, seeking, seeking? If you can never end the lack, then hey, tell me, what's the actual point?"

This question made everyone fall into contemplation, fall into memory, gaze into the infinite, pray into the void.

It seemed everyone was like me, having been searching a long time, knowing the important thing was to move without knowing exactly why. We stayed like that until the sky grew light, and everyone had to go their separate ways.

79. Obsession

After everyone dispersed, only one spirit remained.

Seeing me also leave, he suddenly asked: That Ding is comfortable, what are you worried about, my brother?

Upon closer inspection, it was the old one who had taught me to see through the vanity of fame and fortune.

Do you have a lesson for me, sir?

I just asked you: You've come so far, what are your worries about?

I'm too young and ignorant. Please point me in the right direction.

In your case, it's the old saying: extinguishing emotion brings peace.

How does one extinguish them? This place is a sea of emotions – how to extinguish them! Why can't you stay here, brother?

Where do you mean?

A place with no bitterness or worries, a free, harmonious place?

Where?

A free heart.

May I ask how this heart is without bitterness or worries?

No hoping, no finding, no wishes or desires, so it's naturally without bitterness and worry.

This made me think: then wouldn't you be a vegetable? Vegetables might not be without feeling, so a stone then? If that's the destination, why does the soul travel through the ages, why not let an atomic bomb end it?

Puzzled, the old spirit sensed my thoughts: with no bitterness or worry, with freedom and harmony, this ideology in this place and time, how can I have a clear understanding? Why don't you go and see what's really worth hanging on to here?

Go where? Aren't we always going? We started walking a path, aren't we still walking a path? And won't we still be walking a path in future? As long as we're walking, how can we leave the path?

The spirit hesitated, then seemed ashamed: Path, path, path! What I've pointed out to you is a place of everlasting peace and comfort!

Is there no path there?

The question seemed to throw him off.

It's a final destination, an extreme point. Is it completely silent?

OK, OK, OK. This place is good, this place has a path! If you want to stay here, go right ahead!

You seem angry, sir. I just can't imagine, is there a path that can be walked without bitterness and worry?

But how can a road that never ends be full of concern?

His question left me stupefied.

Sir, I just want you to think what the purpose of endless drifting is.

Eden's covenant! I blurted out.

You, you... you're really obsessed!

I wonder, isn't fixation on being carefree also obsession?

The old spirit saw I was a hard case, threw up his hands and flew off.

All that remained was the heavy night.

All that remained was the surrounding vastness.

All I could do was slowly walk my own individual path, looking into the faraway western sky and feeling sorry for having disappointed the old spirit.

80. In the Police Station

When I found Ding Yi, it was already bright out.
He asked me groggily: *Where is this?*
The police station!
He sat up alert: *Shit, why'd you bring me here?*
I brought you? You brought me!
What do we do?
We explain the problem, that's all.
What problem?
You did it, you think about it.

The officer took off his cap and put a pen to paper. "Do you do this often, brother?"

"No, no, no!" This guy had trouble recalling. "Really, the... the first time, and I really didn't do anything."

"Yeah," the officer said. "You're just wasted."

"And I really didn't want to do anything with... her."

"We don't care if you did anything or not, but you still solicited a prostitute. Do you agree?"

"That girl actually isn't really a bad... a bad person."

"What'd you say? Girl?" The officer laughed. "If you ask me, she's old enough to be your mother!"

"Whatever she is, she's quite pitiable."

"Go on." The officer dropped the pen and crossed his arms with interest.

"It's not that she's poor. The key is this." Ding Yi pointed to his heart. "Lonely."

The officer lit a cigarette.

"Everyone's lonely, don't you think?"

The officer looked at the cigarette, not Ding Yi.

"If you ever sink to those depths, you'd understand. Don't be fooled by their makeup. Really their... their smiles are forced. If you have the chance, you should really talk with them. None of them are bad people. You should really talk... talk to each other now and then."

"Talk about what?"

"Whatever. The... the important thing is to talk. The important thing is to say something really, something from the heart. Usually you want to, but it's not appropriate to talk about... that."

Ha, that word! Good Ding Yi. He's nearly understood Eden's covenant.

The officer seemed undeterred. The alcohol was still making that Ding's lips loose: "You know usually, what things... things do you talk about? Like with your best friend, your very best friend, what kind of things are you willing to tell them? What kinds of things do you even tell your... yourself? But somehow I could with them. It may well be because I saw them as... prostitutes and they saw me as... as... a john. No one's afraid, no one's looking down on anyone, so you don't have to hide."

The officer opened the window, and the glass reflected the great blue sky. A big bird flew freely, white, healthy, but it could never fly out of that glass. It flapped its wings, struggling in vain.

"Some things, some kinds of things, to put it simply that... that kind of thing. You know what I mean?" Ding Yi continued: "Sex, yes, sex! That thing seems the most... most special. That thing seems not just a thing but something else, seems to mean... something else. You know what I mean?"

I didn't think it mattered if he understood or not. The important thing was young Ding Yi was getting his head screwed on straight.

"Something else?" the officer asked. "What else?"

"Maybe freedom. Yes, free... freedom! Of course, you wouldn't necessarily agree. But overall, when that happens between two people, they both seem to... to be able to talk. When you can talk about anything, then anything... anything is possible. And when you feel like you can say anything, wow! You'll certainly think that you don't... don't have to say it. Ah! That feels so..."

The officer picked up the pen. "Age?"

"That feeling, I don't know if you... what do you think?"

The officer raised his voice. "Age!"

"Oh, age. Huh? How old? Shit, why the hell can't I think of it?"

"Occupation or company?"

"I think in the future I might be a... a director or... actor or something. Now I don't have one."

"So now you're idle?"

"Sure, you can say that... elite."

"Enough, go!" the officer said.

"Put it this way, that feeling makes you feel like... bright, feel..."

"Remember, next time don't let me run into you. If I run into you next time, you won't get off so easy!"

81. Or Like the Wind

Outside the police station, the sun shone on everything. In the sunlight came children's singing: "Ah, sweet May, dress the trees in green, take us to the creek, and let us see the violets blooming..."

He couldn't help but sit down, sit in the roadside shade and listen.

"Ah May, sweet May, bring the violets soon..." The lead singer was pure, the accompaniment joyful. "Ah May, May, sweet May..." Variations, chords, different choral sections: "We hope so much to the see the violets again..." The boys and girls had bright eyes, the boys and girls had pure smiles. "Ah come, sweet May, let us play..." And the past, and the future, the countless dreams of childhood. "Ah May, May, let us go to the creek..."

Ding Yi asked: *Where are... they all?*

He looked at the sky, looked at the clouds in the sky, looked at the song in the clouds.

Ah, ah, let us go to the creek, see the violets bloom, see the violets bloom...

What are you looking at, Brother Ding? There! The barber across from us, above the door frame, speakers! My God, I mean are you awake or not?

He kept looking at the sky, looking at the clouds and the song in the clouds.

Then, a long time later, he seemed to take his gaze from the sky and hurled it at the earth: *Fuck fucking May!*

Ding Yi stood up, and we walked into the crowd.

The massive crowd, as thick as porridge, was steaming hot. Only after the wonderful children's song had ended did I notice there were so many people around. Bustling, bustling, but what were they all doing? Where to? One pretentious face after another, one pair of nervous or confused eyes after another, thousands of running legs... what were they all thinking? What were they just thinking, what are they thinking now? What did they just finish doing, what were they going to do now? Don't know. No one asked. No one considered it a problem. But what were they really? Apart from having an image, they creep and wheeze, they're unpredictable. For example, apart from singing the hooligan song, what could they be? They appear and disappear. They disappear and appear. They don't have names, don't have addresses, don't have histories or differences. You have no way of finding out if it's a lot of people or just a small group going back and forth around you. You have no way of knowing if there are many concrete souls or just a short video playing on repeat in front of your eyes. The wind is the same. The light, the leaves, the flowers are all the same – they come, they go, they come and go, they come and go and, having left, come again, so you're born, you grow up, you get old, you disappear... anything else? Is there any other meaning? Rad or rubbish?

We couldn't help but stop again.

We helplessly walked forward again.

We lazily looked left and right.

We stared at a girl walking gracefully to see what would happen. We followed a girl walking leisurely, trying to understand her situation. But in the sea of people she eventually disappeared in a flash, eventually disappeared in a final flash in the crowd or in your life, without history or distinction. I couldn't help but think of that woman's words: "Now I'm here, when I'm not here this woman will not be here... Because of a woman, part of your life has been happy. Or because of a man, part of my life hasn't been very tragic. That's all."

So now, where is she? What is she?

An abstract other person.
An other in a guess.
An other in fear, uncertainty.
Or like the wind, real yet empty.

82. The Importance of Difference, or a Reinterpretation of the Title

I began to realise God's wisdom, realise his vision, realise the importance of differences between people: people, if they're all just people, are no different from a desert.

Wherever you go, whatever you see or hear, everything's the same – the same human form or the same gravel, the same sand and sand dunes, even without clothing and walls – must be a prison. (Oh, that wise old Borges!) Clothing is isolation, walls are blockages. The boundless duplication is also isolation and blockage. In the cell you can touch walls on all sides, in the desert freedom lets you fall in all directions – wherever you go, wherever you end up, everything is repetition, freedom is repetition. It is said the most severe prisons are in the desert. This is worth pondering: no difference, no change, no path or everything is a path. Even though there are no barriers there's nowhere to run! (Is the path clear? No, it's blocked.) Another wise old man, Erich Fromm, wrote a book titled *Escape from Freedom*. Boundless duplication declares the futility of walking, declares the exhaustion of the imagination and the annihilation of hope, while also declaring the preciousness of others.

You'll long for other people, long for what we've always feared: other people.

Long for difference.
Long for novelty.
Long for specialness.
Even if it's difficult, rough. Even if it's dangerous.

So I came to Ding Yi. Ding Yi was one of many roads, not your average road. Ding Yi was an independent soul and unusual person. Ding Yi had a concrete fate and non-abstract era. Ding Yi was an unrepeatable story and a representative of all history. As a result *My Travels in Ding Yi* doesn't stop at reflection and reproduction, but seeks and enquires – seeks and enquires into life's possibilities, seeks and enquires into the full potential of the body.

83. Turning Point

As the alcohol wore off, hunger arrived. At noon Ding Yi hurried to a little restaurant.

Before going in I urged him: *Don't drink, OK?*

Relax, of course!

But if fate were more determined, that little restaurant would show us an acquaintance and thereby make drinking unavoidable, making *My Travels in Ding Yi* reach another turning point.

"Hey, do you still recognise me?"

Right after we sat, someone came and tapped Ding Yi's shoulder.

"You? You're..." Ding Yi tapped his forehead, thinking. "Are you Qin... Qin..."

"Right, right, good memory. Qin... Han!"

"Qin what?"

"Han. Qin, like Qin dynasty. Han, like Han dynasty."

"Oh, right. Right, right. Qin E is your little sister."

"Oh, you still remember her?"

Ding Yi thought: How could I remember you and not her?

Qin Han said: "You looked familiar right away. I thought about it, and hey, isn't that Ding Yi?"

"Thanks for still remembering me."

"Your name's unusual!"

Ding Yi smiled, then quickly looked at the menu on the wall.

"I was two years ahead of you. E was your year but a different class."

"Qin E, she..." Ding Yi really wanted to ask where that valiant classmate was, but he decided to forget it, avoid getting too involved with this Qin Han.

Ding Yi secretly asked me: *Do you know who he is?*

How could I not? One of the red silks and red satins! He was one of the most outspoken rebels, the one who sang the hooligan song loudest.

"Hey, bro, stop wasting your time," Qin Han said. "Besides fried buns, fried rice and fried noodles, there's nothing else here that can fill you up."

"Then fried buns, I guess."

Qin Han took Ding Yi to his table, lit a cigarette, poured tea and ordered fried buns and two appetisers, the intimacy of which made Ding Yi uncomfortable.

"So where have you been these years?"

"Where can someone like us be? Mixed up on the earth."

"Ha, you're funny, bro!" Qin Han sensed the distance of history.

"And you?"

"Same, who can escape earth? Haha..." He tried to narrow the distance.

"Doing what?"

"Well, some people make things, I'm in charge of finding customers."

"What things?"

"Useless things. The only good part is they give people like me a meal."

"People like you? What kind of person is that?"

"A person without prospects, I guess. Or one who lives in fantasies. When my parents were alive, they always said I was a daydreamer."

We discovered that Qin Han was not the old Qin Han. He was much more humble, less domineering, perhaps even too gentle. So much so that Ding quickly gave up the promise he made before entering.

"What do you say bro, want a drink?"

"Yeah, why not!" Ding Yi got excited.

I stopped him: *Drink what, brother? We just spent the whole night downtown!*

"Shit, leave me alone," Ding Yi shouted.

"It's all good," Qin Han said. "Whatever."

"Oh, I didn't mean you."

Qin Han looked around but didn't see anyone else bothering Ding Yi.

As sometimes you regret not meeting a person sooner, or a thousand cups are two few when you're with close friends, so that day Ding Yi drank with his old classmate Qin Han from afternoon till night.

It wasn't good alcohol. The cheap *baijiu*, Erguotou.

As the two hurried to pay the bill first, the hostess came over. "It's not easy to meet up, why not have dinner, then go?"

Outside the window it was already dark.

"Or we can go to my place?" Qin Han meant to go there to keep drinking.

"That's OK," Ding Yi said, holding up a stiff finger.

"I drank way too much the last couple days."

"I have some good stuff, yeah... at least it's better than this."

"I've had my fill. Next time."

"Oh yeah, I have some videos too, things you can't find elsewhere."

"What kind?"

"Let's go, brother. Stuff my friends brought me from overseas."

"I've seen enough of that cheap brothel stuff."

"What? I'm talking about high-quality art film!"

"And your sister?" The alcohol made him bold and he drunkenly asked: "Qin E, what's Qin E been up to?"

"Acting, I guess." Qin Han was wasted too. "I don't think she's done... done anything big."

"Peking opera?" Ding Yi remembered Qin E once sang in a model opera.

"Theatre, film, and some, uh... oh, TV series."

"Really?" that Ding said. "How'd I miss that?"

What are you thinking, brother?

Shit, I'm just asking. Can't I just ask?

I know what this guy was thinking – E is an actress, and he'd been a director for a couple days, so they're practically colleagues.

"She's not famous," Qin Han said. "Let's go, we can go to my place."

"Oh, OK..."

"Don't just say 'OK', let's go."

"So's she married?" Ding Yi had wanted to ask this for a while.

"You mean E? No."

Ding Yi felt relieved.

"She's not married... but it's not that she hasn't married," Qin Han added. "She's divorced."

Ding Yi felt anxious again. "What happened?"

Qin Han shook his head. "Let's go. I'll tell you."

"Who else is at your place?"

"Just me and my shadow."

"E doesn't visit a lot?"

I laughed at that Ding. *You're on a first-name basis now?*

Qin Han said: "You want to invite her?"

That Ding didn't answer, didn't have the nerve.

On that summer night Ding Yi and I went to Qin Han's place. It was a big house. He said his parents left it to him. Inside, apart from alcohol and video tapes, there were audio cassettes, books, newspapers and magazines from floor to ceiling.

"Man, your place is dirty!"

"It's definitely not dirty, it's messy. I hate dirtiness but am fine with messiness."

They cleared a place to sit and kept drinking.

That night at Qin Han's place, to my surprise, my travels in Ding Yi were changed by a film (video).

84. Film: Sex, Lies and Videotape

Director Steven Soderbergh uses a total of four characters.

Graham and John are old classmates. John and Ann are husband and wife. Ann is Cynthia's sister.

Ann is always worrying about little things.

Her psychiatrist asks: "You haven't told John about this, have you?"

"I haven't."

The psychiatrist asks more about their marriage.

Ann says it's fine, just that she hasn't wanted John to touch her lately.

"And before that, how was the sex life?" the psychiatrist asks Ann.

Ann says it was pretty good. "It's not that I don't like it, it's just I never thought it was amazing."

After years of drifting, Graham returns to his hometown and visits John. Ann is the only one home. During the conversation their marriage comes up. Ann says she values security. They have a nice house. John has a good job.

When they have dinner, John is surprised by Graham's depravity. Graham laughs, he disagrees. John asks him whether he wants to see Elizabeth. Graham hesitates and doesn't respond. Elizabeth is Graham's ex-lover.

John is obviously a cheater and soon meets with Cynthia. Cynthia is young, outgoing. She not only treats sex casually but is proud of it. When Ann isn't home, John meets Cynthia again to tease her about the subject.

Meanwhile, Ann has been helping Graham find a place to rent, and they're relaxing in a bar. As they get more familiar, the subject turns to sex. Ann thinks people make too much of it. Women are really different from men.

Graham responds: "Some say a man learns to fall in love with a woman that attracts him, while a woman slowly becomes attracted to the one she loves."

"Wow, that's perfect," Ann says.

The conversation deepens. Graham says he's impotent. As soon as he's with a woman, he can't perform. Ann asks if this makes him ashamed. Graham says it doesn't, maybe a little, but he's different from Ann. Ann asks if he thinks she's ashamed. Graham says it seems that she really cares what people think. Ann says she's seeing a psychiatrist and asks Graham is he sees one. No. Graham says people can't accept advice from someone who doesn't know them very well. Ann says she and her psychiatrist know each other well. Graham asks if they've been physically intimate. No, no, Ann says. How could we?

Graham says: "Sorry, I didn't mean that. I'm saying only people with physical relationships can..."

Ann understands. "You're saying otherwise he can't give good advice?"

Graham smiles and nods.

Cynthia asks Ann about Graham. Ann coldly says that Graham is different. This makes Cynthia more interested. Ann tells her to forget it, Graham isn't the type of person she'd like. Cynthia laughs and says Ann underestimates her.

One day Graham is watching a movie alone and seems comforted. On screen, a woman is talking about her experience masturbating. Ann arrives. Graham quickly turns it off, dresses and greets her. Ann asks about the tapes on the table. Graham says they're private interviews. He's doing a study. Why does each tape have a woman's name on it? Graham says he likes to interview women. Ann asks if she can watch. Graham says no. Graham says he promised the interviewees that he would be the only one to watch them. Ann warily asks what the interviews are about. Graham has to tell that truth, that they're about sexual issues.

"What kind of sexual issues?"

"All sexual issues."

"For example?"

"What they've done, what they want but don't talk about, whatever I think to ask."

Ann is puzzled and hurries to leave.

When Cynthia asks about Graham again, Ann's tone has changed. She says he's a weirdo. Cynthia wants to meet with him even more.

When Cynthia visits Graham she implies that she knows about the videotapes. Graham asks her if she came to attack him. Cynthia says no. Cynthia says that, with regard to men, she's never believed Ann. Cynthia confidently says that whatever scares Ann must be sexual and asks if he's videotaping sex. Graham says no, not exactly. Cynthia says it's a yes or no question.

Graham has trouble explaining. Since Cynthia is so open, obviously so different from Ann, Graham gets an idea. "Why don't you let me tape you a little?"

Sure enough, Cynthia doesn't refuse. She's surprised and excited but, playing coy, asks: "What do you want me to do?"

Talk. Talk about what? Your sexual history, your sexual preferences. Cynthia hesitates. Is it just answering questions, nothing else? Yes, nothing else. This makes you satisfied? Graham doesn't answer. Could someone else watch the video? Definitely not, Graham says. No one but me.

Cynthia talks about something that happened when she was eight: an eight-year-old boy who lived next door asks her if he could watch her pee. Cynthia said if he let her see him pee too, then sure. The two ran off where no one could see. Cynthia did what she promised, but the boy ran off before she was done peeing.

"And you didn't talk about it again afterwards?"

"No. He avoided me that whole summer, then moved. Awful!"

"So when did you end up seeing a man's thing."

Fourteen. Cynthia says she never thought that thing would look like that. She says at first she thought it was independent. When he asked me to touch it, I realised there was a person connected. He said me touching it felt good... Now Cynthia's expression slowly changes. Her gaze and voice get more gentle and she can't help but lean over and lie down.

Graham also slowly lies down on the floor, looking at her thoughtfully before asking: "And then?"

"Then? Then he didn't talk again..."

Cynthia tells Ann about the videotape. Ann is wary and enquires whether he asked her to take off her clothes. Cynthia says no. Did you do it anyway? Cynthia says she did. Why? I wanted to. Why? I wanted him to see me. Are you crazy? He could show it to all his horny friends! No, Cynthia says, he won't. How do you know? Anyway, it's too late, right? Did he touch you? No. And you? No. But Cynthia says she did touch herself. God! Ann says. I don't even do that in front of John! Cynthia says: That's because you can't!

"You don't even know him!" Ann says.

Cynthia says: "I feel like I do."

There are some signs that make Ann wonder if John is having an affair. But John swears he is not, then takes offence, accusing Ann of not being romantic with him and thereby having a reason to suspect him. Ann believes what he says.

John also knows about Graham videotaping Cynthia and says furiously: If Graham needs to get off, why doesn't he buy porn? Cynthia actually really understands Graham. He wants to understand other people, communicate with them. John asks angrily: But you don't have to masturbate in front of him, do you? I do, Cynthia says. I like it! John is furious. Then did you sign a document with him, to guarantee he can't show it? Cynthia says sorry, she didn't. John says she's in big trouble then because she has no legal protection. Cynthia says it's fine, she trusts him. Trust him? Yeah, a lot more than I trust you! John says that's really hurtful, what have I done? Cynthia says you fuck your sister-in-law and lie about it!

"But don't forget, you're also deceiving Ann!"

"That's right, but I never swore before God that I'd be faithful to her forever."

John is speechless. Cynthia tells him to go, saying their relationship should end. John mocks her: Did Graham ask you to say this? Cynthia screams: I don't need anyone to tell me what to do!

When cleaning the bedroom, Ann finds a woman's earring. Ah, it's Cynthia's. Now she understands everything.

Ann goes for a drive and mysteriously ends up at Graham's.

Graham says he knows about John and Cynthia. Ann asks how. Graham says that Cynthia told him during the taping. Ann feels betrayed: Thanks for telling me! Graham apologises, saying he never saw her, how could he tell her? Ann sits down, sighs: Ugh, what a mess, how is everything different than I thought? Graham looks at her helplessly. After a long silence, Ann gets crazy and asks him to tape her. Graham is shocked. No, no, it wouldn't be right. Ann is very eager. What wouldn't be right? Graham says: Because... you're not in your right mind.

"How do you know when I'm in my right mind or not?"

"Well, that's a good question."

Graham is a little embarrassed. Ann urges him, whispering: Do you have to prepare anything? Graham knows it would be hard to refuse, but his gaze urges her to be cautious. Ann whispers: Come on.

At night John comes home, sees that the door is open and Ann isn't home. Just as he's calling for her, she comes back. John cautiously asks her what happened. Ann bluntly says she wants a divorce. Why? You're asking why? Ann says: You're asking me why? John says: I'm your husband, of course I'm asking. Ann says: Get out, get the hell out!

John figures his secret has got out and says: Fine, but where were you just now? Ann says Graham's place. John is surprised. Graham's place? Ann is determined. Yes, Graham's place!

"Son of a bitch!" John flies into a rage. "This arsehole, claiming to be honest!"

Ann looks at John with disgust. John shouts sarcastically: Of course you didn't sleep with him. He's sure about this. But did you shoot a video with him? John's worried about this. Ann ignores him. John screams hoarsely: Speak! Did you film with him or not? Ann calmly says she did. John storms out to get even with Graham.

Graham is already asleep. John drags him up, punches him on his way outside and looks for Ann's video. In the video...

Graham says to Ann: "OK, I'll start. What do you want to talk about?"

Ann asks: "What do you usually talk about?"

Graham says: Sexual issues. OK, Ann says, then sexual issues. Graham asks: Do you often have sex? Ann says: No, not often. Graham asks: When you do, who initiates it? Him, Ann says. Then, Graham asks, do you feel satisfied? Ann says I don't know what you mean. Graham says: Have you ever orgasmed? Ann says she doesn't know. Ann says she doesn't know, so I don't think so. Graham asks: Apart from your husband, have you thought about sleeping with other men?

John bitterly thinks: Here it comes. He grits his teeth and keeps watching.

Ann hesitates a long time before answering the question. Graham says: Should I stop filming? Ann seems to wake up. No, no, don't stop. I want to film. Then, Graham asks again, have you thought about sleeping with other men? Ann says she has. Graham asks: Have you done it? Ann says no. Graham asks why. Ann says, because Cynthia is like that, and she'd hate to be like Cynthia. Graham asks: Then what kind of man have you thought about?

Ann looks at him for a long time: I thought about you.

Graham tries to look away, but Ann won't let him. "Have you thought about me too?"

Graham's eyes seem blurry. "Yes, I have."

What have you thought? I thought about what you're like when you climax. Ann laughs shyly. I'd also like to know. Ann asks: Can you do that to a woman? Graham doesn't answer. He looks sleepy or dreaming. A while later he says he can. Ann asks Graham if he can do it to her. Graham says he can't. Ann asks why. Graham says: Because I can't. Can't or don't want to? Don't want to, so I can't. You said you're not really impotent, right? Right. So you've had sex with other people? Of course. But it made you ashamed, right? No, that's not my problem. Then what is your problem? Unconsciously, Ann has become the one asking the questions.

"The problem is that, when the time comes, I feel like I have to lie," Graham says.

Ann says: Are you lying to me now? Graham says: No, not at all. Ann asks him: Then what else?

"It's just," Graham says, "at that time I can never express myself with words. But that makes me afraid people won't understand me, especially people who love me."

Ann says: So you stopped having sex? Graham says: No, I never thought of it. Ann says if you loved me would you do it? Graham says: No, I haven't fallen in love with you. Ann says: If you had fallen in love then? Graham says the question is pointless. Ann asks why. Graham says: Because I already said. Ann says: But I still don't understand.

"I'm not who I once was," Graham says. "I've changed too much. This makes it really hard for me to communicate with people. I even imagine talking to her and feel so afraid I can't..."

"Her? Who is she?" Ann supposes Graham's heart has been wrapped up in another relationship. "Is it Elizabeth?"

Graham is surprised. He's hardly understood himself. He smiles bitterly. "Probably."

Are you still in touch with her? No, I'm not. Ann says: What do you think Elizabeth would say about your videos? Ann says: She might not really understand, right? Ann continues: Since you hate lying, would you tell Elizabeth about this? Graham doesn't know: Maybe I could.

"Did you come back here to think about it?"

"No, it's because I want some resolution. Some kind of resolution. I hope someone who knows me so well can understand this."

Ann sighs and says it's unfair, coming back nine years later and expecting this resolution. Is this how you're going to keep going for the rest of your life? Ann looks at Graham, her gaze full of passion. What's the real reason, you can't tell me? Graham looks frustrated and helpless, trying to avoid the question. Ann suddenly has an idea, grabs the camera and focuses it on Graham. Answer me! Graham looks away and says: No, no, don't do this.

"Why, why do you tape women talking about sex? Tell me."

Graham avoids the camera. "What do you want me to tell you? My life story? From beginning to end? Unfortunately, even I don't know how I got this way. And also, why would I want to tell you?"

Because I might be able to help you, Ann says. Help me what? Help you resolve your issue. Graham says: Do I have an issue? Compared with you all, I'm living a very healthy life. This, Ann admits, is true. But, she says, you have an issue too. Graham says: But that's my problem. Ann says not necessarily, everyone who gets close to you comes into contact with this problem. Ann says: Me, for example. It is only a matter of time before I divorce John, but my determination now is largely thanks to you.

"Ugh, this is terrible." Graham shakes his head helplessly. "I spent nine years building a life that avoids this kind of thing."

Graham turns and looks into the distance through the window. Ann moves towards him, gently straightens his hair. Graham closes his eyes, allows it or accepts it. Ann caresses him and wants him to touch her too. Ann kisses Graham. Graham turns off the camera...

Only snow on screen. John is dazed, overwhelmed. None of it was what he expected.

John goes outside and sees Graham sitting there. Whether because he doesn't want to lie again, or out of revenge, John tells Graham that he slept with Elizabeth before she and Graham broke up.

After John leaves, Graham goes back inside and smashes all the tapes, then throws them in the bin...

85. End and Infinity

"It's over?" Ding Yi asked.

"You could say so," Qin Han said. "There's still a minute or so."

"What happens at the end?"

"Do you think what happens at the end is important?"

Ding Yi looks at the snow on the screen, like what John saw in the film. I know this guy didn't understand everything, but he clearly felt the film was unlike others.

He secretly asked me: *Seems interesting, you think?*

I thought: He has potential. And asked back: *Which part? Like where, what or how is it interesting?*

He picked up his glass and thought, then complained: "Who the hell cut off the ending?"

"Me, I did," Qin Han said. "You want to know it that bad? Fine, I'll tell you, Ann and Graham fall in love."

"And then?"

"Good question. Then – that's the end! So it's best to cut out those artificial things."

Ding Yi asked me secretly again: *Hey, what do you think?*

I said: *You two discuss it. I never thought there was an ending.*

What do you mean?

Literally.

You're saying everything is fundamentally a lie, there's no such thing as love?

Come on, what are you talking about? I just said you had potential. No ending means no love?

"E has basically the same opinion as you," Qin Han continued. "E also thinks it's better to keep that ending. Otherwise, she says people's lives are too absurd."

"Right!" Ding Yi said. "Would you say E wants to hold onto some hope?"

Great, great! Brother Ding, I've been with you so many years, and this is the soundest thing you've said.

Even Qin Han nodded, but he smiled and said: "But is there, hope?"

"Should be," Ding Yi answered vaguely.

I quickly chimed in: *Of course there must be! What can I say, if there wasn't hope why would I have bothered coming to your place?*

"Of course there must be?" Qin Han emphasised the 'must'.

"Or, there definitely is."

"OK, let's see. What do you hope for?"

"Like what does that film hope for?" *Forget it, Ding Yi. Just practise with him. I can't believe I really met my match today!* "I hope for no lies! At least at one point, at least at one opportunity, people can meet sincerely and bare their souls."

"Not bad. What you're saying sounds good, but I'm wondering, is it possible?"

"Can you not die? But you want to live!"

This question made Qin Han drink and drink. He was certainly unprepared for my interjection.

"Death." It was a long time before he eked out another sentence. "You afraid of it?"

Changing the subject, this guy's changing the subject! But it just shows I touched on the key point.

"What, you're not?" I'll say what I think. He's teaching a fish to swim and trying to beat him at his own game.

Qin Han shook his cup, looked at the red liquid rising and falling along the side, then slowly said: "What's scary about death? For example, everyone's a wave in the water. When the wave dies, the water's still there."

It seemed he'd already thought through this issue.

"And what then?" I asked.

He smiled. "Waves always make a disturbance, water always yields peace and happiness."

"Are you talking about water without waves?"

"I'm talking about eternity."

"Eternal, still water?"

He was taken aback again. "Ah, forget it, forget it. It's not something anyone can understand. The problem is you haven't been there."

I chuckled. *But you have?* "Where have you been?"

"How to put it?" Qin Han glanced at Ding Yi, meaning: Will you understand what I'm about to say? Then he sighed and said: "There, well, to put it finely, there is no pain or trouble, very relaxing. To put it crudely, it's whatever you want, complete freedom, no limits."

"Would you say it's infinite?"

"You could say so."

"But how can you reach infinity?" I asked Qin Han.

I asked further: "Once you arrive, isn't it finite again?"

I asked further: "Infinity means endless, doesn't it?"

His cup trembled slightly. "Yeah... or you could say it leads to infinity," he said.

"Where doesn't lead to infinity? Here, for example – doesn't it lead to infinity? Doesn't every place, time and space, angle and direction, all lead to infinity?"

He began to shake his glass again. There was a hint of surprise in his smile, but soon the smile concealed horror, and he tried to look impassive. "Ahem, forget it, let's not talk about this."

"Can't reveal the secret?" I kept on at him.

He craftily tried to shift the topic. "You still haven't told me what you hope for."

"OK, I'll tell you. You, Qin Han, right now, are my hope."

"How so?"

"Hope is a journey, not a destination."

"You're really stubborn. But I'll bet your hope is fundamentally hopeless."

"Hope is hope, how can it be hopeless? In fact, you mean it fundamentally can't be realised, right?"

"Right, it can't."

"Why can't it?" Ding Yi interjected. "If there is hope, if it is legitimate, how can it not be realised?" (Later I understood, because of Ding Yi's interjection, Qin Han was allowed to change the subject.)

"Sex, for example," Qin Han said. "Do you remember what Graham said? 'The problem is, when the time comes, I always feel I can't help but lie.'"

"I remember, why?"

"With sex as the bait for love, it is destined from beginning to end, to contain deception."

"Destined? Isn't that too certain?"

"Of course it's certain! Because sex has always been survival of the fittest. But what's love? What's it for? Have you thought about that?"

Well, he must be implying it's a symptom of the soul. (Of course I thought about it. For example, if I've always been inspired by prayer, that Ding's always been driven by desire.) It seemed this Qin Han would not be easy to deal with.

He put down his cup, paced back and forth, saying: "Anyone can say sex – sex, sex, sex! Actually sex and love are two different things, which is the cause of all tragedy. Sex is pure selection: selection of the beautiful, of the cool, the pretty, the healthy, the clever, the capable or the thoughtful, the ambitious, the accomplished... in short, advantaged groups. What does advantage mean? It means all kinds of strengths, it means possessing a lot!

Of course not only material things, there's also honour, reputation, power. All in all, advantage means power. People only know that money and power can be exchanged, but ignore the fact that reputation and power can be exchanged. All the advantages I listed can be traded for money and power. This era is dominated by power – where's the room for love?"

Ah, this Qin Han!

"But love, what's love?" he continued. "Love requires you to treat everything equally, all other people, all of God's creation. But when even people are treated like commodities, how can you do that? If you ask me, the things that kill wildlife, cause deforestation and overgrazing, deplete water supplies, make a hole in the ozone layer and so on are all attributes of one act, the act of power, the act of materialism – love is already gone!"

You must admit people really do change.

"Sex and love might as well be like fire and water. Are they compatible?"

"Then you're saying love is impossible?"

"If everyone emphasises sex!"

"Do you think people should become extinct?"

"Sorry, now you're attacking a straw man."

Shit, Brother Ding, your old classmate is impressive!

86. E

So, meeting E, chatting a bit, Ding Yi said: "You're brother's been cultivating himself so much these years he's practically a saint!"

E said: "Have you met his friend?"

"What, after all that, he has a girlfriend too?"

"How could he not?"

"He's practically a monk!"

"What makes you think so?"

"A sense, just a sense. I'm talking nonsense."

"Not all nonsense. But his friend doesn't have to be a girlfriend, right?"

"What do you mean?"

"What I said."

"Say it again."

"If you understand, keep it to yourself. If you don't, don't ask."

"Wow, really!" Ding Yi was stunned.

Those days a lot of things stunned us. First was the film, then was Qin Han's brilliant observations, now there was more breaking news.

"He didn't tell me."

"How would he tell you? Wait till he falls in love with you?"

"Really!" Ding Yi fell on the sofa and laughed. "Fall in love with me?" Ding Yi looked at his scruffy self in the mirror, laughed a while, was stunned a while. "You're not messing with me, E?"

His laugh infected E, and she couldn't help but laugh too. The two of them fell on the sofa and couldn't stop laughing. They laughed until they didn't know what they were laughing about, probably just the other's laughter.

I suddenly felt the return of a long-absent warmth. Two people unguardedly laughing together was such a distant thing! You'd probably have to go back to childhood, back to that snow-swept new year's day, back to when young Ding Yi broke away from his mother and ran naked into the snow, ran among those colourful girls.

"But, but," said E, finally controlling her laughter, "always suspecting others of cheating you is also a kind of lie."

Ding Yi finally stopped laughing and gradually restrained that feeling from developing.

"Don't ask him," E said.

"Come on, am I stupid?"

"No, no, he probably wouldn't care, just we don't ask each other about that stuff."

"Trust?"

"No, habit."

"Then how do you know?"

"As Qin Han would say, everything is just your own understanding or conjecture."

"Then is it true or not?"

"Well, as Ann said in that film, 'You know what's normal and what isn't normal?' Do you know what's true and what isn't true?"

"Does he know you think this?"

"We also don't explain ourselves to each other."

"Also habit?"

"Yeah."

"What has he been doing all these years?" Ding Yi asked.

"But I can actually understand that," E said, "even though I'm not."

"You're not, but you understand?"

"Is it impossible? It's possible, Ding Yi, I'm telling you it's possible. And it's very possible that kind of love is more sincere, more pure, even more noble."

"How?"

"Because it's extremely possible that kind of love relies completely on souls being close."

Right, souls don't have gender, souls are just other.

"Then why aren't you?"

"Habit. I thought about it a long time, and the conclusion was still habit."

Silence. The two seemed to have the chance to look at each other, to examine the marks time left on their faces.

But how can sex just be a habit?

E looked at Ding Yi, seeming to look for something, to wait for something or had already heard my voice in Ding Yi's silence.

"I don't know." Ding Yi had learned from me. "No, no, that should be language, expression, a special language or a necessary ceremony. How can it just be a habit?"

E was stunned for a little while or for a long time. Then she nearly jumped up. "Wow, that's amazing!"

I think at that time Ding Yi and E were like Graham and Ann in the film (when they were in the bar).

"Say it again." Her eyes were filled with expectation.

"Sex should be a kind of special language..."

"Wow! Really, really this is too amazing! I just never found those words.

Ceremony, expression, language... Wow, so amazing! Who said that?"

That Ding looked at E excitedly and just smiled shyly. Of course he knew who said it, but he didn't dare greedily claim credit.

E sat knee to knee with Ding Yi, not concealing the ease she felt after the surprise had passed, or the happiness, even closeness.

By now Ding Yi understood this Ding and this E's love was inevitable.

"But there's something I don't agree with Qin Han about," E said calmly, slowly. "Sex doesn't rely on physiological differences. *(Yeah, yeah, they just mark the body.)* Gay people really can't escape sex, they have different bodies. Different bodies, different sexes. When different souls seek each other, different paths expect to meet, we see original human nature. The importance of gender lies not in sex but in difference. *(Right, right, difference is the soul's situation.)* Or you could say people's fundamental gender is difference. Sex's fundamental meaning is difference..."

Wow, Eve, Eve! Could E be Eve?

"What's wrong?" E realised Ding Yi's breath was quickening.

"Nothing, go on."

"Actually the soul doesn't have sex, the soul is just other. *(My God, great minds think alike!)* As Cynthia said: 'I wanted to take it off. I wanted him to see me.' See what? Body? Who hasn't seen a body? The soul! What you want to see and what you want others to see is really the soul! Because the soul once separated me from you..."

Right, separating after floating on water, separating after leaving Eden was in the end the soul... Ah, there's no doubt Eve has arrived, Eve is already in Qin E! But when did she come?

"E, how long have you thought this?"

"A long time, a really long time."

Ding Yi asked me: *Was it during school? When E gave me that four-inch-wide red cloth, had Eve come? When we were constantly looking at other people, had Eve come?*

But of course, I said. *When the hooligan song started, Eve was still far away.*

E said: "Do you still remember what Graham said in the film? 'The problem is, when the time comes, I always feel I can't help but lie'?"

"Qin Han also asked me about that line."

"What'd he say."

"He said, if sex is bait for love it can't help but contain deception."

"Well, he might be going too far. Why does sex have to contain deception? You're right, it can also be expression! Why can't it be a more thorough, more sincere, more extreme declaration of love?"

"It's just I don't understand," Ding Yi said, "why Graham always has to lie at that time."

"Oh," E said, "I think if he feels he can't fully reveal himself, if he feels it's wrong to fully reveal himself, if he doesn't dare fully reveal himself during that extreme physical expression, won't he feel like he's lying? Put it this way: if during love, making love, you have to divide it up to get a grasp of the scale *(as in 'room skills')* and have to use some common sexual language *(like honesty and respect)*, so you tell me, otherwise how would it be like a lie?"

Ah, amazing! E is so amazing! Did Eve give you this wisdom?

"Did you notice another thing Graham said?" E went on. "'At that time, I can never rely on words to express myself.' Then what does he rely on? Do you know? Sex! Rely on the body, rely on exposure, rely on movement, rely on that language you can't speak during the day, what you can't usually say!"

Oh, is it that word, that extraordinary discourse!

"But if the words are misunderstood as dirty. If that happens and people have to hide, don't you think, you think it makes sense Graham would feel like he's lying?"

Right, right, that's lying, that is lying! Ding Yi was overjoyed and walked excitedly around E's place. Amazing E and amazing Eve, now Ding Yi can say what's good about that film, now we can finally understand that film! Not just understand. I'd say it's a great redress of grievances – the clouds parted, that always buried, desecrated extraordinary discourse can finally see the light of day, can be confident and good, proud and beautiful!

E leaned on the window, comfortably looking outside, looking at the nearby trees, faraway mountains and the sky beyond the mountains.

Ding Yi looked at her blankly, looked at her silhouette on the window, looked at the blue sky beyond her.

The sky was clear, deep. A white bird spread its wings. It flapped its wings gently and finally flew out of the window frame, across the early spring's sparseness and early summer's irritability to the lush, sunny, rainy summer season.

"So bright, the sun's so bright after the storm, the sky's so clear..." a voice named Pavarotti sang all over the world.

87. Doesn't Matter

The third time careless Ding Yi entered E's home, he noticed there was a frame on the desk containing a picture of a laughing girl.

"You were always this happy?"

"No, that's my daughter Asky."

"Asky?"

"She's always asking."

Ding Yi remembered Qin Han saying E had been married but was divorced.

"An illegitimate child," E said, while watching Ding Yi for a reaction.

"No one approved it, but God sent her anyway," E continued, seeming to want to stay on the topic.

"Why haven't I seen her?"

"Who?"

"Asky of course."

"Oh, she's at kindergarten."

The kid really looked like her mother, she'd soon look exactly like E did in middle school.

"How old?"

"Four."

Ah, was E like that when she was four? When E was four Eve was still far away, and I had just arrived in Ding Yi. Four was exactly when Ding Yi and I left the house, walked into the sun, walked among the wind and flowers, right? Exactly when we walked out of the yard, stood on the road outside the gate, because Ding Yi's wonderful naked sprout had been ridiculed by another person, right? At that time was the future already written? Or was it hiding in the little details, waiting for its opportunity? What was the detail that fate finally saw? Emotion like Ding Yi's? Or coldness like Asky's father's? Overall, if a detail is already chosen, the future is basically already written in the present. How is the rest written?

"Why don't you ask about Asky's father?" E finally said.

"Ah, doesn't matter."

"Doesn't matter?"

Ding Yi turned and looked at E, meaning: is this a problem?

But E pressed him. "Who doesn't it matter to?"

"Me, of course."

"I'm saying does it not matter to you that Asky has a father, or does Asky not matter to you?"

She also asked, does finding a partner not matter to you or does the fact that your partner has an ex-husband not matter?

Other people, what has happened in other people's pasts doesn't matter to me...

But you don't want to ask. Does not wanting to ask mean it doesn't matter?

Timid Ding Yi no longer listened to me. Cunning Ding Yi did not listen to me but spoke to E: "Why is it Asky? How could Asky not matter to us?"

"Us?" E stared at Ding Yi, holding the 'us' up to his face and comparing, confirming.

"Yeah, us." Ding Yi was also touched by the sudden appearance of this word.

E slowly turned, held the picture frame, looked, looked carefully, then hugged it to her chest.

Doesn't matter, I'm telling you nothing matters. Why? As long as E loves me, nothing else matters. The more you stress this, Brother Ding, the more I worry...

"Maybe," E said, "we should learn more about each other's past."

"Some other time, E. We have a lot of time."

88. Dream

That night Ding Yi had a lot of dreams. There was E, then the characters in that film, then the long-lost woman in the white dress.

The woman in the white dress suddenly looked like Ann and asked in the tone of the film: "What do you interview them about?"

Ding Yi couldn't help but mimic Graham's response: "Sexual issues."

"What sexual issues?"

"All kinds of sexual issues."

"For example?"

...

Ding Yi hesitated and the woman in the white dress turned into E. E asked: "So I can ask whatever I think of?"

"Of course."

"And you'll answer?"

"Of course."

"About anyone?"

"Of course. Ah, actually... about anyone?"

"No matter who. Anyone. Everyone. All other people..."

"All other people?"

"Yes. OK?"

...

Some time later the woman in the white dress looked blurry before melting into the vast night like before.

John's voice came from the darkness: "Did you sign a document with him, to make sure he can't show it?"

Then Cynthia's voice: "Sorry, I didn't."

Then John's voice again: "Then you're in big trouble, you have no legal guarantee."

Then Cynthia's voice again: "Impossible, I believe him! I wanted him to see me..."

Then Ann's voice: "Are you crazy? He can show it to all his horny friends."

Cynthia's voice: "No, he won't."

Ann's voice: "You don't even know him!"

Cynthia's voice: "I feel like I do know him."

...

"No, no, I don't know, I don't know!" Ding Yi shouted as he awoke.

The night was dark. I tried to comfort him: *It's OK, it's OK, you haven't told E anything.*

Ding Yi's breath gradually slowed down. But I soon reminded him: *You can't not tell E though, you can't not tell Eve, because you can't be even the slightest bit dishonest with them!*

Ding Yi looked at the darkness, looked at the long night. *Yeah, I know.*

What do you know?

Eden's covenant.

If not, do you know what will happen?

If not, Eve will leave E, and Eve will enter someone else.

Good, good. After many summers had passed, this Ding Yi was no longer that Ding Yi!

So the woman in the white dress appeared again, looking and sounding just like E. "So why are you willing to tell me?"

"Because," Ding Yi said, "because you said the soul once separated me from you."

E smiled. "Then can you tell me when you first encountered a woman's body?"

"Fifteen."

"Who was she?"

"Lingling."

"Was Lingling also fifteen?"

"No, she was nineteen or twenty."

"What was it like? Or how did it start?"

"I just wanted to see her, wanted to really... really see her."

"Had you never seen her?"

"I don't know. I don't know if, when other people weren't around... what she would be like. Because during the day, or normally, when you can see her she's always so proud and elegant, and she... when she sat down she always wrapped herself tightly in her skirt..."

"Why's that matter?"

"It... it doesn't matter. But, but it always seemed like there were other people between us, there was always just... just other people."

"So you didn't want her to see you too?"

"Oh no, no, no!"

"Why's that?"

"Because, because Lingling, she would... would look down on me."

"Look down on you? Look down on what about you?"

"Maybe, maybe I'm too young, still not as grown up as her..."

Evasive, Ding Yi, you're still being evasive! I reminded him. Do you really want to lie now? You want to lie to E? Frankly, brother, you were afraid of Lingling looking down on you because you were still named Ding Er!

That Ding's face suddenly heated up.

Right, Ding Er, a cook's son, fifteen years old, maybe not yet fifteen, that summer, one night that summer, before the year that hooligan song was sung, this Ding had already misbehaved. Thank God luck prevented others from finding out, otherwise the hooligan song would have reverberated through Ding Yi's spring. That thing, which had been gathering dust in Ding Yi's heart for years, had almost been forgotten. But I couldn't forget. That memory was hidden in an unspeakable corner and closely guarded thus far. It was closely guarded because the memory was not only considered dirty, crude and ugly... but it was also inescapable. Or because daytime had never been its place. During the day that desire lost its voice. Or also because, no matter how the feeling was shouted, it would die in the boundless dark. Now Graham had touched it. Now Ann understood it. Now E had given him permission and was looking forward to him telling her about it.

That woman in the white dress, Lingling, since I came to Ding Yi, lived with us on the same street, but really Ding Yi was still too young to find this woman. Only when the spring breeze suddenly picked up, suffusing Ding Yi (after a morning on summer holiday) did we discover Lingling's beauty. When young Lingling proudly walked up to us, standing straight, what strongly attracted Ding Yi's attention? Oh, how did her plump chest, waist and hips suddenly become magical? When mature Lingling elegantly, fragrantly passed by us, what made that Ding's soul restless? Oh, gentle gait, bright eyes, every frown and smile full of style! During that short period Ding Yi really liked to play in the street. "Mum, I'm going to go out and play a bit." "With who?" By the time his mum had turned to look, that guy was already gone without a trace. Of course many times his mum found out he was just standing in the street, zoned out. His mum didn't know what he was doing, but I knew: he was waiting for Lingling. Lingling didn't know how he felt, but I knew: if he could just see Lingling, see her once, the day would be a holiday or his dreams would be wonderful.

Ding Yi looked at Lingling's curvy body, but Lingling didn't pay him any attention. Gait gentle, eyes bright, Lingling walked about, then returned home. Ding Yi kept watching, watched the entrance to her house, watched her window, watched the light outside her window. It got dark. Night came. Ding Yi was still watching her, watching Lingling's elegance and arrogance, watching Lingling's fluttering plain white dress, until he began dreaming...

I already said above, because of rediscovering Lingling, Ding Yi regarded the name 'Ding Er' as too crass. Longing for Lingling day and night intensified that feeling, and finally Ding Yi decided to change his name.

But before he could, a summer night came upon him. Below a moonless, starry sky, in an empty little yard, under a blooming sweet olive tree, the night unexpectedly arrived. In waves of the sweet olive tree's fragrance, fifteen-year-old Ding Yi saw the plain white dress glow like neon, saw the floating snow white spread over the dewy grass... What was going on that night? Lingling allowed him to stroke her dress, Lingling allowed his hand to run over the white dress around her body. Ding Er couldn't help but surge with desire: what else will she let me do? But I shouted at him: *Hey! What are you doing?* He quickly pulled his hand away... but in the light of fireflies and the dazzling stars he listened and saw that Lingling wasn't angry at all, so he reached out for her again, reached towards the tempting slopes, the scorching warmth... Lingling's breath seemed to quicken, but she didn't stop him... It was I who stopped him: *Hey, Ding Er! What's wrong with you, are you really this kind of person?* He pulled his hands back again... But the smell of the sweet olive was intoxicating, seeming to pull people's souls from their shells; the silence of the charming night seemed to prevent me from interfering, so that Ding finally got rid of me and reached towards Lingling's open place... Either she had been expecting it or she already heard – young Ding Yi's sprout quietly rose, opened. But Lingling didn't make a sound... until he touched her delicate underwear, until his shaky fingers tried to grip the edge of the silk fabric, only then did Lingling resist him, sit up, in the dance of fireflies and stars re-fasten her dress as if to ask from the depths of the silent night: You're still so young but already this bad?

"And you?" E asked Ding Yi. "What'd you say?"

That Ding was thinking back when Cynthia jumped in to answer for him: "He avoided me all that summer, then moved. Terrible!"

E asked Ding Yi: "So you really never saw her?"

Ding Yi nodded, as if he still regretted it.

"No, no, no," I said. "I saw."

"Saw what?"

"Lingling is missing other people too. Arrogant people like Lingling are the same, they still seek others."

89. Dreams and Drama

Ding Yi told E about this dream, told her all about these dreams we've had since childhood.

She said unexpectedly: "Really, it seems like you could do drama."

"Drama? Me?"

"Drama, you!"
"You think so?"
"I think so."

Really, I also always felt Ding Yi was cut out for that. I always felt drama was the only thing he could do well. He'd shown talent in that area since he was a boy.

"How can you tell I can do it?"
"Because you can dream."
"Ha, anyone can dream!"
"Not necessarily."
"But I can't do anything else."

E said: "If you can do everything but can't dream, you're blind."

E said: "Twenty-four hours every day in reality, three hundred and sixty-five days a year in reality, all twenty thousand days of your life without dreaming, never seeing the flaws in reality, tell me, can such a person understand drama?"

E means drama is actually dreaming! A lot of people do drama their whole lives without understanding this, they spend their whole life imitating reality, boasting about how similar they are. Similar to what? To reality? To the avenue? To the office? To the venue? To the party? To the bathhouse? To the breeders? E is asking if reality has a use for you imitating it. Fundamentally, reality pays no attention to you. If you want to be similar or not, reality goes its own way without a thought for you. But if reality doesn't care about human preferences, E asks, why would we care to imitate it? Isn't it OK not to be like someone else? Can't we be like ourselves, be like the self we wish to be in our heart?

E asked Ding Yi: "Do you remember what Ann asked Graham during their interview and how Graham answered?"

Ding Yi imitated Graham's voice. "It all has to do with sexual issues."
"What sexual issues?"
"All kinds of sexual issues."
"For example?"
"What they've done, what they want but won't say..."

E said: Good, won't say, why? What is it they really want? Won't say, because of the threat of reality! What they want is to escape reality's threat. In this case, E said, why not just get what you want? E asked why we have to compliment reality, obey reality. Reality, why should we have to like you? I'm tired of you, I'm sick of you, I hate you, OK? I don't want to be like you any more, I don't want to follow you any more, and you have no reason to chase me. Is that OK? OK, then there will be dreams, there will be drama, drama will break through reality, drama will expand reality. Where will it expand to, you ask? I'll tell you, E said. Expand to without bounds!

"So I'm telling you, drama is always outside reality."

"Or you could say what drama asks is outside reality."

I said: "But doesn't this mean that drama is always in reality?"

"OK, well said, in reality," E said. "In reality and longing to be outside reality, so drama really is dreaming, it really isn't reality."

"Not reality," Ding Yi said, "but wanting to be realised, right?"

"OK." E and I both applauded simple Ding Yi. "That's drama!"

"But is reality possible?" Ding Yi remembered again what Qin Han had said.

"How could it not be? For example, Lingling can't love you, but this doesn't affect your love, your love for her has already been realised."

"Realised? How did I not know?" That Ding stared with eyes open, foolishly.

Ahem, oh, Ding Yi, one moment understanding, the next moment confused. What E means is, have you loved Lingling or not? I have. OK, having loved is the realisation of love!

"Oh..." That Ding smiled stupidly, enlightened.

E smiled too. "You've loved her, and you haven't been loved – two different things."

"Drama's the same," I said. "Realisation and reality are two different things."

"OK!" E and that Ding high-fived.

She said that's why people thought of a way to make the impossible possible, to make the unrealistic realised, like drama, like dance, like lamplight. E said: What do the theatre and stage delineate? They delineate a free area. What do stage lights illuminate? They illuminate a kind of time. In this kind of time the soul doesn't care what reality wants, it just cares about the possibilities outside reality, what they're like.

I said: "And how they are not."

Ding Yi said: "And caring about what they're like or not!"

O-K!

When Ding Yi said goodbye to E that day, on his way home with me, that beautiful children's song burst forth from the sun again.

"Ah come, sweet May, dress the trees in green, take us to the creek, and let us see the violets blooming..."

We couldn't help but join in: "Ah come, sweet May, hurry and bring the violets..." Then we marched to the beat, walked and sang: "We hope so much to see the violets again, ah come, sweet May, let us go play..." Gradually the pitch rose and we sang happily, carefree. "Ah, May, May, sweet May... let us go to the creek and see the violets bloom."

The people on the street must have thought we were crazy.

90. Call and Song

We kept singing all the way. In Ding Yi's recollection we walked from the afternoon till late at night, while my impression is that we never stopped from late at night until dawn... Singing about May, singing about the violets, we went from one part of the city to another, from one part of the mountains to another, to the winged dawn, to beyond the winged dawn, from now until forever...

People, why do they want to sing? In the beginning, how did people think of singing? To act? To celebrate? To sell, for box office rankings? Obviously not. That can't be why. On the path from Eden to now, while looking at others and searching for Eve, on that solitary, lonely and nerve-racking journey, who are you performing for? Who are you selling to? What are you celebrating? No, that's a call, a path's call.

A call in the heart.

Searching is a call, and loneliness is too. Anxiety is a call, being solitary more so. That mountain, that winged dawn, that horizon, the endless road and endless dreams are all a call.

Since ancient times, folk songs have all been love songs.

Since ancient times, love songs have all been Adam and Eve's wishes – where are you, my sweetheart!

This human body is narrow, constrained. These two eyes are blurry, confused. Only a call can open up this narrow body, only singing can spread like flight – travel with the sky, travel with faith, let the sweetheart in some faraway place hear.

So people sing.

That's why tigers and lions roar, swallows and warblers chirp, apes and wolves howl, horses and deer neigh... are they all spirits trying to open the body, to meet a faraway partner? That's also why wind and rain call, lightning and thunder rumble... The four seasons sing in turn of love's desires and love's harvest.

Right, right, that's why people sing. It's simply not to perform or celebrate and it can't be for the box office. It's a call, even a call for help, man – the song of the soul hitting the walls of its bodily prison.

91. Note: Spring and Rocks For Example

"For example, a young musician plays day and night, calling, even screaming. Why? Because of spring, the soul is still young, and the life force is still like a surging flood – the young soul is imprisoned by the powerful body, the simple soul is blinded by the luxurious body, the hoarse soul is buried by the turbulent body...

Every thing grows, everywhere is the same. At that time the earth wore a costume, the once dead space suddenly surged with energy, the soul was suppressed and breathless, desire was endlessly stimulated. I would say that deafening rock is not for you to listen to but to look at. The soul's hearing is far-reaching and will have to wait until later, wait till autumn. Now the young singers are dazzled, want you to look. Look how strong this young body is, look at the brilliant shape of this beauty, look at the unstoppability of this invisible instinct, look at this talent's gift expressing this splendid spring light. The young singer painted himself anew, shone bizarrely, saying: Look – me!

But where am I? Who am I?

What happened to me? What will happen to me later?

How will I be in the end?

Don't ask this now, this is taboo in spring. Though it's only the weak whisper of a buried soul, it's a threat to spring, an offence. Spring ignores this kind of question. And autumn is still far off – this is spring's good news, spring's encouragement, spring breeze's most enjoyable compliment.

So you see that young singer, sings on the riverbank, on the roadside, in the raucous square, in the gloomy bar, singing from dusk to dawn. The singing ranges from melancholy to happy, from dry to lush, from lonely to madly (but sincerely)... A final breast thumping, excessive grieving, string breaking and microphone tapping (not ostentatiously); eyes burning; voice hoarse and throat roaring like a storm. With colourful feathers like antiquity, they use naked flesh to mark modernity (if it's ostentatious, the spring breeze can tell), use arrogance then obsequiousness, use howls then solicitation, use filth and ugliness to show loneliness, to show difference... Until you recognise the helplessness of a caged beast (but definitely not fake)! But what is really trapped in the cage? Actually spring already saw, already sensed it: me, me and my loneliness.

How will I be?

Where will I go?

Huh, you can see me? I can enter you?

That helplessness makes it impossible for people to stand idly by. But there are only idle bystanders. But listen slowly, you can understand, really it's that weak soul growing up, desiring, searching, trying to open up the body's walls; the young singers are always calling for love. From dusk till dawn, always calling out: love. From ancient times till now, spring has always been like this. Caged in a tangible body, an intangible instinct, a talented gift is nothing but a solitary soul. The solitary soul secretly whispers, there's still not enough power." – **Shi Tiesheng, Rock and Writing for Example**

92. Quotation: Again Like the Spring Through the Summer, and Like Wandering

"So, young lovers are wandering in all directions.

Their hearts are wandering.

In spring, all hearts wander, no matter where people are.

At riverbanks, on bridges, in boring homes and among unintelligible texts. In the affectedly elegant frames of solitary galleries. In the faint thunder of the clouds or the helpless silence of the sun. On the bustling streets, the one who looks most confused.

In the hopeful evening after the empty afternoon, the one hurries between countless lights, eagerly looking around beneath the stars, sprinkling gazes in all train stations, walking past streetlight after streetlight. Counting twelve hours and stepping on her own shadow, which stretches then shortens, stretches then shortens, the one passes by shops as they shutter one by one. Where have you gone? You arsehole!

(You, my destined love! Love songs have been sung like this since ancient times.)

Misty rain on the side street. Misty rain on the window. Misty rain mixed with the sound of music.

Even deep into the night.

The spring breeze never sleeps. An increasingly plump girl. A maturing boy. But ferociously powerful, exuberantly energetic, talent overflowing. Morning sun shines the whole day through. They mess with the police, lie to their parents, ask the teacher unanswerable questions and watch people fighting on the street and justly score each side. Conning their way into stadiums with all their own props, out-and-out football hooligans. They may send lost children home and say to their parents sullenly: "You ask me who I am? What's this got to do with you?" Or they may help up an old man who fell on the roadside, carry him home and say unreservedly to his son. "You're giving me a cash reward? How about a million, so I'll make a fortune, bro."

A flock of white pigeons fly by, melodious.

A flock of colourfully dressed boys and girls are frolicking crazily.

Pigeons coo between sunlit buildings. Boys and girls cycle and run on the streets.

Every year is like this, in the air and on the land.

Reposing with his eyes closed in the sun, the old man knows all about boys and girls.

An increasingly plump girl, a maturing boy – wandering singers or lovers – stand nestled in the heavy rain, silently embracing in the heavy snow.

Spring in the heavy rain and snow. Summer approaches in the heavy rain and snow.

The old man hides in the house. The old man sits in front of the window. This world both excites and disappoints him: we had so many rules in the past, but look at these young people now!

Old taboos are gone.

But are they really gone?

Kissing, hugging, caressing, bathing stark naked in the sunlight, screaming in the moonlight, again and again, moaning and trembling, forceful and gentle, excited yet paralysed...

The body no longer has restricted areas, the forbidden fruit is no longer there.

If the fruit is gone because of freedom – "What can I offer you, my sweetheart?"

The spring breeze swells, the torrential summer rain penetrates everything. But the flesh is a boundary, where else can you enter, where else can you enter? The flesh is a boundary so there is helplessness again and again. Again and again that boundary is clearer.

The flesh is a boundary, you and I are two cages.

If the forbidden fruit has already been released by the flesh – "What can I offer you, my sweetheart?"

All vocabulary has dried up. All movement has withered. All entrances lead to absurdity.

The increasingly plump girl and the maturing boy face each other. But – Where are you, my sweetheart!

The sound echoes in the mountains.

From spring to summer the mountains resound with the madness of rock and roll, and everywhere are hoarse singing voices." – **Shi Tiesheng, *Rock and Writing for Example***

93. Asky

Now it's autumn again. My fifty-fourth autumn in Shi Tiesheng.

These days the sky is high, the clouds are far away and autumn is getting stronger. These days, as soon as I sit at the table, aided by computer memory, I recall *My Travels in Ding Yi*. Bursts of melodious and sparkling piano music float in the autumn sun.

It's Schumann's *Scenes from Childhood*. Played now smoothly, now stumblingly. A mother and daughter appear before me. The aspiring young mother is urging the girl to learn how to play piano, but the girl was impatient, her small fingers fumbling the keys with perfunctory effort... "No, try again!" "Now, I did it!" "Oh man, you had it and now you forgot!" Of course it could be a father and son, father and daughter, or a teacher and student, but my eyes can never resist the image of a mother and daughter.

Because E was once that way. E and Asky were both like that.

One autumn day, one Sunday morning, when Ding Yi and I went into E's place, E smiled at us and indicated for Ding Yi to find a place to sit. E stood still by the piano, fixing her eyes on Asky's fingers, her heart keeping time with the beat. Asky stole a look at Ding Yi and seemed happy to be rescued. But E took a step and blocked her line of sight. "No, no, again!" The girl buried her head once more and played the boring étude again and again – that song is called *Scenes from Childhood*, right? I thought Asky would definitely remember her childhood when hearing this piece as a grown-up. Again and again, again and again, that étude seemed endless. E seemed to have forgotten about Ding Yi, forgotten about herself and *Scenes from Childhood.*

Ding Yi finally couldn't help but ask: "You torture kids like this too?"

E looked up at Ding Yi for a while.

The étude finally stopped.

"OK Asky, that's all for today."

Asky was finally free, and she ran off to the yard without giving us a second look.

E straightened up the room, organised Asky's toys, then mopped the floor, did the dishes, boiled water... ignoring Ding Yi.

I said: *Ding Yi, you idiot, give her some help.*

Ding Yi hurried to the kitchen. "Can I help?"

"Listen," E said, "Asky is not like other children."

"Not like who?"

"Asky must be more capable than other children."

"Why?"

"Because... because I don't have a certificate."

"What's that got to do with Asky?"

"Think about it."

Ding Yi looked at me, puzzled. *What does she mean?*

You don't know?

Because Asky is illegitimate?

Don't use that ugly word, OK?

What's wrong with illegitimate? Are you legitimate? Blessed by authorities?

I said: *Don't be hypocritical. What happened to Ding Er? Why did he change name?*

Ding Yi didn't answer. Mention of this deflated him.

E walked over, sat and said: "Asky still doesn't have any *hukou* [residency permit]."

"*Hukou's* bullshit!"

"But she has to go to school soon."

"She can't stay away from that crap school?"

E didn't answer. She just looked at us, her face turning into a sneer – sneering at Ding Yi? Sneering at herself? Or sneering at the whole world?

The autumn light softly entered the room, all the shadows that moved with it seemed lost in memory. Far away, on the horizon, a place so far away it seemed abstract, some highly subtle commotion was brewing – the autumn wind was departing.

After a long time E finally asked herself a question and answered it: "Why? Because this isn't drama, it's reality."

Then we went to the window and looked at Asky in the yard. Asky was playing happily with a group of boys. She was covered in sweat and dirt.

"Maybe I'm a bit regretful," E said. "Sometimes I feel I'm a bit regretful."

"About what?"
"Maybe she shouldn't have come."
"You mean Asky?"
"Maybe I shouldn't have had her."
"Then you," I said, "should have come?"
"That's out of my control."
"And she is in your control?"
"I could have kept her from coming."
"You came, so you can keep her from coming."
"No, I came, so I know she couldn't come!"
"If you hadn't come, could you know if you should have come or not?"
"What do you mean?"
"Only after someone has come can they think about whether they should have come or not. Put it another way – people only ask whether they should have come because they already did."

E's eyes widened. She looked through Ding Yi and straight at me.

"You have no right to keep someone from coming. You have no ability to decide who should and shouldn't come. You aren't even qualified to consider the question. Because everyone who can ask this has already left Eden..."

E's wide eyes kept looking right at me.

"Asky came from there too. Asky certainly came from there. Or a little girl who certainly came from there happened to be named Asky."

E's wide eyes slowly revealed news of Eve.

"You, me, her and everyone are the result of that separation, are all the path following that departure..."

Not even Ding Yi expected he could have uttered these words. Then he looked at his own image in the glass window, seeming to ask me: What do you say, brother, am I right? But I couldn't pay him any attention. Because I felt Eve fresh in E's gaze. Because I heard Eve restless in E's body. Because I saw Eve had finally discovered me, discovered me waiting for her in Ding Yi for many years.

But I never thought she would actually be so brave – E suddenly hugged Ding Yi.

I never thought she would actually be so passionate – E said in Ding Yi's ear: "You can't leave, from now on you can't leave me..." I never thought she would actually be so crazy – E put her head on Ding Yi's chest and said: "Yes, you can't run, you're under arrest..." I never thought she would actually be so magnanimous, even unconventional – E saw in Ding Yi's eyes that bird in the sky. "Do you still remember what Cynthia said? 'I want him to see me!'"

Ding Yi panicked and said: "Hey, Asky's coming back."

"That's good, she can see what kind of dad she should have."

"Don't, not now, really, Asky will be back soon."

"OK, then let her see how a real man loves his woman."
Asky kicked the door open with a bang.
E jumped up.
Asky rushed in like the wind.

E straightened her hair and dress, gave Ding Yi a smile that seemed to say: Right, this is still reality.

Asky rushed up to E and hurried to tell her some happy news: "Mum, Xiaolang's family's dog just had three puppies, why'd you just have me? Mum, Feifei's family's Dot flew back, it flew all the way back from faraway on its own. Feifei's dad said pigeons can find their way home from the other side of the earth. Mum, I saw ants moving! A long line of ants, so long, so long, so long, each one holding a baby. Mum, if ants are black, why are their babies white?"

E tried to respond, tried to be thorough.

"Why don't you have some water, Asky – want some?"

The girl nodded but quickly added: "I want to pee."

E went and opened the bathroom door. "Come, you want to pee, right?"

But Asky was already peeing, standing up, looking both proud and surprised.

E strode over. "What's wrong with you, you forgot how to use the toilet?"

"Yao Yuan stands to pee. Big Head too."

"Gosh." E was embarrassed.

Ding Yi didn't understand. "She said who?"

"She got it from the boys!"

Ding Yi laughed hard.

Asky looked at Ding Yi laughing and laughed with him, but didn't really understand why, so she asked her mother: "Mum, do you have a little pee pee?"

94. Night Drama

Night is a gifted stage.

Night cut off from day, cut off from noise, so drama's desires sprout.

The roles are fixed in limited space-time, while the heart and soul open to limitless dreams.

Night's drama and day's drama run in opposite directions. For example, when day is putting on makeup, night is removing it. For example, when day's drama wants you to play someone else, night's role is just played by 'I'. For example, if day's drama wants you to disappear into an established role, night's drama is just the opposite, it wants you to step out of the crowd.

For example, a piano lid reflects the moonlight.

For example, a turbulent ray of white suddenly flashes in that moonlight.

For example, E walks to the side of the piano.

The night grows even quieter. The moonlight grows even more distant. Then naked Ding Yi and naked E look at each other. The world shrinks, as if in that quiet distance the path of the past could be seen, that ancient call or song could be heard...

"The forbidden fruit has already been lost to freedom. 'What can I offer you, my sweetheart?'

The forbidden fruit has already been released by flesh. 'What can I offer you, my sweetheart?'

Flesh is a border, you and I are two cages."

So naked Ding Yi and naked E look at each other for a long time, expecting the possibilities of the gifted stage, seeing naked clothing is still there, hearing whether that wandering call has arrived at the night's song.

"Young lovers or old singers, looking at the horizon, looking through the autumn rain.

Looking through that boundary of flesh. Then...

Then the soul leaves the body, the gaze fades into the distance."

Only this way do they slowly approach and realise what that ancient song has always been calling is tonight...

"So the soul comes to the fore, desires become dreams.

Instinct, tempered into a festival of love – sex, receives heaven's gift.

Be they ageing lovers or dying singers, they explore each other, comfort each other.

Free.

Trembling hands seem to check for the forgotten secret language.

Withered bodies, like finding some long-forgotten receipt.

Where have you been all these years?

The mountains echo again, spring's call is finally answered:

I am the secret language you forgot.

You are my lost credentials."

Then, all that follows is madness.

As Graham said: "At such times I always feel like I can't use language to express my feelings."

As Cynthia said: "I wanted him to see me!"

As E asked: "What are you looking at me for? Who hasn't seen a body?"

Right, I want you to see my secret, see my desire, see my hidden wishes... See the vigilance this body has given up, see the isolation this heart has interrupted... Oh, right, right, this is what Eve and I have been looking forward to.

For example, what Graham often asked: "What's the thing you want but don't dare say?"

But also like John's warning: "Did you sign any documents with him? Do you have legal protection?"

But Cynthia answered: "No, I trust him."

Though Ann still worried: "You don't even know him!"
But Cynthia disagreed: "I feel like I know him!"
And as Graham said: "Only people you have a physical relationship with can really give you good advice."
Or like E and Ding Yi naked and mad: "Only this way, only this way can the world's lies be snuffed out."
So it's like Ann confessing frankly in the end: "Have you thought of me? Can you make a woman happy?"
From that shaking Ding Yi, I answered: "I can, E! Of course I can!"
"What'd you say?" Eve asked from panting E.
"I said yes! I said I can. I said is this the ending that Qin Han erased?"
"What ending?"
"I'm saying," Ding Yi said, lowering his voice, into E's ear, "this must be the end of that film, the ending it should have."
...
But in Ding Yi's memory or in my desire, this kind of night would always happen – or would never happen – would have an ending. Just let him/her rise and ebb, each wave higher than the last; just let him/her rage rapidly, one tightly wound around the other; just let his/her inspiration pile up, brilliant and colourful; and just let him/her come out of the rolling mountains to see the sunlit flowers among the shadowed willows...
Eventually the storm calms, eventually the faraway moon rises high, eventually E slowly gets up and walks to the window... Right at that moment, to my surprise, that Ding breathlessly blurted out a comment worthy of a timeless masterpiece:
"E, your bum is so big!"
E quickly turned and stood still, looking at him, surprised, ashamed, but also maybe overjoyed.
Inspired, Ding Yi shouted: "E, you amazing – woman! How can you have such an amazing – bum!"
His erotic compliment reverberated freely throughout the sky, throughout heaven... Then that amazing woman – E and Eve – was deeply moved by the mad reverberation, smiled, twisted, tried to make the plumpness more prominent, make the hidden part more open...
Then Ding Yi and I screamed together: "E, were you always like this – always, before, after, E, where have you hidden your precious gems..."
E's steps gradually staggered... E's gaze gradually blurred... Eve gave her best through E's flesh, bringing that gifted language into the fullest play possible, pouring all the hope and sadness since Eden into this amorous moonlit night, and dedicating Eve's lifelong wishes and secrets to this enjoyable bedtime.
Our screaming became a whisper, became dreamy: "E, you amazing woman, you fox, you shameless woman, you turned out to be this eager, this emotional, this desirous... So are you, were you and will you be

like this? But you hid it so well, you faked it so well! How is it, when I gazed at all those wonderful women, I didn't see you? How is it, when I stared at all those elegant or glamorous women, I didn't find you? Ah, but look at you now – dignified and naked E, elegant and unbridled Eve! I've travelled a thousand miles from Eden, all to look for you. Today you came, it's wonderful that you came... but do you still remember your usual way? Elegant enough to make others admire, dignified enough to make others feel unworthy, noble enough to make others afraid to approach... Could you still be elegant and dignified like that, please? Could you be as restrained as you are in front of others, please? But don't hide your real body again, don't bury your true soul again, don't wear that plain white dress again or that naked clothing..."

So being in the moonlight was like being on stage, naked Eve stepped lightly, walked slowly... So the still dark night was like the clamorous day, naked E gazed and stared, no one else around...

"Right, right, just like this!" Ding Yi and I murmured like a behind-the-scenes narration. "This way I won't fail to recognise you. This way I won't be unable to find you. This way the world will be without the noble and lowly, be without me, you and them, be without overlooked chefs and their sons, be without hooligans..."

The moon shadows shifted, soft, graceful footsteps gradually became dance steps... E and Eve danced like a child, like in Eden, without reservation, extending and flexing, stretching, opening and exposing... The moonlight stroked her expansive bum, illuminated her dark gully, shone on the crucial language or token from Eden...

But what is the dance?

If singing is the soul's call, I thought, what is the dance?

Its expectation has really been deeper than singing! That's not just me calling you, you calling others, more than just us calling each other, it's us calling God together! Calling, and looking up, at the same time letting heaven see you and me – see the limited body's infinite expression, see the imprisoned spirit's unyielding walk and talk, see this twisting waist, see this waving body, see this tapping step, flowing hair and swaying tears... See the lonely sky lend its finishing touch, see desire spread into constant love, or how E and Ding Yi express gratitude for the reunion of Adam and Eve... Yes, yes, that's what dance is! The original meaning of dance has never been to flatter the rich and powerful, nor to entertain people, not to pass the time, not even just you and I to watch each other, it's a call to heaven, truly. Look, you, heaven! Does this seem OK? Does this seem good enough? You see this panting groveller, shouting hump, leaping spirits and trembling hooligan, this wind, this rain, this lightning and thunder, these peaks and gullies... Do these concave and convex flowers keep your promise? Does this talented language speak your heart's desire?

Ah, that amazing night! That mad night, that night of shamelessness or of abandoning shame, that night of unconventional or unrestrained praise. With the moon above and the wind near, people are willing to be hooligans and sluts on such a night.

Then E stopped dancing. Maybe she was tired. She hit the floor with a thump, face full of tears, tears of joy.

Ding Yi took me to the farthest corner of the room, looking at her stupidly.

Later she stood up, walked to the piano and sat silently for a while.

The piano sounded.

The piano sounding, the moonlight gently shone on her neck and shoulders as a melody was being played, the darkness filled with desire to embrace E's waist, the night breeze like an ancient dreamland, gathering at E's fingertips and heart...

The sound of the piano was gentle and profound. E must have known, since separating at Eden, how long Ding Yi's eyes had been looking... The sound of the piano went from profound to playful. Eve must have known, during blinding springs, that sensitive Ding Yi's flower experienced much absurdity... The sound of the piano grew solemn, presumably Eve was sure: Adam came to Ding Yi from Eden, the celebration I guarded for her so many years is here... The sound of the piano became more rushed, became smooth. Yes, God must have promised: you must say those extraordinary human words for him/her, and Eden's parting covenant has reached the moment of fulfilment...

But the sound of the piano suddenly hesitated.

What's wrong, Eve? What's wrong, E? Ah, of course I remember those faraway mountains, nearby trees, remember the winged dawn beyond the mountains... Of course I still remember rushing in the sea of people, searching... Of course I still remember those varied dreams, waking up among countless others, countless days...

The sound of the piano gradually became serene, returned to *Scenes from Childhood*. Returned to when Ding Yi was awarded the four-inch-wide red cloth: Eve, have you always been in proud E? Returned to the approach of that terrible child: E, when I carried that football used only for flattery on my way home were you close by? Returning to the summer night imbued with the smell of sweet olive: Eve, were you in that dignified yet melancholy Lingling? Did you also hold your dress close to yourself like her while always seeing us as other people and saying those heartless words in the dancing light of fireflies and stars? It returned to a more distant summer evening when Ding found it hard to tear himself away from a young woman with whom he had had a good time: E, if I had waited for you the next day under the big tree, would you have not come back like her?

The sound of the piano stopped abruptly.

"Yes, I would." It was my recollection that E shouted like this and jumped away from the piano.

"Yes, I would, I would, Ding Yi." It was my recollection that E shouted like this and rushed into Ding Yi's arms.

"How could I not come back? Look at me, look at me, I'm right here!" As E hurried toward us, Ding Yi remembered how she shouted. "Look at me, I want you to look at me, I want you to always look at me like this. With all your enthusiasm, with all your greedy desire, look all over my body, look into my heart." It was my impression that E shouted like this, murmured like this, through the moonlight, through the darkness, through the past and others, towards me until her hot secret neared Ding Yi's hot mouth and tongue...

Then I flew out of Ding Yi again. Like the big, white bird in the night sky, cheerful, flying freely, neither empty nor panicked... Because just below, in this temporarily silent but ultimately bustling world, there is E's tenderness! Because just below, in this vast sea of others, Eve has already arrived... So I was in no hurry to return. Because nearby E and her amazing moan made Eve fly with me, look at the world with me, look at the earth with me, and look at Ding Yi and E, seeing the two as our beautiful shadow cast on the earth... so I was in no rush to return. Because Eve and I asked each other: That happy man and woman down there – who are they? Because Eve and I answered each other: They're a pair of blessed people! So, in no rush to go back, I flew and flew, flying to the ends of creation, flying to the depths of creation without end...

But in the midst of this delightful flight, I suddenly had a thought: And Yi? Where's Yi? How is Yi? And how is she feeling right now?

95. Contract

This thought made me quickly land. Land, land, land, land... returning to Ding Yi.

Naked Ding Yi and naked E were sitting on the balcony, nestling under the stars.

"Where is Yi?"

Oh, it was E who asked.

"No," E said. "You just asked."

"Really?" that Ding played dumb.

"Yes, Yi, where is she now?" E looked sincerely at the night sky.

"E, do you care?"

"Care about what?"

"Yi..."

"Yi is such a good person!"

"What do you mean?"

"What you mean."

"I don't mean anything else."

"Me neither. I'm just thinking, can people be completely honest and trustworthy with each other?"

E met Ding Yi's gaze in silence, while Eve and I looked at the high wind and moon.

E changed the subject, asking: "Do you think this place is like, uh... a stage?"

"You mean this balcony?"

"No, I mean this moonlight, this darkness. I mean night."

"Night? Stage?"

"A stage isn't a fixed place, but drama must be a unique time. Mere reality, or merely a place to imitate reality, is a false stage. While real drama should be a different kind of life possibility, all kinds of possibilities exist outside reality, or you could say the possible within the impossible. Just because reality contains so many impossibilities, so people dream, fantasise, right? And that's also why there's drama. It's also because dreams and fantasies are that kind of unreality, people want to see if the dreams and fantasies can be realised in another time. Put it this way, drama is this kind of time: it can return the wish daytime stole. Drama is actually this kind of wish: it makes the impossible possible, it makes the unrealisable realised."

"For example?"

"For example a real actor in a drama about first love cannot just perform someone else's love, they have to enact one of their dreams of love. For example there have been so many wonderful love stories since ancient times, but people always think they're just legends. Nonsense, they can't enact them because they're not real at all. So I want to ask: why, as soon as they enter drama, whether actors or viewers, do they all believe it's real and even shed tears over it? Dreams! People expect to realise dreams, and drama gives them this opportunity. To realise without reality! If you want reality you can go to the street and look around, why spend money and go to the theatre? I asked an actor, why do you like acting? He said it's like travel. For example, if you can only be Ding Yi all your life, you can only be like this, this is how it is, but if you can really enter different dramas, you can get a taste of all kinds of possibilities of love."

"Ha, this dude's probably a ladies' man."

E smiled. "Basically. But he's right. Love is such a wonderful thing. It's a shame you can only experience it once, or at most a few times. More than that and you cause trouble."

"You'll hear the hooligan song."

E said: "The subtext he told me is that in drama you can experience this wonderful feeling as much as you want. He asked if it was great that people can always experience love. So he doesn't like to act out conspiracies, fights or stupid comedies. He said those things ruin people. Acting like people are hateful or lonely, always lying, deceitful."

Ding Yi smiled openly. He had no way to predict that, one day, the phrase 'reality isn't reality' would make waves in Ding Yi's life, causing my travels in Ding Yi to take another turn. That's for later.

"Let's make a contract," E said.

"How?"

"No matter when, no matter where and no matter what happens, if things go like this, we'll walk into the moonlight and silence together. That will be our night. It will bring us into drama, bring us into a time when anything is possible, bring us unconditional honesty and trust. During night time there is no shame, hiding or discriminating. All wishes are justified, there's nothing that can't be said. Sound good?"

Ah, amazing E, amazing Eve! Ever since I left Eden, I've been looking for this kind of place. Ever since I arrived in Ding Yi, we've been tormented by this longing!

"Perfect," I said. "Really perfect."

"But this is free, voluntary."

"Of course."

"No one forcing anyone."

"That goes without saying."

"Then now we have a contract."

"No worry, no worry," Ding Yi said. "A contract always needs a ceremony, right?"

"Ceremony, what kind of ceremony?" E asked.

I hesitated when that Ding had another strange idea. "Why don't we sit here till dawn, what do you say, E?"

E was stunned. Arms folded across her chest, she said: "Like this?"

"Exactly."

"Till morning?"

"Until we're surrounded by the eyes of others."

E smiled approvingly.

"And we're not allowed to talk?"

"Right."

OK. E and Ding Yi leaned against the wall, and Eve and I took part in the ceremony along with them.

Until the moonlight slowly dimmed.

Until the starlight gradually thinned.

Until the distant mountains started to appear and there was a faint glow on E's shoulders and chest.

Not until the first pedestrian appeared on the street did the two break into laughter. Ding Yi leaned on the handrail and shouted to the coming day: "Night's drama has concluded, now reality begins." He pulled E, and the two crazies smiled nakedly and leapt back inside.

96. Enemy Testimony

This year, according to what Uncle himself said, when he was desperately trying to prove Fu was a martyr, things suddenly took a turn. Thought Old Liu still couldn't speak on Fu's behalf, an enemy of the past showed up, claiming he could vouch for Fu.

That day Uncle was tending his plants and flowers as usual when someone suddenly called his name. Uncle quickly stopped what he was doing and came out, catching sight of a strange man looking at Fu's picture.

"Who are you?"

The person turned and said Uncle's name again.

"If something's the matter, just say it." Uncle brushed off his sleeves, thinking it was another background checker.

The person smiled and moved closer to Uncle. "You don't recognise me?"

Uncle didn't answer.

"But I still recognise you."

Uncle thought: If you have something to say, say it. People who know me come here for safety, who comes here to make trouble?

"That year you went to see Miss Wu, I..."

A bang went off in Uncle's head, and he dropped into his wicker chair, gaping at that speechless person.

That person lowered his head, took on a respectful expression of guilt as if to repent or make an apology.

Uncle recognised that person. It was the person who had caught him that year. Right, it was the person who had taken a bunch of kitchen knives from the mansion and told Uncle that Fu had already died. That shocking news, Uncle said, had caused him to lose track of where he had been. As he struggled to stay strong, that person had said: "Let's go, please come with us." Uncle had composed himself, asked what they meant. That person said: "What do I mean? I was going to ask you what you mean!" Then he picked up a kitchen knife, unscrewed the handle, and took out a note.

"Hey, you still alive?" Uncle finally took a good look at that person: white hair, hunched back, like someone who had travelled the same road he had.

"Yeah, yeah," that person said. "Still kicking."

"What did you come here for?"

"Well, it's been so many years, wanted to see you."

"See me?" Uncle smiled. "A spy coming to see a traitor?"

"Well, come on. I've already been released from prison. I'm reformed."

"Reformed? If you're reformed, why'd you come here?"

"Should, shouldn't... matter, right?"

"I think you should be careful."

"Oh, yes, no, no. Oh, it's like this. I heard you've been working on Fu's case."

"Who said?"

"Ding Yi. Oh no, Ding Yi's dad. After I got out, I worked in the same dining hall as Ding Yi's dad. His dad made the food, I tended the fire."

Uncle closed his eyes, wondering if he had any reason to come other than make trouble.

"Ding Yi's dad said no one can prove Miss Fu... Oh, no, Comrade Fu's identity?"

"It's not that they can't, they won't."

"I can," that person said. "I can prove it."

Uncle perked up. "You? What can you prove?"

"I can prove Fu was one of you. Oh, no, one of our people. Oh, no, no, your people. Ah, how to put it? In short, the enemy knew for a long time she was undercover."

Uncle's eyes brightened as he thought he was incredibly stupid. Apart from me and Old Liu the enemy also knew Fu was undercover. They can vouch for it too. Why had I never thought of that?

Uncle said: "Can you really?"

"Yes."

Uncle asked: "Do you dare?"

He smiled. "I've done much stupider things. And I'd be doing the people a service, right? I know Comrade Fu was a great person."

As the saying goes, there's always a silver lining. Uncle had not been so happy in many years. Someone was finally willing to vouch for Fu. Fu's story would finally come to a satisfying conclusion. That day Uncle happily bustled about with his old enemy (authentication, certification, testimony, physical evidence), smiling wherever they went.

97. Still a Mystery

But there was something Uncle had not thought of: since the enemy had known for a long time that Fu was undercover, how did they know? Who or what told them? That is to say, someone must have sold Fu out. And who was that?

This made that old enemy terrified: "This... this... this I really don't know. I've already said all I know. No... no way would I hide anything from you comrades."

Then it could only have been Old Liu. The only person who knew Fu's identity, apart from Uncle, was Old Liu. But Uncle only found out as he was facing arrest. Of course it couldn't be Uncle. It could only be Old Liu!

Old Liu, who had previously suffered aphasia from a stroke, suddenly spoke. He said if it was he, Old Liu, then not only Fu would have been betrayed. Old Liu said he was Fu's only contact. He was her only superior.

If Old Liu had sold her out, the enemy should have apprehended Fu. Without doing so, who else did the enemy expect her to sell out? "Sell me out? I sell her out, she then sells me out. Comrades, do you think the enemy are stupid?"

Old Liu said of course there was another possibility: the enemy put out long lines to catch a big fish, scattered nets waiting for someone to come connect with Fu, but the person who connected with her was Uncle. Uncle was also sent by Old Liu. If he wanted to sell out Uncle he could do so directly, why use a go-between? One last thing doesn't add up according to Old Liu: "If I was going to sell out someone, I should have sold out my superiors! Comrades, do you really not understand that the enemy would have figured that out?"

It sounded logical, airtight.

Then who else could it be? Apart from the enemy? Did Uncle sell out Fu? The case officer flatly rejected the possibility because, by the time Uncle knew Fu's identity, she had already died.

Old Liu smiled. "Why could it only have been us? Why couldn't it have been herself?"

"Who do you mean?" Uncle shouted.

Fu. Right. It could have been Fu herself. At least you couldn't logically rule out the possibility that Fu became a traitor long ago.

"No way! There's no way!" Uncle shouted.

The case officer asked why not.

"She, she, she's not that kind of person."

"And?"

"She really... really wasn't that... that kind of person."

That's not a reason. The case officer said it's certainly not proof.

Uncle went home feeling brokenhearted. He'd thought Fu was fully justified to become a martyr. How could she be suspected of being a traitor again?

"Ah, Uncle," Ding Yi said. "How can you be so stupid!"

"Tell me! Hurry up and tell me, Ding Yi, what else can be done?" Uncle grabbed Ding Yi, his face full of anxiety and anticipation.

"Think about it, Uncle. If you were Fu, why wouldn't you sell out Old Liu?"

"Right, right!" Uncle shed some tears, laughed a while, on the brink of insanity.

The case worker agreed, that was reasonable. But then who's the traitor?

"It's me, me!" Uncle said, beaming. "Couldn't be anyone else."

The case worker smiled too. "Don't say that, OK? Your case is ironclad."

"Then can Fu be a martyr?"

The case officer said he couldn't say, nothing could be decided without the full truth.

98. Wild Dreams or the Exile of Sellout Ding Yi

One night Ding Yi and I entered a bizarre dream world.

There were strange flowers and plants all around: trees, buds, blooming flowers... it was like in Uncle's old place. Uncle was sitting in the shade of the lush foliage, weeping to himself.

"What's wrong, Uncle?"

Uncle didn't speak. He kept crying.

A voice seemed to come from the wall: "What are you asking him for? He's the one who sold me out!"

Fu, it was Fu! Her voice floated like a ghost's.

"What, you're saying it was Uncle?"

Fu came out from the picture and suddenly took shape, the snowy woods behind her did too.

Yi or Fu was draped in a white dress, uncertain, wandering, illusory, like steady snowfall.

A chill passed through the old room.

"It was he who sold me out." Yi or Fu's tone or Yi or Fu's appearance told a story of betrayal: "That day I waited outside the small theatre for him to meet up. I'd already gone there in vain several times. Sometimes he didn't come, sometimes he came but the environment wasn't right for us to make contact..."

"Wait, hey wait," Ding Yi said. "What small theatre? Are you talking about that small theatre?"

"Do you still remember the magic? Yeah, that one. That day I thought he wasn't coming again. When I was about to leave I saw him emerge from the theatre. It seemed to be bustling inside, but it was very quiet outside. I walked up to him and asked what show was on. He said magic. I asked what magic. He said, well, the magician still hadn't arrived. I asked him where the magician was from. He told me it was some so-and-so-stan or some so-and-so-sky. I was about to pass the intelligence to him when, next to the house, from behind a tree, a series of strange eyes looked at me oddly. I thought, no, someone has defected, someone has sold me out..."

"You thought it was Uncle?"

"Who else could it be? Who else knew the meeting place?"

"No way, absolutely not!" Ding Yi shouted. "You're wrong. Uncle loves you. He's loved you for a long, long time."

"Then you ask him, ask him if he's a traitor or not."

Uncle struggled out of the flowers, grabbed Ding Yi, grabbed us and pleaded: "Stop, stop talking! I am, I'm a traitor, the only one. I'm begging you not to talk about it any more..."

Ding Yi was stunned. He groaned: "But he loves you, Fu! We always loved you, always loved you, Yi!"

I was worried this Ding was going to go nuts, lose his mind, so I reminded him: *But think about it, Uncle isn't the only one who knows this place.*

Who else?

Come on! Does someone meet up with themself?

You mean Fu? You think it was her too?

When Ding Yi turned to look again, Yi had disappeared in Fu. Fu had to return to the wall.

The Fu in the picture was as before: a hint, a bitterness in her young smile.

But the old room was still unbearably cold and dark. The silent snowscape or the plain white dress suddenly turned into a pale sheet with an emaciated old man sleeping alone under it.

Uncle saw him and jumped up. "Old Liu, Old Liu! Are you finally going to have mercy and open your mouth?"

Old Liu lifted off the sheet. A sign on his chest read: 'Traitor, spy'.

Old Liu opened his bone-white eyes. "I have no way to vouch for her because, unfortunately, she never did any work." Old Liu pointed to the sign on his chest. "If there is proving to be done, she can prove it about me."

"But she was always waiting," Uncle said. "She was always waiting for someone to meet with her, someone to come give her an assignment. She didn't fail to do it, much less refused, just she never had the chance!"

Old Liu shook his head and closed his eyes again.

Uncle pounced on him and shook him. "Then who can I ask? Who can we ask?"

"Ask him," Old Liu said. "He's not a good person anyway."

Now we realised there was a stranger in the room.

"Who are you?" Uncle asked.

"Enemy," that person said, trembling. "One of your enemies from that time."

"What are you here for?"

"I can prove Fu was one of your people. Not long after you sent her to us, uh, no, not long after she was sent to them, they knew she was one of our people, uh, no, your people, one of your informants, undercover agents."

"How did you know?"

"There was a traitor among you, I don't know who. We were like you, uh, no, they were like you, uh, no, they were not like you... jeez, how to put it? The enemy was not like you, but they used similar methods – I'm talking about informants, undercover agents. It's been like that since ancient times, a linear relationship. So someone among you sold out Fu. Fu didn't say it. We really didn't know."

"Then why didn't you arrest and interrogate her?"

"Use little fish to catch big fish? That's another thing that you and them have always had... in common."

"Did you catch anything?"
"We did."
"Uncle?"
"Originally Old Liu too, but we failed to get him. When he saw his contact didn't come back, he disappeared without a trace."

Uncle sat among the flowers, quiet, as if he had had nothing to do with the matter.

But that Old Liu got excited, screamed: "Bullshit! When did I run? That was to... to prevent more comrades from becoming involved."

Uncle shut his eyes, stone-faced.

"Uncle!"

Uncle didn't move.

"Uncle!"

At the edge of Uncle's closed eyes, a teardrop flowed.

"Uncle!"

"Yes," Uncle said, "after the enemy caught us we gave up Old Liu. The case was rock solid. I really couldn't... couldn't stand it. They gave me so much... so much pain."

Then who else sold out Fu?

Uncle jumped up. "You cannot suspect me of that!"

Why not?

"Ding Yi, Ding Yi!" Uncle looked eagerly at Ding Yi. "Tell them, these years, all these years how I've always loved Fu."

Ding Yi put his arm around pathetic Uncle. I said to Old Liu: "But you never thought that Fu attracted the enemy?"

"No, impossible!" Uncle pushed Ding Yi away and shouted: "Impossible, Fu couldn't have done that."

"What makes you so sure? Do you have proof?"

"Yes, of course. Because, because Fu loved... loved me!"

"Even so, there's another possibility. Fu wasn't sold out, but she didn't know the enemy had already discovered her, so the enemy let her lead them to you."

"No, no! I'm saying that just couldn't have happened." Uncle was nearly hoarse. "I was caught outside that... mansion, not that... theatre. At that time, Fu had already... already died!"

Another romantic! Worse than you, Brother Ding.

Then who was telling the truth?

It might all be true or might all be false.

What do you mean?

As far as I can tell, Uncle's arrest could very well have happened outside that theatre.

What?

I'm guessing it was like this: that day Uncle arrived outside the theatre to meet Fu. In order to avoid suspicion he went inside and sat awhile first, looked around to make sure there was nothing unusual, then he came out. I'll add that the one who left before the magician arrived may very well have been Uncle and not X, but as soon as he left he was caught by the enemy.

But Uncle says he was caught outside the mansion.

It's very possible that is Uncle's wishful thinking or dream.

Wish? Dream?

Yes. Uncle has long dreamed that what happened outside the theatre wasn't real. In his hopes, or perhaps in his night drama, everything that happened inside and outside the theatre was all the same, was all magic. This desperate person hoped it was all magic, all just magic, all just something that, after the lights came on, he would find himself sitting in the theatre, find he had never taken a step outside the theatre... or because he was trying to square the circle, or the dream world got mixed up with the real world, Uncle moved the place of his arrest to outside that mansion...

Why, why did he have to move it there?

Because at that time Fu had already died.

I still don't understand.

Think about it. Think about it, Ding Yi. To Uncle, was Fu someone who never lived up to her potential or someone to be suspected of betrayal?

Put it this way, was the traitor at the beginning necessarily Fu?

Not necessarily, not necessarily. It could also be that Uncle betrayed Fu after he was arrested.

No, impossible! Because, because Uncle said he always, always loved Fu.

Have you never forgotten Yi? That Ding looked ashamed, so I quickly changed the subject.

Why can't this be the reason for Uncle's unceasing repentance, why he can never ever forgive himself?

Then what that enemy said isn't actually true?

What the enemy said we only heard from Uncle.

Absurd, truly absurd! Then let me ask you: who really is the traitor?

Uncle, definitely. But there's no way to be sure anyone here is not.

"I'm surely not!" Old Liu shouted from under the white sheet.

That's just by chance, Old Liu! If you were sure you couldn't become one, why did you run away? Why worry about implicating other comrades?

Then the old enemy said with a self-deprecating laugh: "I'm definitely not. I don't think I could be at all."

You're that confident? But they say you are. Enemies, or your own people back then say you are.

Or you, Ding Yi!

I, I am. I sold Yi out, sold out my love... *the person I loved.*

"Bull. This is all bull!" Uncle shouted. "I am, Fu isn't. Only Fu isn't."

Ding Yi and I looked up at Fu on the wall.

Fu came out from the wall again. The person Uncle loved and the person who loved Uncle came down from the wall, her dress like wind ruffling a flower and her voice like rain beating a palm: "If I was like Uncle, beaten black and blue, maybe I would have been. If I had watched him being tortured to death in order not to betray me, I would rather he had done it."

"No! Fu, you aren't. You really aren't."

"But the fact is that's exactly what I am. If, because I'm not, you were killed by the enemy I think I would regret not being one. If, in order for me not to be one, you were tortured to death by the enemy, I think you're better than me."

"No, no, I am, I am! Just let me be the only one. Fu, don't get confused. You're a martyr, a martyr. Listen to me, Fu. You're a martyr, you're definitely a martyr."

"Why?"

Otherwise, otherwise how could I... could I put your picture... put it on my wall..."

The room echoed.

The room was incredibly silent.

Fu and Uncle sat silently under the flowers and cried in each other's arms.

And everyone else immediately disappeared.

It started to warm up. The light shimmered. The breeze blew, urging the sago cycas trees and night-blooming cereus plants to blossom, kicking up that remote as well as close ballad: "Am I the secret language you forgot? Are you my lost credential? What year, what year? Life and death reign."

But what about Yi? that Ding asked me. *Where's Yi?*

Yi's on the frontier.

The wind in the room grew violent, the light became more intense to the point that it overwhelmed everything, making the day completely white... Only Ding Yi's lonely shadow was left, longing.

"Yi! Where are you?"

No one answered.

"Yi's there..."

It was so empty the voice disappeared.

"The frontier, the frontier. You're so far..."

Yes, a kind of exile, boundless.

"Yi – Yi..."

Ding Yi started awake with E next to him.

99. Regarding that Magic

Then I understood: it isn't important if that magic was real or not. The important thing is that it was Uncle's dream or fantasy. Uncle must have hoped that now can be like that magic, the past can come again, time can reverse its flow. Uncle must have hoped that, when he left the theatre at seven-thirty, it was still seven-thirty when he went back, and what happened outside the theatre was just a nightmare; or no matter how long and torturous the nightmare was, the time would always come to wake up. Uncle must have thought that, if it was still seven-thirty when he went back to the theatre, if fate gave him another chance to choose, there was no way he would leave for the meeting. This poor old man, he must have prayed so many times. That magician, that something-something-stan or something-something-sky, cast your spell again, bring time back to the past, bring Fu and I back to our youths! This poor old man must have been hooked by this incredible magic. If it can really be this way, Fu, let's leave this awful place together, even if we have to go to the ends of the earth, even if we have to go to a desert, a remote island, a tomb, I'm willing! There it will always be you and me, no need for others, especially no enemies, and none of 'our people'...

Ever since he watched that magic show, or since he became a traitor rather than a youngster, Uncle mush have entered a dream from which he has never been able to come out or never been thinking of coming out.

A dream is a remote island. That old room resembles a desert. Ah Fu, all the plants on the walls and the ground are planted for you; all the flowers in the room and the courtyard are blooming for you.

At night Fu came down from the wall. During the day Fu went back inside the picture. Or the opposite: when Fu came down from the wall it was night, when Fu went back in the picture it was day.

Uncle's days and nights were thus no longer synchronised with the world's. Or someone else came and made it day. If no one else came, it was night. Or if day was for someone else, the night was the time to meet Fu. So Uncle didn't want to come back from there.

Ding Yi and I were the only people who spent much time with him.

Once Uncle asked Ding Yi: "When you got into trouble that Sunday, where were you thinking of going?"

Ding Yi thought awhile. "I forget. All I remember is one night the snow stopped, and the weather was so good it made you want to go for a walk. I just wanted to go for a walk."

"But I haven't forgotten." Uncle was talking about his own story. "One Sunday long ago, a beautiful spring day. In the bright morning light I bought a bouquet of flowers, planning on going to see Fu."

"But by coincidence," Ding Yi said, ignoring Uncle and talking about his own Sunday, "I don't know how, walking around, I walked into that abandoned garden."

"Right, right, by coincidence," Uncle said. "I didn't find Fu, but on my way back I ran into Old Liu."

"Same here. I never thought I'd run into Yi. But I really wanted to run into her..."

"When he heard I was going to find Fu, Old Liu said I was boring. Time is short, don't sacrifice your career for love. He said how could you be so unidealistic, so unpatriotic? The world is unjust, society is unfair, don't you think you have responsibility? Are you still an intellectual?"

"Yi was drawing a tree. Yi said the tree was so honest, magnanimous. People are so hypocritical..."

"Old Liu was right! Now I see he was right. At least at that time Old Liu was full of passion and pride."

"Yi was right too. Yi said that and I knew she was right. I felt I was like that, all people were like that, all think one thing and say another."

Now Uncle's face changed. He asked Ding Yi: "Then what do you think people can do?"

"Why can't people just say what they think?"

"Oh, no, no." Uncle shook his head. He shook his head hard. "That's impossible. That's not realistic."

"I know, Uncle, I know. Usually it's not realistic, but it could be with some people, right?"

"With who?"

"Friends, family, people you understand, people you trust, like-minded people..."

"OK, say no more." Uncle's gaze softened.

"Uncle, what are you thinking about?"

Uncle didn't answer. A huge butterfly seemed to fly from Uncle's face, so bright, so elegant, swooping around the old, dark room. Maybe all the trees couldn't bear its weight, all the flowers couldn't bear its beauty. That dreamlike butterfly flew out the window. In the yard it kept swooping, swooping. It seemed to feel the sky was too pale, the air too suffocating, so it flew back into the room again, back to Uncle's troubled face and disappeared into the old man's murky eyes.

"Uncle?"

"Uncle!"

Uncle stood up, walked in circles around the room with his hands behind his back, then stopped in front of Ding Yi. "You're still young, Ding Yi. Listen to me if you will: whatever people do in this life is OK, whatever they do will earn them bread – but never, ever have 'your people'!"

"Why, Uncle? You think it's that bad? Not everyone is an enemy, not everyone is an other, everyone has their people who say what they think. What's wrong with that, Uncle?"

"But tell me what does 'your people' mean?"

"Not others, not enemies of course."

"Then what is an enemy?"

"Enemies are definitely... are definitely not... your... your people?"

"Right, right, right!" Uncle patted Ding Yi's head. I thought he would laugh, but he choked up. "Right right right..." Ding Yi was more stupid.

He thought Uncle couldn't breathe from laughter, but Uncle's tears were flowing. "Right right right, right right right right..." he kept repeating. It was unclear if he was laughing or crying.

"Can you stop, Uncle?" He was scaring Ding Yi a little.

"Right right, that's the point, man." Uncle patted Ding Yi's shoulder.

Ding Yi took Uncle's hand. Ding Yi rose and held Uncle's arm. "Maybe I'm right, but don't be angry, OK? Just forget I said it, OK, Uncle?"

"No no no no, you're right. Too right. All day talking and it's the only right thing you've said!"

"Uncle!"

"No no, I'm not mad. What do I have to be mad about? I'm saying you're right. Without enemies, where would 'our people' come from? But, but Ding Yi, listen closely. Where would enemies come from without 'our people'?"

Then Uncle took a breath, pushed Ding Yi away and sat back in his chair.

One old and one young sat like that, quietly looking at the flowers around them, each pondering what was on their mind.

A long time later Ding Yi asked Uncle: "So who are the people to whom you can reveal your thoughts?"

"With people you don't know."

"People you don't know?"

"With people you don't know and those who don't know you."

"If you don't know each other, why would you want to talk?"

"Or with people who love you. If you love them and they love you."

"With Fu? Is it OK with Fu?"

"Naturally. But not you, it should be me!" Uncle laughed crazily, making me uneasy.

Ding Yi thought a moment and said to himself: "Then I believe."

Uncle said: "You believe what?"

"Aunt! You didn't sell her out."

Uncle was stunned. A smile vanished abruptly from his face. The butterfly on his face seemed to move like it was going to take off.

But in the end it didn't. Uncle closed his eyes a moment and got up to take care of his flowers.

Uncle went among the flowers. There was no sound but the click of pruning. Did he forget about us? But suddenly the clicking sound was interrupted by Uncle snarling: "But she's not your aunt, she never made it to become your aunt..."

100. Dream Again

The clicks of pruning resonated louder and louder, making the clipped leaves and flowers sound like footsteps on gravel as they fell.

"Uncle! Uncle!"

The clicking sound increased, snapped stems and damaged vines flying like wind and rain.

"Uncle! Uncle!"

Fragrant dust filled the room, all that could be seen was red mud. The clicking sound didn't stop. In fact it spread farther and farther, reverberating in more and more empty space.

"Uncle, what are you trying to do?"

But in the empty, wild air Uncle was nowhere to be seen.

In the empty, wild air a young woman approached gracefully.

"And Uncle? Where did Uncle go?" Ding Yi asked.

"You mean that traitor?" the young woman said. "He's at the frontier."

"Is the frontier far away?"

"Farther than far."

"Who are you?"

That woman just smiled.

"Yi! You're Yi?"

The woman's smile took on a hint of bitterness.

"E! E!" Ding Yi shouted. "Yi's back! E, come look, it's real this time! Yi really came back from the frontier..."

Awaking, he found E close by.

E still hadn't slept. She put down the book in her hand and smiled. "Dreaming again?"

Ding Yi rubbed his eyes and looked out the window. Outside it was dark, trees creaking in the wind.

"Did I say something?"

"In a foreign language. Blah-blah-blah, blah-blah-blah, maybe a Martian language?"

E was just joking. She didn't blame him. That Ding sighed in relief.

E changed her position, pushed the bedside lamp lower and kept reading her book. She looked peaceful from head to toe, which made Ding Yi ashamed.

But the clipping sound came again, sharp and fierce.

That woman picked up a bunch of plant debris, slowly splicing, making them once again into the sketch of an old cypress.

"Yi, when did you come?"

That woman scooped up the red dirt and fragrant sand from the floor, bowed and gently blew, returning them to the way Uncle dreamed.

"Yi, where did you come from?"

That woman looked up sternly. "Yi? Who said she's back already?"

"You're back, Yi! Look around, where is this?"

That woman looked around and was suddenly surprised. Her gaze softened like Uncle's. "Who are you?"

"Ding Yi. I'm Ding Yi!"

"That person who sold me out?"

Ding Yi was silent with shame.

Then that butterfly appeared out of nowhere – huge, beautiful, flying everywhere like daylight, slowly submerging that young woman, submerging Yi's possible return...

"Yi, where have you been?"

That huge butterfly was like real magic, colours swaying, fear spreading as it fluttered about the old room. Amid the snipped branches it fluttered as if there was nowhere for it to land...

"Don't go, Yi! Come back."

Fluttering or stumbling, that brilliant spirit touched the wall and broke its antennae. Its elegant flight ran into the ceiling, the glass and damaged its wings... The wounded beauty seemed trapped. Then it finally flew back into the picture frame like a trail of moaning disappearing in Fu's bitter smile...

That Ding started awake again. E was still reading.

"Ugh," Ding Yi sighed, looking at the dark night. "She won't come back."

E flashed her book in front of Ding Yi's face and looked at him. "Sleep talking?"

"Nonsense! I never slept."

"Then," E said with a sly smile, "what did I just ask you?"

"You asked... asked me? I think you asked..."

"What?"

"She won't... won't come back."

"Who? Who won't come back?"

The response to E's question was more snoring.

E waved a finger in front of that Ding's face. Having made sure he'd returned to sweet slumber, she turned off the light and, eyes wide open, listened to the sound of the wind outside the window...

"Why won't Yi... come back?" that Ding mumbled.

She suddenly had a thought and turned onto her side. "Hey, did you forget? Change to another time, change time and Yi might be able to come back!"

"You mean drama?"

"Yes, drama! The agreed time."

"This will also... apply to Yi?"

"You shouldn't forget, Ding Yi. In night's drama, at the agreed time, everything becomes possible, everything unreal can be realised."

"Really, E?"

"Of course."

Naughty E giggled, seeing the dude roll over happily and fall into a quiet sleep.

Then the walls before Ding Yi disappeared... From the limitless expanse of night only the smell of flowers blew across his face... Lit by fireflies and stars, naked E danced alone, heaven and earth filled with her unrestrained laughter.

"Come on, Ding Yi, strip! Ha-ha-ha-ha..."

"Hey, now you really are a hooligan!"

"Strip, Ding Yi! When the agreed-upon time with Yi comes, you have to dedicate your flower!"

Naked E and naked Ding Yi danced together, their steps permeating heaven and earth.

"Say it, say those most classic words. Then Yi will come."

"E! Your bum is so, so big."

"Say it again, say it again. You didn't say it frankly enough, not elegantly enough, not sincerely enough."

"E! Your waist is fine, your bum is killer, your bush is dark as night, your feathers can fly."

Then that butterfly flew out of the frame dark as dense night, fresh, elegant, romantic, free. It flew like the spring breeze, the melting ice and snow... It landed on the ground and turned into He Yi.

"Yi! Yi, you came back. Are you really back?"

Yi didn't answer, didn't move, just quietly gazed at Ding Yi.

"Yi, don't leave again, OK?"

Yi still didn't answer and didn't move, still looked intently at Ding Yi.

"Yi! Yi doesn't want to talk to me, huh?"

Then E said: "Do you still remember what Graham said? 'People can't take advice from someone who doesn't know them very well.'"

"I remember, of course I remember. He said 'only people with a physical relationship can...'"

"Right, only then can Yi really come back, can Yi really join our drama."

That Ding walked towards Yi, slowly walked towards her, one step after another... Then he gently touched her white dress, touched the raven black ends of her hair, touched her slender fingertips... Then he hugged her fiercely, hugged her tight like that year in the grove...

But, but he suddenly felt emptiness in his arms. When he looked closely Yi was gone, only the white dress was left. The white dress then flew up, floated up, big as a canopy, white as day...

Ding Yi woke up to a bed and room full of sunlight. E was in the kitchen preparing breakfast.

101. What Asky Asked and Didn't Ask

It should be said that Ding Yi and Asky got along pretty well. Only the little girl's cleverness, or even cunning, often confused me. For example she asked good questions but never how this Ding Yi suddenly came to be in her home. "Who are you?", "What are you doing here?", "Where were you before?" and so on were questions that she not only failed to ask but seemed not to have even occurred to her. Not only that: neither Ding Yi nor I recalled her asking about her dad, never asked and never spoke of him, and the same for other people's dads as if the word 'dad' had never entered into her vocabulary.

One day Ding Yi and E took Asky for a walk in the park and Ding Yi brought this up.

"Really?" E said. "I never noticed."

"I have."

E was quiet, as if trying to remember.

"It's not normal."

"Right, it's not normal." Melancholy grazed E's brows. "But maybe it's because she never had the chance to say it."

"No, that's not a reason. She can't fail to know that word, she's intentionally avoiding it!"

"Intentionally?" E looked at Ding Yi in surprise. But soon the surprise turned to anxiety. It was clear she knew and always knew subconsciously.

As two of them walked in silence awhile, not knowing how to continue (or finish) this subject, Asky ran towards them from afar, shouting "Mum, Mum" with a look of surprise and joy. E set her worries aside and appeared cheerful.

"Mum, hurry and look, there's something so weird over there."

"Oh, all right, but don't be so crazy, slow down."

"There's a snake and a worm and something else I don't know what it's called. You don't have to do anything with them, they can dance on their own!"

"Slow down, tell me slower." E bent down and wiped her sweat. "What, what can dance?"

"I don't know, go see for yourself, over there."

"I think you should rest a bit first."

"No need. You guys hurry and look, it's so weird, lots of people are watching. An old man did it, hurry please!"

Asky pulled Ding Yi and E into the crowd.

Oh, this, a fairly ancient thing: a bowl filled with boiling water, covered with thin paper, wax paper cut into a snake, a centipede, a worm, fish, shrimp, and placed on top. Because the wax layer is unevenly heated, the little things expand, contract and tumble around.

Asky stood enthralled in front of the bowl and watched.

A little later the dance gradually slowed down.

Still later it stopped.

"Did they get tired?" Asky asked the old man.

The old man smiled and held up a paper bag. "These aren't tired."

"Then you make them dance?"

"But they have to eat, right?"

"Then what do you feed them?"

The old man looked up at E.

"OK, buy a bag." Ding Yi paid for it.

Asky was trying to grab the bag. "Hurry, give it to the man and let him make them dance!"

Ding Yi held it over his head. "Let's go, we'll find a place to make them dance ourselves."

"You can make them dance too?"

"Of course."

They found a tranquil lawn and sat down. E reminded Ding Yi that the water in the thermos was almost all gone and might not be hot enough.

Asky spread those things on the ground, looked at them one by one and suddenly fell silent.

"Why don't we go home," E said. "At home Uncle Ding can definitely make them dance."

But Asky seemed lost in thought. She looked up and asked: "Why do they dance?"

Ding Yi explained about the wax's melting point, the tension of the paper, the distribution of heat and so on.

Asky was not at all satisfied. She turned and asked E: "Mum, you tell me, why do they dance?"

"Didn't Uncle Ding Yi tell you why?"

"No, no, I'm not asking those!"

"Then what are you asking?"

"I'm asking why they dance," Asky shouted on the brink of tears.

"Don't rush, take your time talking to Mum." E took Asky in her arms and looked at Ding Yi as if to tell him not to underestimate her. "Do you want to ask why they can dance?"

"No, no, no!"

"K, K, K. Then you wanted to ask why they can jump, right?"

Asky grew quiet, nodded tearfully.

My God, the apple doesn't fall far from the tree!

"Then you tell me," she asked Asky, "why would they want to jump?"

"If I knew, I wouldn't ask you," Asky blurted out.

Ding Yi and E faced each other: how can we say this to her? And: do we know why? And also: what is happening deep within this little person?

102. The Differences Between People > the Differences Between Pigs

Ding Yi went to see Qin Han one day. Before he went inside, he heard him arguing loudly with someone who sounded feminine. Ding Yi whispered in my ear: *All right, buddy, now we can meet his gay lover.*

When he saw Ding Yi had arrived, Qin Han anxiously welcomed him as if he were being rescued, then pulled a chair over. "Sit, sit down, I have a question: what are the two most different things in the world that use the same name?"

There was a flash of deep red light in the room. Someone stood up, beaming, and complained to Qin Han: "What are you doing? You don't let him rest a minute first!" Then that person turned away, probably to make tea.

Ahem, I said to Ding Yi in a disappointed voice. *What gay lover, she's totally a woman!* That Ding ignored me and was even overjoyed for some reason, never taking his eyes from the rays of red light.

"Oh, wow!" Qin Han apologised. "Let me introduce you. This is Lü Sa. Lü Sa, my friend... oh, friend of a friend."

Lü Sa turned and gave Qin Han a look of seeming reproach.

"Oh, right... of course," Qin Han hurried to correct himself. "Friends of friends are friends of course. We all call her Sa."

Sa's face still held a grudge, but she cleverly disguised it as concentration – it seemed that she was entirely focused on the tea set and tea in her hands and hadn't noticed what Qin Han said.

Qin Han moved near Sa, nudged her with his elbow, but she ignored him.

"I'm saying you go by Sa, what's wrong with that?" Qin Han was half joking, half shifting the topic.

Sa smiled reluctantly, but she quietly snorted too.

That Ding seemed to notice something. *Hey, brother, did you notice Qin Han seems afraid of her?*

Not necessarily, I said. *Let's see, don't think it's that simple.*

Qin Han had to persist through the awkwardness. "Ding bro, you still haven't answered my question."

"Your question? What question?" Ding Yi was simply not focused on that.

That brilliant red light drifted over, setting the teacups on the table one by one. "I'll answer for you. What two things in the world are most different but are called exactly the same thing? Is that right, Qin Han?"

"Exactly, even clearer than I expressed it." Qin Han's words of appreciation were quietly meant to comfort.

"Mr Qin Han is always fussing about strange ideas," Ding Yi said. These words appeared to please Miss Sa.

"Mister? He's no one," Sa said wisely and anxiously. So what was it in the end? What could be more appropriate than 'no one', a joke masking discontent.

Did Qin Han not get what Sa meant? He only pretended not to. All his attention was on Ding Yi and his attitude towards that question. "What did you say, I'm fussy? You don't think this question is an issue?"

In the presence of such a sharp woman, Ding Yi thought that he ought to save some face for his host and hurried to say: "Yes, yes, like you said, everything is an issue."

Qin Han said: "Then tell me how many issues are there in life? Besides eating, drinking, shitting and pissing, as well as breeding, is anything else an issue?"

"All right, fine," Ding Yi said. "What really?"

"What what really?"

Sa was enjoying this, her red dress, or rather, pretty face, fluttering as she smiled.

"I can't guess the answer to your question."

"Tell you?"

"Or not."

Sa rushed over to Ding Yi. "People. He's talking about people!"

"People?"

"Yes, peo-ple," said Qin Han, leisurely swirling his teacup as usual.

"People?" That Ding frowned. I'd already understood the deeper meaning, understood Qin Han was not to be taken lightly.

People? That Ding wondered as Sa looked at him hopefully as if to say: It's all on you man, are you going to keep this Qin Han from gloating?

Then amorous Ding Yi silently prayed: Oh, Lord, let us humiliate ourselves in some other way, please, please not now. But the question didn't loosen its grip in the slightest.

Determined to stall, Ding Yi asked casually: "Why not pig? Aren't pig and pig the same?"

Everyone was surprised.

Who knew that Qin Han, stunned momentarily, would slap his thigh, jump up and say in a raised voice: "Marvellous, brother, marvellous. Your line of thinking is even more wonderful."

"Shit, is it worth getting all worked up over?" Ding Yi regretted it, fearing that he might just boost his pride instead of dampening it. He kept looking at Sa.

As for Sa, she seemed to be thinking about something else as she was pacing in the room, teacup in hand and not paying attention to their conversation, her big red dress floating along, causing inexplicable turmoil in Ding Yi.

Seeking an opportunity, this guy asked me: *Sa must be an athlete, you think?*

I said: *Based on what?*

Based on her figure. Did you notice her figure?

What about her figure?

Come on, even track and field athletes – sprinters, high jumpers, long jumpers – are not in such good shape!

Qin Han noticed Ding Yi's thoughts wandering and could tell exactly where to, so he sipped his tea and waited for him.

When that Ding came to, Qin Han said: "Listen, put it this way: the differences between people exceed the differences between people and pigs. Or you could write it this way: people and people's differences, greater than, people and pigs' differences." As he talked, he drew a > sign to mean 'greater than' on the table with a tea-dipped finger.

"What are you getting at? It's nonsense."

"Not at all. It's God's exam question. Solve it, dude!"

Sa came back to listen. With the dazzling red to one side, while Ding Yi lost his presence of mind, Qin Han stayed as cool as usual.

"Well, I'll leave the question for you to answer when you have time," Ding Yi said.

"OK, I'll explain it to you now. First the body. People and pigs have different bodies, let's call it one-zero. When it comes to bodily functions, such as eating, drinking, defecating, sleeping and breeding, people and pigs are the same, still one-zero. Second, people have feelings, but do you think pigs don't? Fine, let's say they don't. Two-zero. Furthermore, people can talk, pigs can't, but this doesn't count. The ability to talk is dependent on the ability to think. People think, animal's don't, three-zero. But don't worry, is thought thought? Thought and thought are worlds apart, no one would dispute this, right? OK then, this world of difference, tell me, how many points? Another example: a stone or a tree blocks your path, what do you do? Walk around, that is what you do. But if it's a big stick, a trap, or a conspiracy waiting for you, what do you do? Where do you hide? All right, now it's easy: people and pigs have three differences. We could list some more, but there is a limit to how many more or less, while the differences between people are infinite."

The house was quiet for a while. Ding Yi and Sa cast a look at each other. Seeing Sa's disappointed look, this Ding felt his manly passions swell, feeling he must take Qin Han down a notch, at least diminish his confidence. He couldn't just let him win outright.

"Is that why you didn't marry?" Ding Yi asked.

Ahem, brother, what's this have to do with anything?

What's wrong?

You ask me? This is how you show your manliness?

Inappropriate?

It's not only inappropriate but... but also despicable!

"Well, that," Qin Han said, after pondering for quite a while. "That's much more complicated than a big stick."

But Ding Yi was still satisfied, since that day he got acquainted with Sa.

103. Drama Season

Night came again.

Midsummer nights are the season of drama. When darkness covers the day, silence blocks noise. E said it was our appointed time.

E's feet stepped lightly.

E's shadow moved.

Turning off the desk lamp, opening the curtains, pushing open the windows to allow the wind and moonlight in – E said it was now.

E said: "What's something you wanted to say but didn't dare say?"

E said: "What's something you've always wanted to do but never have done?"

E said: "What have you always hoped for but felt is hopeless?"

"Then who," Ding Yi said quietly, "are you?"

Ding Yi found E's gaze in the darkness: "Who were you? Usually who are you?"

I said: *And when she isn't here, when she leaves this time and place, who is E then?*

E smiled slyly. "I'm another person. One of countless other people. That woman in the white dress you dream of, for example."

These words made Ding Yi dizzy or made me suddenly drift for a long time. So the momentary line between the past and future seemed to spread infinitely...

When the dizziness or floating passed, Ding Yi looked up to see E changing into a white dress.

"Don't, don't look yet," E said.

Ding Yi obediently closed his eyes.

"Yes, that's right. That's what a good boy's supposed to do."

Right, supposed to. E, you're supposed to be like this: walking over from afar in the white dress, walking out of the sea of people, supposed to drift like a mirage from other people, out of the unknown and out of isolation...

"OK, hey, you can look now."

Ding Yi opened his eyes: E or that woman in the white dress was sitting in the moonlight.

"Now who am I?"

"Lingling, Lingling..." that Ding said softly.

E stood up, letting that snow-white dress gently whirl.

"Are you Lingling?" Ding Yi trembled and retreated, wishing that he had still felt the same awe as he had done before.

"Then who are you now?"

"He's Ding Er." Ding Yi looked abjectly at E, willing to prove himself inferior and unworthy.

E walked proudly like Lingling, walked towards Ding Yi. She lifted herself on tiptoes and stroked his head. "Then who is this Ding Er?"

"A cook... a cook's son."

"You workers really aren't bad, and the four-inch wide armband isn't... isn't bad either, right?"

The night wind came in through the window, quietly closed the door, lifted E's dress.

Ding Yi got on one knee and grabbed the hem of E's dress to stop it from floating so arrogantly and fluttering so... mercifully.

E hugged his head, stroking, combing, hoping he wouldn't tremble so sadly, and would never again think about this... this horror.

Both of them were crying.

Their desire was burning.

E let Ding Yi go, walked as far away as she could, crouched and pulled the hem of her dress around her knees.

Ding Yi's flower quietly opened.

E lifted her skirt then wrapped it tightly again down to her ankles.

The spirits rose in Ding Yi's flower.

E gave a gentle suggestion like a director: "Hey, your turn."

As I said, this Ding's a simple guy and didn't get what E meant.

E raised her voice. "You! How do you want to be now or how should you be?"

As if frightened, Ding Yi's flower suddenly drooped.

"You should take me, no, take Lingling! Take this proud Lingling, this cold-hearted Lingling, OK?"

As if it had got into trouble, Ding Yi's flower gradually withered.

"You should teach her a lesson! You should order her, order her to do what you want, order her to do what she doesn't want to but must do, order her to do what she does in fact want but wouldn't dare do without you – "

"What?"

"All those things."

"All those things?"

"Yes."

Any way is OK? that Ding asked me.

Of course, of course, not going along isn't OK! Because, because...

Because what?

Because the soul once called 'I' was once separated from 'you'.

So what now?

"Undress!" I blurted out.

"Undress!" that Ding shouted at E.

Then proud Lingling in the silence and darkness became naked E. Then naked E in the moonlight became floating Eve. Then floating Eve in the night breeze cohered into the possibility of Lingling, the possibility of other people, cohered into all other people and all the possibilities of love...

"Oh, you really are Lingling?"

"Yes, Ding Yi, I am."

"Then do you still remember that summer night?"

"That summer night and the sweet olive tree."

"And the fireflies flying all around."

"And the sky full of soaring stars."
"But you were so heartless then."
"But now she's already adjusted for her shortcomings."
"But why couldn't you be like this then?"
"Because, because at that time you didn't order her to be like this?"
"That's because you didn't treat... treat Ding Er like this."
"That's because, for Lingling, Ding Er was another person too."
"And if at that time he ordered you like this?"
"At that time why didn't he try?"
"He didn't dare."
"Afraid of something?"
"Afraid... afraid you wouldn't come back the next day."
"Huh?"
"I said I'd wait for you under that tree, but when I went, you didn't show up."
"You're kidding," E said. "Ding Yi are you kidding?"
Ding Yi picked E up. "No way, what am I kidding about?"
"How are you not kidding?" E kicked and struggled on his shoulders. "How did Lingling become that little girl again?"
"What else? That's just, just a matter of time." Ding Yi tossed E on the sofa.
"Ah, Ding Yi!" E suddenly had a realisation. "You would definitely be a good actor and an amazing director..."
"The most important thing is being an amazing lover."
"Oh, yeah, yeah, you're an amazing hooligan!"
"Tell me, Lingling. The next day, why didn't you come back?"
"Maybe, maybe I forgot."
"Forgot? Yeah, yeah, some people can forget, some people can't forget. That's the problem."
"But now I remembered..."
"But the person who can't forget stood under the tree until dark, do you know? The person who can't forget kept standing there, looking at the distant mountains, the sun over the horizon, the gradually disappearing sun, the stars appearing one by one, but the person who forgets never came."
"She won't forget again, OK?"
"He stood there lonely as could be, watching summer pass and autumn come... until winter came, it snowed, there were footprints in the snow, the footprints brought him to a forest... then you came from that forest and asked me: 'How did you know I was here...' Then I realised you hadn't forgotten, you're also someone who doesn't forget. I realised it was my fault, hadn't waited for you patiently enough. I realised since I wanted to wait I should have waited until the land around that tree turned to forest. Since I wanted to wait I should have waited until winter, until after a big

snowstorm, until the footprints came and took me to your side..."

"Yes, even at the frontier I never forgot. She left that sketch of the tree for you." E realised that 'kidding' was wonderful.

But that Ding suddenly fell silent.

"Hey, I'm back!" E said. "You waited and Yi is finally back."

But that Ding was still silent, his whole body seemed to shake.

"After the snow, let's still meet in that little forest, OK?"

Then he put his head on E's chest.

"And, now, there are no other people... just snow, just trees, trees are so trustworthy, snow is so clean... and on the edge of the forest the hooligan song will cease..."

That Ding was completely silent.

"Why aren't you talking?"

"Because I'm a sellout."

"No, you're not."

"I am. I sold out Yi, sold out Yi's whole family."

"But that's not your fault."

"Uncle said he did it because he was afraid of death, but I, what was I afraid of?"

"You were afraid of involving your parents."

"Uncle did it because of severe torture, but what broke me?"

"What you mostly couldn't stand was 'we', 'you', 'them'."

"E, how do you know?"

"All lovers know."

"But in order to become 'you', become 'we', I sold Yi out to 'them'."

"All lovers will go deep into exile because of this, not to the frontier but in their hearts, not to the desert but... but their heart becomes a desert."

"E, how do you... how do you know?"

"Because I'm the same."

"And Qin Han, is he the same?"

"All lovers are the same. But all lovers understand more about love as a result of this exile. And everyone who doesn't love is forever exiled to a place without love."

"But they don't see it that way."

"So they can never, ever understand love."

"Don't you want everyone to understand love?"

"Do you?"

"But that day Qin Han said: 'What use is hope?'"

"How could it have no use?"

"Qin Han asked me: 'Can your hope be realised?'"

"Hope is realisation. Always hoping is always realising."

"Don't you think this is a little helpless?"

"We're always in a state of helplessness. So hopelessness, hope and disappointment – you have to choose one."

"Can you just choose realisation?"
"So you choose hopelessness?"
"Ah, E, you're really cunning."
"No, it's knowledge."
"You're really good at semantics."
"If you can't prove it's semantics, it's really knowledge."
"Right, right, you're really cute."
"So you'd rather choose hope."
"Why?"
"Love is hope."
"What do you mean?"
"People who love are people who hope."
"And those who don't love?"
"They're hopeless."
"Then despairing people?"
"Despairing people say nothing, not even that they're despairing."
"And Qin Han, which is Qin Han?"
"He, uh, he's probably an extraordinary, disappointed person."
"An amazing lover?"
"Maybe."
"Like you?"
"Don't know. I don't know if I can be like him, love the same sex like the opposite sex, love an ugly person like a beautiful person, and even love an awful person like a good one."
"Love a bad person like a good one, how's that possible?"
"If not, where's over? If not, he would say, it's just sex, a beautiful or ugly breast, a noble or ignoble nude body, a holy or unholy arse... but even beasts choose among the strong and the weak."
"That's not true."
"What isn't true?"
"Don't you see a problem with this?"
"What problem?"

104. About ED

One day Ding Yi talked with E about Qin Han's singleness and wondered if it could be because of ED.
"What's ED?" E asked.
"The English abbreviation for erectile dysfunction."
"What? You mean sexual impotence?"
"You don't understand?"
"A sexual handicap, hard to get an erection, yeah?"
"Yeah?" Ding Yi asked back.
"Then tell me," E said. "Are all those that can mate always capable of sex?"

"I don't understand what you're asking."

"Do you think sex is just intercourse?"

"Of course not."

Even a beast can do that simple thing, bro! Apes, fish, dogs and horses all can! Even flowers and trees can!

E said: "Do you still remember what Graham said in that film?"

Ann asked Graham if he could do it for her. Graham said no. Ann asked why. Graham said because he can't. She asked if he couldn't or if he wasn't willing. Graham said he wasn't willing, so he couldn't. She asked if he was sure he wasn't impotent. He said he was sure.

She asked if he had had sex with other people. He said of course he had. She asked if it made him feel ashamed. He said no, that wasn't his problem. She asked what his problem was.

E said: "What do you think Graham's problem is?"

"What is it?"

"Do you remember at the end, what John said to Graham?"

"John said he and Elizabeth had slept together."

"And when Graham and Elizabeth were still getting on!"

"And it seems like Graham already knew," Ding Yi said.

"Yes!" E said. "John thought he didn't know, John wanted to use this to get revenge on Graham, but actually Graham already knew. And that's the very reason Graham left their hometown. So I think that's why Graham has ED."

"And Qin Han," Ding Yi said. "Is that the reason for Qin Han?"

"You might be further off."

"How?"

"It's a long story. The problem is that Graham, or rather, people like Graham, why would he get ED? Do you remember what Graham said? 'At that time I always feel like I can't express my feelings in words.' He can't use ordinary words to express himself. He's saying he has to use his body, break all the rules, use the shameful language of sex or the ceremony of love to express himself. Which is to use the naked body to represent your wish to let go of barriers..."

"That language!"

E was dumbstruck. "That language? What language?"

According to my recollection and understanding, Ding Yi then told E the history and implications of 'that language'.

"Excellent," E shouted. "'The name that can be named is not the eternal name!' The language between speaking and writing, another possibility for communication and exchange, the aspiration regular words struggle to reach! Excellent! You thought of it?"

That Ding struggled to speak, not daring to greedily take the credit for himself – because those words derive from the wisdom of ancient sages.

E said: "Right, since Elizabeth turned 'that language' into lies, Graham can't stand it and left home, and got ED!"

Ding Yi: "So he said: 'I always feel I can't help but lie.'"

E: "So he said: 'I'm no longer who I was, this makes it hard for me to communicate with others.'"

Ding Yi: "He said if that language can be abused, what else can't be a lie? And what else can make Adam and Eve finally recognise each other?"

E: "He's saying if all language is invalid, it'd be strange for anyone not to have ED."

Ding Yi: "So you're saying people with ED might all be great, disappointed people?"

E: "Tell me, why did Graham want to make those films?"

Ding Yi: "Yeah, Ann asked that too."

E: "His heart is far from dead. He still wants to hear true words, especially about love, about what people really say is in their hearts in extreme times."

Ding Yi: "But when Ann truly expresses love for him, he says: 'I spent nine years constructing my life in order to avoid that thing.'"

E: "Maybe he thinks it's better to live in that fantasised truth. He's already terrified of true lies."

Ding Yi: "Is Qin Han like that too?"

E: "That's why I said ED isn't just about sexual impotence."

That reminded Ding Yi of his days of a lifetime but filled with monotony, boredom and fatigue. He thought of his flower's wilted defeats – flesh is a boundary, you and I are two cages. But at some point, in some place, for some reason, this disappointed flower's passion and sensitivity have been restored...

It's because of Eve! Let me remind you, when Eve came to E, and E approached that Ding Yi, we saw an extraordinary woman again!

Is it because of you, E? Is it because of you, Eve?

Of course, of course.

But what is so unusual about you?

Ah, then take a closer look at her.

Then naked E smiled at us and moved to the window. Outside, night was fading. Beside E's flowing hair the morning breeze passed; to the side of her long neck the stars gradually disappeared; between her walking legs distant mountains revealed their shapes... If I were a poet I would make the scene into a poem. But poetry isn't enough to make Ding Yi's flower pulse.

E sat on the floor in front of the window, before her upturned nipples dawn quietly rose. E lay on the floor in front of the window, above her lush hair the rays slowly spread. E and Ding Yi looked at each other, close as could be and as distant as the horizon, as silence buzzed... If I were a painter I would turn this scene into a painting. But paintings aren't enough to raise the spirits of Ding Yi's flower.

Outside, day was coming. I worried that this looking at each other might end, or would it go to the limit? I worried that after years and months, months and years, would the charm wear off?

But just then something was blown to the ground. E got on her knees, shuffled over, bent down and picked it up... Ah, this casual motion! This unrestricted freedom! This ignorant gesture or shameless flow deeply touched that sunken flower. In an instant I was flying,

Ding Yi's wildness shone in the spring light, in the blast of rain... The blast of rain stirred up E's fertile soil, provoked unrestrained screaming or wild howling, inspired Eve's eternal song...

Why is that? I've been wondering for a long time why that is.

"Some people learn to fall in love with the person who attracts them, but others become more and more attracted to the person they love."

In the storm Ding couldn't see E, E couldn't see Ding. But we seemed to be looking farther together, hearing more profoundly to the point of becoming abstract, nearly virtual... Ah, we were no longer looking at each other, we were looking through time together, looking through the past and future, at childhood, youth, spring and twilight, distant mountains and winged dawn, from life to death and from death to life again... That casual moment seemed to take us right back to Eden. That wonderfully abundant bum was no longer a mature attraction but a sign of childishness; that tangible secret was no longer a demarcation line but the truth of return; the gifted figure, skin, organs and desires are signs of your looking back deep into the past and praying for the permanent future... Then the sound of heaven will come, from near abstraction, from near virtuality:

"We are the world, we are the children."

This is the most moving song I heard during my travels in Ding Yi.

105. BDSM

One day Ding Yi and Qin Han talked about BDSM.

Qin Han: "Why do you think people do it?"

Ding Yi: "It's a kind of extreme expression."

Qin Han: "Which means..."

Ding Yi: "It's a kind of extreme form of love."

Qin Han: "That still tells me nothing, but thanks for not saying it's an aberration."

Ding Yi: "Then you tell me why people do it."

Qin Han: "This is E's trade. Don't get me wrong, I'm talking about drama, drama is E's trade. BDSM is actually drama."

Ding Yi: "Yeah? Interesting."

Qin Han: "What's interesting about it?"

Ding Yi: "E said drama is fundamentally potential."

Qin Han: "What potential? Or what has potential?"
Ding Yi: "What usually isn't possible is possible in drama."
Qin Han: "Then what's possible in BDSM?"
Ding Yi: "Love, of course."
Qin Han: "Of course not!"
Ding Yi: "An ex... extreme thing is possible."
Qin Han: "Sorry, I still have to ask what extreme thing is possible? Or what extreme thing was not possible before?"
Ding Yi: "I'd like to hear from you."
Qin Han: "I want to insult you, possible? But now possible. You want to control me, possible? Now it's possible. You don't want to be embarrassed in front of me, I can't degrade myself in front of you, these things that usually aren't possible are now possible. But this isn't the most important thing. The most important things are all these insults, control, embarrassment, degradation, all these things that go on during BDSM are known to both sides as false from the start, as simulations, like drama. In drama I think everything is symbolic. Realism is in the street. And symbolism causes people to make associations, makes them empathise, makes them look forward – ah, but I wish it were the same in reality. If reality was like this it would be so great. Could the bullying, humiliation and domination in reality also be fake? Make the battles in real life fake! At the end of this human drama make them disappear like a nightmare..."

Ah, this Qin Han!

Qin Han: "But is this possible? But look, now – in BDSM or in drama – it's possible, not just possible but necessary! That's the key. The important thing is it's drama from the beginning. You know it will disappear like a nightmare from the beginning, and when the fog lifts, a clear sky will be waiting for you there. As a result BDSM doesn't provoke hatred because the simulated hatred was bound to be restored to love from the beginning, restored to trust, restored to attachment. Drama makes the impossible possible and BDSM – you were right Brother Ding – is a kind of extreme drama, an extreme hope or dream that makes all kinds of impossible things become extremely possible, makes extreme resentment become extreme love."

Ah, this Qin Han!

Qin Han: "To put it another way, that's a model, a model of discrimination, a model a fear, a model of bullying or power, it mimics the truth of hatred when in fact it's enjoying hatred's falseness. You could also say praying for hatred's falseness doubles the enjoyment of true love. Really all myths, legends, are no different. In fact that's why stories of reunion are so charming. Human hope, eternal hope, is all based on this logic."

Well, this Qin Han knows everything, but why doesn't he believe in hope?

Ding Yi ignored me. Ding Yi's train of thought was being led firmly by

Qin Han. "Then why choose sex? For BDSM?"

Qin Han: "Because when sex is no longer limited to reproduction, it becomes the most important ceremony of love."

Hey, hey, Brother Ding, if the previous point is correct and sex becomes a means of reproduction later, then I think sex could very well fundamentally be a ceremony of love, right?

Ding Yi still ignored me. This guy is always interested in questions of minor detail. He asked Qin Han: "Is it actually drama or ceremony?"

Qin Han: "If you ask me, drama is fundamentally ceremony."

This guy's on the right track. Over the course of my long journey, I have found that in most places where ceremony is not valued, drama is in decline; where prayer is not valued, imagination declines – it's like E said: 'Drama will be reduced to a copy of reality.'

"Hey, Brother Ding," Qin Han suddenly asked Ding Yi with interest. "When they say the stage is a small world, and the world is a big stage, I find myself wondering what's the difference between a small world and a big stage?"

"What is it?"

"You guys like drama so much, you never thought about it?"

"Stop beating around the bush. What?"

"In my humble opinion, the characters in the small world all know the outcome while the people on the big stage are mostly muddleheaded, with no understanding of fate."

"Maybe, maybe it's... it's because..."

"Don't give me 'maybe'. There is no 'maybe' here, only destiny. People cannot match fate, that's why it's called fate! The only maybe is this: we are nothing more than a play God wrote."

"You really think that?"

"Really or not doesn't matter, what matters is that people cannot tolerate that possibility."

That Ding listened in a trance, daze, faint, puzzled.

Qing Han's eyes closed slightly as he slowly drank and ate, as if he had now foreseen the outcome of the chess game of life, and was waiting to see how you would play the endgame – to be specific, he was amused by it.

Ding Yi naturally couldn't think clearly, as in foggy clouds or muddy water, so he returned to the previous topic. "Brother Qin, do you think sex is always a love ceremony?"

"Well, good question," Qin Han said.

Then he lit a cigarette as if the mood just struck him: "I think sex can be a ceremony of love or a ceremony of love's destruction."

Ding Yi: "Huh? For example?"

Qin Han: "Uh... Have you heard of the painter Z?"

Ding Yi: "Who? No."

Qin Han: "What about O? Do you know about the female teacher O?"

Ding Yi: "The one who mysteriously committed suicide?"
Qin Han: "What was her name?"
Ding Yi: "Don't know."
Qin Han: "Then I don't' know if she's the one you mentioned or not. O is a true enigma."
Ding Yi: "Whoever she is, just tell me about her."
Qin Han: "OK, you said whoever she is."
Ding Yi: "I said so."
Qin Han: "Deal?"
Ding Yi: "Relax."

Sa came. Sa pushed open the door on tiptoe, a dazzling scarlet light illuminating the room like sunlight – this time not a dress but a red T-shirt and red athletic shorts.

That Ding secretly psst'd at me and said: *What do you say bro, where did we go astray?* He was referring to Sa's athletic shorts.

Sa came in with a big basket of food she had bought: vegetables, fruit, drinks, cold cuts and a variety of cooking ingredients. Presumably she had heard the argument from outside, and so gave Ding Yi a quiet smile and continued sorting out her food, meaning: I won't bother you or Brother Ding, trust me, I always head for the hills when this guy starts theorising. Sa put the drinks and cold cuts in the fridge, put the cooking ingredients in the cupboard one at a time, kept the fruit in the basket, then she brought the fresh vegetables into the kitchen and went out on the balcony. She was obviously a frequent guest there.

Qin Han's eyes were on her the whole time, his expression, really not so satisfied.

Ding Yi, hey, should we leave?
It's nothing, it's nothing.
But you see Qin Han, he doesn't seem very happy.
It's nothing...

"Where were we?" Qin Han said, coming back to himself.

"Maybe," Ding Yi said, "we should change the subject."

"No need, no need, Sa's an open-minded woman. Isn't that right, Sa?"

Sa responded from the balcony: "Based on current circumstances, she's very conventional!"

"Getting groceries makes you conventional? Why don't you say..." But Qin Han left it at that and faced Ding Yi with a smile. "I think we were talking about... oh, that suicide?"

"The teacher O and the painter Z."

Qin Han stubbed out his cigarette in the ashtray and paused before saying: "In my view could anyone be so stupid as this woman who, while her husband was asleep in bed, liable to wake up at any time, went to the next room and had an affair with another man?"

Ding Yi: "Maybe, it's possible."

Qin Han: "Let's forget stupidity, forget dissolute women, forget husbands and wives who have long become indifferent to each other. To my knowledge O was someone who thought love was important. O had painstakingly divorced her ex-husband in order to marry Z. If, later, she realised it wouldn't work with Z either and was without love or had never been in love, then why didn't she find someone else? Wouldn't leaving Z solve the problem? Why would she do that? She wasn't someone who could get by in marriage and showed lack of respect in sex?"

Ding Yi: "Are you sure this is all true?"

Qin Han: "Presumably. And as we agreed it doesn't matter who."

Ding Yi: "Then how do you think it happened?"

Qin Han: "There's only one clue: O always said she would never fall in love with that third person, the guy who, according to legend, had an affair with her. They say this was written in black and white in her suicide note."

I heard Sa walk over quietly, the sound of her footsteps passing through the kitchen and into the living room. She stopped behind Qin Han. It was quiet for a moment, then I heard Sa speak urgently and somewhat nervously: "O also wrote that, if she had loved in this world, she had only loved Z."

"If she had loved!" Qin Han didn't look at Sa but followed her words. "Did you hear that, Brother Ding? She said if she had loved! She said in this world! If she had loved in this world, she only loved Z."

Ding Yi: "What do you mean?"

Qin Han: "There's only one explanation."

Ding Yi: "So? Don't be so mysterious."

Qin Han: "I believe she wanted to do that deliberately."

Ding Yi: "Deliberately? Why?"

Qin Han: "Because it's a ceremony of love's destruction. As I just said, sex can be a ceremony of love or a ceremony of love's destruction. O either wanted to get revenge on Z or call all love into question. Or she felt both love and hatred for Z or she had completely lost hope for human love."

Ding Yi: "And that third person?"

Qin Han: "Oh, I think it was complete mockery. Not only did she mock that third person, but also all the 'so-called' love in this world!"

I noticed that Sa's expression was both focused and confused. She looked at Qin Han a moment, looked at Ding Yi a moment, was absorbed in picking her nails for a moment, as if solving several problems at once.

Qin Han: "I think something had happened before."

Ding Yi: "What happened?"

Qin Han: "Something unrelated to Z but a matter of life and death for O."

Ding Yi: "Be more specific."

Qin Han: "You'd have to ask O, but O's already dead. Or ask Z, but Z disappeared afterward to no one knows where. But if you did find Z, he might not be able to tell you. Because, because if Z could've understood O, O wouldn't have died."

Then I discovered that Sa seemed surprised and suddenly looked up but only for a short time, before slowly looking down again. Then she turned and left. But Ding Yi discerned that Sa had at some point changed into a white dress.

But when exactly? Ding Yi asked me.

I said: *It probably doesn't matter exactly.*

"Right, it probably doesn't matter exactly," Qin Han said. "But it was certainly something and not necessarily something physical. It could have been something metaphysical."

Ding Yi: "Don't get philosophical on me, OK? Talk like a person."

Qin Han: "That is to say, not that ordinary, specific, for example, something that law can resolve. Rather it occurs in the heart, desperation. Love is also desperate, but so too is no love. I mean people are fundamentally born desperate!"

Ding Yi: "Brother Qin, aren't you talking about yourself?"

Qin Han: "This has nothing to do with me. But it is certainly my understanding, my hypothesis. My understanding and my hypothesis are mine alone, they have nothing to do with Z and O, have nothing to do with what had happened any more."

Ding Yi: "Brother Qin, the more you talk the more mysterious you sound. You should really study philosophy."

Qin Han: "Take me, for example, what am I? I am my understanding, I am my memory, I am my impressions, I am my thoughts, I am my emotions... Apart from this what am I? Where would you find me? Take you, Ding Yi, for example, because we've been talking, you now have more memories and impressions, but your thoughts and feelings about them are completely your own. However you think and feel about it, this world will have that thinking and feeling Ding Yi, but what happened is in the past, gone like a musical note, but it hasn't disappeared, it persists in your thoughts and feelings, it persists in many people's memories, in a series of overlapping musical notes it continues, overlaps, changes and evolves into a movement."

Ha, he says so too – note and movement!

Ding Yi: "Brother Qin, have you been studying philosophy all these years?"

Qin Han: "I wouldn't use the term philosophy so lightly. I'm just a person who can't but think, who can't but feel and wonder."

Travelling soul! Not bad, my fellow. It's like the song from around here: "The sturdy north wind blows, the yellow sand slowly passes... I'm a wolf from the north..." That endlessly travelling soul also passes through the north wind and the yellow sand, through Qin Han. And it seems that soul's trek has been more full of hardships than mine, has travelled farther than me.

"What?" Ding Yi was still stuck on specifics. "I think Z and O might have had something?"

Qin Han stretched his limbs, stood up and walked around, took a look in the kitchen and said in a deliberately loud voice: "Ooh, so good, Ding Yi, you're in for a treat."

But the only sound coming from the kitchen was that of chopping vegetables and Sa's humming, no response. I'm sure she was thinking: shove it!

"No, no, I still have something to do," Ding Yi said.

This guy was observant, could see Sa's meticulous preparation was for sharing the meal with Qin Han – whether it would be a happy night or not, it was at least something looked forward to.

Qin Han again tried to mask his embarrassment with casualness and, turning to Ding Yi, said: "Like BDSM, you say it's an extreme form of love, and it usually is, but it can also be an extreme form of hate."

Ding Yi: "You mean the painter?"

Qin Han: "Whoever."

Ding Yi: "Right, right, anyone."

Qin Han: "If, I'm saying if, the dominant one doesn't enjoy this falsehood but admires its truth, what he hopes for is not love, not the disappearance of hatred but the realisation of conquest. Who's the clearest example of this?"

Ding Yi: "Who?"

Qin Han: "The submissive one."

Ding Yi: "The female teacher found out the painter was like that, didn't she?"

Qin Han: "Don't know. I never said that. I just know my suspicions and doubts. Now I can confirm you also have some suspicions and doubts. That's all."

Ding Yi: "So that's why you don't get married, is that right, Brother Qin?"

Qin Han: "You're back to that subject again! I'll say it once more, this has nothing to do with me."

Ding Yi: "But all your impressions are you, how can it have nothing to do with you?"

Qin Han: "Part of my impressions is: if, at Z's place, that extremity was reality instead of drama, the satisfaction of the dominator and the simulation of revenge, then O, that female teacher O, would probably say things like that."

That day, before I left with Ding Yi, Sa didn't show her face again, only her shadow swaying in the kitchen and on the balcony, swaying to her intermittent humming.

While Qin Han was showing Ding Yi out, several more guests arrived.

"Great, great," Qin Han greeted them, "tonight we're going to eat well."

"Frozen dumplings or instant noodles?"

"No, no, a proper dinner."

Oh, Ding Yi and I sighed, *poor Sa!*

106. Shi Tiesheng Interjects

Tonight, as soon as I sat down at the computer, that Shi clamoured in my ear: "You really believe in the soul?"

"Of course," I said. "Otherwise who am I?"

"Who are you? You're kidding, who else but Shi Tiesheng?"

"But I'm not just Shi Tiesheng!"

"Based on what?"

"Based on the fact that I can still be what you are not, or what you think you are not. I also know things you don't know, or things you know but aren't willing to recognise. So I'm in places you are not, because you won't recognise, because of intentional and unintentional forgetfulness, I can go to places you can't."

"The soul! Then tell me, what is the soul?"

"I already told Ding Yi."

"What's it like? What shape?"

"I have no way of telling you."

"Ha!" that Shi mocked. "Why can't you?"

"It's not that I can't, it's that there's no way. Because language is the soul's creator, the creator certainly cannot be bigger than its creation. Do you think a wave can speak of water? Can a cloud speak of the breeze?"

That Shi lowered his head, silent.

"But," I said to Shi, "a wave is an expression of water, a cloud is proof of wind."

"What's it prove?"

"It proves the concreteness of the vastness."

"Where are you?" That Shi narrowed his eyes again, looking disdainful.

"The finite and its infinite journey in the infinite."

107. A Kind of Drama: Strange and Interval

The stage is still that kind of stage with the agreed-upon time and the agreed-upon desire. The actor and director are still those two, Ding Yi and Qin E; they're the playwrights too.

The script was all in their hearts. The plot and dialogue are not fixed, but they were all in their hearts.

This kind of drama makes people excited.

The sunset makes people excited. Because the night is arriving and the day that follows is like birds that come to rest and gradually quiet down or go into the darkness and disappear.

There was no need for props. Lights, scenery and costumes were not needed, only to vacate the house.

They just had to draw a 'T' on the ground to divide it into three parts.

"This look OK?" Ding Yi asked.

E said: "OK."

E said: "OK, like this."

Then she stepped on both ends of the horizontal line to make a gap. "This is a door." She meant there are no gaps in the walls.

Then the two of them, outside the 'wall' or the 'door', approached from either end, dressed to the nines.

"This is the street." E tapped the ground outside the horizontal line with her toes.

"Lots of people," Ding Yi said, motioning all around.

"Right, and they're all other people."

Two people passed by each other.

The two passed again, tilted, even looking at each other, but were total strangers.

"As I said, you could be a good actor," E softly praised Ding Yi, smiling slightly at him.

Ding Yi stared again: "Not only that!"

After a few more times back and forth, E stopped and pulled Ding Yi to her side.

"What?"

"A station. The two of them may well have seen each other at a station, became close like this."

"And he noticed her." Ding Yi looked at E.

"Yeah? How?"

"Even, maybe, followed her."

"You mean it?"

"Probably." Ding Yi touched the centre of his chest. "According to Buddhism, having hatred in your heart is equivalent to murder."

"Why?"

"You mean hatred?"

"No, I mean why follow her?"

"Isn't it obvious? Because, because of her elegance, dignity, grace."

"Did he have 'evil' thoughts then?"

"No. Really. Didn't dare have them."

That guy's serious look made E unable to refrain from laughing.

"Shh," Ding Yi said. "We're on the street and don't know each other."

The two leaned back on the wall and sat side-by-side on the ground to symbolise being on a bus. The woman tried to maintain distance. The man looked steadily ahead.

"Do you want us to both use different names?" she asked.
"Oh, no need. No one's watching."
"Then we are each other's audience?"
"Hey, well said!"

Then it was like they were among the masses again; the two of them got off the bus, hurried, discreet or even indifferent.

Ding Yi: "That wasn't only well said, it also seemed... to have another, deeper meaning."

E: "Like what?"

Ding Yi: "Could it mean, appreciating each other?"

E: "Yeah... but that wouldn't seem enough. Just appreciating doesn't seem to be enough."

Then the two of them walked to their own houses, that is, the gaps at either end of the horizontal line, stood for a while, then passed through the doors.

After going inside E used her toe to point at the vertical line and tap above it. "Remember, this is a wall, we can't see each other now."

That Ding acted as if he didn't hear.

"Did you hear me?"

"I shouldn't be able to!"

E muttered something angry in an appreciative tone.

Ding Yi went into 'his room', took off his backpack, removed his jacket and stern expression, and tumbled onto the sofa. (Note: there is no sofa, just the base of a wall. All objects hereafter are virtual.) He closed his eyes, sighed and took out a cigarette, lit it, crossed his legs and blew out a long stream of smoke... a bachelor tired from a long day, lonely, sad.

E smiled genuinely, then made herself serious again, no, free again. Her expression and body both relaxed. She got rid of her high heels, was in no hurry to change into slippers, and even pulled off her stockings and threw them aside, leaving herself barefoot.

Ding Yi was there puffing on his side of the line.

"Next," E said quietly. "What do we do next?"

"He's thinking of a woman," Ding Yi said, his tone like dramatic inner monologue, "a strange woman. Maybe the one who had just sat next to him on the bus. He was thinking of her. Thinking of her elegance, dignity. Was wondering if she was that proud at home, that arrogant? Are such extraordinary women always so reserved, alert, impenetrable?"

E got what Ding Yi was implying and started to take her clothes off.

She calmly stripped, perhaps even carelessly, tossing her clothing on the bed one piece at a time, on the floor even.

Then she sat down naked and thought about something. Then she went into the 'bathroom', pretended to bathe, simulating before she bathed, and the feeling of afterwards, the comfort... like the enjoyment of turning the pages of a bestseller. The detail, yes, the detail must be true, but the storyline must be possibility. This scene must be slow, patient, indulgent with time, lavish beauty. Every detail passing: noble yet ordinary, indulgent but peaceful.

Or there could be a children's song sung softly: 'Oh May, hurry sweet May, let us go play... the fields dress in green... go to the riverside, watch the violets bloom...'

Ding Yi sat up and strained his ears, then walked to the vertical line and looked.

"Ah, sweet May, go to the riverside... hey, that's a wall!" E reminded him.

"Shh," Ding Yi said. "This is his imagination, no wall can stop a person's imagination."

"Then me?"

"She's unaware. She wants to keep being herself, unrestrained, extravagant. She wants to brazenly bare it all. Because this is a man's imagination. On the other side of the stage you act out his imagination, act out his desire and 'evil' thoughts. That elegant travel companion, the cold and yet pretty woman on the bus, now she's in the imagination of the man she ignored: her wonderful, big arse doesn't evade him, is not hidden, has no fear, no shame. Shame is evil you know? She's even... even unembarrassed about letting out a fart."

"Shut up!"

"You're not being a good theatre person."

"But I didn't."

"Farts are language too, you know? One that can't be spoken to others. A book called *Who Cut the Cheese?* says that some tribes allow their members to fart among their own people but are banished if they do so in front of outsiders."

"But I really didn't just now."

"This is a much better way to say it; that you didn't is another matter. But now you're his imagination, near to the freedom and dreams of his desire... He hopes the dignified, decent woman is as ordinary as he is, common, not so cold, not so reserved... of course, of course, she's still elegant, dignified, elegant and dignified but ordinary, common... that way he has hope. That way a lonely, ashamed man has hope, can hope and can imagine..."

E crouched down, held her legs.

Her long hair hung over her knees.

The line from her neck to her hips was a wonderful arc. The arc reminded me of children, of a foetus in the womb, of the beginning of life in an empty world... Right, once that wonderful arc unfolds itself, it will unfold with it a history of alienation, a dangerous situation, a distant dream or a hard journey...

"Yet every person is destined to join this history." Ding Yi spoke flatly, no longer like a monologue, more like a voiceover or instructions coming from an unseen world. "And a wonderful woman, she, well, she should appreciate herself, praise herself. Not so stupid like men, fighting to seem strong, doing the stupid things they don't have to... And an elegant, ordinary woman is hope this world can't do without, a great parable or sign. So, so she wants to walk in front of the mirror, deep in the night, when day rests and falls into a fast sleep, in the silence of the moonlight, and wholeheartedly admire God's creation, wholeheartedly long for His trust... Men cannot avoid going crazy and women are drifting spirits. Women want to take care of these ungrateful boys, make them come back, make them learn to come back, make them come back to where they started, and know how to admire, know how to bow before a woman without shame..."

Ah, good, Ding Yi! Well said, really well said. I didn't come to you for nothing. I don't dare say what will happen in the future, but now I know me and that Ding are already one. God's spirit walked on water, the eternal soul is filling Ding Yi, like wilderness in its mature season, like the white bird spreading its wings, free, healthy, humble and romantic, flying in the wind, flying in the wind...

E began to cry, began to enter the play.

Eve, moving or stationary, was unhindered.

Though standing still, in Ding Yi's eyes E and Eve were doing a beautiful dance. Even when sitting, in Ding Yi's eyes E and Eve were singing songs...

"Come," E called. "Hurry!"

"But, this wall?" Ding Yi pointed at the vertical line with exaggerated hesitance.

"But this is also a woman's imagination," Eve said, opening her arms. "To act out my imagination the wall can't hinder you!"

Ding Yi strode over the 'wall'.

You can imagine the rest, whether elegant or wild, it was all singing, it was all dancing, it was all dreaming and screaming, it was all soul meeting beyond flesh...

But doesn't this scene have some humour, one well dressed, the other calmly naked? But before they went to the mirror, the scene became unexpectedly shocking, much appreciated: behind E and Ding Yi or between being well dressed and naked, daylight quietly spread like the gates of heaven opening narrowly, like the winds of Eden blowing over the earth... The two stood side by side, speechless for a long time, the same sentence in their hearts: have you ever seen such peace? Have you seen such peace amid such humour?

Oh, oh, I have, I have! In an Edouard Manet painting called *Luncheon on the Grass*: a naked woman and two well-dressed men sitting on the grass in the forest, comfortably resting, chatting. In a stream not far away, a woman bent over the water to play lifts the bottom of her skirt... What a peaceful picture, what shocking peace! Who are they, who are they all? When and where? Did the painter dream of Ding and E or has this ancient wish been ongoing, forever the dream of the human world?

108. Untitled

When they fell breathless on the floor E said: What next?"
"What what next?"
"The end? A good ending is the most important thing for a play."
"Oh, the end... someone knocks on the door!" Ding Yi remembered the recent night without walls.
E sat up, surprised and shouted: "Who is it?"
No one answered.
"Maybe the postman."
"Yeah?" She strained her ears.
"Afraid to look?"
E hurried to find her clothes.
That Ding couldn't help but laugh. "I don't mean now, I mean in the end."
"The end?"
"Aren't we talking about the end of the play?"
"Gosh, you scared me."
"Are you that timid?"
"Shut up, look at my embarrassing appearance!"
"Nothing wrong with this, especially if you're on the 'street'?" Ding Yi patted the floor next to him – at some point they had rolled outside the horizontal line.
E laughed and jumped up and stepped on the horizontal line. "I've been sitting right on the 'street'? I want to stand on the 'wall' too!"

109. Script: Empty Wall Night

Soon Ding Yi wrote a script called *Empty Wall Night*.
"But," he said to E, "there can't just be two characters this time."
"Ha," E smiled, "then I'm afraid it will always just be a script."
"Why?"
"You're asking why? Unless you take multiple wives or I marry all the men."
They laughed. Ding Yi started to tell her about his idea.
"During the most boring days of my life I often left home alone, wandering all day, it didn't matter where to, resting when I was tired then walking again. When I was resting I stared at buildings the whole time, feeling they were really mysterious. Have you ever looked in that way?"

"Mm, go on."

"When you look you feel there's something mysterious, and funny, and that this world is filled with sorrow. Window after window, light after light, a story behind every closed curtain, each family staging their own play. The rows of windows all stacked up, how could they be so close? But in reality I knew they were very, very far away, so far that they would never find each other."

E took a cup of tea and sat in a wicker chair. "Mm, keep going."

"If it weren't for those walls of five or fifty inches thick, what do you think would happen? You would see that the people on either side often sit face to face, looking eye to eye, even lying next to each other in bed, sleeping... You might even worry their dreams would mix, influence each other, become intertwined, jumble into one. But in fact, if you want to get around a wall it's easier said than done, even if you trek around the earth and back you might not reach the next door. You can get to Africa or the South Pole in a dozen hours, but who can say how long it would take to get in next door? It'd be much easier to get close to penguins in Antarctica, go to space, it's not impossible to walk on another planet, but if you want to visit your neighbour, visit the person who sits face to face with you all day, could you be certain of getting there? You could try for a lifetime and fail!"

"Good thinking," E said.

"The so-called 'our world', the so-called 'under the same blue sky'? Actually you're just walking on a perplexing road, an extremely narrow road! One road after another, some are winding and occasionally intersect, some are intertwined but distant, some are leading to opposite ends never to meet."

(Shi Tiesheng agreed here with Ding Yi and couldn't help but interrupt: "Right, for example, me – Beijing is so big, I don't say I'm from Beijing, I used to be from Beixinqiao, then Yonghegong, now Shuiduizi. Beixinqiao, Yonghegong, Shuiduizi are all Beijing street names." I said not necessarily, did you cover the entire Shuiduizi? I said: "I would only say I've been to Ding Yi, now I'm passing through you.")

"But it can be very, very big," Ding Yi said to E. "Your imagination, your hope, your soul's dreams, your laughter and play... can take you very, very far, through unforeseen vastness!"

Nice, Ding Yi! I quietly praised him again, praised him for finally seeing that the places I can go to are not limited to the places you can go to, just as Eve's journey exceeds E's reach.

"For example?" E impatiently took the script from Ding Yi's hands.

"For example, the first scene is in the evening," Ding Yi said, excited like a hemmed-in animal, "or maybe later. Regardless, the sky isn't too dark. At that time people's feelings still haven't broken away from the daytime, there are still daytime rules to be followed.

"The whole stage is like a residential area, a residential building. But there are no walls. But there are still some horizontal and vertical lines that represent walls in the strict sense. Just like road lines – what do the police say if you ignore them? 'Hey! Your driver's licence, and the car, leave them here. What, you in a rush? You gonna crash into a wall cos you're in a rush? And you won't be able to drive that car any more, man, you think the wall won't smash it?' You certainly can't argue with the police that you haven't hit anything, the car hasn't been smashed, because in view of the consequences your car is smashed, and you can't go anywhere. It's like this: the vertical and horizontal walls will divide the stage into seven or eight, or at least five or six units.

"This first scene, I'm thinking, is called 'near yet far'. Of course, the horizontal and vertical lines aren't actually walls, they just convey some horizontal and vertical concepts. Really all walls are just concepts. Walls are man-made, isn't it easy for people to knock them down? But it's not easy, really knocking them down is actually not doable, just like the way you can't drive your car."

"Amazing," E said. "Definitely dramatic."

"I dreamed I was sitting against a wall when I suddenly felt nothing behind me. I turned to look and saw that the wall of the building behind me was gone. The people in the building, high and low, left and right, were still going about their business as if they didn't noticed the wall's disappearance... Nonetheless, I could still see where the walls had been, the invisible demarcations. How? Because of people's expressions, because of people's movements. Based on people's gestures you could tell that the wall was still there. For example, they had an air of calm because they were expecting to be tightly enveloped by four walls. For example, if they suddenly stopped laughing, unlike before, it meant they had already crossed the wall into another situation. You couldn't just see where the empty wall was, you could even tell how the isolation was different. Some were more relaxed, indifferent. Others were much more rigorous, needing to be meticulous. For example in order to cross over this demarcation, you just have to put on some shorts, to span this demarcation you have to dress neatly, smile nicely. You will find that only in solitude do people enjoy full liberation, or rather, the highest level of freedom."

"Bravo, bravo," E applauded gently but in exaggeration.

Ding Yi said: "Like naked clothing, now we have invisible walls!"

Ding Yi said: "Really, there are invisible walls everywhere. We're walking between invisible walls most of the time. On the street, at the store, moving among the masses, wherever you are, even making toasts among distinguished guests, you still may be between invisible walls."

Ding Yi said: "So people need a home. Homes are incredible! No other people, no one to disturb you, no one to watch you or nag you. Within the walls built with brick and stone or that give you cover, envelop you, everyone is free, peaceful and does whatever they like. But! Is that really the case? Please look at the second scene.

"The second scene is the opposite, it's called 'far yet near'. When night falls and everything is still, when people enter the dream world the drama really starts or the real drama starts. Now look, though in reality people are distant, in dreams people are eager to approach each other. At this time the whole stage is filled with dreams and hopes. Where can you find something more real, in the day or night? In reality or dream? In the isolation of walls? Or the calmness of restriction by the concept? Or are unpredictable dreams more able to tell us our true feelings and true wishes?"

"Good, really so good!" E was enthralled.

Ding Yi kept talking. "Really what's real, what's unreal? Why are restricted actions considered real while unbound desires considered unreal? If the former were called true, then we should call the latter true wishes! We should act out these true wishes. If from ancient times to today these true wishes can only sneak around at night, then now we should have men and women act them out under stage lights. As you often say, let's make the impossible possible, realise the unreal!"

"Ah," E shouted, "so brilliant!"

"And it could be really, really rich," Ding Yi said.

"Yes, yes," E said. "There are really so, so many possibilities here."

"It has as many possibilities as exist in reality," Ding Yi said.

"Then I think," E said, "what you've written so far is enough."

"Yeah, the rest can be improvised."

"If... I mean, if all the roles were played by non-actors that would be amazing."

"So everyone would play themselves?"

"You think?"

"I mean usually they're elsewhere, in clothes and walls, following the rules of reality..."

"And when they get here, they'll enter drama..."

"Enter a dream world, where they can realise things that are impossible elsewhere..."

"Yeah! They can realise what they want to do but don't dare try, say what they normally don't dare say..."

"Yeah, yeah."

"You think there are any other problems?"

"Problems? No, no problems. This kind of drama gets its meaning from having no problems, not having a slew of rules, the best thing is to do it according to your true wishes."

"Really amazing, really..."

"Unprecedented!"

"So what kind of roles have you imagined?"

Ding Yi said: "A lonely and self-loathing teenager, the sort who usually gives people the impression of being a coward, but it really isn't so, really he's full of energy. Like if he's had a long secret crush on a woman, a mature woman, he often looks through her window, watching her resting in bed, to the point that he even knows her outfits, but she hasn't noticed him, doesn't even know he exists. It could even be that the reason he's crazy about her is that she's never found out about him! And now he goes into the room he's longed to enter, goes up to that woman – dream or drama gives him this opportunity, this courage, you could even say it gives him this right..."

E: "There could also be a former couple, for whatever reason they abandoned each other, but really they couldn't forget each other, so here with the possibilities drama allows, they finally meet again, in the freedom dreams create, they speak frankly..."

Ding Yi: "Yes, as God gave humans the right to live, drama gives them the freedom to love. Here, at this time, in this arrangement, the room the teenager has been hoping to enter can no longer refuse him. That elegant, arrogant woman can no longer despise him, cannot ignore him, just like you can't stop a person from dreaming..."

E: "So right! The rules here are: dreams become reality. However you have dreamed, you can be; whatever possibilities dreams have you can enact; however they are in dreams, they can be in drama; this way, after years of separation, in this hazy night without walls, they can talk openly about the past..."

Ding Yi: "Right, this way the person he has been longing for can be like what he dreamed, listening to the teenager's loneliness and wretchedness..."

E: "All the grudges of the past will dissipate too, they'll be pushed outside of drama and thrown into the rubbish heap of reality... Like he and she go back to the beginning, back to that time before suspicion, back to Eden..."

Ding Yi: "That white dress won't float as arrogant and unattainable. That teenager can also grow up... I mean when the arrogant dress is shed like a wave, that lonely, self-loathing teenager will finally mature..."

E: "Like Graham said: 'Only people who've had a physical relationship can deeply understand each other.' Otherwise you can't give the other one helpful advice..."

Ding Yi: "But that's no longer a spring dream, it's mature drama. We've always hoped for this kind of drama. But during the day, here and there, during the majority of our lives we act out such awful roles. Like those crappy directors who read something in a trashy book and say: 'Drama is my life', shout loudly to direct you, correct you. What they know is day, they don't understand night..."

E: "And regarding the old couple who meet again, I think, even though they've both aged over time, even becoming really old, when they have their frank meeting the sight of each other will be as moving as when they were young..."

Yes, as the song goes: 'People all say I'm getting old, Maggie, it's hard to move now. Time is like a ruthless pen, writing lines on my face. They say we're old, Maggie, like bubbles washed among the waves, but you're still as young and beautiful as you used to be... We sing of the happy past, Maggie, sing of our youthful past.'

110. Note: Autumn and Writing, For Example

"Summer was coming, the sun quietly entered the house, the shadows it made moving like memories. Far away on the edge of the northern sky, so far it seemed abstract, listen carefully and you could make out a subtle disturbance lining up, opening, buzzing eagerly – it's the first autumn wind, the first stirring of autumn wind.

Nearby, nothing has changed. People still wear shorts, wave fans, as summer heat lingers over verdant vegetation. Only the insects seem aware, due to autumn's approach, they stay up late singing.

In the days after, if you kept listening, the faraway sound slowly changed a little, seeming to jump or laugh, comfortably, magnanimously striding closer, like after exchanging greetings at a crossroads then going on a date.

The approach of autumn wind could not be blocked, forcing the sun to hold back its indulgence. As a result the leaves and branches fell, bodies weakened, all fleshy bodies ran into trouble. Strong instincts, talented abilities, fierce energy, mad desire and will had to give up their previous conceit and doubt their past assurance. Thus the spirit shone.

As a result, autumn is the season of writing.

The season of understanding songs.

When groans and moans replace wild rock and roll, when wanderers return from wherever they were.

Heaven and earth, mountains and water, as well as human hearts are made empty and leisurely by the awesome pace of the autumn wind.

Leaves fall.

Or incessant autumn rain.

Mature lovers or old singers gaze at the horizon.

Look forward to autumn waters.

Look forward to flesh's boundary.

Then souls meet outside the flesh, the gaze dissipates in the distance.

Everything is sparse, everything withered. As the powerful body is covered with imprints of history, and the promise of talent smells the breath of death, the soul breaks out, turning desires into dreams.

Instinct is tempered into the ceremony of love – sex contains heaven's will.

The drizzle is like a song.
Falling leaves graceful, like dance.
Ageing lovers or dying singers do what they like.
Feeling each other, trembling hands search for secrets of a forgotten language.
Comforting each other, haggard bodies counted an inventory of lost credentials.
Where have you been all this time?
The mountains echo again. The call finally has an answer:
I am the forgotten secret language.
You are my lost credentials.
What year is it?
Unavoidable life and death.
Autumn is the season of writing."
– **Shi Tiesheng, *Rock and Writing for Example***

111. Note: Autumn For Example Again, and Even into Winter

"Autumn, even into winter, is the season of writing.
Until death.
Until dust buries time, time seals past waves.
Then an old man arrives at a bustling cabaret, walks to the seething square, sits in a corner, sits where one in their twilight years should sit, feels the unyielding spring wind.
Feeling the arrival of another generation. Whatever their shape, attitude, wildness or extremity, the old man understands.
No matter how they shout, rush or fail, the old man knows it's fine.
Do you want spring to listen to the autumn wind? Could it be that young men and women should see death? No, they just awoke from it. God wants them to forget death and forge a new season, reaffirm the journey.
They arrive on schedule.
They must stir up spring, its fanaticism, its arrogance, its various modes of unrestraint and traverse countless summers. Only when they have experienced public life, the instigation of instinct, the torture of love and the way physical limitations stifle talent... at the end of a long summer can they hear autumn's wind.
And this old man walks to his final resting place. Letting the autumn wind take him to the wilderness, seeing the golden rice, listening to the ripening fruit fall, smelling the vast rising fragrance of the broken sunflowers...
The winter arrives, at the wide-open wilderness.
Birds migrate south.

Life is dormant in the ground, the heart and soul stretch towards the sky. Towards infinity.
But infinity cannot be reached, souls converge on the eternal road.
God's spirit moves over water.
Another cycle.
Another separation.
The migrating flock promises to return, this cycle of separation...
The promise of search, the promise of love's drama."
– Shi Tiesheng, *Rock and Writing for Example*

112. Ding Yi's Cunning Ideas

Ding Yi was pretty foolish, reckless, but his cunning ideas numbered no fewer than anyone else's. For example, he didn't share any of the *Empty Wall Night* script with Qin Han but seized the opportunity of Qin Han's absence by showing it to Sa. I think I have to say another word about this: it doesn't seem like a big deal, at worst the guy's not a great friend, at best it shows the narrowness of male (or same sex) instincts. But if this narrowness is allowed to lurk and get out of control, the consequence likely runs counter to the ideals of *Empty Wall Night*. In the right climate this seemingly insignificant narrowness can swell, inflate... Whether this inflation will lead to a loss of reasoning is unclear, but like the aforementioned butterfly effect, it could take my Ding Yi anywhere.

Hey, Brother Ding, did you hear that? But that guy's attention was all on Sa, he completely dismissed my warning. Ugh, wait and see.

"You wrote it?"

"Yes, I wrote it."

Sa sat on the grass, first out of politeness, she skimmed it, but soon she started reading seriously, confusedly, strangely, with wrinkled brows.

Ding Yi sat next to Sa, stretched out his legs, which were clearly shorter than hers; his knees were not as high as hers either.

"Sa, with this body you must have been a track athlete, right?"

"Yeah, why?"

"Sprinting?"

"I was a sprinter, then I changed."

"Changed to long jump?"

Sa looked up from the script at him. "How'd you know?"

"I can tell."

"How?"

"Your body."

Sa's gaze returned to the script. Then she stopped and looked at the beautiful long legs beneath it. Then she changed positions, placing her chin on her knees with the script spread between her legs as she continued turning page after page.

Ding Yi used the change to say to me: *With regard to body, E really can't match Sa.*

I said: *What are you getting at, man?*

Nothing, nothing.

Then what do you mean by that?

I don't mean anything, really. What do you think I mean?

I said: *I just know people don't generally say things for no reason.*

Ding Yi got a bit angry. *Damn, I just made a statement, a statement of fact!*

Sa looked up from the script and gave Ding Yi a confused look. "What do you mean by that?"

That guy was surprised and took a while to regain his senses. "Oh, you mean the script?"

"What were you saying?"

"Oh, oh right, I was saying... saying this script."

On the grass wild flowers spilled. In the sky clouds tangled. The sunlight shimmered and dimmed alternately. The distant mountains seemed bright and close one second and covered by clouds the next.

"Yeah," Sa said, looking at Ding Yi.

"Oh, yeah, what?"

"This script?"

"Oh right, the script, this script, uh... E said she's afraid it will always just be a script."

"That doesn't matter."

"Then, then what do you mean?"

Sa looked at Ding Yi and gave him a gentle, sincere smile. "I'm saying what does this script mean? What are you really thinking?"

Ha! I suddenly understood something: the affection this Ding Yi got from women was closely tied to his silliness. Put it another way: this Ding made me realise men's clumsiness or stupidity attracts women like magic! Or put it more directly: I expected this Ding and Sa to fall in love at the same time, though to this point it had only been happening half consciously.

On the grass the light and shadows of the clouds kept fluctuating. Ding Yi explained *Empty Wall Night* to Sa from beginning to end, talked about his vision, talked about the things he told E. Of course he was a gentleman and left some things out.

Sa listened without moving.

"Sa?"

Sa's eyes fell.

"Sa?"

Sa's mind seemed elsewhere.

"You OK, Sa?"

Sa sighed, stretched out her legs, leaned back on her arms and looked at the sky. The clouds were entangled, making shapes. Sa sighed again.

"Well," Ding Yi said, "these are just some thoughts of mine, don't worry if you disagree."

Sa gently shook her head as if to say: No, no, maybe it's written pretty well. Especially the far yet near and near yet far are quite moving. "This really seems like me and him," Sa said.

"Who?"

Sa looked at Ding Yi, not answering, meaning: You don't know? You can't not know.

Sa said: "No matter how close you are to him, you always seem so far away from him, so so far away."

Sa said: "You seem like you'll never get close to him, never walk to his side, enter his heart."

Sa said: "No matter how close you are to him, so close, you don't see him clearly."

Sa said: "I often dream I'm chasing him and chasing him, running to the point of collapse, but he's still just slowly walking ahead of me. Or finally when I catch him, able to see him, his silhouette, movements, voice and even sense the right smell of him, everything's right, man, my heart says I've got you! My heart says I've found you at last! But... but you can't see his face clearly. You can't see his face clearly. I can see his hands, his feet and the clothes he always wears, but I can't see his face clearly, can't see his expression clearly. Even the eyes are his eyes, nose and mouth are all so familiar, but put together they don't seem like his."

Sa asked Ding Yi: "What do you think of him – Qin Han?"

Sa asked Ding Yi: "Being his friend for such a long time, what kind of person do you really think he is?"

Sa first said: "Maybe we aren't meant to be. Like in that song, you know that song?"

"Which song?"

Sa said: "'I have chased you a thousand miles, but you don't care. I've already changed into someone else, but you're still you.' Then she hummed: 'Time and again, I ask myself, if I really love you...'"

I recognised it as the song she was humming to herself in the kitchen that day.

Sa said: "It sounds like something out of a film, it's all acting, but I really feel this way. It's not only time and again, but I've asked myself a thousand times if I really love him or not."

Ding Yi said: "Do you really know him? I mean all about him, do you really know him thoroughly?"

To my surprise Sa got angry. "Do you? Do you really know all about him? Do you all really know all about him? I told you he loves both men and women. He loves the ugly and the beautiful. He loves everyone. He says love should be for everyone, otherwise it isn't love, otherwise it's just sex. I'm telling you, who's a saint? He is! Have you noticed what else is in his house besides some books, videotapes and DVDs? Have you noticed? You must think I bought that food for the heck of it, but I'm telling you, not true, not true! It's just because he didn't have it, he just had frozen dumplings and instant noodles."

Ding Yi and I faced each other. I said: *Yeah, like I said, the ancient soul in Qin Han has experienced hardships, wandered a long distance and now seeks beauty.*

Ding Yi said: *Sa's beautiful.*

"You guys don't understand him," Sa said. "Know why?"

"Why?"

"Most people think he's gay, even E thinks so."

"He isn't?"

"Of course not!"

"Then why..."

"For what? He just doesn't want to explain it you. He just doesn't discriminate against gays like most people. He says people who discriminate against gays really don't understand love. He says gays are actually purer, nobler."

Ding Yi said: *Hey, did you notice E said this too.*

Shh, I said. *Listen to her!*

"Qin Han said: 'Love doesn't come from gender, and love isn't in the world because of gender. Things just based on gender are not love but attraction, at best. At worst even animals, plants and minerals are attracted by yin and yang.'

"Qin Han said: 'Sexual attraction is necessary for reproduction, but if it's mere sexual attraction why talk about love?'

"Also, Qin Han didn't say this, but I think, why is sex sometimes not attractive?"

I told her what Graham said: "'Men fall in love with the women they're attracted to while women become more attracted to the man they love.'"

Sa thought a moment, then shouted: "Oh! Who said that?"

"From a film."

"What's it called? I have to tell Qin Han."

"I watched it at his place."

"Oh, really?" Sa was a little taken aback. "But dividing men and women like this, I doubt Qin Han would like that, he never thought it was a gender issue."

"But sex really is a language, right?" Ding Yi said.

"Language?"

"An extreme expression and... and a unique discourse."

Great, Brother Ding you said it at just the right moment! But Sa didn't notice, Sa may not have understood.

Sa just questioned 'unique': "People have been praising love since ancient times, right? Love is the most wonderful feeling people have, no one could disagree, right? So Qin Han asked me, if that's the case, then why does this most wonderful feeling have to be limited to the narrowest range?"

Ding Yi and I were at a loss.

Sa said: "First it's limited to gender, then it's limited to a monogamous relationship and given to the smallest number of people. Qin Han said: 'Is this how you treat something wonderful? It's actually how you treat something criminal.'"

Ding Yi wasn't sure about this, Ding Yi laughed to himself. But I already sensed this was an extraordinary question, a wise question. And this could become Ding Yi's future and affect the rest of my journey with Ding Yi.

Sa told Ding Yi not to laugh. Sa said: "I laughed at him at first too, felt it wasn't worth refuting. But he said it may make sense when it comes to preserving the race and passing on property, but what about love? It's all sex, sex, sex! Just mating and breeding, just the labour force and stocks and that's it. But 'Remember this', he said, don't complain when you get into a marriage without love; don't blame this ism or that ism after you have your children and grandchildren without enjoying love."

Finished?

Sa seemed to be finished.

Ding Yi had missed out on an important line of thought, that is, the key question Qin Han asked and Sa reported: since love is the most wonderful feeling, why limit it to the narrowest range? But I think this guy with his worthy intelligence could not have completely missed this point.

The distant clouds were becoming rain. The nearby trees were summoning the wind.

Birds in flight suddenly thought of home.

Ding Yi and Sa seemed not to notice the changing weather, even their sitting postures remained the same.

Sa took a silk ribbon from her pocket and held it, letting it flutter in the wind.

Ding Yi and I both thought of that four-inch-wide arm band. But Ding Yi was much stronger now. He said: "Sa, can I ask you a question?"

"Ask!" Sa seemed to already know what Ding Yi would say.

"I feel, uh... feel you aren't really... very happy."

"Wrong! I knew you would ask that."

"So you are very happy?"

"Of course."

"Then how did you know I would ask why you aren't very happy? Why didn't you guess I would ask why you're always so happy?"

Sa's face turned red, and she became angry. "Because, because you silly people always ask that."

Ding Yi's response was excellent. "Then now you should admit I'm a smart person, right?"

Sa was speechless.

"So you can also tell me why you're always..." – the guy deliberately paused, gazing towards the wind rising in the distance – "always this un-hap-py?"

Sa nearly exploded with anger. She couldn't stand it any more and pushed him fiercely. As far as I can remember, this was the first physical contact between Sa and Ding Yi. Of course that Ding wasn't angry, the emotional guy even enjoyed it, the genius ladies' man even felt honoured. Ha, now I dared to claim this Ding would hold Sa in his arms sooner or later.

Sa turned away.

The emotional one ignored her.

Sa softly cried.

The genius 'gardener' knew he should let her go.

Sa stood up and started walking home.

This romantic class leader was so shrewd. Look at him, staying a few steps behind, quietly accompanying.

The rain arrived. The wind blew the rain horizontally, turned the leaves over, chased the birds away. The whole world was drowned in the roar of heavy rain.

"Let's get some shelter for a while," Sa said.

You see? He had to let her talk first! But Ding Yi wasn't using some trick or technique – I've said he's honest, but I've also said he has natural talents that are hard to give up. It wasn't skill, it was instinct, ability acquired at birth! (I couldn't help but again think of that scary child, its ability to build power, which probably also sprung from their genes?)

Running up the hill, running into a small pavilion, they were completely soaked. What to do? Don't be like the ones in romance novels: the man, being a true gentleman, turns his back, as a true gentleman he brought some extra dry clothing, and he starts shaking and shivering, but out with tenderheartedness or unsavoury intentions must let the woman change into them... This Ding had internalised this after years under my instruction: don't be like that, vulgar!

Only then can tasteful things happen, and they must happen.

Tears and rain mixed, which was good – Sa had nothing to be embarrassed about.

She said: "I'm not happy, just because I'm not so advanced."

She said: "I really can't manage to feel the same love for all things."

She said: "Really, it's nothing. And I'm really not that unhappy."

She said: "I'm pretty happy with Qin Han."

She went on: "It's all my fault. It's my own problem, has nothing to do with Qin Han."

Ding Yi asked: "Then what if you weren't with him?" He seemed to have had the question ready a long time.

Sa quickly followed with: "It really isn't worse than not being with him!" This sentence seemed to have been buried a long time.

I thought, if at that time I asked her why, it would strike a nerve. But Ding Yi indicated for me not to worry: *Don't be so aggressive, can she really take it back at this point? Haste makes waste.*

Oh come on, Ding Yi, don't be too fucking much. At this rate you'll be ready for politics in no time!

In fact with no one asking, Sa began talking on her own. The three main points were: first, she worshipped Qin Han, believed him to be a saint. As a result she would always love him, even if one day she had to leave him, she believed she would still love him. Second, Sa's pain did not come from whether Qin Han would marry her or not, or who Qin Han loved, but rather from her inability to be so advanced. How to explain it? For example, the fact was Sa did not like or even disliked Qin Han's so-called friends (she called them "his really weird friends"). She hoped they'd leave, be less close to Qin Han, stop always coming to savagely torture him! She believed that Qin Han wouldn't be happy unless he lived with her, wouldn't be healthy, wouldn't be able to live well. Third, perhaps because of Qin Han's influence, Sa thought that sex really is an awful thing, the body's just a stinking husk, never clean, and sex is most interested in the dirtiest body parts. "Do people have to be like that?" Dirty and ugly, cruel and ridiculous – did they have to be that way?

"Not being like that, only love is left – is that not enough?"

"Do you think it is?" I asked.

"Why wouldn't it be?"

"Do you think it's possible?"

"Maybe one day when we're all old," Sa said, looking at the misty rain, falling into a reverie. "Then we may be able to, able to relinquish the body's control, no longer be driven by hormones. And really, what the hell are hormones anyway? Can you believe such a little thing could fix people? I really wish I didn't have them, it would be much better without them. People always want to stay young, but I'd love to hurry up and get old. Being old I'd be rid of that mess. Two old people, or if Qin Han has his way, a group, a group of old people, a group of cute old people, without jealousy, without suspicion, without you, me, them, everything coming from the heart, spiritual communication between them all, the soul's needs... that way, that way I feel Qin Han's dream would be possible."

"But that way," I said, "there might be no passion, right?"

"Really?"

"People all like piles of wood or clay sculptures stupidly filling the world?"

"How could it be like that? It couldn't. Are we forgetting the present?"

I said I didn't know, didn't know how people without desire would be. Ding Yi continued: "Really, even trees have desire, flowers and grass all have desire, all objects and spirits are desire."

That made me think of the beginning of life. For a moment I seemed to have returned to my state prior to coming to Ding Yi: like water shouting in the sand or wind blowing in the soul, desire gathering in the void... Consciousness undying, gently wobbling, floating, undulating, gently exhibiting or fancying... At that time it seemed like there was a voice saying something, rising and falling, here and then gone, hard to make out... Or it was just an idea, like a yearning, almost a fear...

"Then, you're saying this will never be possible?" Sa asked.

"Only in drama is it possible." Ding Yi took out up that script again.

Sa tilted her head to look at it, then looked seriously at Ding Yi.

Ding Yi: "E said drama is the time when everything that isn't possible becomes possible, the place where everything that isn't real can be realised."

Ding Yi: "More precisely it's a kind of agreement, an agreement between hearts."

Ding Yi: "The agreement is outside of reality, the agreement happens in dreams."

Ding Yi: "Drama doesn't imitate the truth of reality but the truth of real dreams. There, in drama, or in the agreement, people can express their hearts and carry out their wishes."

Ding Yi: "Then you come back to reality. Outside the agreement you have no choice but to obey the rules of the daytime."

Ding Yi: "But at night, in drama, in that kind of agreement, you must be your authentic self, remove your physical and mental armour, remove your packaging, remove your naked clothing, because once..."

"Naked clothing?"

"Oh, I'll tell you about it later. Because once you try to hide, try to disguise yourself, once you're insincere, feeling that being sincere is shameful, then the drama ends. Once you feel that spiritually or physically you have to take cover, like when Adam and Eve left the Garden of Eden, you're already outside the agreement, you've already walked out of drama and into the rules of reality..."

Sa listened, entranced.

113. Ou

After the rainstorm Ding Yi and Sa walked home, their clothes drying in the blazing sun. On the way Ding Yi felt something had been left unresolved – what was it? When they were about to part, it came roaring back to him.

"Oh, right." He stopped walking. "You still haven't told me something."

"What?"

Ding Yi hesitated.

"Tell me. I hate it when guys beat around the bush like women."

"Me? You mean me?" Ding Yi laughed.

"What are you laughing at? Out with it!"

Ding Yi hurried ahead. "I'm saying, hey, listen..."

Sa giggled, stopped and listened to him.

Ha, I once again understood that Ding was straightforward after all. This straightforwardness, not just his natural talent, allowed him to gain the trust of a good woman.

"I'm saying, oh no, it's what you said – what makes you say Qin Han isn't that... that kind?"

"What, what kind? I say you're as faltering as a woman and you don't believe me. I'll tell you: he has a girlfriend!"

"Really?"

"Stop acting surprised, maybe you do?" Sa lifted her legs and continued walking.

Sa was speaking freely, which made Ding Yi secretly happy.

"Who? Where is she?" that Ding asked as he chased Sa.

"Here!" Sa pointed to her heart to say in Qin Han's heart.

"How do you know?"

"If you don't believe me, fine."

They walked a little more, then Sa asked without stopping: "Do you know Ou?"

"Ou?"

"You never heard him talk about her?"

Ding Yi shook his head, thought a while, then shook his head again. "Woman?"

"Come on!" Sa was furious. "Are you stupid or acting stupid?"

Sa said one afternoon she went to see Qin Han. She knocked on the door and got no response. She opened it and went in and saw Qin Han lying on the couch sleeping. Sa didn't disturb him. Sa pulled up a chair and sat down, looking at him. That afternoon was unusually quiet. The sun eased into the house, spreading over the window sill, spreading over the back of the sofa, spreading over Qin Han's body. Sa said she had never looked at him so closely, so calmly and so alone. (Now I realised something had happened – why was Ding Yi's heart hurting so much? *What's going on with you, brother?* He lowered his head, then looked up again. *Nothing's going on, why don't you stop making trouble?*) Sa watched Qin Han that way, watched his extended expression, watched his steady breathing... she said at that time he was truly him. Sa said at that time Qin Han was clear, distinct, detailed, perhaps even complete, and finally conformed with the Qin Han in her heart. (That Ding's heart grew even more hurt.

I said: *Yes, yes, how can our 'first-class romantic leader' bear his title being taken away by Qin Han?*

That Ding hissed disdainfully through his teeth: *Shh!*

I quickly said: *Oh, yes, Brother Ding, since you've sailed the seven seas, how come you can't handle a splash?* He didn't respond, probably meaning: Shut up and listen!) On that quiet afternoon, Sa said, so quiet you could hear sounds from the distance, the northern sky, places so far away they seemed abstract, some small commotion forming a row, opening a line, buzzing with eagerness...

"Ah, it's autumn wind!" Sa said it was certainly the autumn wind setting out. Sa said she suddenly felt Qin Han before then was like this autumn wind, somewhere on the horizon, setting out from somewhere, and the Qin Han sleeping in front of her was as serene as that afternoon, quiet, the warm sun slowly moving over him, slowly moving between his eyebrows and moving in his dreams. (*Brother Ding, doesn't she mean her eyes really never left that old Qin Han?* Brother Ding just cleared his throat and even strained his mind thinking for a long time about what even he didn't know.)

Sa said that afternoon was clear as a pool of water, gurgling like a stream, vast as if it had a long history... bewildering everyone into sleep, everyone into a dreamland at that serene noontime, like the rest of the world... Only the autumn wind whispered in her ear, only the autumn wind buzzed eagerly, like a deep anxiety in the dream. (I said: *Mr Ding, is Sa composing a poem?* Mr Ding didn't hear me this time. I felt Ding Yi was a bit like Peter in the film, who was also hurting when he watched Ann's video.) Sa asked if he had ever closely watched someone dream. Dreams have foresight, can see everything around, are causally related to surrounding events, logically. Sa said, when an awake person is not aware of the changes around them, the dreamer seems to have already noticed everything. Sa said, when nothing was changing on the serene afternoon, she noticed Qin Han's breath was gradually speeding him, his expression was suddenly distorted, then he groaned, struggled and his forehead began to sweat... Sa wondered if she should wake him up, but then either upstairs or next door something hit the ground or the wall with a loud bang. Qin Han's struggle reached its height at this moment to the point where he couldn't bear it any more and had to wake up as if his dream had been a story that coincided with the one upstairs or next door, the events occurring simultaneously. (*Have you heard of this?* that Ding asked me. I said: *Maybe, the soul? Can you compare it to hope? But there is one thing: if Qin Han's dream wasn't a nightmare, that sound could have catered to him and created another message.*)

But it seemed Qin Han's dream really was a nightmare. He screamed and sat up, squinting and grabbing around him. Sa said she couldn't believe it: "He grabbed me."

Qin Han tightly grabbed Sa and didn't let go, shouting, horrified: "Ou, Ou! Ou! Where are you Ou? You're OK, right..."

Sa held him. Sa held him tightly. Sa couldn't think of anything to say to comfort him, just held him and held him tightly. Sa said there was nothing more pitiful on earth than that. Sa said she had never seen a more pitiful sight. Sa said not even every pitiful thing added together could match the expression in Qin Han's eyes...

"And then?" I asked since that stupid Ding couldn't even speak full sentences.

"Then? Then he really woke up."

Then Qin Han broke free from Sa and slowly calmed down. Then he got up, drank some water and casually said: "Ahem, was dreaming." Then he smiled, completely back to his normal bearing or demeanour.

"So different you wouldn't recognise him," Sa said.

"And then?"

"And then you and I should both go home!" Sa shouted, her mood apparently still trapped by that never-ending afternoon.

Ding Yi decided to hit her where it hurt. "I'm saying Ou, who is she really?"

"Like I would know!"

"Didn't you say she was Qin Han's girlfriend?"

"Well if she isn't his girlfriend, who is she?"

"Then how do you know?"

"Are you an idiot? How?" Sa was about to curse.

But suddenly I felt that Ding smile to himself – how strange, for a moment I really didn't understand why.

"What else?" that Ding asked.

"Jack shit, you already know more than I do!" Sa turned, left and jumped on a bus.

114. Good ≠ OK

When Ding Yi told E about Sa, Qin Han and Ou, she said: "It seems to me that Sa is hopeless."

"What, Qin Han really isn't gay?"

Haha, I understand! Ding Yi's words pretend to be concerned but are really cunning: since Qin Han has another in his heart, Sa obviously has no hope with him. If so, doesn't Sa have a lot of hope with Ding Yi? But he wouldn't necessarily admit it. He sniffed in some air to indicate he couldn't stand my misunderstanding, hated my conjecture – *How can you be so mistaken about people?*

"Do you know Ou?" Ding Yi changed the subject.

"I wouldn't say I know her," E said. "I've heard about her."

"Is she really Qin Han's girlfriend?"

"She was."

"What went wrong?"

"Don't know."

"Now where is she or how is she?"

"That Qin Han may not even know."
"How so?"
"How not?"
"He never told you about all this?"
"After Ou disappeared he just told me one thing: all is empty. Actually he said something else after: humanity's biggest mistake is seeing reality as drama and drama as reality."
"What's that mean?"
"On the surface it seems to be about me, but I sense he's referring to someone else."
"Referring to Ou?"
"Who else?"

But I see what Qin Han said as significant. In my opinion it's very important, in my opinion it's not limited to what he refers to. It's a shame Ding Yi and E couldn't notice.

But suddenly Ding Yi thought of another thing Qin Han had said. As I've mentioned, given this guy's romantic genius, he wouldn't easily forget such a thing: "Since love is human's most beautiful emotion, why does it have to be limited in quantity and scope?" It's strange that, since Sa jumped on that bus, that question jumped into Ding Yi's mind, lingered, filling Ding Yi's mind with reverberations and creating another series of questions: why can't his beautiful emotion expand? Why is it limited to couples?

Can't there be love between greater numbers of people? Could it be that more people can't love each other? Qin Han was right, only property inheritance should be handled that way, only the reproduction of the species would require it. But love! Why would love that transcends economic and reproductive motivations be like that, what is the need to be like that? It's simply absurd, simply foolish. How many people say 'universal love' but mean something else? What does 'universal love' really mean? How is it different from the expansion of love? How does it seem to be making a boundary? Pointing out a distance, a kind of defined distance, a kind of not-too-close, not-too-far, just right distance? Who has the right to limit it like this? If people are too alienated it's bad, if people are close it's also bad. Under whose authority was the 'right' distance established? Why do we have to listen to them?

One day Ding Yi asked E these questions.

E was with Asky practising piano. "I can't say now, if I said, it wouldn't be the truth."

Ding Yi glanced at Asky. "Does she understand?"

E laughed slyly. "No, not just her, the daytime. Now I can only say: if reality is reality, it can only be accepted, don't ask in absolutes."

Only when night came, when Asky was asleep, when they entered the agreed-upon hour together did E say: "Now you can ask. Now's the time when you can ask anything. Now I can answer without restrictions."

E sat on the windowsill, looked at the lamplight and starlight outside.

Ding Yi walked up and down in front of her. "Then tell me, three, four, five or six people loving each other – what's wrong with that?"

"Who said there is?"

Ding Yi stopped walking, his eyes brightened. "You think it's OK?"

E turned towards him, "Not so fast mister, not wrong doesn't mean OK."

"Since it's good, what's not OK about it?"

"Look what you asked! It's like a poet asking a politician. Let me think, let me think how a politician would respond... Oh, they would definitely say this: Look out for theatre people, people who make art, look out for poets, and whatever you do, don't let them be in power!"

Ding Yi started to pace up and down again. "Then why did you say there's nothing wrong?"

E faced the stars but kept her gaze on Ding Yi. "Because in fact everyone thinks so."

That Ding stopped and turned. "Are you sure?"

E said: "Do you remember what Graham asked Ann?"

Graham asked Ann: Besides your husband, have you thought about making love with other men? Ann hesitated a long time: Yes, I have. Graham asked: Have you really done anything? Ann said no. Graham asked: Then what kind of man have you thought of? Ann looked at Graham a long time, said I thought of you... have you thought of me too? Graham's gaze softened: Yes, I have. Ann said: What have you thought of? Graham said: What you're like when you climax.

E said: "That is to say, people don't all just think of one person."

E said: "Everyone thinks of lots of people, even at the same time."

E said: "But is it not love? Of course it can be love. Apart from one, the others, can't be love? Self-deception, pure self-deception. But just that one is allowed by reality, the rest cannot be realised, that's why it's called unrealistic."

"But that's just in reality," Ding Yi said.

"Right," E said. "In reality there can only be unreality."

"But in drama," Ding Yi said, "can't everything... everything can be realised, right?"

"Is that so?" E's heart suddenly seemed to grow heavy. "Maybe it's like dreams."

Ding Yi was very excited but tried to contain himself.

E noticed Ding Yi's excitement but only smiled faintly, perhaps with a touch of bitterness or ridicule. But soon E turned her face again towards the city gradually dimmed or the starry sky gradually alight, her soul seeming to fall into the past.

"Hey, then do you think Sa can or can't?"

"Sa? Oh, her…"
"OK, you think?"
"You mean drama?"
"Of course, just drama."
"Empty Wall Night?"
"For example, yeah, *Empty Wall Night.*"

E thought carefully like a director, taking her time to think of Sa; E had seen her, but her image was blurry.

"Why don't you ask her first?"
"I'm asking you first."
"I…" E hopped off the windowsill, walked silently along the horizontal and vertical lines awhile then looked up and said: "OK, no problem for me."
"Wow, you're awesome!"

But I could see there was still a hint of ridicule on E's face, a hidden smile, even cynicism.

E said: "I think we've been talking a long time about something good in theory but that we'd hate in reality, no? Which is also a wonderful play!" E seemed to have broken free from the past or deliberately broken out of her annoyance and bitterness, which made her seem sharper than usual, more open-minded.

Ding Yi said: "Relax, it's just drama."
Ding Yi said: "Relax, sex isn't a factor here."
E said: "Really? If that's really what you want, I wouldn't be able to relax."
Ding Yi quickly said: "Oh, oh, of course it's not love."
"That's even worse: with neither sex nor love. Tell me, what are you trying to realise with this drama?"

Ding Yi's mouth hung open. I silently laughed at him: *Are you an idiot? Why don't we just tell the truth!*

E said: "Thus the unreal is realised, thus the impossible is finally becoming possible, just because that's what people usually want but cannot want, what they usually want to say but don't dare say, and what is usually extraordinary is dangerous at the same time…"

115. Title Interpretation

For a long time afterwards, Qin Han's question became the theoretical basis or moral support for Ding Yi's multi-directional lust. "Since love is humanity's most beautiful feeling, why does it have to be so restricted in scope? Why not let her expand as much as possible? Constrained, limited, restricted, only allowed to be good and honest, not talk freely – is that how you treat a beautiful thing? It's how you treat plagues and catastrophes!" He talked about simplified or expanded versions of this theory with

E, with Sa, with himself, with all kinds of ethicists and theorists in an attempt to prove the question was not only extraordinary and beautiful but irrefutably true. The reason could be that my so-called travels in Ding Yi initiated this question and were its extension. It both amazed me and gave me boundless enthusiasm and hope.

Or to put it another way, travels in Ding Yi may have been my past life and also may be my future life, but it was more likely I was travelling in a particular Shi and that question stimulated my imagination and gave rise to my heart's desire. This desire must accompany me into my lives, since this desire is the 'I' of those lives. This desire is more boundless than heaven, older than earth – the boundless sky and old earth may vanish, but the desire is everlasting.

Now I can say where I am.

Now I can say where this ancient travelling spirit is.

He is in this Shi and in that Ding, and especially in Qin Han's question. Yes, yes, I'm in everything I've heard and seen, in everything my thoughts and mind can reach. And in other places where I encountered the strange. Or encountering thick barriers, became confused. I encountered a never-ending siege. And precisely this never-ending siege made an immortal soul become possible, made this limited existence eternally named 'I'.

116. Some Clouds

But in my view, theory and philosophy are just ways to interpret one's own lust.

"I think therefore I am"? Really I am therefore I think! Do you think of your existence? Thinking is just a faint and mysterious communication or of this vast and mysterious existence. Take Ding Yi, for example. Do you think that's why he took that question so seriously, just because its logic was impeccable? No way! Life looms larger than theory. The guy definitely thought the question was precious because its logic played into the hands of this first-class romantic!

As getting a little lost brings a sense of direction and being in a vast desert reveals the significance of an oasis, after learning the aforementioned question this Ding was suddenly enlightened, rejoicing day and night: Ah, where were you before? How had I not thought of you? He even studied his script day and night, coming up with more drama. As a result he had as much freedom and authenticity awake as in dreams, his mind and body open like the midsummer sky, blue and bright, clear and brilliant...

But I would like everyone to pay special attention to that wisp of cloud: not only did he not let Qin Han read *Empty Wall Night*, he also never discussed its ideas with him. This is quite important. I had asked Ding Yi why he hadn't talked about it with Qin Han. That guy hemmed and hawed about him, trying to convince himself that it was his busy schedule that had made him negligent. Do you believe, everyone? So I said this passionate butterfly flapping its wings in confinement seems very important. Who knows when and where its flapping may cause a storm or if it will capsize the boat that is my travels in Ding Yi.

117. Empty Wall Night With an Audience

Still in that bare living room. But this time it wasn't divided by horizontal and vertical lines, colour was used instead. The floor was painted red, blue and white to distinguish three areas. Where the different colours met were 'walls'.

It was still night, it was still that agreed-upon hour, but there was another person: Lü Sa.

This wasn't simple.

Sa was in the white area, moving, standing or sitting, to show she was on the street; or you could say she was in the audience; but the main thing was not part of the plot.

Being outside the plot did not mean being outside the drama.

Being outside the plot just means not participating in the acting. It doesn't mean she was not participating in imagination.

Not participating in the plot but participating in imagination, that is to say: an audience is an indispensable part of drama. Furthermore, non-participants in acting may still have an impact on the acting.

Like passersby, like reality existing outside the plot or outside the theatre are all imaginative resources for the actors, are potential energy for the plot or why the drama was created. As a result, Sa's presence was by no means irrelevant.

Sa as a passerby or an audience member made the drama that night unique.

In fact you could say Sa was present as a potential performer, like a character with a famous name who never appears onstage. Because Sa as the audience wasn't just an imaginer but one who was imagined – could be felt, cared for or wondered about by a performer at any time. She imagined the performers' thoughts and feelings, and the performers also tried to understand her heart, while she influenced the performers, influenced the plot or became a potential dramatic persona.

Being a potential dramatic persona was a right granted to an audience by the drama, not the admission ticket. The essence of drama is that it's not just the performers and established plot that have the right to tell; in fact the audience also tells. There is a theory of aesthetic reception stating that beauty comes to be in the response or blending of performer and audience. That's why there is a kind of theatrical future expectation: the audience directly, happily and freely attends the plot. It is said that there are some 'avant-garde dramatists' who have done experiments in this area.

But tonight's drama was not pioneering. Tonight's drama was relatively traditional. As for the audience's – Sa's – attendance, it was still just Ding Yi's hope, not yet reality.

(That unwilling-to-be-left-out Shi Tiesheng enigmatically interjected: "Not that realistic or not that dramatic?" Good question! I said: "Not that realistic, so not that dramatic." That Shi laughed to himself: "So tonight's drama succumbed to reality?" What a trickster! But don't worry. "Not so real, so more dramatic!" Shi didn't respond, just looked suspicious. We'll let him go for now.)

The script had not been changed. Everything was as previously envisioned: E acted like a woman Ding Yi desired, while Ding Yi played a man E longed for. They both dreamed of the other, both became the other's fantasy. In sum, to let the distance of previous looking or peeping disappear in the dream world or let their shelter dissolve by agreement.

It started like this: in the evening or after nightfall on either side of the wall (where red and blue intersected) were a single man and woman. They both sat at tables. (Note: the props were all imaginary so the two actually stood or sat on the ground.) The tables faced the same wall so E and Ding Yi actually faced each other closely. They were face to face without seeing each other. The woman dressed in front of a mirror but seemed to be looking silently at Ding Yi. The man was playing with a video camera – head lowered as if about to go headlong into E's arms.

Next, either unbearably hot or lonely, the two left their houses (going from red or blue to white respectively) to walk around. Sa was there too – on the 'street', maybe cooling down, but her gaze was focused like an audience member's. When E passed, she quietly said: "Hey, we might know each other. If we do, let's say hello." Sa didn't realise the words were for her until E was already 'far'. 'Far away' Ding Yi and E met face-to-face, they glanced at each other, but they did not speak, making their expressions more solemn, cautious, even indifferent.

Sa couldn't help but cheer. "Yes, yes, it's really like this!"

"Really like what?" E asked with a smile.

"You can easily say 'hello' to an insignificant person. But if you unexpectedly meet someone you've been expecting for a long time, you don't dare be so casual, say a word, you..."

"What?"

"Pretend to be pathetic!"

"You mean you and Qin Han?" E asked and walked 'farther'.

Sa smiled happily. Smiled happily and nodded happily.

"Shh," Ding Yi raised a finger and shook it at them.

Next, the man and woman went home (to red and blue). Two downcast people, two preoccupied people, two lonely people lay on the bed, staring and thinking, thinking a while, thinking a long time, they themselves not knowing what of...

Sa dimmed the lights accordingly.

The man's voice-over monologue began: "Night, why is it still not near?"

Then the woman's followed: "Dreams, why have they still not come?"

The monologues repeated again and again like night talking or sounds of nature, before growing indistinct. The lights went out.

Now they seemed to be really in a theatre, surrounded by silence and darkness. Once their eyes adjusted to the darkness, the cool bright moonlight became visible on two patches of the floor near the windows, where streaky tree shadows wavered. "The moon peeps into the windows, casting its shifting light on sleepless people," therefore causing Ding and E to toss and turn...

Sa got a bit nervous, unable to guess what would happen.

Sa sat in a corner the moonlight did not reach, trembling somewhat: "Hey, can you wait a minute? I... I have to go to the bathroom."

Sa didn't dare move. Holding her breath, tilting her head to listen, she hoped she hadn't broken any rules.

"Attention audience members who wish to use the bathroom, attention audience members who wish to use the bathroom," Ding Yi said dully like an announcer.

"Ladies and gentlemen, if you wish to use the bathroom you may do so. No need to ask the director."

E laughed. Then Ding Yi laughed. Sa took a while to understand what was going on.

The laughter made her relax a little. "I'll be right back."

Ding Yi: "Yes, yes, no one will think you'll go and not come back."

E closed her eyes. E heard the guy's unusual excitement.

When Sa came back Ding Yi was standing on the edge of the blue zone. The man peered obsessively at the woman in the red zone, peering at her solitude, her sleep as if peering into her heart and dreams... And the sleeping woman must have also been confused, fantasising, longing – as a result E was disturbed and couldn't sleep, now stretching, now curling up, now on her back breathing deeply, now on her stomach breathing shallowly, to the point where she lost all elegance and dignity... her emotions making the man's heart tremble with fascination, or waking up the voice of Ding Yi's heart: "Ah, you're that proud woman? That cold neighbour who looks down on everyone?"

"Hey hey, that's a wall," Sa stood up and shouted. "You can't see her!"

Ding Yi raised his head and his eyes, as if reciting his defence: "But this is imagination, no wall can contain a man's imagination." This old refrain was just the right line for that night or a divine promise from the unknown world.

Then Sa saw: the man walked through the walls, towards the woman, close to her as moonlight, looking at her, surrounding her like the night wind, teasing her... Then Sa saw: the man lifted his video camera, wanting to fix her truth like a mountain, engrave her indulgent, innocent sleep into eternal memory, inscribe it on the future, even carve it on the past... Then Sa saw: the man's arrival ended the magic of sleep, in the possibility of dreams the woman opened her eyes peacefully, sat up, accepted him, allowed him, went along with his caresses...

"You're kidding right, E?" Sa shouted. "That's his fantasy, you're supposed to be asleep and not know!"

"But it's not just the man's imagination, Sa. It's the wish of all women who seem cold and arrogant!"

So the man and woman in the dream or Ding and E in the drama, hugged and kissed, intoxicated.

Where have you been all this time?

The mountains' echo reverberates...

Then the man and woman in the night or the Ding and E at the agreed-upon time, moved gently, sorrowfully.

E: "Where have you been all these years since you left me?"

Ding Yi: "Ah, do you still remember that sweet olive tree? I was there, I was there waiting for you all my life."

E: "But I often dreamed you were next door. Right next door, but seeming far off on the horizon."

Ding Yi: "But you never came. I waited until sunset, the sky filled with stars, but you never came."

E: "Maybe next door is farther than the horizon? Maybe the horizon is a bit closer than next door."

Ding Yi: "If at different times we arrived at the same place, then it's like us arriving at the same time at different places."

E: "If having different feelings we are in the same place, that's like having the same feelings on opposite ends of the earth."

Ding Yi: "Since I saw you dance, I've been looking for you everywhere. Since you wrote your name on my hand, I've been looking for you."

E: "You should look for me at our old house. But not during the day, do it at night, in the promises you made."

Ding Yi: "But you stood me up. You never came. When the stars grew bright, only that white dress was dancing."

E: "I often heard your distant sounds from next door. I often heard the sound of your past words in the present, and heard the sounds of your future there too. Can we really only be separated by this distance?"

Ding Yi: "Yes, that's because that white dress floats too elegantly, too coldly."

E: "That's because you're too easily hurt."

Ding Yi: "That's because you dance too elegantly, too arrogantly."

E: "That's because you're too quick to beat yourself up."

Ding Yi: "That's because your name is too noble, too different."

E: "That's because you're too afraid of loneliness, too eager to be strong."

Ding Yi: "That's because your parents stood onstage, for whatever reason, they were standing onstage after all."

E: "That's because you forgot our first home."

Ding Yi: "First home? Where?"

E: "Maybe distant Eden."

Ding Yi: "But that time the white dress didn't exist!"

E: "But that time we also had no nobility or noble names."

Ding Yi: "Right, right, then everything was naked."

E: "That time we were just called Adam, just called Eve."

Ding Yi: "Then who are you now?"

E: "Then who are you now?"

Ding Yi: "Tonight Adam has reached the man next door."

E: "Tonight Eve has also reached the woman next door."

Ding Yi: "Now Adam wants to do what the man next door has always wanted to do but hasn't dared."

E: "Eve now wants to say what the woman next door has always wanted to say but hasn't dared."

Ding Yi: "Yes, all that was impossible is now possible?"

E: "Yes, all unreality can be realised."

Then the night wind sang, the moonlight danced... Then the neighbours in dreams or the couple from the end of the earth, again asked each other: Where have you been all this time? The echo reverberating in the mountains... Then the agreed-upon man and woman or the free Ding and E felt each other, their trembling hands seeming to speak the forgotten language; they comforted each other, close like recovering the lost credentials... So on this 'empty-wall night' the ancient call finally received its response: I am your lifelong secret language; you are my everlasting credentials...

118. Untitled

But from the passionate drama of that night, Sa learned that Ding Yi was emotionally turbulent, experienced with almost all the women he liked – from childhood to the present. While in E's dialogue only one name was hidden – from beginning to end it's been him.

119. Naked Clothing

That night of drama was unusual. For example, 'off' wasn't spoken, not at all. It had all the intimate movements, all the moving information, all the unconventional plots or plot possibilities, the only thing it didn't have was that key word.

Clothing is a wall, could it still be called wall-less night?

But! I told Ding Yi: It's like that 'naked clothing' Roland Barthes discovered, have you come up with another possibility? Next I reminded E and also Sa: The reason nakedness is clothing is because the soul is still obscured, so is it possible for clothes not to cover the soul?

"Right, right," that Ding said to E. "Nakedness can be clothing, why can't clothing be naked?"

E said: "Awesome, awesome, the important thing is to open the soul, as long as the soul is open!"

Then Ding Yi and I and Ding Yi and E rejoiced at the discovery that the night of drama had yielded an unprecedented creation: clothed nakedness!

But Sa didn't see it that way. Sa had a different notion. Sa understood that crucial phrase should come. What should have come did not come, Sa knew, all because of her – the presence of a passerby, the presence of an outsider. Yes, all because she couldn't sink into the night, the drama couldn't expand, the agreed-upon peace was still threatened by reality. Because she was a designated spectator, an outsider who would not enter the drama, whose desire for clothed nakedness was still un-naked clothing, that 'off' word still evasively never came.

Otherwise it would come.

Otherwise it must come.

Later, Sa said at that time her first impulse was to tell Qin Han, why sex is unavoidable, is important, even essential. Sa thought she understood what she saw and heard, what sex implied to every kind of desire, and why that 'off' word must come.

An extreme wish!

An irreplaceable expression!

An extreme wish requires extreme language. That is to say, extreme action is required to enact extreme wishes, to bear your extreme expression, so lovers can confirm what they say and hear is extreme. Otherwise a grand season may be confused with mediocrity, a meeting awaited for a thousand years may be placid. Otherwise how could Adam and Eve recognise each other? How would lovers or dying musicians be distinguished: you and other people?

So later, when Ding Yi said sex is fundamentally a language, Sa kept nodding.

Still on that patch of grass, fireflies flying, sky full of stars, Ding Yi said: "Have you thought that, in fact, it's a kind of expression, a kind of statement."

Ding Yi and Sa sat facing each other. Her face was unclear in the dim starlight, but the fireflies in flight were like Ding Yi's mood.

He said to Sa: "It's even a ceremony, from then on someone opens themself completely to another, someone takes on another's complete opening."

But Brother Ding, that can't be a lie, right?

A lie?
Like what Peter did to Ann, like what the painter Z did to the teacher O.
Oh... yeah, yeah.
Qin Han even said that could be a ceremony for the end of love...
"Right, that could also be a lie."
"Lie?" Sa looked at Ding Yi in surprise.

That guy was silent for a moment, then suddenly got an idea. "Sa, do you believe that lies also start from here? Because... because protection also starts here, aggression, resentment, suspicion all start here. So love also starts here. Peace also starts here."

Sa couldn't stop nodding again.

Ding Yi wasn't finished. "Because leaving Eden, with that beginning – either the beginning of lies or the beginning of love."

Ding Yi's spirits rose. "Why do people love? Because of loneliness. Because of distance. Because you've been surrounded by other people since you were born."

He asked Sa: "Do you know the lyrics? Why are the stars as crowded as the people on earth? Why are the people on earth as distant as the stars above?"

"Mm," Sa said quietly to indicate she knew the song, she liked the lyrics or something else? Or it was just a casual response to show she was listening.

"Folk songs, do you like folk songs?" Ding Yi cleared his throat and sang a line: "Big slate stones over white clouds, the hardship of life is missing another."

"What do you think? There's another." That Ding stood and opened his throat. "If you're my brother give me a wave, if you're not my brother go your own way!

"There's still another, the most imaginative: I miss you so much my eyes glaze over and the ground looks like a mare..."

"Why a mare?" Sa asked.

"To ride it and go look for him!"

That Ding slowly walked around the lawn, growing smugger with each and every step. Of course I knew what this boy was thinking, this boy always had firm confidence in his intellect, then he must have felt that an incredibly lucky spirit was backing him up. As a result the situation was worthy of music, for example some old songs like *The Country* or *Heat*...

Sit down, Ding Yi, I said.

Yeah, yeah. That Ding sat down, quietly saying to himself: *It's time to be calm, hold your breath.*

Hold your breath?

Yeah, be smooth, take it easy, be open-minded, the guy said to himself. *Don't be so impudent, don't be so unrestrained. Of course you can be cool, but you also have to be a little bit simple...*

I said: *Son of a gun, you're being cunning. I didn't ask you to sit for that.*

He said: *Go, go, go, you're over worried.*

I said: *At this moment, you're still pulling a smart trick, bro, do you think it's right?*

He said: *No I'm not, I'm not.*

I said: *Yes or no, I don't think even you yourself have any idea.*

That guy ignored me from then on.

He said to Sa: "So people thought of making a contract."

He said to Sa: "So love is an agreement. From now on we are not other people."

Sa looked at the starry sky, the depths of heaven that even stars can't reach.

There was no moon, or it couldn't be seen.

"But," Ding Yi continued, "Qin Han's question is really good."

"What question?"

"If it's a beautiful feeling, if everyone praises it, why minimise its range as much as possible? Only one-to-one really makes no sense!"

The moon hid in the clouds or hid behind the buildings.

It's said that all the stars that can be seen are larger than the moon.

Ding Yi said: "E said that's why people invented drama."

Ding Yi said: "E said that's why drama cannot imitate reality. On the contrary, reality responds to drama."

Ding Yi said: "It would be unthinkable to enact daily life onstage!"

Ding Yi said: "Typical people, typical environments. May I know who tells us what is normal?"

Ding Yi said: "What drama wants is not the typical but the possible! Real drama is a kind of – no – all kinds of, every kind of life. That is to say..."

"I know." Sa stood up then sat down again, wrapping her legs in her skirt.

"What do you know?"

"The agreed-upon time, and place, oh, no, time and place are not important, the important thing is the feeling, a kind of cherished desire, everything is possible there, everything can be realised."

Ding Yi was stunned, for a while he didn't know what to say. I gloated. *You're showing off...*

"Then," Sa turned and asked, "am I OK?"

"What do you mean?"

"You know!" Sa sounded very certain.

"I know? I know what?" That Ding acted surprised, trying hard to seem innocent or calm.

"You're asking what you know? Don't you want to ask if I can join your drama?"

Seeing Sa cutting to the chase, Ding couldn't but hum and haw, not knowing what to say.

Fortunately Sa wasn't interested in pressing him, and her thoughts seemed to stray elsewhere.

Ding Yi tried to justify what he said. "I'm just saying, if it's a beautiful thing why... why try so hard to shrink it?"

"No, no, I never said you were wrong."

Ding Yi was evasive. "It's just E said, E said..."

"No, no, I never said E was wrong either."

Ding Yi resisted and shifted. "E said drama doesn't want to imitate reality but..."

"But reality wants to approach drama, I know. I'm just saying I'm talking about myself! OK?"

Ding Yi was silent.

Sa lay down and looked at the starry sky for a long time. "You said all the stars are bigger than the moon?"

"What do you mean?"

"Nothing, just asking."

Then Ding Yi also looked up. "Yeah... right, it's actually true."

"Then you know all the 'actualies'?"

"At least about the moon and stars I know."

"What about satellites?" Sa smiled proudly.

"That doesn't count," Ding Yi said. "Satellites don't count as stars."

Sa's smile slowly faded. Sa's smile seemed to float into the depths of the sky. The meaning seemed to be: this question doesn't need to be debated again. Or: debating this question again, it's still one question. Or there's another possibility, which would be impolite to say: can people know all the actualies? But you men always think you're omniscient.

While Ding Yi was feeling a bit embarrassed or discouraged, Sa seemed to have already counted the stars or forgotten about the moon as she looked up hard, eyes bright, at Ding Yi.

"Maybe I'm OK?" she said.

"I really think I'm OK!" she said.

"If I'm OK," she said, "I think I can understand Qin Han."

It didn't look bad, everything seemed to be going well. Only Sa's last sentence made Ding Yi feel disheartened inside.

120. Title Interpretation

Ding Yi, I'm sorry, but I still have to say it, does what you're doing count as seduction? Does it count as taking advantage?

Ding Yi said: *Taking advantage of who?*

Ding Yi said: *Qin Han never had that intention [with Sa], E also said Sa has no hope, so tell me, who am I taking advantage of?*

I said: *That's wrong, then you don't seem open and frank enough.*
Ding Yi said: *How the hell am I not open, not frank?*
I said: *Anyway, I sensed something fishy, something filthy in what you said. I felt you seemed to be conniving somehow.*

Ding Yi just grumbled, but that Shi quietly laughed again.

The laugh was so infuriating! I thought Ding Yi can be reprimanded by me, but you're not in a position to sneer at him, so I told that Shi: "Ding Yi is deceased, a brother who can't defend himself, why don't we be a little more kind?"

That Shi closed his mouth and pretended not to laugh, but it was clear that he was trying hard not to laugh, anyone could tell he was still laughing. This is really so infuriating, so annoying, so awful! Really cunning, two birds with one stone: it showed Shi's magnanimity and suggested Ding Yi's ridiculousness was impossible not to laugh at.

I was really kind of regretting telling *My Travels in Ding Yi* to Shi.

Fed up, I said: "Do I dare ask, Mr Shi? How about you?"

"What's wrong with me?"

"That Ding's feelings, are you saying you've never had them?"

That Shi stopped laughing, put on the face of a gentlemen, but the sneer in the corners of his mouth remained.

OK, OK, now I think I have to explain the title of the book again: the so-called *My Travels in Ding Yi* could be considered a path my life took before Shi Tiesheng, and could also be seen as a way I comprehended life from inside Shi. It could also be seen as biographical sketches from when I was in Ding Yi and could be understood as the various thoughts I had in Shi. Put it this way: without the travels in Ding, there wouldn't be the thoughts in Shi; without the thoughts in Shi, alas, wouldn't that time in Ding be wasted, an absurd encounter? Might it be better to be an ape, fish, dog or horse, or a soulless vessel? Just like mighty Shi, so many Ding travels, many travels' thoughts!

"What's up with that again?" that Shi Tiesheng said. "What's wrong with me thinking about him and laughing about him?"

"Sure, but why just laugh at him?"

"Who else should I laugh at?"

"I told you, I was in Ding Yi, I can't get around that."

"So you're saying I should laugh at you too?"

"Exactly, but now I'm in Shi Tiesheng."

That Shi was surprised and feeling fooled, shouted: "That's bullshit, I have nothing to do with you and that Ding Yi!"

"But I'm staying in you now and experiencing him?"

"But you... you better not fucking write it!"

Ha, I hit the nail on the head! But this is none of your business! The so-called *My Travels in Ding Yi* says: Ding travels, Shi thinks, my journey never ends, my thinking is boundless.

121. Three-Person Drama

Three-person drama, no doubt, makes people nervous.

They just pretended to be calm, had a few innocent questions and answers or laughs. But as that agreed-upon time approached they were silent. It was like they were going to a dangerous place, opening a blockade or falling into a magical kingdom as all three held their breath, faced each other in the darkness... subconsciously delaying, resigning themselves to fate.

Between them were the red, blue and white areas. Ding Yi, Qin E, Lü Sa, each occupied one. In another corner was the window, the misty moonlight, the blurred shadows of trees.

You can imagine it, destiny on the line: just taking one step forward you cannot return to where you were. Just go a step further and you hand yourself over, hand yourself over to two and not one – you thought you understood, but you really weren't sure that you could forever hang on to the one that knew and accompanied you – one of other people. As irreversible as time, or unchangeable as history. Really this is history: things develop a little more, and you'll suffer the consequences, you'll have to abide by the agreement, honour your words, and you'll hold in pledge your privacy, your secrets, your weaknesses... just like Uncle said, you'll have 'your people'.

Even though they often brought up beforehand: we're free, now and still will be after.

We choose freedom, without reluctance and without compulsion. What our drama is and will always be seeking is precisely freedom and love.

Despite this there's still anxiety.

A so-called point of no return means: from now on you can't deny your desire or lust's multidirectionality, you can't dress up to hide your loneliness, your vulnerability and your longing for others. At least in front of these two people, that's how you have to be.

But what did Uncle say? "Fu, well, let's leave this awful place, whether we go to the ends of the earth, whether we go to a desert, a remote island, a tomb, it's fine with me. There, it will always be you and me, no other people, no enemies, none of 'our people'."

Amid that anxiety or giddiness, I sensed a danger: the plural you is always greater than the singular you; we may never be as safe as me; and has all along been plural in number. I think subconsciously Ding Yi, Qin E and Lü Sa all feel this vaguely.

But love's expansion is so seductive!

Time passes in minutes and seconds, everything is final.

The tricolour ground is empty, silence shouts there.

On the empty, moonlit tricolour ground, screams and shouts jump and dance.

So in the blurred shadows of trees on the tricolour ground, 'off' finally comes. That trembling sound is like an on-schedule command, first reached E, then Sa, then Ding Yi.

But their naked bodies clung to their corners, not daring to step forward.

They stood silently, not even daring to look at each other.

They're silently praying: let the moonlight dim more, let the tree shadows blur more. Or: get brighter, moonlight, light up our desires! Tree shadows, shake, don't let us back down!

Sa bravely walked into the moonlight.

Ding Yi and E heard her dance-like steps.

Moonlight and wind made the tree shadows sway over Sa's sculpted body, sway over her quivering chest and long legs, sway over her plump arse and blushing face...

Then E suddenly shouted the words of Ding Yi that moved her: "Sa, your arse is gorgeous!"

This was a gentle order, all expectant souls must raise their spirits!

Sa, as if no one was around, or as if in front of all her lovers, bared herself without restraint – she turned her beautiful body into a silent language, filled all her potential gestures with great expectation, made all her talents and secrets available for all to see, let her wild heart ask the night: Hey, who am I? And you and him, who are you all?

Then the silent, dark night responded: I am Lü Sa, expecting love... I am Qin E, rife with desire and vulnerability... I am Ding Yi, desiring to be weaker... We are ancient travelling souls, endlessly searching for each other – Adam and Eve...

122. Imagination

I want to leave the rest of what happened to the reader's imagination, let anyone who is willing or able to imagine, imagine. Because after all, drama doesn't rely on other people but imagination – life's limitless imagination, desire's limitless possibilities' imagination. While three people's drama relies on extraordinary imaginative powers, relies on broad-mindedness, pure desire and the most daring agreement.

Ding Yi, Qin E and Lü Sa on that red-, blue- and white-coloured ground performed an extraordinary scene. In the red, blue and white rooms Ding Yi, Qin E and Lü Sa were extremely bold.

I want to leave their extreme boldness to your imagination. For example, imagine according to all the legends and tales ancient and contemporary, foreign or Chinese, imagine according to all the endless desires held since ancient times. Imagine according to the sentiment of 'saying what you want to say but don't dare, and doing what you want to do but don't dare'. Imagine according to what you want to imagine but don't dare imagine, what you want to say but only say in dreams. You can also do so according to the 'raw footage' available everywhere – because, one, sex all looks pretty similar; and because, two, sex is all imagined pretty differently.

Ding Yi, Qin E and Lü Sa's night was wonderful and filled me with admiration

Ding Yi, Qin E and Lü Sa's night was wildly imaginative and deeply touched me.

I want to leave those overflowing imaginings to the reader's imagination. I'm OK with knowing that the night's drama was outside the day's constraints, an agreement between hearts. Just want to know it wasn't simply a matter of flesh, and maybe not simply a matter of energy, it was a matter of the soul. Just like the holy spirit walking on water. Just like now, God finally freeing man and returning them to Eden. Just like Adam and Eve seeing through the snake's lies, renouncing the lure of the tree of knowledge, the prodigal son turning back, to enjoy again the fruits of the tree of life.

In my imagination Ding Yi, Qin E and Lü Sa's drama was incredibly rich.

In my imagination the sex is more poetic than meritorious.

But I can only leave it to each's imagination. Because this drama was fundamentally not for you to see but for you to hear, to imagine, to attend with your imagination. And because, when imagination is lost, people's hearts weaken and they rely on the flesh, they ignore language and focus on vessels, and they force an endless path to heaven into a lurid zone.

If you're not willing to imagine, can't imagine or don't value imagination, then simply put this book down.

They say the other area is real, just requires the movement of the vessel.

123. That Shi Asks Me: Lewdness and Dirtiness

If you imagine, if that extraordinary imagination makes you feel the threat of lewdness or dirtiness – for example Shi asked me: "What is lewdness, what is dirtiness?"

I said: "Do you think sincere nakedness is lewdness? Reckless baring is dirtiness?" I said: "If so, then you grip your clothes and walls, grip your secrets and loneliness, let imagination die."

Sex looks similar but is imagined differently. Was there lewdness in Graham's tapes?

But precisely from John's perspective – from Ann's rightful husband's perspective or Laura's secret love's perspective, you see dirtiness.

Lewdness and dirtiness aren't necessarily related to flesh, while deeply moving words could be lies; it may even be that deeply moving words are all lies.

Night has no need to deceive. Night is night, no need to flaunt something else. So night is the time to tell. Or in order to tell, night must fall.

When Ding Yi, Qin E and Lü Sa sat naked in the moonlight and where the red, blue and white zones met, feet against feet, their toes made a 'Y' shape as the night wind blew, I didn't see lewdness. When they looked at the agreed-upon night, let the wavering tree shadows dance over their naked bodies, let their eyes wander with impunity over each other, I certainly didn't see any dirtiness.

Really in my view E and Sa's conversation was free, E and Sa got along intimately, while Ding Yi's feelings were incredibly intense. Really in my view the two women's gaze was as full of openness and sincerity as Ding Yi's gaze, revealing attraction or even longing, then Ding Yi felt more grateful and satisfied than ever...

I asked him: *How is it, brother?*
Amazing, amazing, thank you, thank you.
Fate has been a little too good to you, huh?
Yes, yes, thank you, thank you!
Maybe you should feel a little guilty?
Yes, thanks, thanks...
Don't just stupidly say thanks, say a sentence!
The sky is wide, the earth is broad, brilliant and bright, brother I just feel the sky is wide, the earth is broad, brilliant and bright!

Yes, yes, the sky is wide, the earth is broad, brilliant and bright, our usual dream. From never knowing its past to not knowing its future – it seems its reward has already been reaped! Then I looked around, saw the starlight, moonlight, the wind blowing the trees – all gifts fate had given Ding Yi. Then I closed my eyes and listened, heard the distant clamour, the silence near, the old hardships and present peace – all mercy that God bestows on people! I wanted that Ding to put his hands together and pray with me: let my travels in Ding Yi go on like this, on and on, on like this forever, or let it end here.

124. Weird and Shameless

If you want to give your imagination a jolt, think of when you've been harassed by 'weird' or oppressed by 'shameless'. For example, that Shi asked me this before or attacked me with it. I said: "Then have you thought about why people have shame? What is normality based on?"

This made me think of when Ding Yi and I first encountered the world: strange gazes glimmering in the tree shadows, gradually gathering around, watching, pointing, sniggering... One voice said: "Wow, look at him, just standing naked in the street!" Another voice said: "Ha, not a bad little thing, you let it stick up for people to look at?" Then the naked boy felt embarrassed, a shiver ran down his body and he instinctively covered his little bud... Is this shame? But why be ashamed?

Then I remembered Eden, remembered setting out from Adam, saying goodbye to Eve: naked Adam and naked Eve left the garden, holding hands as they awaited an unpredictable world. Then they also suddenly felt a shiver, felt embarrassed, let go of each other's hands, drooped completely... And just then fig leaves floated down, the leaves that first covered the two different flowers... Why? What for? Because people understood shame and were banished from Eden, but the question is: why do people feel shame?

I've thought about this a long time but haven't been able to understand. I've been wondering for years.

But look at animals, all animals? When they – for example apes, fish, dogs, horses – expose the weakest part of their bodies to one of their own, what are they expressing? Right, right, expressing affection. What else? Yes, yes, expressing surrender! Strange, how are affection and surrender expressed the same way? Could it be that affection contains surrender? Or do affection and surrender express each other?

If I say yes, I doubt you'll believe me. If I say hate contains conquest, you'll probably believe me, but if I say love contains surrender, you won't believe me. If I say love is a kind of extraordinary surrender, you'll probably be baffled. If I say the cure for conquest is extraordinary surrender you may feel the logic is novel, but is it correct?

If I change the sentence and say the cure for hate is love, the original cure for hate is love, the final cure is love, I think you would definitely agree, even praise me.

Ahem, that's where the problem starts: people are so drawn to love, but people are so unwilling to surrender. The problem starts here: people are so weak and are also so unwilling to recognise their weakness, especially during the day.

Especially during the roaring, transpiring day!

That's why night comes. Night is the time to pray for love and hope for surrender, the time to sacrifice love in dedication to surrender. Because night is telling, it's when the soul enthusiastically breaks away from the day's coercion, when the preference for surrender grows.

But what does the night want you to surrender?

Love is not surrendered for cruelty but for people's weakness.

Since God separated man from chaos, man was destined to be weak. Since God separated men from each other, man was destined to be weak. God created differences through separation, thus creating the world: on the first day he separated day from night; on the second day he separated sky and earth; on the third day he separated the sea and land, and on the land separated all kinds of plants and animals; on the fourth day he separated the sun, moon and stars; on the fifth day he separated the birds, beasts and reptiles that fly in the sky, swim in the water and walk on land; on the sixth day he separated people, dividing them into man and woman; on the seventh day God finished his creation and rested: "And God blessed the seventh day and made it holy; because on it he rested from all the work of creating that he had done." **– Old Testament, Genesis**

But there's a problem. Since God already separated man and woman on the sixth day, how did he later take Adam's rib and turn it into Eve? Ah, that clearly means that, on the day of rest, God didn't want people to work hard, take a break from living blindly. It clearly means God wanted people to remember Eden on that special day and have the opportunity to examine themselves and consult others. It clearly means the separation God made on the sixth day wasn't just between animal-like male and female vessels, but inexpressible emptiness, only after a long journey can people and life be separated, can the soul and flesh be separated. For example, Ding Yi and me.

That clearly means that this way people aren't bound to lifelong foraging, wild wandering, mindless breeding...

But this way, weakness comes.

But this way, love also comes.

But with separation and weakness come strength and conquest.

So hate comes.

If, during the day, you can't surrender, can't show weakness, then at night you're eager to tell.

Dreams, for example, are telling. Lewdness and dirtiness, for example, weirdness and shamelessness are all telling. Night replenishes your ability to tell; sex is extremely tremendous. So night's telling cannot mix with day. Insincere speech and sex without feeling are lies. During night's agreed-upon time the only lie that exists is lewdness. Night drama should be open, cheerful, be hopeful and sorrowful, acknowledging weakness and preferring surrender, the only conquest is dirtiness. But don't surrender to day.

Don't surrender to conquest. Surrender to night's call, surrender to the limitless distance and nearby deformation, because surrendering to weakness, surrendering to soul that longs for love and can love...

125. Uncle For Example

Uncle for example. That person (and all old people) who can't escape shame for example. For example one and all of those who live with regret because they were afraid of torture, who feared death and so lived with broken souls.

For example Ding Yi, Qin E and Lü Sa's boldness that wanted to endlessly expand the wall-less night. For example they wanted to invite those suffering souls into the drama, wanted those cruel realities to become fictitious models, wanted Uncle's dream to become possible. For example they wanted to use their naked bodies and naked souls to comfort each other, and comfort Uncle: traitor, even traitors need love! For example they wanted to use all their extreme words with each other and say to the old man: Forget man-made honour and disgrace, forget human good and evil, use this blessed moment to get closer to Eden! Ding Yi, Qin E and Lü Sa, for example, used all the lewdness and weirdness they could imagine to announce, to announce to all the lonely souls: We were, we will be, God's messages searching for each other! And liberated by night's drama in our true roles!

And this all relied on imagination.

Because after all, this kind of drama isn't for watching, and I don't want to write it for you.

Because seeing is narrow, while listening and thinking are wide.

So I want you to think. Imagine Uncle's drama, and the drama of Fu and others. Imagine the performance of Ding Yi, E and Sa. Imagine their imaginations and be imagined by them... For example in that room divided into red, blue and white, Ding Yi mentally incorporated (performed) Uncle's reality, incorporated a lonely soul sentenced to loneliness, while E and Sa were (pretending to be) other people – honourable or just other people... For example, during an 'empty-wall night' in the real virtuality of the agreed-upon time, E's heart flow (performance) was Fu's history, flowed into a homeless travelling spirit, while Ding Yi and Sa were (pretending to be) other people – peaceful or lucky other people... For example, when inside some time's magic, Sa sincerely prayed to become (and presumably did become) a marvellous magician, become (or symbolise) a saviour of sufferers, while Ding Yi and E both (acted as) other people – other people who let history incite them...

For example, when Uncle walked along that white road, E and Sa were the eyes on the road – contemptuous insiders ("Oh, this traitor"), familiar, yet dodgy people ("Oh, this human shit heap"), curious strangers and fearful children ("Hey, look, look, that old guy's a traitor")... Ding Yi seemed to hear the hooligan song again, or hear other people shouting together: "Look, it's him, he's the guy who lost his things to others and then asked for them back!" "Look, he's just standing there naked on the street!" So Ding Yi could only lower his head and speed up, and Uncle could only hurry back home...

Ding Yi hurried to the red zone, as Uncle hurried to the yard full of plants and flowers.

Uncle panted. Uncle prayed distractedly, could only ever pray hopelessly. Meanwhile, E and Sa entered gracefully through the wall – E in a white dress to arouse Ding Yi's childhood fears; Sa in a splendid dress like the colourful butterfly that came and went, rose and fell on Uncle's face. Fear or butterfly crossed the junction of red and white, came before Uncle.

White E said: "I am Fu, do you still remember me?" Splendid Sa said: "I am another person, honourable and just!" White E said: "You traitor, you think you can escape the eyes of the honourable and just?" Splendid Sa said: "The eyes of the honourable and just cannot be blocked by walls!" White E said: "Our keen gaze can see through you completely!" Splendid Sa said: "See through your walls, see through your clothes, directly see your shame!" Ding Yi had to submit, tremblingly strip, even his naked clothing, stripped everything off until Uncle's scarred body and scarred soul were revealed... So you should imagine, imagine those whipping sounds floating into the universe, shouting, insulting, pleading... Yes, those scary sounds, those humiliating sights floating into the universe by not dissipating as, along with you, memory or prayers entered the night's drama – just as Qin Han said: turn into a simulated model... So the cold torture device instead turned into a dear wish; so that cruel punishment seemed to sign a tender agreement; so the parts of the universe in deep pain could be reborn, reconstruct the ancient dreams that have gone through catastrophe... As long as you imagine, with the help of the night's false model, cry for lost reality. With the help of the gentleness nearby, pray for the distant wronged souls... Yes, imagine: did not youth's excitement determine old age's shame? Did not living life mark the world's eternal scars? As long as you imagine like this, as long as you listen to what these scars tell, this shameful prayer, these dreams dead as Uncle, that cruel model will collapse, hatred lingering in the depths of the universe will vanish... Then the girl Fu's ghost will be resurrected, time will reverse, white E and splendid Sa and spring-like Fu and dusky Fu's name will come together, Uncle will be rescued in my travels in Ding Yi... If Fu turns around a large frame (there very well could be such a prop), Sa goes in, face showing a sad smile, spring-like Fu can return to the world.

If E comes out from behind Sa, slowly walks towards Ding Yi, gently strokes his hair, dusky Uncle may reunite with his dusky lover. But don't speak. E and Sa with their honour and justice, with their peace and happiness, don't want to speak. Just be quiet. Just be quiet, quiet and quiet... Let the white or splendid dress flow in the breeze, let the beauty of youth fade and come into view, let that child's fear and current prayer depend on each other, and think of Eden, and approach Eden's frankness and shamelessness... That way Uncle can be saved, a shameful old man may find peace in his garden.

Fu can be saved too.

Fu's spring-like secret language, dusky care and even her life's hopes can be saved too.

Let Sa take off her splendid dress in the red, blue and white room, be at ease, flow, relax, all kinds of ways, that is to say: Sa's sincere wish – like that magician – opens time's path, or time uses Sa's wish to open Eden's door. If the splendid dress flutters in the wind, the sincere wishes flood the quiet night, that is to say: time disregards past and present. If naked Sa and her naked imagination dance like the waves, that is to say: all the ignored lives have received the grace of enchanted time, buried souls can now be resurrected.

(As Jesus said: "Your time goes by the clock, but mine does not, now is not the time to go to Jerusalem.")

If time is more than the clock, Fu's soul can be resurrected in E's body.

If time is more than clocks, why can't E be Fu?

If E takes off the white dress, goes from the red zone to the blue zone, then Fu can wake from day's burial and enter the second life of the night. If E peacefully waits there then it's Fu who's softly singing. How often has she sung to herself before finally singing to – to sing to Uncle: See the bright sunset, shining golden light, breeze on the sea, blue waves ripple, before night falls, come on my little boat... If this singing alarms the neighbour, a long road may be shortened instantly by the magic of time, Ding Yi can make Uncle's dream float. If two souls passing through Ding Yi and E hug, kiss, look at each other with tears in their eyes, then the ever-unyielding time would be moved by this... Then Ding Yi could think of the girl A Chun, think of what that little princess said: "Hey hey, I haven't died! Look, how am I dead..." And Uncle? Ah, who knows how many times he's dreamed of this kind of drama!

Sa quietly sat to the side, let time stop walking.

Sa watched Ding Yi and E, let time again allow Fu to reunite with Uncle.

Time quietly flowed. Time was enthusiastic.

If time isn't just clocks, the present is the time to go to Jerusalem. If time isn't just clocks, Adam and Eve can use any male or female vessel to easily express their dreams and longings experienced during their separation. If time isn't just clocks, everything will return to the beginning of creation: the soul's boundaries disappear, breaking down 'you' and 'I', converging with the holy spirit on the vast waters...

So Sa knew she was sure to participate – only time can compensate the mind dismantled by time.

So Sa knew she was destined to meet Ding Yi and E in expansive love – only time can recall those dreams lost over time.

As soon as Sa hugged E and Ding Yi locked in an embrace, youth celebrated, old age was praised, ancient dreams came true in the flesh of the three...

Then all unconventionality was unrestrained, everything lewd could be lewd.

Then heaven and earth were quiet with their delight, the moon and stars shone in their shape.

If time isn't just clocks, all the day's stigmatisation will be consecrated by night. E, how did your arse get so glorious? Sa, how did your pubic hair get so wild? Why is Ding Yi's flower so volatile, so high spirited? Yes, yes,

I know, of course I know about Ding Yi's desire: that's for your trembling breasts, your rising and falling waist, your wonderful peaks and valleys, and your buried vigour in the valley or the bubbling springs of the heart...

Ah, no, definitely not just for the delicate or charming hole, or that glistening dew or violent wind, but for all the opening mysteries, be so free for them, open freely and sacredly... And that freedom is not just one-way, that trust isn't just two-way, but goes towards multiple others, towards boundless nights and boundless thoughts...

So during this kind of time behind the curtain or far away, next door and the door next to next door, an angelic elegy is heard: "There's a linden tree outside the door, next to the old well, I've dreamed countless dreams in its shade..." This song flowed in the quiet night, not resting like time: "Today was like days past, I wandered deep into the night... Ah, friends, come here, come and be peaceful and happy..." This song flows into spring: "By the river, where the cranberries blossomed, a young man caught my eye, but I couldn't say what was on my mind, couldn't tell him that truth on mine..." This song flows into old age: "The years are like ruthless pens, writing lines on my face, they call us old, Maggie, like spray washed away by the ocean, but you're still as you always were, young and beautiful..." Flows to the northern grasslands: "The full moon rises in the sky, why are there no clouds nearby? I'm waiting for the beautiful girl, why have you still not arrived?" Flows to the western plateaus: "Brother three is nineteen, sister four is sixteen, people say they're a perfect match, tell her to meet him at the crossroads..." Flows to home villages: "Come sit next to me, don't leave in such a hurry, remember Red River village, your hometown, and that woman who loves you so..." Flows to faraway rivers: "Hey, hello, the wind blows my sails, girl, I want to meet you... Before I come before you, you must keep me in your heart..." Flows towards distant oceans: "Sweetheart, I'm willing to voyage far with you, fly like a dove, free over the sea... Oh, beautiful dove, please come to my side, we've flown over that blue sea towards a faraway place..."

Ah, all the traditional songs are love songs, all love songs are laments – what's a lament? By lingering on the dead, praying for that beauty! So all laments are prayers, praying to drift towards the horizon and converge there: "The carriage comes down from the sky, takes me back to my hometown... the carriage comes down from the sky, takes me back to my hometown."

126. Ding Yi's Ideal Life

In the living room of the apartment marked by red, blue and white, Ding Yi and E had an ideal life. They did their own thing during the day like foraging birds flying into a sea of people, disappearing in the mountains of buildings and valleys of streets, then went back there for the evening, using simple objects and luxurious imagination for the other half of their time.

Sometimes Sa would come too.

They created so many passionate dramas together, along with some uninhibited, unrealistic plots that I've already forgotten. Maybe writing down those things makes me feel embarrassed. I worry writing really could indulge people's eyes and stifle their brains. Or only when one day the audience spontaneously closes their eyes, hearts bent on hearing the divine, can I describe the details of those dramas.

I insist on calling it drama, the only other thing to emphasise is sex looks alike but is thought of quite differently. So the night's drama really relies on imagination, that is, in this fearful human world, the weak, lonely souls can seek and depend on each other and pray together that God gives them peace and reunion.

Or as a famous philosopher said: "People on earth should dwell in poetry."

Poetically question history, see the future and poetically reconstruct reality.

So for a while they fell in love with adaptation, adapting plays, films and even novels, and moved to their tricolour stage. I remember they were daring and even adapted some classic plays; I wouldn't say their adaptations were great, but I respect the pure motivation and wonderful imagination to this day and can't help but smile.

For example, they didn't give that revolutionary mother in *Struggles in an Ancient City* the opportunity to kill herself. They let her live, let her fall into the trap of the enemy's coercion then return to see what fate had in store for her son. Another example: they changed the famous traitor in the middle of *Red Crag*, made him ignorant and uncontaminated by love. Naturally he had no time for a lover, they even made him contemptuous of 'puppy love' and thus take advantage of the enemy's mistake and escape, then see if he could come back and be a hero.

Hey, Ding Yi, you think this makes sense?
What, you don't think it makes sense?
What do you think you changed?
Nothing, brother, it's the same fate with a different name!
Yes, man, but that doesn't make sense?

They ignored me from then on, happily continued their adaptation.

Once they adapted *The Gadfly*. Originally the Gadfly was intended to survive, so that Arthur and Gemma recognise each other and reconcile with Montanelli. But while acting, the three of them hated that Rivarez. When the Gadfly buries his face in Gemma's arms and drags out his trembling weakness, then looks up, regaining his usual composure, or rather puts on that mask that can never be taken off, Sa suddenly couldn't keep acting.

Sa shoved away half-kneeling Ding Yi and shouted: "Why's he like this? Why can't he tell Gemma everything? I think he doesn't love her at all, what do you think, E?"

"Yeah," E said unhurriedly, sitting in the moonlight. "I thought the same thing."

Sa said: "I think he enjoys torturing people!"

"He wants revenge," E said. "Not only revenge on Montanelli, on Gemma, he wants revenge on everyone. Have you guys seen him be good to anyone?"

"Because he's suffered," Sa said, "he wants the world to suffer double."

"Right," E said. "Use others' confessions, others' apologies, pain and suffering to vent his resentment, satisfy his vanity, wrap himself in the image of so-called man."

Sa said: "He said he wouldn't complain, but hasn't he complained a lot? He uses people who love him or uses the love others have for him to vent his resentment and elevate himself. Ding Yi, can such a person fall in love at all?"

"He primarily wants to be a hero," E said. "Wants to be someone like beloved Rivarez and the Gadfly, and that loving and lovable Arthur has already been wiped out by thirteen years of insults."

"So what do we do?" Ding Yi asked from his position kneeling on the floor.

E said: "I'd say there's no way Arthur can come back."

"So what then?" Ding Yi said, looking up.

Sa said: "We have to make the Gadfly say the truth, come completely clean. Only that way can Arthur come back."

"Or," E added, "can Gemma recognise Arthur? Gemma definitely wouldn't recognise him as Ramirez."

"Right, right," Sa said. "The suspense at the end doesn't necessarily come from the Gadfly not wanting to tell the truth but from the deep fear in Gemma's heart. He doesn't dare recognise him, she can't imagine that Arthur's pure face could return in the Ramirez mask."

"Amazing, Sa, amazing!"

Ding Yi buried his face in E's arms again, then looked up. "Gemma, Gemma, look closely. Have you not noticed I'm the Arthur you loved and who has always loved you?"

"Weak, weak!" Sa laughed. "I've never seen such a weak performance, Brother Ding."

E also bent over with laughter.

"Then how should I say it?"

The two women sat together in the moonlight, laughing at him, not answering.

I had to remind him: *Did you think dead-end language could express such an extreme wish, Brother Ding?*

How would you say it?
Did you forget how Graham said it?

Naked E and naked Sa stood up together and shouted at him: Ramirez, give me back Arthur! Ramirez, give me back Arthur! Ramirez, give me...

Another time they adapted Shakespeare's *Othello* for some reason. They delayed that self-abased and therefore suspicious Moor a few minutes because of some incidental thought – for example it's very hot out, so he wants to rinse off – before falling upon irreparable tragedy, and that few minutes not only changed the fate of the protagonists but also the whole ending of the play. To put it simply, those few minutes Othello entered an unprecedented corner, even transcending our limited space-time, he unknowingly walked into the end of the play, thus hearing Desdemona's death and Cassio's confession in advance. The alternate ending was when dishonest Iago spread rumours about him, when they reached Othello's ear like the wind again, he discovered his trick provided the answer to a longstanding puzzle of his master's. Seeing the Moor not enraged, not pained or mad, but looking at him disdainfully, hand on hilt, Iago burst into laughter, realising that his conspiracy had fallen apart.

"You laughed too late, sir!" Othello held his sword with its tip against his throat.

"Not necessarily," eloquent Iago said. "There are no problems of earliness or lateness in classic drama."

"OK, then I'll give you another minute to explain."

"Since you were able to see the drama's ending ahead of time, why can't I go back to the drama's beginning?"

"...!"

"So, my commander-in-chief, you can't kill me."

"Should I try?"

"Try it! Unless you can kill your own low self-worth and paranoia, I will come back to life again."

"Based on what?"

"Based on my omnipresence, one hint of your suspicion and I'll return."

Othello, suspicious of the crafty sycophant, killed him with his sword. But sure enough he heard Iago's sinister laugh throughout the sky, earth and wind: "Othello, Othello, your luck came only once, but I'll always be lurking around you..."

127. Asky's Dream

One little thing once mystified Ding Yi and E. The weekend they painted the living room floor red, blue and white Asky came back from kindergarten, happy and laughing the whole way, but as soon as she came she didn't make a sound.

"What's wrong, Asky? You don't like this?" said E, pointing to the floor.

Asky shook her head, didn't speak.

"If you don't like it," Ding Yi said, "we can change it back to how it was."

Asky shook her head, still not speaking.

"Then why are you unhappy?"

Asky sighed, her sigh was as rich with meaning as an adult's.

"What's really the matter, Asky, did something happen at kindergarten?"

Asky shook her head again and went into her own room.

Ding Yi didn't stay over that night.

The next day E called. "Hey, guess what Asky was up to last night? She said she dreamed of that kind of room before."

"What kind of room?"

"A room with the floor painted red, blue and white."

"Really? And?"

"She said the blue represents waves, red an island and white a flock of seagulls."

"Then why was she unhappy?"

There was silence on the other end of the phone for a moment.

"Hey, hey. E, are you OK?"

"I'm fine, I'm fine. Uh... OK, I'll talk to you later."

"And Asky? How is she now?"

"Asky, she... Oh, fine, she's talking and laughing again."

"What's really going on, E?"

"Oh! OK, I'll talk to you later."

"No, tell me. Asky definitely said something else."

"She said, she said that when another person appears on that red island, the room... is empty."

"What's that mean? What does the room have to do with the island?"

"I don't know. Asky said she couldn't remember."

128. A Question

That lovely time was like a long summer, and when the autumn wind began to blow they didn't notice. As far as I remember the very beginning of that autumn wind was starting when E asked: "Who really is it that's making love in that drama?"

One day E went to Ding Yi's house in a courtyard. She said she had been to Asky's parent-teacher meeting and passed by on the way back. When she saw the words 'To be demolished' written in big characters on the wall, she was curious and therefore came in to see what was going on.

"Will they really demolish?"

"Of course."

"When?"

"Soon I hear."

"Uncle and your parents?"

"All looking for new places."

E sat on a bench.

I remember the yard was full of blooming pomegranates, green leaves and red flowers filled the sky above the house. Ding Yi sat under the tree, with manuscript paper spread out in front of him, intensely focused on his script.

After sitting a while, E suddenly asked Ding Yi: "Like in a film, the male actor X plays the lead role A and the female actor Z plays the other lead B. And if in the movie A and B are husband and wife, or lovers, and there's a scene in the movie where they make love. Then can we think of asking, for example: 'Are A and B being physically intimate or X and Z?'"

Without much thought, Ding Yi turned his head and said: "A and B of course."

I saw Qin E take on a serious expression and thought I should remind Ding Yi: *Hey, hey, listen close. Why did E say 'for example'? And something about 'a film', 'think of asking', she's not done, brother!*

But this Ding was quite focused on his script and didn't pay me any attention.

"I meant in reality," E said, "in reality."

"In reality?" That Ding looked up. "Right, it's still A and B in reality."

"I mean really! Who really had relations, who and who?"

"Really?"

"OK, OK, in reality then. In reality A and B don't exist, right? A and B are fictional, right? In reality there's only X and Z."

"Oh, oh..." Silly Ding Yi seemed finally to have caught on.

E looked at him silently.

Ding Yi said: "You mean, in reality, it's those two actors?"

E didn't speak, her gaze softened a little like she was counting those countless pomegranate flowers.

"Put it this way." Ding Yi put the script down. "Of... of course it's X and Z."

E still didn't say anything, her soft gaze a bit like the butterfly on Uncle's face.

What do you say, brother, something a bit complicated going on?

"But it's fake!" Ding Yi said.

"Oh, fake, fake..." E nodded slightly, as if agreeing or mocking, but she followed up with: "Then who is fake with who?"

"Of course X and Z."

E went silent again. The butterfly seemed to struggle, wanting to fly into, or penetrate, that tree's scarlet.

"What, you think I... with Sa?"

"No, I'm talking about X and Z." E crossed her arms, her mind seeming to be elsewhere.

That Ding asked me: *Brother, what is she really getting at?*

I said: *Brother, seems like you're in a bit of trouble.*

That Ding felt somewhat wronged: *I was just speaking what came to mind! But everything you said was a lie!*

What was a lie? I just said X and Z are actors, so... so it's fake.

I said: *That's absolutely right, isn't that naked clothing? If the day's drama can't be trusted and the night's drama is fake, doesn't that mean everything's a lie?*

That Ding shook his head and complained: *But can I say X and Z are... are real?*

I laughed. *Why not? Aren't you saying what comes to mind?*

That Ding added: *If Sa and I are real, then me and E? If I'm real with one, two, three, four, five, six, seven, gosh, brother, how is that OK?*

How's it OK? Since love is people's most beautiful feeling, why can't it all be real? Isn't the point of the drama to make the impossible possible, realise the unreal?

That Ding pondered awhile, helpless, then finally confided in me: *If it can all be like that, brother, tell me, is... is drama still needed?*

Well, yes, yes. I tried not to sound shocked. But I still held on to hope: *Can't, can't be, E can't be that narrow-minded!*

So that Ding reminded me: *Then why is she asking about 'in reality' and adding all those 'for examples'? And why isn't she talking about* Empty Wall Night *and instead talking about 'a film' and 'can we think of...'*

Ah, I smiled bitterly. I thought this Ding was silly, always honest, who knew he knew everything and almost even tricked me! But hold on, was he just pretending not to understand? It didn't seem like it. Before, this guy's schemes have never escaped me, what happened this time? Well, could be instinct, this human tool's bright instinct! His prior lack of understanding and later all knowingness were both real; sex is the instinct of the flesh, his strategic sensitivity was unconscious I'm afraid. Wow, these travels in Ding Yi really were no fun – who knew where that 'butterfly' would fly, where it would land, when and where it would cause a storm?

As far as I can remember, midsummer passed quickly.

Colourful flowers began to fall, and the sun changed its angle without hesitation.

E opened her hands and caught the falling scarlet petals as she muttered to herself: "Oh, I hope there are some things that can be true."

That Ding was shocked a moment, then he hurried to ask me: *What, what, what'd she say?*

I said: *You thought everyone was as narrow-minded as you? She said she really hopes some things are true!*

"Right, E?" That Ding didn't dare believe it. "Do you really think that?"

E gently blew away the petals in her palm, eyes avoiding Ding Yi. "Otherwise what's the point of us?"

"Really? E do you really mean it?" That Ding looked unsettled.

E spoke one phrase at a time. "I hope, everything, can all, be true."

"You mean X and Z can also be... true?" There was fire in his eyes.

E looked calm as water. "I mean our drama, our agreement, isn't it aiming for truth?"

"E, you're too amazing. E, you're really incredible!" That Ding jumped up, eager to hug this great woman.

But E moved, leaned on the tree, looking bitter.

"E, what's wrong?" That Ding trembled, afraid of further complication.

E closed her eyes as if wanting the butterfly in her heart to split in two – the distant, sad one to hide in the flowers, the near, fresh one to take flight, fly into the future, fly into possibility and bring about the shocking 'truth'.

"E?"

E opened her eyes.

"E?"

E smiled.

"Ah, E, you scared me to death..."

"You're afraid I changed my mind? Did I say I would?"

Ding Yi really didn't know what the right response was. I quickly reminded him: *No, of course not! Brother, what are you dawdling about, hurry up – say 'No'!*

"Relax," E said, "it's not about me changing my mind, not about a guarantee or lack of it. Right, like Peter said, there's no legal protection."

"Then... then..."

Then, then! I said. *Then bullshit, are you an idiot?*

"Otherwise," E continued, "the two of us reaching this point, on this planet, what's the point?"

That Ding really was an idiot, standing there awkwardly, dumbstruck. Meanwhile, the bees and butterflies danced among the flowers, meanwhile branches and leaves swayed, meanwhile countless stories happened in the world, and that Ding was still staring at E, doing nothing.

I said: *Could you make a move for me, at least give E some kind of response?*

Then he finally smiled, not as good as crying, then, like a hero in a bad film or a fool, hugged E and rambled: "E, are you talking about us? Me and you, you and Sa, Sa and me, us and you, you two and me, us and her, is that what you would... would mean?"

I remember the flowers fell red, each like a drop of blood. I remember the flowers fell like rain, floating onto E's face like a line of tears...

129. Yi's Return

Yi came back very suddenly. The pomegranate tree bore green-white fruit, and one afternoon Yi seemed to fall from the sky. Actually Ding Yi was in his little room continuing to write *Empty Wall Night* when he suddenly heard a familiar sound in the yard. "Excuse me, does Ding Yi still live here?"

Mother replied: "Whoa, what a pretty girl! Where'd you come from?" "Well, ma'am, I'm his classmate, Ding Yi... is he back?" This voice is familiar, so familiar, who is it?

Ding Yi opened the door and went out and all he saw, in the shade of the pomegranate tree, was a graceful woman standing in a plain white dress.

"Yi? You're Yi?"

"Hey, Ding Yi!" Yi turned, looking as surprised as Ding Yi.

"It's really you, Yi?"

Yi slapped Ding Yi on the shoulder. "Hey, you're just like before."

Yi walked into the house and looked around.

Ding Yi stopped in the entrance, too shy to follow.

"Do you think I look old?" Yi asked.

Ding Yi looked at her as if from a great distance.

"You guys don't recognise me, do you?" Yi said.

"Have I really changed that much?" Yi asked, while looking at herself in the glass of the bookcase.

Before the wind blew the door shut, Yi blocked it. Then Ding Yi finally went in.

"When, Yi, when did you... did you come back?"

"Oh, a few days ago. You?"

"Me?"

"All the way I wondered if you had come back too. Ah, thank God we're both here now."

Yi put her palms together, closed her eyes and murmured something.

I said quietly to Ding Yi: *We're in trouble again, brother, Yi thinks you were sent to the frontier too.*

Ding Yi's head swam, his whole body wavered, like he was completely unmoored.

"So great, so great!" Yi sighed with relief and continued looking around the walls, floor and tables.

That Ding felt his vision fading to black, he held the bookcase to steady himself – why did Uncle seem to be reflected on its glass?

"What's everyone else doing?" E asked. "Are our old classmates OK?"

"Oh, oh, doing all kinds of things." Ding Yi said, then walked away quickly for tea.

While he was in the kitchen boiling water, that Ding asked me: *What now, brother?*

What could I say? *Just be honest, can a sellout like you run forever?*

Luckily Yi didn't bring up the past again. Yi's attention was caught by the script on the table.

"Whoa, you're writing novels?"

"Oh, no, not novels."

"Then what is it?"

"Uh, just fooling around." Ding Yi hurried to grab the manuscript and close it.

"Whatever it is, maybe I can give you some material?"

"You still draw?"

"Dunno."

"Then your... your dad, is he OK?"

"He's passed."

Ding Yi's head echoed and echoed, then Fu appeared in the reflection of the bookcase.

Yi said: "My dad, he feels he hurt you the most."

"Me?"

"He hated involving other people more than anything, but he ended up involving you."

"Oh, no, no..."

"That night, after they caught us, my dad went to the revolutionary committee. My dad asked if they were just trying to get documentary evidence on him. So, 'Tell me, what do you want me to admit?' he said. 'But you can't torture those kids!' He said he taught his daughter to be honest, and he wanted to keep teaching her that, so he couldn't deny things he had said. My dad slapped the table and asked them: 'Where did you young guys learn these tricks of interrogation? Learn to widen the net? If no one taught you, then I'm right: evil human nature! If you just learned it, then I'm also right: this is a shit era! So there, I've admitted everything I've said, can you let the kids go now? Especially that boy, this has nothing to do with him...'"

Yi said: "But my dad was too honest, he thought if he admitted it, you and I would be OK."

Yi said: "The day we left here until we got on the train, my dad kept asking them about you, asking if the boy named Ding Yi had been sent back home or not. But they said they couldn't gossip about other people because the revolution isn't a dinner party."

Yi said: "Until the end, my dad never forgot your situation. He told me: 'If you can get back, you must see Ding Yi.' At that time my dad had a little bit of freedom and heard we'd be able to go home soon."

Yi said: "Those years my dad wanted to send you a message but was afraid of involving you again, or involving your whole family. My dad asked me to tell you, this stuff has nothing to do with you, he takes responsibility for everything. He wanted to tell you that, no matter what those people try to get you to admit, you can blame it all on him."

Yi said: "He told me to do the same, but I told him if I had done it, what would I have become?"

Yi said: "Then he hugged me and said nothing for a long time."

Yi said: "Then one day we saw the Yugoslavian film, *Walter Defends Sarajevo*, you remember it?

"There's an old watchmaker in it, do you remember what he told his daughter? He said: 'Some people want to stand out, some people want to wait. You, my daughter, are still young, so you must wait.' That made my dad weep. I'd never seen him cry before.

"Then he said: 'This, this, I always wanted to say to you!'"

Ding Yi quietly walked out the door.

Yi didn't stop him.

That day Ding Yi walked alone for a long time. He didn't know where, didn't know if he was off the hook or not, or if the old sin of Yi was too great.

When he got back, Yi was already gone. She'd left a note on the table: 'Read your masterpiece without your permission, sorry. I'll be back tomorrow. I want to talk to you about the ideas in *Empty Wall Night*.'

130. Yi's Doubt

"You don't think I'm writing erotica, right?" Ding Yi pretended to wonder.

Yi, on the other hand, looked serious. "No way. Furthermore, furthermore I understand your wish, or, that is, your ideal."

"Really!" Ding Yi slapped his thigh and nearly jumped up. "I knew you'd be different, definitely not stupid."

But Yi was not affected by his excitement, an element of worry seemed to mix with the seriousness. Yi picked up the manuscript like she was looking over a financial statement. "But I hope this always, always remains an ideal."

"Huh?"

"Always just a beautiful ideal."

"Why?"

"Otherwise it could be dangerous."

"Dangerous? Dangerous how?" Ding Yi's smile was no longer so confident.

"Dunno." Yi looked at Ding Yi, as if trying to see the answer in his face. "Just an intuition..."

"Intuition of what?"

"In your script there seems to be lurking a kind of..."

"What?"

"Terror."

"You mean fear?"

"No, terror. The terror I've seen with my own eyes."

"Seen with your own eyes?" Ding Yi lowered his eyes, thinking she was talking about the border.

"Empty wall night!" Yi said. "Your 'empty wall night' is just a, uh... how to put it? Well-intentioned, naive dream."

"Yes, a dream!" Ding Yi said quickly. "But dreams aren't necessarily unrealisable."

Ding Yi wanted to change the subject to his drama and avoid the border.

"But on the border," Yi said, "I encountered that kind of nightmare. A real empty wall night. Do you know what a real empty wall night is like? Up all night, frightened, at any moment someone can come in and ask what you're doing, what you're thinking. Or they take my mum and dad away, leave me there alone waiting for them to come back. Waiting until I fall asleep, then suddenly start awake again, or think I'm awake and see I'm sleeping in the wilderness, nothing covering the ground, surrounded by wolves with their eyes gleaming in the dark and owls laughing like weeping among the trees... waiting for my dad to come back, waiting for my mum to come back, I finally realise it's a dream, a terrible nightmare..."

"But this isn't the same, Yi. I know you suffered a lot on the border, but our drama is not the same as that. In your dream walls vanished because you're afraid of losing protection, but we remove them in our dream to eliminate isolation, to destroy hostility..."

"But that's the danger. Listen to me, Ding Yi, that's the terror. You want to eliminate isolation but eliminate protection instead!"

"No way, no way, definitely not."

"How can you say definitely not?"

"Because, because everything is voluntary. Right, these two kinds of wall-less nights are this: on the border it was by force, in drama it's voluntary!"

Yi closed her eyes for a while then spoke as gently as she could. "You think being voluntary is enough?"

"I prefer to."

"Uncle did it voluntarily back then too!"

Ding Yi was shocked. "Yi, you think Uncle's a bad person too?"

Yi shook her head. "But he did it voluntarily. The person he sold out and the person who sold him out all did so voluntarily."

"Then you think people are unreliable?"

"Ding Yi, let me tell you a true story. On the border those people wanted my mum and dad and lots of people like them to confess to the leaders, wanted them to voluntarily write down all their thoughts."

"This isn't the same," Ding Yi shouted. "Yi, this is completely different."

"They said: 'You have to trust the leaders, be loyal to them, take the dark corners of your heart, the deepest parts of your soul, especially those unspeakable thoughts, and explain them to the leaders. What do you think my parents did? They were extremely devout. They did so completely voluntarily, thinking that, if they expressed their loyalty, they would win their...'"

"Yi," Ding Yi shouted. "I'm telling you, can I tell you why it's not the same? Their allegiance was one directional, but ours is multi-directional."

"Can I finish, Ding Yi? The leaders even made my parents do the same with each other, be honest with each other, supervise each other, hide nothing from each other, make the word 'selfishness' vanish in a flash. The best way to do so was to bring everything into the light. Those innocent old people really believed it and really did it, told others their most secret thoughts... but do you know what the result was?"

"I know, I know, but it's still not the same. Yi, listen to me." Ding Yi tried to make his tone more neutral. "The opening of our hearts happens on equal terms, there's no commander or manipulator – your mum and dad were forced!"

Now Yi stopped talking like surging waves coming to rest in a silent, deep pool, suddenly falling.

"Yi, do you understand now?"

Yi's gaze seemed to fall into that deep pool as well. The currents beneath the pool crisscrossed, converged, separated in unknown places and then flowed to even more unknown places.

"Yi?"

Maybe the deep, dark pool was too deep and dark.

"Yi?"

Or the undercurrent had flowed too long and far.

"Yi, I know you've suffered a lot, suffered too many deceptions, but you haven't lost your faith in humanity, have you?"

Yi's body had returned to her hometown, but her soul was still drifting elsewhere. Yi's lips trembled a moment. Ding Yi didn't hear what she said, but I heard. "Can't your drama encourage the growth of a leader or manipulator?"

Oh, that frightful child! Did Ding Yi still remember?

131. The Legend of Danqing Island

Later Ding Yi asked me: *Are you sure Yi said that?*

I said: *For sure she said that.*

Ding Yi said: *How come I didn't hear it?*

I said: *You didn't hear it because you weren't willing to hear it.*

And then we saw Qin Han, and Qin Han smiled. "Hmm, interesting. I actually agree with Yi."

"Huh? What about her?"

"To be honest," Qin Han said as he took a sip of his drink, "I really admire and appreciate your drama."

Hah. Qin Han already knew everything, Ding Yi couldn't help but feel awkward.

To cover it he tried to change the subject. "What do you agree with Yi about?"

"Have you heard of Danqing Island?" Qin Han asked.

"What? What island are you talking about?"

"A nameless ocean island. It's called Danqing Island because, some years ago, the poet Dao – written with the character that means island – and two of the women he loved, the painters Dan and Qing, went there to escape the hustle and bustle of the city. According to them, they were a lost group hoping to find themselves on that barren island."

"Really?" Ding Yi asked, eyes growing wide. "This really happened?"

"So I've heard."

"Who? Who were they? Really famous?"

"That doesn't matter."

"Where? I mean what barren island?"

"Does it matter?" Qin Han said. "You always seem interested in the unimportant things."

Ding Yi stared a moment, then asked: "You're saying those two women both loved him?"

"Probably. At least that's what I heard. What do you think – enough?"

"Why are you asking me if it's enough? How would I know." Ding Yi was a bit sensitive.

"Oh, sorry, that's not what I meant. I was thinking that, in order to maintain a pluralistic love, would that be enough or not?"

"I don't know what you mean."

"Look," Qin Han said as he brought two wine glasses on the table together, "two people make how many relationships? One." Then he pushed another glass over and asked: "And when you add another?"

"What?" Ding Yi stared stupidly at the three glasses.

"When you add another glass, the number of relationships doesn't just increase by one."

Ding Yi still didn't understand.

"Three people make how many relationships?"

"Oh, I get it. You're saying the two women also have to love each other?"

Qin Han took a sip of his drink and gave Ding Yi a thumbs up. "Of course, and there could be more."

"Then they, I mean the poet and the two women, were like that?"

"If not, it'd just be a barren island."

"Whoa! That really happened?" Ding Yi was truly in awe, delighted, inspired. But I noticed there were some overtones in what Qin Han had said, and asked again: "What do you mean by 'there could be more'?"

"Since there can be more, why not add even more?"

"Right," Ding Yi said. "Why not some more and then some more?"

Qin Han said: "Who are you asking?"

"You of course?"

"How would I know."

"Didn't you say what Sa said? You said that, since love is the most beautiful thing in human life, we should expand it, not constrain it, right?"

"Right, I said that, why? You find an answer?"

Ding Yi stared, dumbstruck, frozen.

I couldn't help but sigh again and again. I just said to Ding Yi, you didn't hear because you didn't want to hear. Now it seems this logic can be extended: you hear what you want to hear, if you want to hear something you'll hear it. As long as you want to, you can turn a doubtful question (Qin Han's) into an affirmation, even a call to action.

"OK, OK." Ding Yi shook his head helplessly. "Tell me what happened on Danqing Island."

"The poet and his two women... no, no, putting it that way would offend. They stress equality, so I should say 'the three of them'. The three of them fled the hubbub, left the mainland and made their extraordinary home on a small southern island, happily read books and poetry, raised snakes and scorpions for income, and planted vegetables to eat. There was plenty of wasteland on the island, where anything could grow. There were numerous small fish and shrimps in the ocean, and all kinds of plankton, it wasn't difficult to raise anything. Whole scorpions make good medicine, snake meat and gall are ingredients of traditional medicine, snakeskin is even more useful, people came to buy them regularly and they used them themselves. The people on Danqing Island believed they didn't need too many possessions to live, simply having enough was true wealth.

"They were determined to live a life quite different from that of the rest of the world, cherish simplicity, cherish wisdom, cherish love. As the great philosopher said: Live poetically... Right, isn't this poetry? That's poetry. Otherwise, tell me, what is poetry?"

"Then, now, they?"

"I'm talking about now."

"And?"

"That's all I know."

"Wow, I don't believe it!" Ding Yi was amazed.

Ding Yi asked: "You know them?"

"People I know know them."

I sensed a hint of something else in Qin Han's words, but Ding Yi was ready to leap up in excitement. "Amazing, amazing! If it's true, then it's really amazing."

"Yeah," Qin Han said, "if that was all."

"What do you mean?"

"But they, I mean Danqing Island, can't answer my question."

"What question?"

"If it can be more, why not even more?"

"I don't get what it has to do with the poet Dao."

"I understand people's desire."

"Who's the poet really?"

"You're asking who he is again. I'm telling you, it doesn't matter."

"Then," Ding Yi said, "I don't see anything wrong with it."

"Right, it's even better, but this drama!"

"Drama? But you just said it's real, you're kidding me right?"

"It's real, but it can only be drama," Qin Han said. "You should understand drama."

"I don't know what you mean."

"Limited – to use your language, 'agreed-upon--time'. Limited time, limited space, limited people and limited power."

"Power?" Ding Yi laughed. "I'm afraid you misinterpreted the text, our drama aims to be rid of power!"

"Then openness, the mutual opening of souls you discuss, doesn't imply some kind of power? You hand yourself over, OK, whoever you handed yourself over to gains a kind of power. Then from whoever you gave yourself to, you ask for the same kind of power over them. So I think Yi's question was right – are you sure this doesn't contribute to power?"

Ding Yi: "I just don't understand what you're saying."

Qin Han: "Fine, we can talk about it again when you do."

Ding Yi: "Like Danqing Island, you don't like it?"

Qin Han: "I'm just saying they can't answer my question."

Ding Yi: "What would you do in their position?"

Qin Han: "I still think Yi was right, let it remain an ideal, an incredibly beautiful ideal."

132. Title Interpretation

There's another way to understand *My Travels in Ding Yi*. It is about a scene of my dream deriving from my hearing about Danqing Island on that journey through a certain Ding.

'The legend of Danqing Island' is so widespread, with different versions, no one can differentiate rumour from truth. And regarding the poet and two painters' actions, there are differing opinions, mixed reviews. Just like all difficult-to-examine history, though there must be a sole truth, a variety of conjectures circulate.

That's the special characteristic of history, the special characteristic of all complicated things.

Complicated things must all become fable: if I hear it then I think it, if I think it then I will it, and vice versa. In sum, you don't hear because you don't want to hear, and what you do hear you can hear from those complicated things.

So a real rumour is likely more important than the sole truth – beneath it all, all kinds of conjecture have created the true world. So sometimes I really can't tell if, by passing through a certain Shi, I experienced 'my travels in Ding Yi'. Or because passing through Ding Yi I dreamed of Shi, and thereby was able to tentatively come up with this 'memoir' thing.

133. Uncle Leaves

One day Yi called and asked Ding Yi if he knew where Uncle moved to.

Ding Yi was surprised. "Uncle moved?"

"What, you didn't know?"

"When did it happen?"

"How do I know?"

"Who told you?"

"I went to visit him, but the courtyard was gone, now it's a restaurant."

"Are you serious?"

"Stop, would I kid about this?"

That made Ding Yi remember he hadn't seen Uncle in a long time. Since Ding Yi's family moved from the small street, we'd visited Uncle once, and now it'd been more than a year.

"Yi, are you free in the afternoon?"

"Four, is four OK?"

"OK, four. I'll wait for you at that intersection."

When Ding Yi arrived before four, Yi was already there. The general appearance of the street hadn't changed, there were just more cars. They walked down the street and saw from faraway a flag bearing the character for alcohol, 'jiu', signifying a bar or restaurant. As they got closer, they saw more words: 'No more advertising needed.'

Yi stopped. "Here."

Ding Yi looked all around.

"Right?" Yi asked.

Ding Yi nodded silently.

"Has to be?"

"If you walk thirty feet farther, opposite is the place I was born."

The place Ding Yi referred to was in ruins, with several horse-drawn carriages from the villages coming to pick up bricks.

The two of them found an out-of-the-way spot at the base of a wall to stand and look at the restaurant. Sure enough good alcohol needed no further advertisement and though the sun was still high, diners were already gathering. Well-dressed hostesses stood by the door, bowing to and welcoming the patrons.

"Are we just gonna stare?" Yi said.

Ding Yi walked forward to ask: "Excuse me, when did this restaurant open?"

"Welcome," one of the girls said. "Today is our one-year anniversary celebration, all prices are twenty per cent off."

"Excuse me, do you know where the person who used to live here moved to?"

"I'm sorry, I haven't been working here long."

"Is your boss around?"

"My boss is at headquarters."

"Do you have the number?"

"I'm sorry, do you want to eat?"

Ding Yi turned and walked back, lit a cigarette.

"Ah, didn't you say you quit?"

Ding Yi quickly snuffed it out.

Then, an old man staggered out of the door to a courtyard nearby. Ding Yi ahemmed, wondering how he could be so stupid. Then he hurried to greet him.

"Hello Mr Fu!"

Mr Fu squinted at Ding Yi.

"What, you don't remember me?"

"You, you're... Oh, the second son of the Ding family?"

"Ding Yi."

"Ding Yi? Why do you look like Ding Er?"

"Do you know where Uncle moved to?"

"Uncle? What uncle?"

"The old man who lived diagonal from us." Ding Yi pointed at the restaurant. "Right there."

"Oh, you mean that traitor, good at growing plants?"

"Right, right..."

"Don't know." Mr Fu shook his head, ready to leave.

"Uh, Mr Fu." Ding Yi stopped him. "Do you know who would know?"

"Ah, there's only a few of us old people still on this street. The others all left, all went to those damn buildings. God protect them, don't let those buildings suffocate them!"

Mr Fu left. Ding Yi and Yi spent the afternoon going from house to house asking but came up empty-handed. People just knew Uncle sold the inherited courtyard for about ten thousand, then left, but no one knew where to. Only when Ding Yi asked did people remember: this Uncle or that traitor was really different – where he went to with that money and even when he left not one person on the street knew.

"And those flowers, where did they go?"

Everyone told Ding Yi: "A man came and hauled them off in a truck."

"Did Uncle know him?"

"Ah, he helped him. Otherwise who would dare touch his plants?"

But who was that man?

134. Asky's Father Arrives

Summer was almost over, the gentlemanly autumn sun arriving. The ivy covering the wall outside E's house saw flecks of red and yellow amid the green. Ding Yi spotted Asky from far off and only then realised it was Sunday.

Asky was playing in the sand in front of a building, someone else's home being renovated. There was a man next to her.

When Asky saw Ding Yi, she ran over. "Uncle Ding, another uncle came!"

The man came over and offered his hand. "Hello, Asky's told me a lot about you."

Ding Yi had to offer his hand. "You are?"

"Qin E's friend, old friend, Shangzhou."

"And your last name?"

"You got it, Shang."

"Oh, oh, Shang Zhou, you just said."

"The weather's really good today."

"Oh, yeah, yeah, autumn, refreshing."

Then it seemed they'd run out of words. Asky played in the sand.

"OK, you guys play, I'll go... Oh, go talk to her about something."

When Ding Yi arrived E was facing the window, apparently watching Asky and that Shang Zhou guy for a long time. She must also have seen Ding Yi and Shang Zhou exchange their greetings.

"Shang Zhou," Ding Yi said as he sat, "why haven't I heard you mention him?"

E was still facing the window.

"Classmate or co-worker?"

"Neither." E didn't look at him as she turned and went into the kitchen. She did some stuff in the kitchen then carried out a plate of fruit.

Ding Yi's inquiring eyes never left E's face.

E sat next to Ding Yi. "He's Asky's father."

"Who?"

E motioned towards the window without raising her eyes and started peeling fruit.

The room was quiet, you could hear the sound of the fruit being peeled and Asky laughing as she played.

A long time later Ding Yi finally came up with a question: "Where'd he come from?"

"Abroad."

It was silent for a long time once more.

E sliced the peeled fruit and arranged it on the plate then rubbed her face, looking tired.

"Did you tell her?"

"What?"

"Asky?"

"Do I need to? You see how much they look alike."

"Then..."

E gazed at Ding Yi, then quickly looked away.

The kettle in the kitchen squealed like a police siren. E rushed to it.

Asky kicked the door. Ding Yi got himself together before opening it, but she was alone.

"Sorry, mummy, I had to kick the door, look at how many things I have!" There was a bucket, a can, a shovel and spoon, and also a dessert made of sand.

"And Uncle Shang?" E asked, looking outside.

"Went home," Asky said. "He said he'll come play with me again."

Ding Yi and E stared speechless at each other.

"This uncle's really been to a lot of places," Asky began to rave. "He said he'd been to the southern hemisphere, that is the southern half of the earth. He's also been to the South Pole, it's really, really cold there, and the only place penguins can live. But the tropics are really, really hot, because the sun shines there directly. He said he's also been to Africa and the desert, and took a boat on the world's biggest river. He said if I want he'll take me when I'm older... Mummy, are those places far from here?"

E stood dumbstruck, seeming not to have heard what Asky said.

"Far, of course they're far," Ding Yi said, "very far."

"Have to take a train?"

"Take a plane."

"Really! Mummy, I want to take a plane, I still haven't taken a plane."

E suddenly shoved Asky.

Asky was stunned, her eyes quickly filled with tears, but she shut her mouth to keep herself from crying.

E was horrified and hurried to hug her.

But Asky broke away and went to her room, closing the door behind her.

"What was that?"

E shook her head and sighed. "Well, this kid's really grown up."

Ding Yi went into the room to comfort Asky. Who knew that, when he came in, she would quickly dry her tears and comfort him. "I'm OK, I just want to be alone a bit."

Ding Yi almost laughed out loud, wondering what film she got that from.

Asky pulled a cardboard box out from under the bed, touched all her toys the same way and made herself smile, made herself look pleased.

Ding Yi played with Asky awhile, with all kinds of stuffed animals: a deer named Graham, a wolf named Peter, a raccoon named Ann and a duck named Cynthia...

"Who gave them these names?" Ding Yi asked.

"Mummy and me."

"Why?"

Asky looked at the ceiling and thought about it. "Why are you named Ding Yi? Why am I named Asky? Why is Mummy named Qin E, why is Mum's brother named Qin Han?"

"True, true." Ding Yi kissed Asky.

Asky said: "You can now, but in a few years you won't be able to kiss me like that."

"Why?"

"Then wouldn't you become like Peter?"

"What about Peter?"

"Peter's a little hooligan."

Jesus, Ding Yi and I said to ourselves, the power of day is unstoppable!

"OK, I'm leaving." Ding Yi stood up then stooped and said into Asky's ear: "In a little while say sorry to Mummy, OK?"

"Of course I will, but she has to say it first."

"I'll say it to you."

"Nothing to do with you, that new uncle caused it."

Ding Yi was shocked and couldn't help but creep out of the bedroom.

135. Shang Zhou or That Moor

Ding Yi: "Why didn't you ever tell me about him?"

E: "Because you never asked. You don't care."

Ding Yi: "I don't care?"

E: "One time I asked why you didn't ask about Asky's father, you said you didn't care."

Ding Yi thought about this, it was shortly after he met Qin E.

I said: *But why didn't you ask later.*

He thought about it: *Yeah, why not?*

Think more, what was that 'I don't care' about?

About Asky. E already had a child, and whether she was a virgin or not, I've never cared.

Really?

Of course! Those idiots who obsess about virginity just want to satisfy their vanity, what else? It's just stupid!

Right, God originally wanted people to respect chaste language or the grandness of the ceremony, not to have an excuse for discrimination.

OK, OK, I said. *And now, what now?*

Ding Yi said: *What, what do you think?*

Why does it seem like you still care?

That guy hung his head and thought a moment: *I think, I think the problem is this: before I came, whatever happened was other people's business, but afterwards... it's different.*

How is it different?

Hey, brother, that's what you said – that's love's language, an extreme expression and confession!

I said: *Right, but what does this have to do with before and after?*

Of course it's related, you can't just be extreme with everyone, can you? And you especially can't be extreme with everyone at the same time, right? Before I arrived, whatever she had done with anyone else had nothing to do with me, but afterwards it just wasn't the same. When you've given yourself to me and I've given myself to you, everything's different. Now what you did with whoever else, especially extreme expression and confession, no longer has nothing to do with me!

Why?

Maybe it's because too much extremity can make extremity become normal, powerless.

Then I must ask, you and E and Sa were all extreme at the same time or all unextreme?

That's not the same.

How so?

He ignored me again. He always avoided me at those times.

He said to E: "Then now I'll ask again, is there still time?"

E didn't respond, but her face darkened as if to ask why he would say it like that.

"I mean, can I?"

"Of course."

But Ding Yi was at a loss for words.

"This Shang Zhou guy, really, uh..." It was E who broke the impasse. "Really I've always thought he's a good person, kindhearted, very smart, extremely capable..."

"Powerful?" Ding Yi blurted out.

"No, no, just the opposite," E said. "He used to be very unconfident. A proud, unconfident, angry and weak person."

"And now?" Ding Yi's tone clearly contained sarcasm, meaning only kindness, cleverness and capability are left?

E didn't notice or didn't care and kept on. "He was born in the countryside and was able to get into university with incredible test scores, then stayed in the city after graduation. I met him when I was at my lowest emotionally. Then I couldn't direct any productions in the theatre troupe, no chance, and didn't want to direct anyway. Out of a hundred scripts forty-nine were comedies, forty-nine were tragedies, one didn't pass review and another couldn't get funding. I often went to the park nearby to read. Then, then..."

"Just like in fiction, you met a young scholar."

"What attracted me wasn't his brains, I didn't even understand what he was studying. What attracted me was his energy, specifically his enthusiasm. It was like he never heard of pessimism, never heard of impossible. Yeah, that's what intrigued me, maybe because it's exactly what I was lacking. Once, when I complained life was boring, guess what he said? He said: 'Ahem, you've just had the appetisers – the main course is still to come!' Hey, are you listening?"

"I'm all ears, you're describing a perfect person."

"There are no perfect people. I'm telling you, Ding Yi, I've never believed there are perfect people in this world."

"God, what do we do?"

"Ding Yi!"

"OK, OK, go on. Go on?"

"I think you're like him a little now."

"Like perfect?"

"I'm not joking!"

Ding Yi felt he had gone a little far himself and tried to sound sincere. "OK, like him how?"

"Unconfident."

"Me? Unconfident?"

"Someone unwilling to really listen to another person is definitely unconfident."

Ding Yi was speechless. I said to him: *Amazing E, you really got it!*

Ding Yi said: *Shut up, troublemaker!*

I said: *What trouble? If I wanted to make trouble, I'd say you were more than unconfident!*

"Lack of confidence," E said, "is what ruined us. Got a cigarette? Give me one."

E twiddled the cigarette between her fingers, smelled it, went to the window, faced the distance and closed her eyes... It seemed that there, in E's heart, in the faraway, abstract place, a butterfly flapped its wings... or in time beyond clocks a storm was brewing.

"You must remember *Othello* right?" E said.

"Sorry, I'm not as great as him," Ding Yi said, hurt.

"Then I finally understood Shakespeare's greatness. Lack of confidence is the cause of hatred. Lack of confidence could be the cause of all tragedy. It made people completely irrational, didn't give Desdemona the chance to speak."

"Are you talking about that Moor?"

"And Shang Zhou."

"What for?"

"For a play in which I acted."

"What play?"

"For example, a man X played by actor A, a woman Y played by female actor B, A and B are husband and wife, or lovers, and during the drama they love each other, hug and kiss. Which leads to the question: the two people having physical relations – are they A and B or X and Y?"

"And then?"

"This Othello isn't too much like the Shakespeare one, he chose to leave."

"So what do you think," Ding Yi said, "I should choose?"

E couldn't help but yell: "That's your business!"

Silence.

It made one think of the Gadfly and Gemma. Think of the scene they adapted together, how to get Arthur to return from that silence.

"Sorry, sorry." Ding Yi walked up to E, patted her shoulder. "I'm saying, can I still choose our agreement?"

E enjoyed his touch and let her tears answer: of course.

"When it comes time for me to choose to leave, please let me know, OK?" Ding Yi said.

"And before that," Ding Yi added, "I'll still choose our agreement."

E hugged him tightly. The two of them kissed tearfully. The scene also made me think of Spring and Autumn, think of Autumn's dance and the spell of the accompanying piano... think of the stars and fireflies, think of Lingling's white dress... think of Eden, think of the vast silence outside of Eden, think of my many lives and endless search...

136. News of Uncle

One night afterwards Ding Yi happened upon a news report on the TV: a gardener had twenty night-blooming cereus bloom in one night, visitors came in an endless stream and all left amazed. When the gardener was interviewed, he said the flowers were all given by an old friend. And panning shots showed multiple palms in the background and many other familiar-looking flowers and plants...

Ding Yi quickly called Yi. "Hey, hey, hurry, put on the TV."

"It's on. What station?"

"I don't know, here it's ninety-nine."

"Ninety-nine, ninety-nine... ninety-nine has a magic show on."

"Wrong! Oh man, hurry and look, the channel with a reporter interviewing an old man."

"Why, what's going on?"

"I think the old man's the guy who took Uncle's plants away."

"Based on what?"

"Hurry up and find it, have you found it?"

"No?"

"Gah, it's over, it's over, don't bother."

"Oh, maybe I caught the end."

"What?"

"A night blooming cereus. The TV said it's a night blooming cereus."

"Right, that station, did you think they looked like Uncle's?"

"It's an advert now."

The next day Ding Yi went to the TV station to inquire and soon found the newsroom. In the afternoon Ding Yi and Yi used the address they were given to visit the old gardener's house.

"Did Uncle give you these flowers?" Ding Yi asked the old man.

"Uncle?" the old man shook his head.

"Oh, traitor, did a traitor give them to you?"

"What do you have to do with him?"

"Friends, Uncle's old friends."

"Older than me?" The old man laughed and went on: "But you're actually right, these flowers are all his, he wanted to go far away, and he made me the flowers' foster parent. Are you Ding Yi?"

"You know me?"

"I worked with your dad, your dad cooked, I kept the fire going."

"Oh, it's you, you're that..."

"Right. Now I'm retired. Haven't seen your dad in a long time, how is he?"

"Fine."

"What, is there a problem with these flowers?"

"Oh, no, no, we just came to ask if you know where Uncle went."

Then the old man invited them in, found two somewhat dirty cups and made them tea.

"He just said he was going to the shore, didn't say anything else."

"What shore?"

"Right, I said the shore's big. Can you go around and cover it all? Drink."

Ding Yi picked up the cup, looked at it and put it back down. "Does he know anyone there?"

"Oh, right, an old classmate, named, uh, what was it... Ai Kesi?"

"Do you know X's real name?"

"Just Ai Kesi, I don't know if they have another name."

"Oh!" Ding Yi slapped his head. "I know, I know!"

"Who?" Yi asked.

"Magician, that magician!"

"What magician?"

"From E city, you forgot?"

"Right, right, a foreign city!" that old man said, taking the monophonic E as the Chinese character pronounced 'E' but meaning 'foreign'. "I thought of it as soon as you said it, nice, nice, foreign city, he talked about him."

137. E City

Ding Yi and Yi visited E city. As Uncle said: picturesque small city, sitting against a mountain, facing the sea. As that magician described: green mountains and waters; the vast sea merged with boundless sky; flying wind and clouds; seagulls and waves sound in harmony.

They walked through the whole city in one afternoon, found all seven cinemas, two theatres, but didn't see Uncle. The seven cinemas and one of the theatres were all showing trendy films, only the other theatre said it still put on the occasional magic show. Ding Yi walked around the theatre but saw no trace of Uncle.

Yi asked the doorman: "Have you seen an old man recently, coming here a lot?"

"What a question!" the doorman said. "The only people who come to see magic, apart from old women, are old men."

Yi laughed. "Young people don't come?"

"Young people live in magic, why pay for it?"

Ding Yi said: "We're looking for an old man who looks a little... a little abnormal."

"Ah, I hope you don't take it to heart. By the way, who can you be sure is normal these days?"

"Sorry." Ding Yi lowered his head, thinking that this could be a sage.

The doorman asked: "How is he abnormal?"

"Oh," Ding Yi said. "I think if he saw you, he'd definitely ask about a so-and-so-stan or a so-and-so-sky."

"You talking about time magic?"

"Whoa, you know!"

"I heard my grandpa talk about it, but..."

Ding Yi quickly handed him a cigarette. "Oh, yeah, go on, go on."

"But that was decades ago, I just heard it did exist."

"Is your grandpa still with us?"

"What are you talking about?" The doorman laughed. "Even my father died several years ago!"

"Then the theatre from that year is this one?"

"It was here, but the original was torn down. This one's only been here a few years."

In the afternoon Ding Yi and Yi went to the shore, like that so-and-so-stan or so-and-so-sky suggested, lying down on the soft, clean beach, limbs extended, facing the sky, letting the sea breeze and sunshine cover their bodies...

"How is it, Yi?"

"How's what?"

"Does it feel like the magician said?"

"What?"

"Like going back to childhood and sleeping in your mother's arms?"

"Mm, not quite, but it feels pretty good."

"Close your eyes..."

Yi opened her eyes very wide and looked at the sky. "Where else can we look for him?"

"If only we could enter another time."

"Another time?"

"Because 'your time is clocks, but mine isn't'."

"You really believe that magician?"

"What do you think he came so far to find?" Ding Yi said. "The method to turn back time!"

"How is that possible?"

"But Uncle believed it."

"If we assume it's true, it's just magic after all, in the end wouldn't that so-and-so-stan or so-and-so-sky come back to reality?"

"But this is his only hope," Ding Yi said. "If every route is a dead end, all lead to humiliation and loneliness then, think about it, what else can he believe in?"

"Ugh, what a tragedy!" Yi sighed.

"But for people to live they must have some kind of belief. Sometimes it's impossible to forget."

"Right, right, actually my mum and dad are that way too."

"They believe in magic?" Ding Yi asked jokingly.

"But," Yi said, sitting up. "We, I mean me, you, Qin E and Lü Sa can't believe in magic."

"No, ours is drama."

"But how will this drama end, Ding Yi, have you thought about that?"

"Yi, lay down, lay down, right, like that, relax your body, completely relax... Right, right, think of the magician's words, imagine a smooth, full voice: ah, no one around, no one in the world but me... The waves roared, the wind flies like magic, the salty water refreshes your spirit, the shifting clouds seem ancient... Do you feel it, Yi? We are those clouds, those waves, that wind... Hard to distinguish, hard to distinguish, we are everything we can see... Yi, do you feel how beautiful this is? Yi, why can't we get away from the city like the poet and painters, flee the hubbub, come build a life in a place like this? Build an extraordinary family here, you, me, also E and Sa, all of us together, here, till we grow old, old and white-haired, without suspicion, without discrimination and discord, only mutual trust, mutual appreciation and work of course... We don't need a lot of possessions, basic things are enough, just live a wise, simple life... Yi, are you listening to me?"

Yi closed her eyes.

"Yi?"

There seemed to be tears in the corners of her eyes.

"Yi!"

Yi opened her eyes. "Yes, of course it would be great if it could be like that."

"Yi, do you really think so?"

But Yi did not look happy as she stared blankly at Ding Yi for a long time.

"If it sounds good, if it sounds promising, Yi, why not go do it?"

Yi closed her eyes again.

"Yi, can I ask you a question?"

"I know what you're going to ask."
"What?"
"Why haven't I married yet."
"No, no, you don't necessarily have to marry, but why haven't you…"
"I'm fragile by nature."
"Fragile. You're fragile?"
"I'm not like you think, that strong."
"Nonsense!"
"Then I'm nonsense."
"OK, even so, but doesn't that mean you need love even more?"
"I'm afraid. Really, I'm so afraid."
"Afraid? Afraid of what?"
"Love is a risk."
"Risk?"
"It's the most dangerous thing in life."
"Whoa! Yi, you're really funny…"
Yi stood up, dusting sand off her. "Should be going. There's a train back tonight."

138. Power

On the train back the two of them beat around the bush, obviously with things on their minds that they wouldn't say outright. Ding Yi steered the conversation towards Danqing Island, the possibility of that life, and his drama. Yi always sidestepped him.

Yi didn't want to talk about that. Yi wanted to talk about her past on the border, which Ding Yi didn't respond to.

"OK, sleep then," Yi said. "It's late."

"OK," Ding Yi responded but didn't move.

Yi lay down, turned away from him.

The train sped along and Ding Yi looked out the window, bored.

The night beyond the window was vast, the wind rushed between the wilderness and stars, whistling by. I wondered if, between the wilderness and stars, there were overlapping shows onstage and thousands of souls roaming around in the dark — "Ah, night like water, dreams like boats, drunken paddles swaying, heart flowing unhurriedly…"

That drowsy Ding Yi asked me: *Hey brother, can you tell me where you are again? Or where my soul actually is?*

Now?

Yeah, now for example.

Now he's in your soul's question… Now he's in your thoughts about my response… Now, because your thinking is confused, he's moved to the dark night you watch.

Brother, can you be a little clearer, sum it up?

The soul is always where the finite and the infinite interlink.

They say the soul weighs twenty-one grams.

Ha, that precise?

Someone did a test, in the moment people die, the body weighs twenty-one grams less.

Why does this have to be about mass and not about linkage? For example, waves and the wind. For example, tides and the moon. For example, your care for Uncle. For example, the passion you have for Yi, for E, for Sa, the difficulty you have forgetting Spring and Autumn, Lingling and that white dress. For example, our memory of Eden and our hopes and prayers for the future that leads we know where...

Maybe so, but what does that mean?

First of all it's a fact, this fact demands meaning from us. Or put it this way: ask here for meaning of the fact that is not to be explained.

Isn't this fact a little absurd?

That's why God said to Job: 'Where were you when I created the earth?'

What's that mean?

It means: 'Who do you think you are?' You think you're someone? You think God should favour you?

Yeah, yeah, I know that, but it can't stop me from feeling absurd. Can I ask why we had to come to this world?

People didn't have a reason, they were thrown into this world.

Unreasonable, simply unreasonable! It's like we're just a chessboard, and the game has already been played!

So don't look for reason on the board, maybe you can sit outside the board and see its beauty.

That's an unhelpful note, a pretentious annotation.

A note, OK, very interesting! A note is language, a thought, a hope, which bears meaning. Once I walked a path named Sisyphus, that place was absurd! From morning to night we pushed a boulder up a mountain, then it rolled down again, and from morning to night we pushed it up again, the boulder rolled down again... Until one day we saw Sisyphus's shadow cast by the setting sun, and we read a beautiful note from the screen of the sky. And only then did we realise how beautiful that path became again...

Still resignation, brother, I think it's still resignation!

Sorry, God doesn't care if it's resignation or not, just like infinity doesn't care how finite you are. God just cares about giving you a reality, wants you to find beautiful value in your despair. And isn't that exactly what you've been hoping for – realising the unrealisable?

Well, brother, what you're saying sounds rational, but...

But what?

What is the basis of our belief that love is meaningful and hatred is not?

Love makes people search and meaning is inherent in the search, while hatred interrupts the journey, isolates people, makes them lonely, and isolated notes are just noise, noise that cannot be expanded.

So why love isn't expanded as much as possible but confined as much as possible?

"Don't you want to sleep?" Yi asked, turning around. Yi still hadn't fallen asleep.

"Oh, Yi, can I ask you another question?"

"Shoot."

"Why is love, the most beautiful feeling in the world, confined as much as possible instead of expanded as much as possible? Confined, confined, confined, until it's confined to one-on-one – then people are satisfied?"

"You asked this a long time ago."

"But I never got a proper response."

"Does the question necessarily have a response?"

"At least in theory it should."

"Not having an answer isn't a kind of answer?"

"Sorry, I think that's sophistry. I think being unwilling to answer such an important question is a disgrace. People sing her praises, but treat her with fear like she's a scourge. This has to be a cause of shame to the human race!"

Yi's eyes widened. There was light outside the train window, rows of lights like a school of fish appearing at shorter and shorter intervals – maybe a station ahead. The lights slid over Yi's face, over her wide eyes, where some type of fear seemed to pulse.

Then a bright light shone. Yi covered her face with her hands.

In the lights, souls stood and walked – who knows from where, going where, or linked to where, caring for where, affected by where.

Then the train whistled and rolled into darkness again.

"Yi, are you asleep?"

"Oh, I can't answer your question."

There was a long silence. The light in the carriage was dim, it wasn't clear if Yi was sleeping or not.

Ding Yi could only spread his blanket and prepare to sleep himself.

Then Yi said: "Maybe people don't necessarily fear love's expansion..."

"Then fear what?"

"Power's expansion."

Ding Yi looked around, wondering if she was sleeptalking.

139. Citation and Conjectures

"Why must there be sex? The answer seems incontrovertible – the reason why ninety-nine-point-nine per cent of multicellular organisms engage in sexual reproduction is that it's the best way to pass on genes to the next generation while maintaining diversity. But this explanation has a fatal flaw: sexual reproduction is a short-term waste.

Imagine a group of fish living in the same pond, competing over a limited food supply. They initiate sexual reproduction and as a result each generation includes males and females. Assume a fish has found a way to reproduce without sex, all its descendants are female and they all give birth to female offspring. Some generations later those that reproduce without sex will outnumber their sexual counterparts and eventually make them extinct. In the short-term battle for survival, sex is a serious disadvantage.

Of course over the long term that's not the case. In the absence of two genders that mate and shuffle genes, a species accumulates harmful mutations and before long goes extinct. The majority of single-sex organisms only last some tens of thousands of years. But this isn't a satisfactory explanation for the near ubiquity of sexual behaviour. Natural selection doesn't care about generations in the distant future. In order to win the battle, sexual mating must have immediate benefits. This is difficult to explain...

Maybe something can explain this puzzle. Gender is ubiquitous, not because it brings long-term advantages but because it is difficult to abandon once it has evolved. Some biologists believe the pattern of cell division that forms sperm and eggs evolved very early in the history of life and only later became the means of reproduction. They say gender is so deeply written into life's operating system that it is impossible to give up. This is a very promising but incomplete answer. From a certain perspective this explanation only passes the mystery to another area: how did gender first evolve?"

– **Reference News, *'Top Ten Mysteries of Life'*, 22 December 2004**

So when I was in Ding Yi or Shi Tiesheng, I had three hypotheses: 1. It's not for short-term competition, nor for long-term survival, but for a varied path. 2. Variation confuses people, seduces them, makes them ignore what's in front of them – like God's expectation of Dr Faust: go listen to the revelation in the confusion. 3. Since it only became a means of reproduction later, it's obvious: the two genders were not originally for reproduction but to find each other and unite to always look forward to the continuation of the journey, or continue to look forward to an endless journey.

140. Return to E City

E left a phone message: "Come see me when you get back."

Ding Yi hurried to her place, worrying the whole way: maybe Asky's sick or got in trouble again? Asky was always making trouble. Once she ran into the classroom at night and covered the white walls in drawings. Another time she put three raw eggs under her blanket and accidentally crushed them all. The teacher asked why she put eggs in her bed, she said she wanted to hatch birdies.

There didn't seem to be an issue though, E was sitting in front of the window, reading.

Spotty autumn light beat peacefully on her body.

"What's up?"

"Nothing."

"I thought something happened."

"Be seated first."

It sounded like something had happened, so Ding Yi didn't take his eyes off her.

"Asky has to go to school," E said.

"Really? She's already seven?"

"Six, she should start next year."

"Oh, is there a problem?"

"She'll understand everything."

"What do you mean?"

"I'm afraid she'll be discriminated against at school. What will she think when other people ask about her father?"

Ding Yi's fingers tapped the table. E went to the bathroom, obviously giving him time to think.

When E came back Ding Yi said: "She has me, can't I be her father?"

"Would she believe it? She's always called you 'uncle'."

"Whatever we do, Asky will know the truth in her heart."

"What should we do?"

"Go get a marriage certificate."

"You? And me?"

"Doesn't matter. Having it doesn't matter, not having it doesn't matter, a piece of paper."

"No, I mean Sa, what would Sa think?"

"What about Sa?"

"She loves you. You don't think Sa loves you already?"

Really, Brother Ding, I'm not so sure am I?"

But he avoided my question and took forever to come up with a response to E's question.

"Yes... I think so, maybe... Oh, but if it's for Asky, Sa should be able to understand."

"You think everyone's like you?"

"What about me?"

"You think everyone can always live in drama?"

Ding Yi paced silently, from red to blue, from blue to white...

E changed locations, sat in a corner where the sun didn't reach, leaning against the wall, watching Ding Yi.

Ding Yi walked onto the balcony, stood a moment then walked into the bedroom. After walking around the bedroom, he came out and went into Asky's room.

"Ding Yi," E said from the living room, "maybe... maybe we should live a normal life."

Ding Yi looked at Asky's toys – Graham the deer, Peter the wolf, Ann the raccoon and Cynthia the duck... Then he slowly sat down, slow like an old person.

Yes, brother, I've been expecting it, he said.

I said: *You've been expecting what?*

This day would come, I long expected this day would come...

The sunlight seemed like an old person too, through the window panes, in the shadows of the tree, next to those furry toys, and in the memory of the old clock's tick-tock, slowly moving... In the distance, so distant it became abstract, a commotion stirred, the first autumn wind.

"Normal," Ding Yi seemed to say to himself, like sleeptalking, and like he was addressing E. "You mean daytime?"

"But Asky has to go to school," E answered.

"Why does she have to... have to go to that crap school."

"That's what you think."

"And you?"

"No one can make that decision for her."

"But can you make a normal... decision for her?"

"It can only be this way, Ding Yi. Later she can choose for herself. We must let Asky choose for herself."

"This isn't Shang Zhou's decision is it?"

"Hard to say... but it's not as simple as you think."

Ding Yi came out of Asky's room at a sleepwalker's pace and stopped next to the door to the living room.

"He, I mean Shang Zhou, came again?"

"Yes. He said Asky could go to school abroad."

"That's true."

"True how?"

Ding Yi laughed, half bitter, half mocking.

"What are you laughing at, I hate that so much," E shouted. "Just say what you're thinking."

"I'm laughing at myself. No, I'm like that Moor."

"You thought you weren't?" E stood up angrily and walked to the balcony.

One stood on the balcony, the other leaned next to the living room door, in between were the red, blue and white areas of the floor, dancing tree shadows, tranquil autumn wind, the peace the autumn wind brought from the distance.

This peace made it hard for them to think of something to say.

A long time later, E finally said: "Why don't you go, I want to be alone for a while."

Ding Yi walked up to the couch, picked up his bag – his slow, silent movements like sleepwalking.

"Let's both think it through again, OK?" E said.

When E turned to look, that guy was already gone.

"Ding Yi? Ding Yi?"

The doors were all closed.

"Ding Yi? Ding Yi?"

All the doors seemed never to have opened.

What's wrong, brother?

Nothing.

141. Disappointment or Omnipresence

Ding Yi walked into the autumn wind alone. It seemed to be full of Iago's rumours, it seemed full of Othello's heartache, it seemed full of Cassio and Shang Zhou's shadows.

Brother, what's wrong with you?

Uninteresting! he said. *No fun! Boring! Tacky! Vulgar!*

Why not say jealous?

Me? Jealous?

Who else?

No, this isn't jealousy.

If it isn't jealousy, what is it? What do you think jealousy is?

I'm telling you this isn't jealousy, it isn't, it isn't! This is...

Is what?

Disappointment! Ah, now Qin Han can gloat, now he's right. Brother, tell me, can there be some things in this world that are real? Can there be some things to trust in that won't drift away in the wind?

You, the great disappointed?

I'm not Qin Han. I'm just saying, if even E is like this, even Eve suddenly thinks of leaving, tell me, brother, does any of this still have any hope?

But to me your disappointment really isn't that grand.

I never said it was great, I just want truth!

This is truth. This is actually truth. A true life and your true jealousy!

Then how do you think people should be? Resigned to adversity? Go with the flow? In order not to be disappointed, simply avoid having hope? In order not to hurt, simply be numb? If someone tells you to go, there's another descendent of Adam, you'd leave like that? If someone tells you to go, show's over, you'll get up and go home? If someone says your stuff isn't precious, it's rubbish, garbage, abnormal, you take your bloody heart and stuff in a bag and throw it away?

Did E say that?

What, you didn't sense it? Wait and see...

So the dust blew, and Ding Yi was whipped by Iago's rumours like a violent wind – yes, yes, you hear what you want to hear. So like the leaves,

Ding Yi's journey fell into Othello's anger – "Iago is omnipresent like the wind, one glimpse of your suspicion and I'll return." So fog covering thousands of miles and bitter rain falls non-stop – yes, yes, what you think is real becomes real: Ding Yi's autumn seemed to hold Cassio's falsehoods and the unforgivable betrayal of Desdemona...

142. Title Interpretation

One possibility is Shang Zhou's appearance was only temporary, and E wouldn't go with him; regardless of whether Asky could go with him. Another possibility made Ding Yi suffer, tested his drama: E still loved Shang Zhou. E always thought of Shang Zhou, thought of the day when that man who had travelled so far from home would return, one day return to his wife and child.

They were both possible.

But fate would only allow one.

That's why *Travels in Ding Yi* could be *Ding Yi's Travels*, that is the path fate chose for a Ding. *My Travels in Ding Yi* could also be *My Ding Yi's Travels*, the path I imagined fate chose for a Ding.

Two possibilities may be equally likely, but for him I chose the latter.

Poor Ding Yi, it may have been better for you to land in another's imagination. But unfortunately, or fortunately, this time you were destined to walk into mine. (Maybe we're all just someone else's imagining – that wise old man, Borges, once said.)

Just as the 'night's drama' is always acted out in someone's dreams, imagination is also a kind of reality. You thought the night was just endless silence? You thought the night was lifeless? No, no, in the depths of night thoughts become dreams, dreams ride the wind... The wild call is not dispelled by the day's arrival but annihilated, and thus became *My Travels in Ding Yi* or *Ding's Travels*. As for the other path, the last resort is thus interrupted, or from another place enters the hustle and bustle of the day, or the joy of the day. That is because I'm just a possibility, a possibility that is also a limitation.

143. Reality's Drama

Still that balcony, where the agreement was made. Still that way: moonlight, starry sky, Ding Yi and E sitting by the balcony rail, the dense lights around them stretching into the boundless night. The difference was falling leaves, dry branches brushing the windows.

The difference was also the night's drama wanted you to let go of your imagination, tonight's drama just wanted you to accept.

But it was still the agreed-upon time.

The past was not far away. The echoes of the past rippled through the clockless time: "Regardless of when, regardless of where and regardless of what happens, as long as it's like this we'll enter the moonlight together, enter darkness, which is our stage. Night brings us into drama, brings us into frankness, brings us into a time where anything is possible. There is without cover, without shame and without discrimination, then all desire is proper, all words can be said. Sound good?"

"Does that mean something happened now?" Ding Yi said, breaking the silence.

"You can ask anything," E said.

"Ask what?"

"Any question. Anything you think of."

Listen, you listen, that Ding said to me. She's so calm!

What, is there something wrong with being calm?

Could it be a trap?

My God, why would you think that? Isn't this the truth you wanted?

What, this is truth too? It seems like a planned retreat to me!

Watch it. Is there something wrong with change? Change is true too.

Whew! Thanks...

"Are you saying," Ding Yi asked E, "you still... still love him?"

"It's not as simple as you think."

"Yes or no!"

"I think I've at least never hated him."

"You still like him, right?"

"Originally I thought I couldn't, but this time, this time... really if there wasn't that inferiority, that need to be stronger than others, Shang Zhou was... oh, did you see how he played with Asky?"

"Stay on topic, he was what?"

"Don't be so aggressive."

"OK. Go on, go!"

E sighed to herself and spoke more slowly. "I think you probably saw how well he got along with Asky, how simple, focused, it was as if he'd just come to play with her, had no other demands, had no other hopes, had come all that way just to enjoy that time... that, honestly, really moved me."

"You're emphasising Asky, that Asky needs him."

"Yes. I can't let myself ignore that."

"What about you? Do you want to go back to him too?"

"He came back to me! Oh, and... and I said, primarily, I just think... just think Asky should have a normal life."

"I think you should admit you still love him. Or you've already fallen in love with him again!"

"Yeah?"

This "Yeah?" seemed to leap out of E's mouth with fear and anxiety.

She seems to have mixed feelings. Am I right, brother?

I said: Could be, maybe, yeah... yeah?

What could be, maybe, I'm telling you: yeah!
"Yeah?" E softly repeated the question, her face seeming both relieved and more tense.
Brother, you still think 'could be', 'maybe'?
E turned and went inside.

In the empty living room, the moon cast shadows of swaying trees, and E's footsteps and sighs crossed the red, blue and white floor sections.

"You should admit," Ding Yi said, following her, "that the one who wants a normal life is you!"

"Yeah?" E's expression showed she was contemplating the same thing. "Yeah?" She asked herself more than Ding Yi. "Yeah?" Or she was asking the empty room, asking the silence.

"There's no reason to be so shy about this 'normal life'," Ding Yi said behind E. "Really it's... it's that you can't resist the temptation of the day, can't shake off that mediocre life!"

"Mediocre?"

Hey, brother, don't you hate people calling you mediocre?

But he couldn't hear me any more. "Yes, mediocre! Comfortable, safe, secure, by the book, but you know it's also a dead life, don't you, E? Lifeless, no passion, no imagination. Like a machine that functions for decades, a lifetime, one step at a time.

"And what is life then? A task to be completed so you can get your reward – job titles, reputation, international speaking tour, coming back and making money, buying a house and car, having kids... then the children grow up and do it all over again."

"You think people who live like that are mediocre?"
"Don't you?"
"You think someone who lives the way they want to is mediocre?"
"Depends on the life he wants."
"Only the life you want to live isn't mediocre?"
"That's not what I said."
"Then what kind of life do you think isn't mediocre?"
"You already know."
"But I'm confused. I'm confused, please enlighten me."
"You don't have to use that tone. Without using that tone I can tell you: a life that's passionate and imaginative like our drama, like... in short, a life full of romantic desire."
"Then what romantic desire do you have exactly?"
"Not letting you fall into mediocrity is one!"
"What if, what if I have that freedom?"
"Freedom to fall into mediocrity?"
Brother, aren't you being a bit hypocritical?
"That's just what you're saying," E said, "but what you're saying no longer adds up."

"How so?"

"Your life full of love, now, now seems full of hate."

"Hate? For who?"

"For people who don't want to live like you, people who've affected the life you want to live."

"Not true, not true, that's just love!"

"It's love?"

"It's love."

"Oh, I'm listening."

E took a drink of water and looked seriously at Ding Yi, awaiting his theory.

"Like if someone loves you, the person closest to you, like... like your parents, could they watch you sink into a swamp?"

E's eyes widened, saying: What, you're done? Then she almost spat out the water in her mouth with laughter before holding it in and swallowing it.

"What's so funny?!" Ding Yi said.

E kept staring at him, wide-eyed, saying: Oh, Ding Yi, you've really surprised me!

"What? I'm just making a comparison."

Brother, what kind of comparison is that? Talk about paternalistic! Your mum and dad love you, your aunts and uncles love you, your brothers and sisters love you, does that make you a pet? Mean you do whatever they say?

"Forget it, fine," E said.

E thought a moment and said: "Then let me ask you, if I... if Shang Zhou and I go... go live that kind of life, would you hate me?"

Silence. In the gloom and silence, the sound of distant commotion and nearby bells could slowly be heard – 'tick-tock, tick-tock' is always this steady.

That Ding squatted, lit a cigarette, then sat down, sat in the blue area.

E quietly stood in the red 'next door' area.

No 'off' came, of course it couldn't. The question was would it come again later.

In the silence, the two of them looked at each other. Or maybe the empty wall between the red and blue became tangible, grew taller, closer and isolated them?

"Give me one too?" E said.

Ding Yi gave her the cigarette in his hand. OK, OK, there was still no barrier in between. Ding Yi lit another cigarette and slowly blew out some smoke; the smoke swirled, coiled through the moonlight and disappeared in the darkness.

"No, that's not hate," Ding Yi said. "It looks like hate, but it's love, it's my desire not to fall into mediocrity, not to let Sa fall into it either. And we want to make all the mediocrity in the world... move towards love."

"You? Because of you?"
"And you."
"Ding Yi, you've changed."
"How?"
"Who do you think you are?"
Ding Yi looked at himself in the window glazed with moonlight.
Right, how did you suddenly turn into a tough guy? E's right, you really aren't how you used to be.
Come on, is it me who's different or her who's different?
"E, do you regret it?"
"Regret what?"
"E, do you know where we are? Have you forgotten our drama?"
"No, I can't, it's unforgettable. But, but it's just drama, Ding Yi!"
"Just? E, what's just drama?"
"I'm saying since it's drama, just because it's drama, because…"
"Because what?"
"Because it can't be reality!"
"So you like reality, E?"
"Ding Yi, you're really a bit like Qin Han."
"Ha, you're bringing him up again!"
"You don't know why he erased the end of that film. He didn't want to see reality but preferred to stay in dreams. While you, Ding Yi, you go even further, you want to turn a dream into reality."
"No, it's not just a dream, it's an ideal from childhood. E, you once said, we all said, love is an ideal. I really can't stand your logic, acting like dreams have to always remain dreams. People are also ignorant in that they all have dreams in their heart, all have desires, but because everyone doesn't believe they can be realised, they aren't, and they really do always remain dreams. Then, looking back, you say it was just a dream, just drama, not real, not normal, so each generation can only walk in reality's circles, forming a phantom wall!"
"I think you're a bit like Uncle too. Uncle believed time could flow backwards, and you think drama can become reality."
"But I'm just talking about us!" Ding Yi said, grabbing E's shoulders. "You, me and Sa. We can't give up, can't follow the crowd into a mediocre life!"
"Qin Han was right about at least one thing."
"What?"
"The essentials of drama. Finite time, finite space, finite characters and finite p-power!"
Right, Yi said it too, I reminded that Ding. *The fear is not of love's expansion but power's expansion.*
"Damn, you listen to him!" Ding Yi shouted, shaking E's shoulders.
"So I should listen to you?" E tried to get his hands off her and failed.

"The key is us," Ding Yi said. "Do you understand? The key is you. The key is what you want!"

"The key is," E said, looking at Ding Yi, "whether I can want what I want or not."

Ding Yi slowly let go, slowly let his hands drop.

E sat in the room's farthest corner, closed her eyes. A long time later she said: "Maybe I've always been a mediocre person."

Ding Yi laughed.

"Ding Yi, you'd better, better consider me a mediocre person."

"Then what are we talking about?" Ding Yi laughed like Rivarez, laughed and turned to leave. "Then what is there to talk about…"

144. Reality or Nightmare

"That's just drama." Those words stung Ding Yi.

For many days after that, like the early spring of the past, Ding Yi's mood was like dust that had blocked out the sun, and he was surrounded by wilderness. "Just", "just", "just…" This word really broke his heart.

I should say I understood him.

Or that I wanted to help him but couldn't.

But the autumn light was good, with exceptionally thin clouds and a clean sky. Once the autumn wind spread, it was no longer as urgent as when it first began but evolved quietly and came to affect everything. The sun's angle changed, passing through wilderness, passing through endless land, passing through each plant and tree… leaving long shadows everywhere; the moment it sank under the horizon, it showed how quietly it passes. The autumn water smoothed the waves, migrating birds called out between the water and sky – the flocks fulfilling their annual commitment. The leisurely deer, calling cranes, falling leaves… Life on earth eagerly listened to the call of the season.

But before long they would all want to leave.

The wilderness would soon become withered and empty.

Yes, all things must come to an end, that's just drama.

I was the only one who accompanied Ding Yi, sitting inside with him, or wandering around. I said: *I! accompany – you! I'm your only reliable brother.*

Really? Thanks. But we have alcohol too… yeah, alcohol, can't do without it at a time like this. That guy pulled his head into his collar, alone in the harsh autumn winds, even dissolving his heart in alcohol, staggering into nothingness.

I tried to fly out of him, turn the guy's drunkenness into my travel time. But it didn't work, this guy held me tight, asking me questions as he drank.

Brother, tell me, is it just drama? Is it just a dream? I'm always fucking dreaming wishful dreams, all the time, right?

Brother Ding, you're drunk again!

I'm drunk? Only if you can prove what I said... doesn't qualify as a... a question.

Yes, it's a question, even though you must call it a day today.

It's OK so long as it's a question. And you're not drunk, either. So I'll ask again: Can this world have... have things that are completely real? Are there or... aren't there?

There are.

OK, you're a good man. Then let me ask: what... what is real?

Well, E, she wants to live the life she wants, do you recognise that as real?

If you... put it like that, someone can change their mind as they wish, you think they're real?

Of course they are, she's not fake.

Then someone isn't honest with themself, are they... they real too?

You mean E?

Let's not talk about her, let's take someone, someone for example.

E wasn't dishonest in anything she said, was she? But people can change, E's free. You've said everyone is free, so are you being honest now?

I... shit, you mean what you're saying is fucking... right, huh?

Brother, you've got to face reality, otherwise how can you talk about what's real or not?

Hey, it seems like I fucked up, huh? I'm telling you this... isn't OK!

What are you going to do about it?

People have to take responsibility for what they say.

Will you take responsibility for freedom?

Screw, screw fucking freedom! All this freedom then... then what can be real?

Oh, right, you think E just changed her mind, but she didn't change, I think you changed.

I changed? No way!

Early on, drama was something E chose freely, now she wants to live a normal life that she chose freely too. Did E change? You changed, Ding Yi, you changed by not allowing her to be free!

That guy was quiet, he started chugging alcohol, started crying. The alcohol went in his belly, tears flowed down his face, the wind blew and stung it.

I tried to fly away from him again. That flight would feel amazing, so wonderful, not being dragged down by his embarrassment, not subject to his limitations, his windswept nightmare, I could be anywhere I wanted – wilderness, fields, villages... jungles, glens, mountains... simmering deserts, river sunsets... but no. Maybe because he hadn't been drinking for a few years, my flight technique was rusty; I tried a few times without success and heard that Ding calling me.

Brother, brother!

What's wrong?

Don't you think this thing is... is a little screwed up?

What thing?

Not... not giving people freedom... of... of course a little like that.

What? Speak clearly, what?

A little, uh, easy to create Uncle. But all without freedom, man... man, tell me, where can we go now?

Well, no need to say it, that Ding had a knack after all. So I came from the void to Ding Yi or those waves of invisible desire coalesced into that body, why? Because that limitless freedom was also lonely, also boring; like the desert we talked about, each step is the starting over, wherever you go it's like you're moving in place. Good old Borges really had foresight: space minimised by walls is a prison, space arbitrarily expanded into desert is also a prison. Yes, yes, boundless freedom is like a boundless desert, where can you go? This guy's last question really stumped me.

Luckily he didn't ask again. Ding Yi had fallen asleep. Even sleep couldn't stop this guy drinking. While snoring loudly, he muttered about alcohol...

He dreamed of a murder.

A murder in the desert: a bloody pale dress dyed red... but he couldn't see the victim, and there was no one else around, he could only see the bright red of the blood staining the paleness of the dress as it fluttered in the breeze below the blue sky... he saw neither the victim nor the perpetrator. When he looked at the place where the endless sand and sky met, the bright red seemed like a tree growing, the pale white like a flower blooming... Then he heard his own heartbeat, saw his own feet – toes, ankles, two feet moving together, walking, towards the bright red tree and the pale white flower... He wanted to go look, take a closer look and see what it was, or who it was, what had really happened there. But suddenly the wind raged, blowing dust and sand, first some grains of sand smacked him in the face like lashing whips, then that forceful cold wind hit his body, forcing him to crouch forward, shivering... It wasn't good though, he saw blood. That whiteness had come towards him, that bright red spread to his feet... He tried to scramble backwards in horror, but it seemed as if someone was pushing him forward... Then that white and red flew up like giant butterflies, blotting out the sun, making the world spin, emitting a deafening clicking sound like Uncle's pruning... He struggled to get away, back up, but it was like someone was pushing him, the pruning clicks got closer and closer, faster and faster, the butterflies then turned and flew towards him, fluttering into his head, hitting his face...

"Brother, hey, brother!" Someone really was pushing him.

The guy sleeping was lying with his face on the ground, trying to ward off the butterflies.

"Hey, hey, Ding Yi, Ding Yi, wake up!"

Only then was he startled upright, sat wide-eyed.

It was Sa. "Brother Ding, what happened?" Sa held a handkerchief out to cover his nose.

That guy pushed Sa's hand away unhappily, the snow-white handkerchief stained with bright-red blood.

"What happened, you fell?"

"Oh, uh... drank a little too much." The guy finally snapped out of it.

"Go to the hospital?"

"Bah, it's nothing. What are you doing?"

"Looking for you, all looking for you!"

"All?"

"E, Qin Han and Shang Zhou."

Yes, made a fool of yourself now?

Surprisingly, that Ding got angry and shouted at Sa: "Did I hire all of you for that?"

145. Sa's Questioning

Still on that same lawn as before, Ding Yi looked depressed and asked Sa with that saddening question of E's, asked her if she thought it was "just drama".

"Since it's called drama," Sa ventured, "it's drama of course, isn't it?"

"Just or can only be – you'd better use one of those modifiers," Ding Yi said coldly.

The grass was still all green. The wildflowers, however, were gone, only their dried husks remained, shaking off seeds as they flew in the wind.

"The whole statement is like this," Ding Yi said, "since it's called a dream, of course it's just a dream."

"Isn't it?" Sa forced a smile.

"Yes, yes, who said it wasn't?" Ding Yi sighed and dropped back down.

A drifting grass seed landed on Ding Yi's nose. He stuck out his lower lip and blew, causing the seed to fly up. Ding Yi stared at it without blinking. It was like when he used to stare at unacquainted women in the crowd, he stared and stared, stared as the seed drifted into the tree tops, floated to distant mountains, each of its fine hairs glistening in the sun... But there was a sudden gust and the delicate figure disappeared – it was there, it must still be there, but no one knew where fate would take it.

"Then why not be blunt," Ding Yi said, "just call it nonsense, just call it junk, call it crap – it's really shit drama."

"Not necessarily," Sa said. "If it's in pursuit of dreams, it's not just a dream."

"Sophistry!"

"How is it sophistry? If it's a forced dream then that's a different kind of dream."

"What about giving up dreams?"

"Giving up whose dreams? Yours? E can't have her own dreams, old or new?"

"Wow, God! I get it, I get it, now I finally get it, everything can be easily explained, all beautiful language can be ruined by anyone!"

Sa looked at the distant mountains and the fleeting colours of dusk behind them, and seemed to become confused.

I thought of that sentence again: the fall of man is language's beginning.

But who can vouch that something is fallen?

Who can vouch for freedom and dreams?

Is it free dream or dreams' freedom?

Wow, God...

"Ding Yi," Sa said, "I always wanted to ask you something."

"Do it while I'm still kicking."

"Didn't you always ask why the most beautiful feeling isn't expanded? Let me ask you: Shang Zhou, for example, can he also join your drama?"

I heard that Ding's head ring. I felt a chasm in his heart, enticing people to fall, and fall into it... When he opened his eyes he saw blackness, when he closed them, endless red...

"Ding Yi?"

"Ding Yi!"

"Then why not ask... ask him?" that guy replied perfunctorily.

Cunning, how cunning, brother!

"No, I'm asking you." Sa stared at Ding Yi.

What'd she say?

She asked if Shang Zhou can join us or not.

Right, right... what do you think?

She asked you!

Me?

Yes, she asked Ding Yi!

This... this I'll have to think about...

"Ding Yi, Ding Yi?" Sa called.

"Ding Yi, Ding Yi!" She pushed him.

"Brother Ding, maybe I shouldn't have asked?"

Ding Yi opened his eyes, the glory of the setting sun seemed cold, its brilliance false. He turned and sat up, looked at Sa, saw she seemed to be drifting into the setting sun and its afterglow, drifting farther and farther with that question...

While he was faint, stuck to the ground, becoming a flat and thin thing...

Brother Ding, didn't you say you weren't jealous?

Oh, oh, so, I'm still a h-hooligan after all, aren't I?

How would I know?

Then... then let this arsehole die then, let me go with you...

"Brother Ding, why don't we go home."

146. The Tragedy of Danqing Island

Before the year was over, the air buzzed with a rumour that a tragedy had happened on that little Danqing Island: the poet Dao killed the painter Dan. The media quickly confirmed the rumour.

The poet Dao killed the painter Dan then threw himself into the sea. The painter Qing's whereabouts was unknown.

Ding Yi hurried to visit to learn more about it.

"What happened?"

Qin Han didn't answer, he put his hands in his pockets and seemed to recoil.

Ding Yi shook the newspaper in his hand. "Is it true?"

Qin Han sat down, shaking a leg, nodding slightly.

"How do you know?" Ding Yi asked.

"Same as you."

"Then it's definitely true?"

"Basically, should be."

"Should?"

Qin Han looked up at Ding Yi. "I'm saying the ending."

"What for?"

"Actually, no one knows what for yet."

"I'm asking why you think it basically should be."

"I'm just saying this isn't beyond my expectations."

"The painter Qing, where is she?"

"Yeah, that's a problem."

Ding Yi suddenly remembered his recent dream. "How did she die?"

"What? You mean Ou also..." Qin Han seemed surprised.

"Ou? No, no, I'm saying Dan, how did Dan die?"

"Oh, oh, Dan," Qin Han seemed to heave a sigh of relief. "Dan... oh, right, seems she bled to death. Last night a friend called, said she bled to death, such a remote island, so, so no help could arrive in time."

Blood, brother, did you hear that, blood again!

Yes, yes, this is really a bit strange, Brother Ding, you still remember what night that was?

But it was the desert, not an island.

Maybe, maybe it was an illusion, like a mirage?

But Qin Han said it was real! By the way, ours was but a dream.

But that time you were drunk out of your mind, brother, can you be sure it was just a dream?

Maybe that day I really flew out of Ding Yi? Maybe when he was falling down drunk I went elsewhere, to Danqing Island? There's another possibility: other souls out and about that night spread similar news – told me, on their timeless journey, a similar story they heard and witnessed, a story that in the desert instead of on an island. Or as it spread the story became a fable that could have happened anywhere.

Ding Yi asked: "Was the painter Qing not there when it happened or did she leave after?"

"Now that I think of it, that island isn't far away," said Qin Han, answering a different question.

147. Painter Qing

Afterwards Ding Yi felt stranger.

Ah, death, I said, *often has to do with blood.*

No, Ding Yi said, *the strangeness isn't the blood but when the painter Qing came up, Qin Han heard Ou.*

Must be a slip of the tongue. Meant to say Qing, Ou came out.

I'm afraid it's not that simple. Did you notice he seemed a bit out of it?

Oh, for sure.

Sa hurried over to say goodbye to Ding Yi.

"I'm leaving tomorrow."

"Leaving? Where to?"

"The south."

"Alone?"

"And Qin Han, I'm going with him."

"With him? Does he need your company?"

"I think he should have someone with him now."

Ding Yi tapped me. *What'd I just say? Something's on that guy's mind.*

"The south is big, where specifically?"

"An island."

"Danqing Island?"

Sa nodded.

Ding said: *What do you think's going on?*

I said: *Hell if I know.*

"Going to the funeral?" Ding Yi asked.

"Not just that," Sa said. "He seems to really... really want to know where Qing is."

"Does he want you to go with him?"

"No. I think he needs someone."

"Yeah? He has so much to worry about?"

Sa nodded again and started to cry.

"Does he want me to go with him, too?"

Don't kid, brother, this is too serious.

"I think," Sa said, wiping off her tears, "now he really needs someone to, someone to be with him..."

"What really happened?"

"I'll tell you later."

Ding Yi sat down, stunned.

"Then, I'll go?" Sa adjusted her backpack.

Ding Yi didn't seem to hear.

"I have to go." Sa looked at her watch.

Ding Yi's eyes seemed lifeless.

Sa left. Ding Yi seemed not to notice, other words rang in his ears: now I'm here, wait until I'm gone, that girl will be no more...

In the emptiness that huge butterfly seemed to flap its wings again.

But Sa turned back. "I guess I should tell you."

That butterfly stopped in midair or waited in clock-less time.

"Do you know the painter Qing's surname?"

Ding Yi shook his head mechanically.

"It's Ou. Ou Qing."

148. Nightmare Confusion

The desert is dim.

Heaven and earth seem to have returned to antediluvian times.

Amid the blood-red clouds and pale white fluttering, wrapping around the poet Dao's blame and question that sounded akin to entreaty.

"Dan, you're leaving me too, aren't you?"

The water seems to have been sucked dry by the sand. The poet Dao's voice is hoarse...

"Dan Qing left without saying goodbye, like a knife in my heart. Dan, you want me to die too?"

The soul seems to have been blown away by the wind. The poet Dao's anger is weak –

"Is death a scary thing? No, it's a lover's fate. But, but you can hurt me, can make me die, but you can't treat our Danqing Island like this! It's a dream I've had since I was young, a dream I had since my life started. What, you all forgot? Our vision, our vows, our dreams, how could you forget so soon? In my eyes you are beautiful, you are goddesses, you have always been the truth! But I am not. Only I am not. I was always an ugly child, an ugly child dreaming of you his whole life, only wanting to be with you his whole life, having only this one glorious thing his whole life. What 'poet', just a boring title the mediocre day gave me. No poetry can approach my dreams, none is more precious than those dreams, none more beautiful than you in my dreams, none can make me happier than you have, make me nobler. I know I'm unworthy of both you and Qing, but I can die for Danqing Island's beauty. I'm begging you, Dan! Don't leave, don't only not leave but bring Qing back. Then I'll be fine with anything. Then let my infatuation fly off with the wind, drift along the water, wherever it wants to go is fine. As long as Dan doesn't leave, is still on this island, with Qing, with Dan and Qing and this little island, the world can still be a beautiful place. Let me go, let the painstaking efforts we made on this island remain with you. That way, even if I disappear, even if I die without a burial place, my dream will not die, no matter where my soul wanders, it will find satisfaction in the existence of Danqing Island. It will be as happy as before.

"You know, seeing you two together without suspicion or jealousy, without vitriol and so without caution, made me so content, so grateful for fate's blessings! Why? How could you not know why? Because that's where beautiful women should be, where noble souls should be, where my Dan and Qing should be. A beautiful place isn't necessarily this little island's exact latitude and longitude but the dream I've had since I came into this world – not just a hope or dream, not that mediocre mainland hope, that silly thing that can be built in reality's hierarchy. I'm saying the place we were born to be is definitely not that awful mainland, that boring day! Dan, please don't go back to that place. Dan, please don't go, you and Qing should stay on this island where you should be. Let my wish surround you, protect you, let my wandering soul forge ahead for you. Dan, please find Qing and bring her back too, live from farming, enjoy poetry and painting, isn't that what we said before? If in the end I can't reunite with you in heaven, then let me wait forever in the sea, guard the island, wait for you to rain down, float on the water... And let that mediocre mainland always have a place to admire and leave an immortal dream for their mediocre reality..."

"But I want to live a normal life!" In the floating of a wisp of pale white, E's response suddenly floated.

"Just so Asky can go to school?" Ding Yi asked.

"No, not just for Asky, for myself too."

"What's normal, E, tell me what normal is."

No response, just floating.

"E, this if falling, you've fallen! Is it like the poet Dao said: Is our oath that easy to forget?"

"No, I think you forgot. Do you still remember what our oath was?"

"Love!"

"But free love!"

Only sand, sucking the water dry; only wind, hissing the soul away. Ding Yi slumped down on the endless, yellow sand.

Brother, that Ding asked me, *didn't I let E and Sa be free?*

Brother, I said, *can't E freely fall in love with Shang Zhou? Can't Sa freely leave your drama, go accompany the Qin Han she's always loved?*

Wow, you really know how to talk, you really know how to talk, old friend! But let's cut the crap, no matter what the thing is, we add 'free' to it and it's good?

I just know it's real, it's the truth you wanted.

No, I don't want that kind of truth!

"Then you'll get what you didn't want – power!" Yi's voice suddenly called from the blood-red clouds.

"Power?"
"Yes, the power you said you wanted to renounce."
"Why?"
"You can see. Or actually, you already have seen."

The blood-red cloud changed shape, surged, gathered, tore, ascended and sunk... strands dipped into the yellow sand, dyed the wind, and that pale fluttering in an instant became a blood-stained dress... blood-red drops like flowers, blood flowing like branching trees, flowing and bleeding like a dirge, spreading at Ding Yi's feet... Then the painter Qing's cry was heard, the painter Dan's gasping, and the heavy swoosh of the axe on Danqing Island... The sound of the axe spread throughout the sand, spread throughout the wilderness, echoed 'thud-thud-thud' between heaven and earth... Wind and sand, strands and clusters of cloud became thousands of butterflies, large as buckets or small as sand, rough like chisel-work or delicate like embroidery, blindly flying with the sky of lamentations... Ding Yi and I also seemed to turn into butterflies and fly, lost in the colourful yet barren group...

149. Poet's Last Word

The media report was very simple: the poet Dao hacked the painter Dan to death with an axe, then drowned himself in the sea. The painter Qing's whereabouts is unknown.

Some tabloids also published the poet Dao's last dispatch:

"All words are ruined by the king of the day.
Only eyes of night can distinguish beauty."

150. E's Letter

Beneath a copy of the newspaper that published 'The Danqing Island Tragedy' was a letter, apparently written by E. It read:

"I've gone, I don't know where to settle down for now. Asky went with Shang Zhou. She's as excited about those faraway places as she is about fairy tales. I'll always remember our drama, people should always remember their heart's dreams – 'remember' said where they should be. Take care, as we said: keep faith in this world. By the way, I'll add one more thing: Qin Han will never marry Sa. He has promised himself to Ou not only in this life but also in the next."

No heading, no complimentary close, no date.
What's it mean? What's she mean?
I said: *You mean the last sentence?*
Yeah, yeah, I forgot, that Ding smiled coldly. *What she wants is... a normal ending!*

E means well.

Means well? Her brother Qin Han promised himself to Ou, his sister wants to leave me in Sa's care, is that it?

What are you talking about, what is that nonsense?

That Ding shook his head and didn't answer, half-smiling.

His look became strange, his eyes less and less focused. I felt his body stagnate, though his blood flowed, his pulse beat, his hands and feet were cold, a chill seemed to penetrate his flesh with a hiss, and his chest and abdomen contracted, burning, he stumbled left and right, with no direction.

Hey, Ding Yi!

That Ding just laughed, cried, wailed, stomped his feet... The sight reminded me of his tantrum when he wasn't allowed to bathe with the little girl or his sorrow at Snow White's death, but this was an emergency, dangerous and unprecedented. As I was saying to myself 'Something bad will...', that guy collapsed.

What's wrong, brother? Ding Yi! Ding Yi, wake up, wake up! Hey, someone, help...

But there was no one around. While I was anxious and at a loss, he opened his eyes, rolled over and looked self-deprecatingly out the window. Outside the window was the faint white light of a winter's day.

Brother, is it serious?

What serious? What anything else serious can there be?

If you need, let's go to the hospital!

That dark tunnel? Forget it.

I'm afraid you'll be in danger if you don't get help.

I thought you weren't afraid of death? Didn't you say you'd still exist after I die?

Oh, poor brother Ding you forgot again, it's if you die, I'm still me.

Whatever, whatever.

The guy laughed quietly. *Do you think there's anything worth staying for in this capricious and precarious world?*

That's the most horrible thing in the world. As the saying goes: nothing is more lamentable than desperation. Looking back, how many dreams failed because of this, how many talented people came to nothing, how much hard work was wasted! As the king of the day destroys words, he cuts people's futures short – cashing in on his pact with Morpheus or the plan they made to cheat together.

Ah, between freedom and dream, where does God's finger point?

151. Dream Seeking

The traditional Chinese medicine diagnosis was qin and blood stagnation; yin and yang imbalance.

Western medicine doctors believed he was suffering from the pale, filthy flowers in the abdomen that were poised to bloom again.

Ding Yi and I were again in a cave-like ward where it was difficult to distinguish between night and day. I tried to carry out my duty. Since I promised not to leave, of course I would stick with him. And that Ding Yi was attached this time, unperturbed as he closed his eyes and said: Let my drama have a normal ending. So when the nurse asked him to take medicine, he took it. When it was time for an injection, he got an injection, he went where the doctor took him, let whatever lights had to be shone on him shine. Whatever they did to him, he never asked why.

Ding Yi, what are you doing?
Brother, we should let medicine win a bout.
What do you mean?
Did you forget what sore losers they were last time?

The dazzling white and deep green gowns came and went, their cold or soothing hands all over Ding Yi... The female residents looked afraid, the female doctors took him for granted, genial old professors gave orders and stood back, but their instructions were not carried out too well... Ding Yi had to strip again and again, again and again had to be exposed in front of others. I realised this guy was well accustomed and experienced – despite all the brushing wind and waving trees, his weather-beaten flower remained as immobile as a mountain, as if he had been alone – the wind moved, the trees moved, but the flower stayed still as if alone.

I couldn't help but murmur: *Is this a bad or a good omen?*

That Ding smiled calmly: *Take the chance to go your own way, let me be their good teaching aid.*

He dozed off during the conversation.

The professor shook his head slightly. The male and female residents got the hint and put that Ding on a small gurney, a white sheet covering him from chest to toes. If it weren't for his pale, gently snoring face being exposed, he'd have been ready for the crematorium.

What's up, brother? Ready to die?
No, expecting to dream!
That's my department, brother.
So why don't you go?
I said: *Where can I go?*
He said: *A faint candle turns into dissipating ashes.*
I said: *You know the path you'll take is endless?*
He said: *I'll dream and chase souls. I'm not thinking of returning.*

The gurney rolled smoothly and swayed slightly like a boat on water, through dark passages, through secluded caves, amid sighs of lamentation, beyond faint lights... So we suddenly dreamed of water and mountains overlapping, suddenly dreamed of flowers and willows mingling...

152. Dying Dream

"Mum said Autumn is a hundred times prettier than me."

The girl, Spring, led Ding Yi through the quiet hall, through the blooming begonias, looking for the secret source of the piano sound.

"Who's playing the piano?"

"Big Brother."

"Your brother?"

"No, no, Big Brother."

As if coming to a realisation, Ding Yi asked Spring quietly: "You can tell me that secret now, right?"

Spring grinned, a long time later said: "You really want to know?"

Ding Yi tilted his ear closer. Spring's breath covered Ding Yi's face. "They, they sometimes..."

"Sometimes what?"

"Sometimes neither of them have clothes on."

"Really?" Ding Yi was bewildered.

Spring looked at him and giggled, seeming not to fully understand but have a grasp.

"When?"

"When they play piano and dance together."

"Lying!"

"Autumn, Autumn!" the girl Spring called her big sister. "Autumn, am I lying?"

Then Autumn walked out of the strong spring breeze, not answering, just taking Ding Yi's hand to dance. The steps seemed magical, he had no choice but to follow her... The plain white dress fluttered like a tree full of flowers, flying triumphantly like a spring surge...

"Is what Spring said true?" Ding Yi asked.

Autumn didn't answer, just kept dancing.

"Spring said you're a hundred times prettier than her."

Autumn just kept dancing, didn't respond.

"Can we also do what... what Spring said?"

The trees and wind were calm, the rushing spring silent. Ding Yi realised the girl in front of him wasn't Autumn but Lingling. Lingling took Ding Yi's hand and wrote two characters on it, then her elegant form suddenly vanished like smoke in the night air or hid in night's black cloak.

Next, it was like a darkened theatre where scenes were being changed, out of the darkness came narration like Qin Han's. "Whoever you give yourself to, you're also asking that much power from them... whoever you give yourself to, you're also asking that much power from them... whoever you give yourself to, you're also asking that much power from them..."

Ding Yi opened his hand and looked, thought it was 'Lingling', but it was 'traitor' on his palm.

Ding Yi slumped to the ground as if falling into a deep, dark well, helplessly falling, falling... falling faster and faster. Had he fallen into a black hole that even time can't escape?

Luckily someone caught him.

He looked and found him to be long-lost Uncle.

"Where am I, Uncle?"

"Clock-less time."

"Did you really find a way to make time flow backwards?"

Uncle shook his head, then nodded, nodded and shook.

"Tell me, Uncle!"

"I'm here to tell you something else."

"What is it?"

"Don't be a traitor, try hard not to be a traitor. But I'm telling you, man, some kind of traitor, I'm saying there is one kind that knows love best."

"Did you find Fu?"

Uncle nodded and shook his head, shook and nodded.

"Where's Fu?"

"In clockless time."

"Is she a martyr?"

"She's a lover."

"Uncle, can you take me back?"

Uncle's figure gradually faded.

"Uncle! Can I go back to clock time with you?"

Uncle's figure gradually melted.

"Uncle! Uncle!"

A flash of light, as bright as day.

An old man appeared where Uncle disappeared, white-haired but face indistinguishable.

Who's this? that Ding asked me.

The old man taught me to see through the world of fame and fortune.

How have I never seen him before?

You were sleeping. Oh, no, you were drunk that day.

"Oh, is the old gentleman OK?"

"You see?" the old man said. "This Ding's already awake, anything left to say?"

"How can you tell this Ding's already awake?"

"Didn't you hear him say, I'll dream and chase souls, I'm not thinking of returning?"

"There's a difference, mister. You left out the previous sentence: I know the path I'll take will be endless. So this Ding already knows: even a dreaming soul is still on an endless path, so where is the road you spoke of, a road of extreme happiness with neither pain nor worry?"

"Then how can not thinking of returning home be explained, isn't that what he said?"

"Haha, haha... where is the point of return on the endless path? Where is the end? And also, where does infinity end? How can an end be infinite?"

"Proud, arrogant, absolutely arrogant!" The old man was a little annoyed again.

"I'm terribly sorry, master. Please pardon your humble student!"

"Youthful pride shuts your eyes! Have you sensed a murderous intent arising from the recess of that Ding's heart?"

"He's become murderous? I hadn't detected that yet."

"Resentment arising in the heart means murderous intent! Could it be that he doesn't have to commit an atrocity like the Danqing Island tragedy, does he?"

That shocked me. *Really, Ding Yi?*

That Ding was quiet, still faintly dreaming. I put my face on his body, my ear to his heart, and sure enough heard the thump, thump, thump – the anger of a resentful heart or the vengeance of a hateful axe?

Brother, what's wrong?
Brother, I have said, if you can hurry up, your work is done!
What are you panicking about?
I... I... I see the poet Dao's hate and can really... understand.
Ding Yi!
I think the painter's betrayal is really... really unbearable!
Ding Yi, what are you going to do?
Who knows!
Ding Yi! What are you thinking?
None of your business, none of your business any more...

"Ah, pathetic, sad, deplorable! Life is bitter, life is hard, life is full of endless troubles..." The old man sighed as he shook his head before vanishing as wind and clouds.

Looking at the place where the wind and clouds departed, I contemplated how all of the events can be summed up in a word – is anything harder than living? But, but do troubles die with death? Where does death in the end take you? Apart from nowhere. Apart from complete nothingness. Apart from not feeling utter nothingness. Apart from not feeling the lack of feeling of utter nothingness... But, but I suddenly remember my reason for being me: minds don't die. I also instantly remembered the words God said to Job: Where were you when I created the world?

But the thumping of that Ding's heart calls for no more contemplation. That hateful axe was already approaching chaotically, urging me to leave quickly.

153. Goodbye Ding Yi

That vicious plant, maybe because of constantly bathing in worry and resentment, finally came into full bloom. The sinister branches and vines grew with each passing minute, developing wildly, occupying barbarically, finally winning an overwhelming advantage over life supplies and its defences. I had no choice but to leave Ding Yi.

Brother, that Ding used his last energy to ask me: *Was I wrong again, was Eve not in E?*

I said: *No, Eve was in E, but the truth is Eve is in Adam's heart, in his blood, is his half, is his endless search.*

Are you still going to look for her?

Of course.

Why?

Because I'm her half too.

You really think she exists?

Because of Adam's search, Eve must exist. Just as those migratory birds promise to return, Adam and Eve promise to look for each other...

Ding Yi slowly closed his eyes.

Suspended above or wandering around I couldn't bear to leave for a long time.

Ding Yi, once so full of life, was now dead. The fierce, wicked, arrogant vines did as they liked, after sucking Ding Yi dry they were also exhausted, withered, like the ruins of an ancient city-state.

Qin Han and Shang Zhou carried Ding Yi's remains to a mountaintop. *Thank you, thank you Qin Han and Shang Zhou!* I hope it was the green mountain Ding Yi and I first saw together. And while the fleeting overflow is still in the farther distance, I'd like to take Ding Yi's dying dream to continue our pursuance of its brilliance.

Everyone worked together and dug a grave under a big tree for Ding Yi. *Thank you, thank you, friends!* I hope it was the big tree of the little girl, the crabapple of Spring and Autumn, the Osmanthus of Lingling, the old cypress of Yi, the moonlight tree outside E's window, the starry tree above Sa's grass, and Uncle's cycad, the pomegranate in that Ding's yard, and the old jujube tree in the birthplace of that Shi...

Everyone then brought the wooden box called a coffin to the grave. *Hey everyone, everyone, please, everyone, don't let such an ugly box touch my Ding Yi! Throw it away, throw it away, throw away this unsightly thing!* I hope Ding Yi won't be constrained in the next life. I hope on my future travels I can still remember Ding Yi's ideals, or be able to comfort his dreams and wishes.

E, sitting on the edge of the mountain, looked ecstatically at the sky. She seemed to hear my request, walked over and patted the coffin, said: "OK, forget it."

"What, forget it?" Shang Zhou said.

"Yes, forget it!"

"Then what?" Sa asked.

E leaned forward and looked at Ding Yi, touched his hair, dusted the dirt off his sleeve. "Let him go like this, he spent his life wanting to be open."

Thank you, E, thank you, Amazing E!

Everyone then put Ding Yi directly in the ground.

Thank you, thank all of you...

"Shouldn't we leave a marker?" Sa said. "Otherwise, how can we find him later?"

Qin Han said: "'I gently go, as I gently came.' That's what he said, you can't find a better epitaph than that."

"No," Yi said. "I remember he also said he didn't even want something like that. Right, E?"

"Right. He said he wanted peace, even to be forgotten, go read that poetry."

"But that way," Sa said, "I'm afraid we really will forget where he is."

E looked up at the sky again, where a big white bird was leisurely flying. Everyone then looked up, saw that bird like a dream, flapping its wings, so elegant and so graceful, like a spirit floating on water...

Thank you, my friend! Thank you, my loved ones!

154. Danqing Island

Leaving Ding Yi, I flew against time. First, I went to say goodbye to E's living place, goodbye to those red, blue and white floor sections: dim moonlight, tree shadows, others saw an empty room, I saw sincere dreams still being performed there...

Then I went to say goodbye to the lawn where we had long conversations with Sa: grass dotted with wildflowers. Others just say Ding Yi is overly sentimental, but I know his passion isn't just reactive but also crafty...

Then I went to say goodbye to Asky's room: Bless you, Asky! Whether your future is normal or unique, please don't forget that *Scenes from Childhood* song...

Next, I said goodbye Yi's ancient garden: on the snow-covered ground a set of young footprints attracted another and thus a blazing, dangerous kiss hidden in the woods...

Next, I said goodbye to Qin Han's place: leaned on his beloved tapes, alcohol and instant noodles. Yes, brother, who knows what will be this world's drama. So don't lose hope...

Then I went to say goodbye to Uncle's garden: in that old enemy's house, the plants were able to flourish...

Then I went to say goodbye to Spring's fairytale play, Autumn's dance room; goodbye to the little street where Ding Yi first saw the world, and the first little yard, little room where I first came to Ding Yi... Before my departure, I even remembered to visit the young couple next door to ask them to take care; the couple's bodies and souls had used to be at odds.

Then I flew horizontally through time to find Danqing Island.

Either the legendary remote ocean island or the exotic legend that happened to that remote ocean island was in the vicinity of time.

Thought is faster than time.

I arrived in the blink of an eye: the blue sea wrapped around the clay-coloured land, waves with silver edges heaved and heaved as if sighing for it, as if alleviating its pain, or as if clearing up its inner perplexities...

I slowly descended, as the island slowly grew larger.

Only when I heard the waves roar without seeing their swells did I realise the island really wasn't that small. White gulls flew overhead, cheering. I greeted them: "Hey! Is this Dan-Qing-Island?" They flew down like a flock of sprites but didn't land, just grazed the treetops or hovered over the ground, their cheers became desolate, depressed lamentations... Then, on some signal, the birds all turned at the same time, converged and flew away together.

I knew they wanted me to follow.

The white flock had black wings like funeral mourners.

I got between them, flew over the trees, hills, wasteland, beach and waves... They circled the island ritualistically, or wanting me to see every inch of the island upon which the poet and painters had placed their hope... Then they landed like paper flowers, scattered around rugged seaside rocks.

Where is this?

They just wailed gu-gu-gu.

Is there anything else worth seeing here?

They were suddenly quiet, looking uncomfortably up and down.

Unhurriedly I inspected the island among the rocks, birds behind me.

There didn't seem to be anything. I didn't see anything among the rocks.

The birds all took flight again, flew onto a crag, landing and taking flight again, unwilling to leave.

I knew they wanted me to be up there.

Up, up, up... Ah, now it was clear: the part of the crag facing the sun was embossed! Looking around it seemed the tops of all the rocks had reliefs or pictures – different shapes on each side, each face with wonderful colours!

The faces were of mortals, the bodies of normal people... The carving was not necessarily delicate; the drawing was not necessarily realistic, as if everything was improvised, just a vent to let out thoughts and feelings, or just for the joy of working, for ease of action, and for the freedom of breathing. Axes and chisels wielded freely were merely intended to expand lives, blending them with the surrounding wind, clouds and waves into a song of heaven...

But gradually I saw something strange: all the faces looked confused, anxious, cautious, even fearful, and all the bodies were unruly, wavy, proud, exaggerated, even exposed... How could it be? Why? What does it mean? Just improvisation? But could improvisation be so consistent? Think about it, close your eyes and think about it: what's the alternative? What's the alternative? Open your eyes and look again: in that case the faces and bodies are beautiful! If, by contrast, the bodies were confused and cautious whereas the faces were unruly and exaggerated, would that be ugly?

But why is it this way?

Right, Graham said it: At that time I couldn't rely on language to express my feelings.

Likewise, E once asked: "If you can't rely on language, what can you rely on?"

And E soon responded: "Rely on the body, rely on exposure, rely on movement, rely on the day's unspeakable language, speaking the way you can't usually speak!"

I remember at that time that I, within Ding Yi, was beyond myself with joy: "Yes, yes, rely on that language – the language outside words and sounds, another communication possibility, the thoughts and feelings words have trouble sustaining..."

That's why appearances are unreliable.

That's why thinking is difficult.

So, close your eyes to reject daylight, wear 'no clothes' to dream your dream, meditate by arresting your heart and let your soul roam under the cover of night.

So watch the white clouds fleeting, listen to the waves lapping; bathe in the light of the sun and moon, and expect to reach the celestial path soon.

Then Qin Han's questions appeared on those cautious faces. Then Yi's anxiety emerged in their fearful expressions. Then Qin Han's thoughts landed on the group of huge rocks, and Yi's experience following the white birds or black wings spiralled in the sky above Danqing Island, and flew...

It was time for me to go back.

Return to the vast water, return to the empty space.

Return to the clockless time or writing nights.

Just as the poet said: "All words are abolished by the king of the day." That is the soul's return to night, the time to again forge a language or a path.

155. Title Interpretation

As the water howls in the sand or the wind blows from the soul, a mind in illusion – is undying like me. Gently wobbling, floating, wavering, spreading or thinking... when suddenly that once wavering, faint voice became clearer: "Can only life be used to prove death, existence used to prove nothingness, limit used to prove infinity, the rest you'll understand..." I waited to hear the conclusion, but the voice was gone.

Then a bell reverberated. There appeared bright-white paper blinds, darkened window panes, waving shadows of trees in sparkling sunlight, then coming to sight were four walls, a ceiling, a chandelier, as well as an antique clock.

I woke up in Shi Tiesheng.

Or you could say I woke up from a Shi's dream into a Shi's reality. So-called 'Ding Yi' was just a possibility; a possibility, realised in a 'writing night'. So 'travels in Ding Yi' was just a phrase; a possible phrase sauntering and chanting in the night and startling from sleep in cautious day. Put it this way: Ding Yi and Shi Tiesheng's timeless relationship was at most a special coincidence, overlapping thought.

156. Postscript

There's one more thing to say. I was about to fly from Danqing Island when I saw Qin Han and Lü Sa rushing over.

"Hey hey, why are you just coming now?"

Hey, yeah, Ding Yi's gone...

I could only watch them walking and stopping amid the rocks, pointing, searching... Finally they seemed to find something. At a rock that was not the smallest but not the most obvious, they took a closer look, now whispering, now looking up in silence. I gently landed next to them and saw a message someone had quickly carved on the rock: 'Everything is possible, but I'm here.'

"It's her," Qin Han said, "it's Ou Qing's handwriting."

"What do it mean?" Lü Sa asked.

Qin Han didn't answer, just shook his head slightly.

"Where did she say she is?"

Qin Han then blew the dust off the inscription and gazed at it for a long time.

October 2002 to July 2005

ABOUT THE AUTHOR

Shi Tiesheng (1951-2010) was one of the most prominent Chinese writers of the second half of the 20th century. Born in Beijing in 1951, he attended Tsinghua University High School before being sent down to Yan'an, Shaanxi province as part of the Cultural Revolution campaign to re-educate urban youths in the countryside. An injury to his spine in 1971 left him paralysed from the waist down. On returning to Beijing, he wrote as a way to process his grief and explore the world.

His first work of fiction was published in 1979, and he went on to write a number of acclaimed books, including *Notes On Principles* and several short story and essay collections. Shi's 1985 novella *Like a Banjo String* was turned into a film by the acclaimed director Chen Kaige. In January 2018 *The Complete Works of Shi Tiesheng* was published by Beijing Publishing House, comprising twelve volumes of his novels, short stories, essays, scripts, poetry, letters and interview transcripts. His essay *The Temple of Earth and I* is considered a masterpiece and is taught throughout schools in China.